Melted BY A *Man*

ANDREA ANDERSEN

This book is a love letter to unlikeable women.
For the women who are told to smile more, and frown less.
For the women who have been told that they're too combative.
Too bossy.
Too serious.
This book is for the Girl's-girls.

It's also for the women who just want to be thoroughly and properly dicked down.

Prologue

JACQUELINE: MANY MONTHS EARLIER

MY NAME IS JACQUELINE WILLIAMS, and I was going to have a one-night stand.

I *wanted* a one-night stand, which was the most important thing.

I was a warm-blooded woman who enjoyed the consensual touch of someone who desired me.

Other women did this all the time, I wasn't special for trying this out.

"Who are you staring at?" My brother, Marco, asked as he brought his cheek against mine to see where my gaze landed.

"Him," I replied with a nod. My nerves were skittering in my veins from simply acknowledging who my attention was focused on.

"Oh, good choice." Marco nodded in approval. As twins, we were close. As a gay man and straight woman, we were even closer than normal. Talking about boys was something we did as early as teenagers before he officially came out to our father.

Since coming out, Marco had found his confidence.

Whereas, I still hadn't.

"Thanks," I grinned, looking back and rubbing my sweaty palms on my skater skirt. I felt like a fraud. Like I wasn't dressed like the thirty-year-old woman I was. Was I even allowed to dress sexy? I desperately wanted to. Something about slacks, pencil skirts, and business casual just got old.

"What are you going to do?" Marco asked. He sipped from his old-fashioned as he stared at the back of the man's head. He sat at the bar, so I couldn't see his face entirely. I had caught glimpses of his profile in the hour we had been sitting here scoping out possibilities for a no-strings-attached hookup. His back looked handsome, though. He wore a black leather jacket with dark jeans. I also decided on him because he looked about my age, which was difficult to find here. Either it was all college-looking students (hard pass) or much older men (hard pass).

"I'm not sure yet," I said, pressing my lips flat together, trying to channel even a fraction of the confidence Marco had shown before approaching the dark-haired man at the bar. "Do you have any pro tips?"

"None that would apply to you," Marco quipped, giving me raised eyebrows when I frowned at him in disappointment, "Gay men are very direct. Very little talking takes place. Dating apps have ruined basic communication skills."

I sighed, determined to see this through even if my brother did not help me.

"What if I just ask for his name? A fun fact?" Most of my social skills consisted of what a professional like me would say to employees. I hadn't had a casual, outside-of-work, flirty conversation with a man in a very long time.

"His name is not a bad start, but a fun fact feels like an interview," Marco raised one perfectly manicured dark eyebrow at me, "While you are technically interviewing him to ensure he qualifies for entry under your skirt, you don't want to make him feel like he's *in* an interview."

I nodded, trying to seem more...chill.

"How about—"

"How about you start by walking up there and sitting on the empty stool next to him?" Marco emphasized his advice with a dramatic shove, making me almost fall out of my seat in our booth.

"Okay!" I whisper-hissed as I shoved him away from me and fixed my skirt to ensure no part of my butt was falling out of it. I brushed my hands over my top to flatten any wrinkles. I wore a long-sleeved crop top, just enough crop to show an inch of skin on my waist. Nothing dramatic. The high-waisted flare skirt I wore helped me feel more comfortable with the look. The neckline was square and much lower than I normally wore, but I was both excited and nervous about dressing so provocatively with intention.

This was about taking charge of my sexuality.

About me practicing confidence.

"Just remember," Marco grabbed my wrist before I turned around to make it over to the handsome stranger I hoped to seduce tonight, "*You* are the catch. He's the one who should be lucky and grateful to have an opportunity to touch *you*. If he isn't interested, it is his loss."

I gave my twin a nervous smile and nodded. Then, standing straight, I took a deep breath to steady myself.

I was the catch.

I had worth, and value, outside of looks and confidence, and sexual experience.

"Go get 'em," Marco released my wrist and nodded to

encourage me to get a move on, "I'll be keeping an eye out in case you need help."

I exhaled a nervous breath before tucking my loose hair behind my ears. I usually wore my hair up for work because it was one less thing to worry about during the busy workday. Having it down and styled in loose waves was outside of my comfort zone but in a good way. I forgot how nice my brown hair looked. How I had natural highlights from the near-constant sun exposure living in southern California.

I tried to channel the confidence I usually felt while listening to *Carly Rae Jepsen's* "Cut To The Feeling" as I strode across the bar to approach the stranger. I hadn't propositioned someone before. I had personally been propositioned many times, but I never took charge like this.

I nervously pulled the stool out, sat, and tried to sit as a calm, collected woman would. Casual, but with an air of authority. I leaned forward and rested both of my elbows on the bar top, hopefully showing off the curve of my back and the low cut of my long-sleeved shirt.

"What can I get you?" The young bartender asked. As he approached, I noticed that his eyes dropped to sneak a glance at my cleavage. It was so fast, it felt almost accidental. I smiled at him as I pretended to think for a moment.

"A piña colada would be nice," I replied, still building up the nerve to look to my right where the handsome stranger still sat, sipping...something. I couldn't tell what it was yet in my peripheral vision. I figured that if I ended up striking out with this man, at least I would have a fun fruity drink to help me get over the rejection.

"Coming right up!" The bartender rapped his knuckles on the counter as he stepped away and started to work.

I just sat there; my muscles taut as I rested my elbows on the bar top. I turned to admire the bar towards my left, kicking myself for not even looking at him yet. *C'mon, Jacqueline. Just start with a glance. You don't even need to say hello, yet, just basic eye contact would be a good start.*

I inhaled through my nose and held my breath as I slowly forced my neck to comply with my plans. I turned slowly, pretending to glance at the young bartender who was mixing my drink on the right side of the bar.

And that's when I got my first full, real look at him.

He was already staring at me, a glass of beer at his lips as he met my wondering gaze.

The breath released out of my lungs in a woosh, and I immediately panicked about whether he noticed that or not.

I hadn't seen a man that took my breath away in a very long time, and yet, here he was.

Perhaps I set my sights a little too high tonight. He was undeniably gorgeous. Maybe even out of my league.

Damnit, I scolded myself, I'm *the catch.* I'm *the one he should be thanking for this opportunity* I'm *about to give him.*

"Hello." The man set the glass down after taking a sip, his clear blue eyes on me in a way that immediately made me feel vulnerable.

"Hi." It took every muscle in my body to make that a friendly, small greeting, and not a wheeze from his direct attention.

He had dark, almost black hair that was casually styled but may have had his fingers run through it a few times. His icy blue eyes were lined with thick lashes, supported by high cheekbones and a sharp nose that pointed towards light pink, hydrated lips that didn't have any evidence of nervous chewing or skin peeling.

Must be nice, I thought to myself.

Thankfully I hadn't nervously picked at my lips recently. I even wore lip-plumping chapstick tonight because I had very high hopes for myself.

His jawline was perfectly defined against his neck.

I could see a hint of collarbones sticking out of a Henley-styled shirt underneath his open leather jacket, and I realized right then, in that very moment, how viscerally attracted to a nice set of collarbones I was.

"Do I have something on my shirt?" The man asked, glancing down at himself before meeting my eyes again. His lips were twitching, as if he was hiding a smile.

"Nope," I replied, but my brain halted a little bit at the British accent he had just spoken with. It wasn't a Mr. Darcy-sounding British accent like I heard in movies and TV shows. It was a little messier and more casual. I wanted to guess that he had a cockney accent, but I wasn't quite sure.

I wasn't prepared to be completely knocked off my game. Attractive men were one thing, attractive men with British accents were almost unfair. I fought the urge to toss up a peace sign with my fingers and run out of the bar in embarrassment.

"You've just...been staring," the man replied, humor lacing his tone.

My blush crept up my neck, into my cheeks. I prayed that he didn't notice, but I was already on the verge of sweating. He probably wouldn't be excited about no-strings-attached orgasm exchanges if I was already sweaty.

"Just...enjoying the view," I replied. I locked onto those clear blue eyes of his, shocked that I dared to say such a thing. *Who was I? This was Marco, not me.* But I didn't take it back, I didn't apologize. I just met his gaze and waited for his reaction.

His lips finally pulled into a smile then, and my heart stuttered at the sheer beauty of this man.

I almost fell off of my barstool when he shifted his weight and held a hand toward me to shake, "I'm Leo." Marco's words immediately filled my head, *First things first, does he have a moanable name?*

...I thought, I could moan "Leo", but I couldn't let myself focus on that for too long.

As I took his hand, I smiled back at him, probably too widely, but I was living off of the insanity that I managed to make him smile. "I'm Jacqueline."

"Lovely to meet you, Jacqueline." His gaze quickly swept over my body sitting on the stool next to him. I wasn't too familiar with flirting with men at this point in my life, but when he rested an arm on the bar next to us and set one of his booted feet on the rung of my barstool, I wanted to punch the air with the success that he, too, must have liked what he saw.

"Any fun plans for tonight?" I asked, twisting in my seat as well and crossing one leg over the other. The movement rode my skirt up my thigh a little bit more, and I fought the reflex to tug it down.

"This is it, unfortunately," Leo replied. He rubbed his thumb against his bottom lip as he studied me, "I'm only in town until tomorrow night."

"That's perfect," I whispered, making his dark eyebrows jump up.

"And why is that?" Based on the smirk he gave me, and the way his hand made a fist so he could rest his cheek against it in a way that had no business being as sexy as it was, my jig was officially up.

"I...um..." Well, at least I knew when my air of confidence had officially run out. I drummed my fingertips on the bar top, a movement Leo clocked as he waited for my response, "I was wondering if you could help me with something—no pressure though." I pressed my lips together to keep myself from blurting out more. To keep me from saying something like, *Are you interested in getting freaky tonight, good sir? Perhaps a bit of canoodling to release some pent-up stress? You know what? I'm sorry to bother you, I'll see myself out.*

Game, to no one's surprise, was something I did not have.

"I'm happy to be of service," Leo replied, not pronouncing the *h* in "happy". He was so calm. I suddenly felt so put on the spot. What did I say now that didn't turn him off or scare him away? Would it be this easy?

"Are you sure?" I asked, leaning closer as I checked my surroundings to ensure no one else was listening to this train wreck of a seduction, "It's a little embarrassing." I bit my lip and blushed harder when I saw Leo's eyes land on my mouth.

"I doubt it," Leo replied to my lips. He didn't pronounce his t's half the time either, but I enjoyed the sound of his accent. If I wasn't specifically attempting to learn how to orgasm with a casual partner, I would have loved to stay here and hear him talk as much as possible tonight.

"It's not something I like to brag about," I added, licking my lips and internally squealing at how he mirrored the movement with his own, "But I'm feeling a little bit...lonely."

"Lonely." His gaze lifted to meet mine again; something sparked behind it and heated my blood.

"And I'm trying to put myself out there," I continued, glancing down at my nervously twisting fingers. I looked back up and saw that I still had his full, undivided attention.

"I see," was his only response. He didn't give me any more than that; he just sat there, confidently resting one of his feet on my barstool, one elbow on the bar top with his cheek resting on his fist. Not a care in the world.

I wondered what that was like.

"So...if you're interested..." I started to clam up, swallowing around a nervous lump in my throat. I stopped my fidgeting as soon as I saw his hand reach forward and wrap around both of mine, halting my movements.

I glanced up to meet his gaze again, and his expression was a mixture of emotions my frantic nerves made difficult to read.

"Not to be too forward," he responded, gently squeezing my fingers with his hand, the warmth of it seeping into my skin, "but I am *very* interested, Jacqueline."

The grin that pulled at my cheeks was instant, something about the immediate validation from him filled me and made me straighten my spine a bit more. Leo smiled as well, continuing to hold my hands in his grip when I didn't pull away.

"That's...good." I nodded.

And then we just sat there in silence.

"Just so we're clear," Leo leaned forward, casually scooting his stool a little bit closer to me, "You're trying to pull me, yeah?"

I furrowed my brows at his terminology, "Pull?" The visual I had was immediately filthy, and part of me wondered if I even remembered how to give a hand job. It couldn't be that hard, right? Like riding a bike, or something?

"Sleep with?" he explained, as his gaze fell to my lips again.

Oh.

"Yes." I nodded, leaning in a little bit more when his gaze lingered on my mouth.

I needed to wear this plumping chapstick way more often.

"Good to hear," he nodded, his grip on my hands loosening just enough for him to trail his index finger over my knuckles, "Though you should probably take the lead, love."

Oh my god, he did the thing. He did the English guy thing, using "love" as a term of endearment. Even though this was a hookup, I felt my insides turn to goo. This man was dangerous to someone with as little experience as me, but I couldn't find it in me to care. Somehow, the stars were aligning and Leo was picking up what I was laying down. He seemed just as enthusiastic as I was on the inside.

"Oh..." I spoke, glancing to the side nervously to figure out what the next step could be. My forgotten piña colada was sitting in front of me, and I wondered how long it had been there, "Do you...want to try kissing me first?"

"Try?" Leo asked with a note of humor in his question.

"Well..." I lifted a shoulder, "We should probably see if we like how the other kisses, before exploring this...further." I winced a little. Was I being too analytical about it? Was this professional Jacqueline sneaking in, interviewing him like an employee and not a person I was interested in fooling around with?

"Ah, very practical." Leo nodded as he sat a little straighter, releasing his grip on my fingers and shaking his hands out. He even went as far as to crack his neck and relax his shoulders, as if he was preparing for a type of athletic activity instead of just kissing me.

"Are you good?" I asked through a nervous giggle.

Leo intertwined his fingers and stretched them out in front of him, winking at me as he replied, "I'm just preparing myself. I don't want to miss out on anything if I don't do this just right for you." He pronounced it like "any-fing" which was oddly adorable, for a man I wouldn't describe as adorable in any way. He was attractive, sexy, and confident. Everything I wanted to be.

My lips parted in surprise.

I'm the catch, I repeated to myself as I grinned at his theatrics.

"Take your time, as long as you don't slobber all over my mouth, we should be good." I played along, my nerves easing the slightest bit.

"Got it," Leo nodded, making a face as if he was taking a mental note. He pulled one arm across his chest to stretch, closed his eyes, and said, "You've got this, mate." I laughed again, covering my mouth to smother the sound, "You've done this before. You know how to kiss a woman. Don't psyche yourself out just because she's gorgeous." I blushed, rolling my eyes at his little act. "Why she even singled you out of all the blokes here is none of your business," he continued, his brow pinched in concentration during his pep talk, "Just kiss her."

"She's waiting," I replied, amused with the show.

He opened his eyes and grinned at me, a grin that promised *things*. Things that made my insides fill with butterflies. Things that lit up nerves and stirred a warmth in my lower stomach.

"My apologies." He shook his hands out one last time and settled in his seat, sitting with a straight back with his hands planted on his thighs, "Lay it on me."

I immediately felt insecurity creep into my spine again,

but with a hopefully subtle shake of my head, I mentally slapped myself to get it together.

Just kiss him.

Just take his face and...put your mouth on his. How do you expect to do anything else if just kissing a man intimidates you this much?

I leaned forward, waiting for him to lean in as well to meet me halfway, but he just sat there. A friendly, open expression on his face as he waited ever so patiently.

"Actually, um..." I blinked, trying to calm my racing heart, "I think you need to kiss me." Leo's brows twitched up, before nodding and reaching forward to take both of my hands in his again.

"Is this, okay?" He asked. His thumbs brushed smooth circles on the backs of my hands. It was embarrassing how little contact with him sent my heart into cardiac arrest.

"Mhmm." I nodded. He smiled as one of his hands slowly started traveling up my arm, the brush of his fingertips created goosebumps on the skin underneath my long sleeve as he slowly made it to my shoulder.

"And this?" He asked as his eyes held me hostage. He leaned closer, his long legs resting on either side of mine.

"It's good," I whispered, my breath caught in my throat as he leaned even closer, using his other grip on my hand to tug me a hair closer to his body.

Damn, he smelled amazing. It wasn't a strong smell, but the smell of a man who bathed and washed his clothing often, *thank god*. Soapy, with a hint of clean linen. His hand on my shoulder barely brushed the exposed skin from my wide-neck shirt. His fingertips teased me as his warm hand slowly came up to cup the side of my neck, his thumb resting on my jaw, "...And this, Jacqueline?"

"It's, um," I inhaled through my barely parted lips, desperately trying to control my breathing, "Really good."

"Good," he murmured, leaning in, and using his grip on my neck to angle my face for him. We were an inch or two apart now. My hands rested on his thighs as he guided my movements. He had hard muscles underneath his denim. My own fingertips flexed as I struggled to wrap my head around how turned on I was simply from his touch.

"Are you ready?" Leo murmured as his eyes became hooded.

"As I'll ever be," I whispered. His lips pulled back in a quick grin, before he finally, finally closed the distance.

I held my breath when his lips first pressed themselves against mine. I was frozen, every muscle in my body aware of his touch and his lips as I adjusted to their smooth warmth. It was probably only a second or two before he brushed his lips against mine again. He adjusted the kiss so that my bottom lip was tucked between both of his, nipping gently.

I didn't recall closing my eyes, but I was thankful that my body thought to do so, allowing me to focus on how amazing this simple kiss felt. I removed one of my hands from his thighs to clutch the open panel of his leather jacket, tugging him closer to me as I responded to him.

I wondered if he knew that he was teaching me with this kiss.

Letting me know just how slow or fast to kiss back, and how much pressure to apply.

His grip on my neck flinched when I tugged him closer again. His other hand came up to cup the other side of my neck, angling my head to deepen the kiss.

When I tentatively tasted his lip with my tongue, I heard a low sound rumble in his throat at the contact.

And that was when I pulled away just a hair, just enough to create space and for our eyes to meet so close together, "... Was that good?"

He blinked, his eyes hooded and darker as he stared back at me, murmuring something that sounded a lot like "fuck me" before he placed his lips on mine again.

I groaned at the additional pressure he added this time. I opened my mouth and met his tongue with my own. I forgot all about being in a very public, crowded bar. How my brother was probably still in that booth across the way, watching to make sure I was safe. None of that mattered, all that mattered was Leo's mouth on mine. The way his tongue slid sensually against mine. How his grip on my neck and jaw felt like the most natural, wonderful feeling in the world.

How good it felt to simply be *held*.

Without thinking too much about it, I slipped both of my hands underneath his open leather jacket, resting them on the sides of his cotton shirt and feeling the hardness underneath.

"Are you enjoying this, Jacqueline?" Leo asked against my mouth, nipping at my bottom lip once again before I had a chance to respond.

By some miracle, I was able to mumble some form of, "God, yes," against his lips.

He smiled against me, before pressing a firm kiss against my lips once more and pulling back. His hold on my neck dropped as he trailed his fingers down my shoulders and arms again. He rested his hands on my wrists, gently removing them from his sides.

I was panting.

I was in way over my head.

But I didn't care. That was the whole point of tonight.

"Want to get out of here?" I was pretty sure I gasped the question.

In response, Leo abruptly stood and pulled his wallet out to throw some bills down on the bar. *Oh crap,* I forgot I had ordered a drink and never touched it. I started patting around in the pockets of my skirt for some money to pay, but he shook his head at me before taking my hand and pulling me off of my barstool, "You're covered."

I smiled and mumbled, "Thanks," before tugging against his hold, "Wait, wait." I almost forgot the most important part. And part of me panicked, wondering if I was about to ruin this before we got to the fun stuff, "I need to take your picture."

Leo lifted an eyebrow before a grin took over his sharp features again, "For safety?"

I nodded and took out my phone, laughing when Leo dropped my hand to pose with both of his hands on his narrow hips, his boyish grin doing things to my insides.

I sent the picture to Marco, with Leo's first name. I also added a "British accent" mostly to brag. Once I pocketed my phone, I took Leo's hand again and let him lead me out of the bar.

"This is going to sound a little tacky," Leo spoke as stepped out into the warm night. Summer was going to end soon, but the warm days would last well into November, "But my hotel room is only a block away."

"No one else is staying with you?" I should have asked beforehand, I realized. *What if he was married? What if he had a partner waiting for him?*

"No, I'm alone," Leo replied. He still held my hand but waited for me to engage. To let me lead the way. I grinned, looking down at how large his hand was in comparison to mine, how his fingers interlaced with my smaller ones. I hadn't held hands like this in a very long time, and it was both heartbreaking and rejuvenating to relearn just how much I loved this kind of casual intimate touch.

With a deep breath filling my lungs for confidence, I took the first step forward, silently encouraging Leo to take the lead.

Chapter One

JACQUELINE: PRESENT DAY

"THAT'S IT," *he murmured against my neck. I shivered, releasing a groan I normally would have tried to swallow but didn't feel the need to this time. I arched into him, relishing the heavy weight of his hard body on top of me. I tried to meet him thrust for thrust, but the hold he had on my hands sent my blood racing, my thoughts scattered into nonsensical fragments, and my body eventually fell lax, surrendering to him, "Do you like it when I talk you through it, Jacqueline?"*

I had suspected for quite some time I needed intimacy like this, but this was the first experience I had to test the theory. So I nodded against the comforter while moaning an affirmative because words were lost to me.

"Bloody hell," Leo grunted against my skin, "You're so beautiful like this."

IT WAS against company policy to slap a strip of duct tape over the CTO's mouth.

But I still wanted to.

Everyone was laughing outside of my office, while behind the closed door I wore my earbuds and turned up my music, determined to drown out their ruckus. I was in the middle of processing new teams of software engineers and sales reps, drowning in onboarding paperwork. It was all done digitally, but it was paperwork all the same. I wanted to focus.

But I couldn't, because *he* stood just outside my office, barely visible through the glass next to my door, throwing his head back to laugh at something his cousin had said to him with a smirk.

How did he fit in so well, so fast?

I had worked here for almost three years now, and I was just barely starting to form friendships.

Sure, I used to argue that work wasn't where I should bother to form friendships. If I wanted friendly companionship, I could be more social outside of this nine-to-five.

Unfortunately, I was very antisocial. The only real friend I had was my ex, so when I finally left him, I had no one.

I was an introvert, but I was also capable of becoming so, so lonely.

I didn't want to be lonely anymore, and I was finally starting to consider myself friends with other women in the office.

But Leo Turner was already friends with everyone.

He made it look so effortless.

I shouldn't have been surprised, though. I knew him. I knew him before anyone else did. Before he even interviewed at Sun Steer Technologies.

Suddenly, he turned his head and his clear blue eyes landed on me. He caught me staring at him through my office window.

He grinned.

I frowned and pointed to my earbuds with a raised eyebrow.

Leo's lips formed an 'oh' and suddenly he was walking back towards his own office, Mary and the others following him as they all continued the conversation elsewhere.

My phone rang, buzzing on the top of my desk. I paused my music to answer the call, allowing Brandon Moore's voice to fill my ears.

"Are you busy?" The CEO of Sun Steer Technologies asked.

"Not terribly," I replied, glancing at the work on my desktop. *I guess I could use a break.*

"Are you in your office?" He asked.

"Yup," after my reply, the call disconnected. I pulled out my earbuds and secured them in their case when a knock sounded and my office door opened.

I used to think Brandon was pretty cute.

In a basic white man sort of way.

He had dark blonde hair that brightened in the summertime, blue eyes a couple of shades darker than Leo's, and a sturdy build slowly becoming more defined since he started joining our former CTO at the gym every morning.

There were rumblings from Sun Steer employees that Brandon had an arrogant personality, which I understood to a degree, but I thought that Brandon and I were more similar than not.

We had different modes.

He and I fell into work mode very easily, which could be off-putting to those who liked to shoot the shit on the job.

Brandon smiled shyly as he stepped into my office, and behind him, another new hire followed.

Sun Steer's new Chief Financial Officer, Nicole Young, was beautiful.

She had short black hair that was half an inch above her shoulders, sometimes she wore her hair wavy, and other times she ironed it straight. She wore straight-cut jeans more often than not unless she had important meetings scheduled. Nicole also had a sleeve of random patchwork tattoos all over her arm, and it felt like every day she wore a short-sleeved blouse to work, I discovered a new one.

Today, I noticed a cartoon raccoon holding a little bouquet with large puppy-dog eyes added to her bicep.

I was confident that wasn't there last week.

She plopped into the first chair across from my desk. Brandon grabbed the back of the other chair and pulled it a little farther away from Nicole, before taking his own seat and propping an ankle on his knee.

"We wanted to ask if you would be interested in hiring someone to support you." Brandon usually went straight to the point. It was something I appreciated because it made his expectations of me clear. He didn't start with pleasantries, pretending to care about anything personal going on in my life.

Some called that behavior cold, but I thrived from black-and-white conversations.

"I was telling Brandon that you've been so busy with all the onboarding you've had to run," Nicole crossed her arms over her chest, giving me a kind smile, "And that we have the budget to hire one or two people for the Human Resources department if you're interested in that."

I nodded my head, suddenly thrilled that I was being offered help until a familiar sinking feeling settled in my gut.

What prompted them to have this discussion?

What did I do to make them feel like I needed help?

They're disappointed in you.
They're upset with you.
You're not doing enough.

"Oh, I'm okay," I smiled and fidgeted with my fingers on my desk, trying to look more confident in the moment than I was, "I can handle it."

Nicole tilted her head, considering that response, "That's great, but you shouldn't have to. We're going to reorganize a lot of the company to accommodate almost doubling the number of employees in a year. You shouldn't have to handle a company this size on your own."

I nodded, pressing my lips together, something in my chest tightening from her words.

She's lying.
They're trying to let you down easy.
You should have anticipated this.

"I'm okay though," I pressed, "I appreciate you thinking about me, I do. But if you have something else you want to use the budget for that's more pressing, I can run things just fine on my own for the time being."

Brandon gave Nicole a look, one I couldn't decipher before she inhaled a breath and blew it out of her mouth. She sat forward, bracing her arms on her knees as she raised an eyebrow at me.

"Hiring additional employees to help support you is, in fact, pressing," Nicole's smile was kind, and I tried desperately to find any insincerity behind it, but I couldn't, "While I agree that you probably could handle what's coming in the future with grace, we don't want to wear you out. Think of this as a preventative measure, so you don't get overwhelmed with the potential workload."

I nodded along, letting her know I understood where she was coming from.

I glanced down at my fingers, trying to remember what my therapist had instructed me to do the next time I caught myself in a spiral like this.

"Ask the questions," Mariam encouraged me, *"No one can read your mind. It's better to ask and know what they're thinking, instead of second-guessing the interaction later."*

"Can I ask," I cleared my throat as I lifted my gaze to stare at Nicole, her dark eyes still looking at me with kindness, "Did I do something wrong?"

Both of my coworker's brows furrowed, Brandon already shaking his head as he shared a concerned look with Nicole, "What? No. You've done nothing wrong, Jacqueline."

He's lying.

He wants you to fix it without having to hold your hand through it.

"Trust their answers," Mariam's words filled my head again, making me inhale a deep breath to calm myself, *"You have to trust that people will be honest with you, Jacqueline. Not everyone is Vincent."*

It was Nicole's turn again to chime in, "We don't want to hire support for you because we don't think you can do your job," she sounded sincere, but I was still a little skeptical because I was pretty sure I was broken, "We want to hire support so that you'll feel comfortable taking a fucking vacation day."

I blinked, ignoring the reprimand on my tongue for her language at work because she was technically my superior, "Oh."

"You haven't taken a day off in over a year, Jacqueline," Brandon added, "You only took the day off when the rest of the company already had it off. You have almost a month's worth of sick days added up because you've never taken a sick day either."

I frowned, "...Is that a problem?" I had a feeling Brandon took as many sick days as I did. It felt hypocritical coming from him.

"For a capitalist society, no, not really," Brandon replied, frowning a little.

I was immediately confused.

Nicole shook her head at him before looking at me again, "What he means to say is," Brandon looked a little embarrassed at her need to step in, "It's important to us for Sun Steer employees to take breaks. To unwind and maintain a healthy balance. Working eight to ten-hour days, five days a week, fifty-two weeks a year, isn't sustainable. It'll eventually catch up with you, whether you want it to or not."

Why did I feel like crying?

I thought I was doing so well, I thought I was meeting expectations.

Maybe even exceeding them.

Turns out, I was just messing up again.

"Oh," I didn't know what else to say.

"You're not in trouble," Nicole sat up, lifting her brows at me with what looked like an encouraging smile, "We are proud of you and want to do everything we can to keep you happy here. We don't want you to look for work elsewhere because we aren't providing enough support for you. That's why we want to hire more people to work in Human Resources."

Trust that she will be honest with you, Jacqueline.

"Got it," I was starting to feel embarrassed from all the reassurances Nicole was giving me, "No worries. I just wanted to make sure I wasn't slacking anywhere."

"Not at all," Brandon shook his head, "You're probably the hardest worker here."

"Definitely," Nicole pulled her buzzing phone out of her pocket and smiled at the screen, "Are we good here? My partner is waiting for me downstairs to have lunch."

"We're good," I replied, while Brandon hummed his agreement.

"Excellent," Nicole stood, leading Brandon out of my office with one last look over her shoulder, "If there is anyone you know who you think would be a good fit, let us know. If not, we can start looking for potential interviewees whenever you're ready."

"Alright," my smile wobbled, "Thanks again."

"Of course." And with that, the two of them left my office, closing the door behind them.

I exhaled and dropped my head in my hands, I could feel my arms trembling.

They're not mad at you.

They like you, and they want to keep you around.

Trust that they'll be honest with you, Jacqueline.

I don't know how long I sat there, breathing through my anxiety over a work conversation that, logically, I knew shouldn't have triggered such a physical response from me. I felt like there was a firm grip on my lungs, attempting to crush them against my heart. I felt heavy, so heavy.

I needed to lie down.

I eventually stood up and left my office, turning off the light and shutting the door behind me. I turned the corner, out of upper management's wing, and walked past the empty front desk.

Thank god, because I didn't think I could handle keeping up with a casual conversation with Signe right now.

I finally made it to my destination, the label on the door bringing me a hint of relief when I saw the unoccupied sign hanging from the handle.

Sensory Room.

I practically threw the door open before quickly flipping the sign to "occupied" and shutting myself inside.

I flicked on the oil diffuser resting on a small bookshelf on the lefthand wall, next to the only light sources in the room. A small lamp, right next to a pink salt lamp. I walked past the bean bags and kicked off my shoes to feel the soft rug underneath my toes. I bent down to the linen basket, digging out my preferred blanket that smelled like the oil diffuser, inhaling the eucalyptus and lavender scent as I held the material toward my face.

Wrapping myself up and remembering to set the thermostat for this room to sixty-nine degrees, I finally made my way toward the very back. Where the warm, muted lamp light barely made it. The dimness immediately felt like a weight off of my eyes.

A hammock hung in the corner, and I folded my body inside, letting the canvas support my weight.

I inhaled the scent of the blanket near my face again, focusing on the gentle sway of the hammock I settled in.

You're safe.

You're at work, and you're safe.

No one is mad at you.

You're in your head again.

I struggled to repeat those words in my mind, desperate to shake the last of this panic from my body, but realized I needed something else.

"Hey Siri," I gently called from my swing. The gentle beep of the speaker let me know the device was listening, "Play Jacqueline's Playlist."

"...Playing Jacqueline's Playlist," Siri responded. A second later, instrumental music gently filled the room. The low volume made the music a calm sound. Enough to drown out my thoughts, but not loud enough to overstimulate me again. It was a playlist designed specifically to bring me down to earth. It wasn't music I generally reached for on my own, it was music I only listened to specifically for these moments.

What I normally preferred to listen to would have been too much right now.

I hadn't needed to use this room in a long time. The last time I used it was when I learned that Leo Turner was accepting the position of Chief Technology Officer.

That was about five months ago.

Breathe in through your nose, out through your mouth.

I ground my teeth together and exhaled through my nose instead.

You're safe, Jacqueline.

No one is upset.

You're freaking out over nothing.

You did nothing wrong.

Though the words were true, my body couldn't comprehend them. I pulled my phone out and set a fifteen-minute timer, another tactic Mariam gave me when I first started seeing her.

Having a hard and fast stop time for my meltdowns helped me feel more in control. I would allow my body to feel what it needed to feel for fifteen minutes, and then when the timer buzzed against my stomach, I would force myself to get it together to make it through the rest of the workday.

Then I could go home and dress down and cry.

Crying is good, Mariam told me, *Crying is your body's natural way to help relieve all the extra cortisol in your brain. Crying isn't a bad thing. It doesn't make you weak. It's what your body is designed to do to help you regulate your emotions.*

Which was cool to know and all, but crying made my eyes puffy, my nose run, and my skin flushed. It wasn't something I could do quickly in the middle of my workday without causing concern.

So this fifteen-minute timer would have to do. I let my body shake, my teeth grind, and my fists clench. I soaked in the herbal smells and sound of the calming music, allowing my eyes to open and take in the dim, quiet, calm space around me.

I focused on the back-and-forth, gentle swing of the hammock that cocooned me.

Deep breaths, Jacqueline.

Just fifteen minutes of this, and then I could make it through the day.

Just fifteen minutes of this, and my heart rate would be at a healthier beat again.

Just fifteen minutes of this, and I could go back to who I needed to be.

Chapter Two

LEO

"CAN YOU—" Jacqueline gasped as I sucked on the pulse point between her shoulder and neck, she shivered underneath my hands as my fingers teased the warm skin at her waist, "Lead?"

"Lead?" I repeated against her neck.

"You know, like," she removed one of her hands from my shirt as she flapped it in the air beside us, flustered as I teased her skin with my lips and tongue, "Take charge. Be in control. Tell me what to do—if you're comfortable with that."

I paused only momentarily before standing tall and pulling her flush against my front, more than comfortable with this goddess' shy request, "I can, as long as we have a safety word. Do you have one in mind?" I cupped her jaw and tilted her face up toward mine.

Her lips parted as she locked her eyes with me and breathed, "...Glacier."

"No." My cousin didn't even bother looking up at me as she deleted a line of code on her screen.

"Why not?" I pressed, sitting on the edge of her desk and twirling a pen in my fingers.

I was towering over her, clearly an authoritative figure, and yet when Mary Jiang gave me a look down her nose while sitting at her desk chair, scrunching it in irritation, she still felt taller than me.

"Because I have plans," she replied, turning her dark eyes back towards her screen.

I grabbed a lock of her dark silky hair and tugged it once before her hand immediately swiped at me.

"You see Jamie daily," I argued, "but we've hardly hung out since I moved here."

"I hung out with you for like two weeks straight, when you first moved here."

"That was to help me unpack."

Mary rolled her eyes without bothering to look up at me as she replied, "Actually, no, that was for me to unpack for you."

I rolled the pen between my fingers again, watching it glide back and forth over my knuckles, "You're better at interior design than I am."

"True," Mary nodded, "but it's no excuse to weaponize your incompetence. I have plans. Go away."

"C'mon," I adjusted my grip on the pen so that I could bounce it in between my thumb and middle finger rapidly, "Hold my hand while I make new friends."

Mary scoffed.

I grinned.

"You have never needed help making friends since the moment you were born." Mary tapped on her keyboard with her black-painted fingernails, locking her screen, then bent down to grab her bag, "You'll be fine." With that, Mary stood and started marching toward the lift. I tossed the pen I was fidgeting with on her desk and followed, undeterred by her dismissal. We turned the corner to where the front desk sat directly across from the doors, seeing Signe Lange and Jamie Hansen chatting.

For as long as I've known Mary, I never would have pictured Jamie being her type. Usually, Mary dated women who looked more like her. Women who wore a lot of black and had some tattoos, maybe facial piercings. Grunge clothing usually filled their wardrobes. One time Mary dated a woman whose hair was dyed the colors of the rainbow; eyebrows included. It was badass, which made sense because Mary usually dated badass-looking women.

Jamie was shorter than Mary, smaller, with medium-length pale blonde hair and blue eyes. I didn't think I'd seen Jamie wear makeup once since I started working here, and today she wore a pale pink blouse with a cream-colored floral print, French tucked into her straight-cut jeans.

There must have been something special about Jamie, something that made her a badass in Mary's eyes, because Mary seemed more at peace in this relationship than she had in any of her previous ones.

"You ready?" Jamie asked her girlfriend, before giving me one of her timid smiles, "Hi, Leo."

"Hello," I gave her my signature smile, the smile I crafted during my early twenties that generally worked on women, "Is there any way you could let me steal your partner for tonight? Actually," I raised my eyebrows as if the idea had just come to me, "Would you like to join us, too?"

Mary was already shaking her head at Jamie, who just grinned and raised a blonde eyebrow at me, "What are you doing?"

"You see," I leaned against the front desk, catching Signe's eye who was giving me some raised eyebrows of her own, not bothering to hide her smile, "I'm starting on a new recreational rugby league, and I can be a bit shy at times—" Signe snorted nice and loud, and I held up a hand to cover her face from my view as I continued to plead my case, "and I would feel much better if I had my dear cousin there to help me break the ice."

"You just don't want to look like a loser with no friends." Mary rolled her eyes and looped her arm through Jamie's, tugging the smaller woman toward the lift.

"Maybe we can—" Jamie started, but after Mary punched the call button, she cupped each of Jamie's cheeks and turned her face to look her in the eye.

"No," Mary shook her head once, "Don't fall for it. He's a grown man in his mid-thirties. He doesn't need us to hold his hand. Do you want to go watch a bunch of men in booty shorts get all dirty and sweaty while they wrestle with each other under the guise of sportsmanship?"

Jamie grinned between her squished cheeks, "Do you want an honest answer?"

"Why do you think I even signed up?" I added.

"Wait," Signe chimed in, pulling my hand down with her own so I would look at her again, "Are you meeting at Laguna Field?"

I lifted a brow at her, "Yes..."

"Zaid is going tonight," Signe grinned, "I'll be there, too."

"Oh excellent," I high-fived the office manager, before flipping off my cousin, "Enjoy your date night."

"I will." Mary grinned while Jamie giggled and allowed herself to be tugged into the lift.

"Mr. Turner," a feminine, alto voice echoed towards us, and I felt something zing down my spine from the sound of my name on her lips. I turned, noting the way Signe immediately put her hand up over her mouth to smother her smile as I saw the woman who suddenly appeared out of nowhere.

"Ms. Williams," I replied, with a formal nod. I was standing taller, a reaction I usually had when Sun Steer's Director of Human Resources referred to me by my last name.

"Need I remind you that vulgar gestures like that go against Sun Steer's code of conduct?" Jacqueline raised a dark eyebrow at me as she approached the front desk Signe sat behind, "Something the CTO should know already?"

I took a moment to drink her in because when it came down to it, I was a simple man. A man who still struggled to wrap my head around who was standing in front of me, versus the woman who approached me at a bar all those months ago.

Jacqueline's hair was up in a tight bun, not a hair out of place. A bun that I immediately wanted to undo because I knew how beautiful her dark brown hair looked hanging loose at her back.

I knew how her deep, dark eyes looked without the shield of her thin gold glasses, hooded and glassy and utterly hypnotizing. I knew how her skin looked flushed and the sounds she made when I angled my hips *just* right. How her eyes widened after she came, looking adorably surprised every single time her body pulsed erratically around me when she reached her pleasure.

I knew Jacqueline Williams' body intimately, and I was confident those memories would forever be seared into my brain.

Today she wore an outfit that was somehow both my favorite and also my least favorite.

Because it included a pencil skirt.

Even though the skirt was perfectly modest for the workplace, I couldn't help but get stuck on how each step she took teased the outline of her soft, smooth thighs. Her arse that I knew for a fact fit perfectly in the palms of my hands.

"Mr. Turner?" I snapped my eyes up from her legs, grinning on instinct even though Jacqueline was all but openly glaring at me. Her brows were lowered, her lush lips were turned down in disapproval, clutching an iPad to her chest as if to shield herself from me.

Were those dark circles under her eyes?

I hadn't seen Jacqueline Williams smile at me since that one night we shared, and every day that I went to work and failed to see her lips pull back in that joyful expression, I felt like the biggest failure.

"My apologies," I placed a palm over my heart, looking her in the eye, "No more vulgar gestures in the office."

Jacqueline raised a dark eyebrow at me before turning towards Signe, dismissing me without a word.

I tried not to flinch from her cold shoulder.

"Cheers." I nodded to the two women and started to walk back toward my office, shoving my hands in my pockets in an attempt to still them. I was always fidgeting, but around Jacqueline, my hands physically itched. The constant restlessness inside me burned hotter in her presence.

It wasn't until I made it back to my office, leaving my door wide open so that the hum of the other Sun Steer employees in the building would filter in, that I opened my drawer and pulled out another pen to twirl in my fingers.

I slumped in my desk chair, clicking my monitor to life.

I started working at Sun Steer Technologies almost five months ago, needing a change. Packing my life up in

London and moving to Orange County, California. There were perks of doing this, of course. Being closer to my cousin and childhood best friend, Mary Jiang. Living in a place where the weather was nearly perfect at all times. The thrill of starting over in someplace new.

The fact that my one-night stand was the Director of HR was just a small con, a teeny-tiny awkwardness to my day.

We never spoke about it.

Even when I showed up at the office to interview for a new position the night after she made me see gods, I saw in real time how she threw her professional mask in place.

The message was clear; never speak of that night again.

So, I haven't.

Though I was confident she thought about it as often as I did.

Because, as Americans say, Jacqueline Williams was constantly on my ass.

As soon as I spoke out of turn, or made an inappropriate joke, Jacqueline was there to scold me. Even if I was in a conference room speaking to my team, she would go out of her way to shake her head at me through the glass wall and glare.

I hadn't seen Jacqueline behave so strictly to anyone else in the office.

It felt personal.

Thankfully, everyone else seemed to accept me into the fold. I established a good relationship with my team early on, making them feel comfortable approaching me with questions or concerns regardless of how busy I was. I never wanted to seem too superior to anyone else. I wanted to be one of the guys, so to speak.

Jacqueline was the very last person at Sun Steer I

needed to win over, and I was confident that as soon as I did that, my daily stress levels would be reduced.

I wouldn't feel the need to look over my shoulder every time I threw the word "cunt" around, because apparently, that word was severely more offensive here than in London.

I wouldn't feel the need to grab anything—literally anything—to keep my hands busy whenever she stood in my presence.

Maybe we could even be friends and socialize with the others after work.

Even if I was sure I would never be able to get the expression she made when she clenched around my fingers out of my mind.

I was such a prick.

That problem of mine was probably the exact reason why it was important for Jacqueline and me to keep our distance from each other. For her to throw up this prickly wall between the two of us. She was a gorgeous woman, probably used to men not taking the hint.

I didn't want to be that kind of man.

The kind of man who couldn't be professional after knowing how it felt to be intimate with her.

The kind of man who felt entitled to her smiles or flirting simply because she had consented to intimacy with me the one single time.

The kind of man who constantly got a hard-on any time she bent in one of those torturous fucking pencil skirts.

No, I knew I wanted to be better. That I was capable of being responsible and mature. Safe. I never wanted her to feel unsafe because of what she shared with me. I understood that certain things she consented to with me had been immediately revoked as soon as we shook hands and pretended that we were meeting for the first time during my interview with her and Signe.

I wasn't expecting to feel personally targeted by her wrath as often as I was, but I desperately tried to cut her some slack.

I was a man.

She was a woman.

Things were different for us.

Things weren't as safe for her as they would be for me.

I understood the dynamic, especially in my managerial position.

I dropped my head in my hands, massaging my temples before scrubbing a hand down my face, desperate to pull myself out of those tempting memories that sometimes still haunted me in my dreams.

The sound of her voice.

The feel of her skin against mine.

"Shit," I grumbled, then immediately lifted my head to double-check that Jacqueline wasn't walking past my door at the exact moment I released a curse.

I bent down and opened the mini fridge I had installed under my desk on day one of working here, pulling out a can of espresso and flipping the top open, before I took a healthy chug. I had meetings today, and I didn't want to be tired or distracted.

I pretended that the caffeine would last this time. That it wouldn't burn out within thirty minutes of me consuming the beverage. That I wouldn't be capable of taking a three-hour nap within an hour of drinking it.

I drummed my fingers on the can for a few moments while I tapped the space bar on my work laptop again, seeing the large number of unread emails that I needed to attend to.

Then I checked the time on my phone, seeing a few interesting headlines on the local news apps I had downloaded—

"No," I grumbled to myself, turning my phone over face down on the desk, "Focus, mate." I settled into my seat, sitting straighter as I forced myself to open the first email and read.

The caffeine started to hit, and I used that temporary high to help motivate me to check off as many tasks as I could that day.

Chapter Three

LEO

"Oh GOD, OH GOD," *she was panting beautifully, heavily, while laying prone on the hotel bed on the brink of orgasm, "Please, please, I need—"*

Like I'd ever stop after I started to feel her inner walls clench erratically around me, seconds from reaching that bliss.

"You're taking me so well, Jacqueline," I encouraged, watching her jaw drop and eyes squeeze close. I rewarded her by swiping my thumb over the hardened tip of her breast, "Come for me, love. You've earned it."

THE GROUP of people gathering at the center of the pitch looked promising. Zaid Ansara and I dropped our bags next to his girlfriend on the grass, who had plopped herself down on a picnic blanket, and pulled out a laptop covered in a variety of stickers.

Why anyone would ruin the sleek, clean look of a laptop with stickers that would fade and peel over time, was mind-boggling.

"Were you on a team back in London?" Zaid asked, removing his glasses before drinking his water bottle.

"Off and on," I shrugged, lifting my back leg to stretch a bit before we joined the others, "I was more competitive in university, but now I mostly play on occasion to stay in shape." I glanced over at Zaid as he bent down to kiss Signe on the lips once in farewell before he stood taller and walked with me to meet the team, "Were you on a team?"

"No," Zaid lifted a shoulder, "I only ever played recreationally."

"Could have fooled me," I glanced down at his biceps, to his muscular form, "Are those hot girl muscles, then?"

Zaid chuckled, not offended by my banter, "I like exercising, it helps calm my brain."

"I get that." I held my fist up, and he knocked his knuckles against mine right when a whistle sounded. None of us were in any sort of uniform, just a variety of men in athletic wear. Mostly shorts. There were a lot of toned, male thighs to be seen. I smirked to myself, thinking about how Mary would gag at the sight.

Damn, I did need to make more friends.

Thankfully, Zaid seemed to be cool with us both conveniently signing up for the same rec league. I was a little worried that things would be weird between us when I came in to fill the position he used to have, but then I learned very quickly that I was doing him a favor by accepting the position of Chief Technology Officer.

Because he hated it.

Zaid and Signe welcomed me to the company with open arms, which helped make the transition a little easier considering I'd be spending forty to sixty hours a week there.

"Listen up everyone," I glanced around to find the owner

of the whistle that called everyone's attention, Zaid and I stood near the back of the crowd since we seemed to be the last ones to arrive, "Welcome, and thank you for signing up. I am your captain, and this is the Laguna Rec Rugby League. If you meant to sign up for pickleball or soccer or anything else, speak now or accept your fate." I stepped to the side, finally finding the owner of the voice.

A lean, smaller-framed person was standing in front of everyone. They had short brown hair that was pulled back with a thin headband to keep the longer locks on top out of their face, a face that had sharp cheekbones, and a defined jaw. Their septum ring glistened in the sunlight as they turned their head. When their dark blue eyes scanned the crowd of men in front of them, I squinted mine to see if I could make out the shapes that were shaved into the back of his or her head.

"Um," someone raised his hand near the front, "I thought this was the men's league."

The team captain turned their head and made direct, unblinking eye contact with the blonde who voiced their statement.

"I'm sorry," the team captain shook his or her head, "Did you have a question, or..."

I smirked, and Zaid coughed a bit to hide his laugh.

"Are we going to be playing with women, too?" The blonde waved his hand to vaguely gesture at the captain. I tilted my head at the person, since they were in charge of this gathering. Though they were smaller in comparison to some of the men here, I definitely wouldn't mistake them for weak. I could see the toned arms and rounded shoulders because of the cutoff t-shirt they were wearing, and the way they held themselves made me think they were an athlete.

"Oh, I'm sorry," they placed a hand on their relatively flat chest before pointing to the blonde and addressing the rest of the team, "Does anyone here identify as a woman? I'll be writing everyone's preferred pronouns next to their name." They held a clipboard with a list on it in the air, before someone standing directly in front of me started shaking his head, "For example, at the top here you'll find my name, Taylor Desmond. My pronouns are they/them." The man in front of me threw his hands up in the air at the same time most of the other men in the group nodded their heads in understanding.

"I don't care if you identify as a couch, or an orange, or *them*—I don't want to practice against someone biologically weaker than me and get yelled at when I inevitably hurt them."

Taylor frowned, but before they had to defend themself again, I stepped forward and slapped a hand down on the bigoted man's shoulder, making him jump as I spoke loud enough for my voice to project over the team.

"Oi," I squeezed his shoulder, the message clear in my grip as he squirmed and turned his head to look up at me with concerned eyes. I was easily one of the tallest people here standing at six five, "Nobody is forcing you to be here, mate. If our captain is a problem for you, I suggest you find something else more misogynistic to fill your afternoons."

He turned around after my advice, facing the rest of the team. There were probably about fifteen players, and all of them had a variety of disapproving expressions as they studied the man under my grip.

After a moment, he shook me off of him, "I haven't played with someone like you before," he nodded to Taylor, who stood tall and still, "I don't want to fuck something up or do something wrong."

"Do you feel threatened playing a recreational sport with me?" Taylor asked, lifting their chin.

"N-no." he shook his head. Again.

"Are you genuinely worried about hurting me, or are you worried you won't be able to toss around any slurs or problematic jokes with your boys in my presence?" Taylor added, making me raise my eyebrows.

"I'm not a homophobe," he shook his head again and crossed his arms against his chest, "I've just only ever played rugby with other men."

"Then welcome to your first day on a gender-inclusive recreational rugby team," Taylor smiled, but I could see the tension in their dark blue eyes from here, "Rest assured, I can take a hit. If I couldn't, I wouldn't fucking be here forming a *fucking* rugby team, my guy."

I grinned, falling a little bit in love with Taylor. Their eyes landed on my smile, and I saw their lips twitch with humor before they finished off strong, "Does anyone else have any concerns about my body or my pronouns?" The team was silent, Zaid and I exchanged a look with smirks and raised eyebrows, "No? Then let's run a couple of laps to warm up." They tossed their clipboard to the side and took off running, right past the group of players. The rest of the team slowly followed suit, but Zaid and I stayed and watched the man standing before us, who let his eyes trail after everyone else.

Then his dark eyes met mine again, waiting for something from me.

I nodded my head once at him and said, "Cheers!" before I clapped him on the shoulder and followed after Zaid.

"Damn," Zaid shook his head as he jogged next to me, the both of us taking up the back of the group. The player with the bigoted questions raced past us to join the men he came with, "Every time I think we've made enough progress as a society, I'm reminded that we still haven't."

"It's shit," I agreed, glancing up at Taylor as they stopped their jog to encourage everyone else to run faster. As soon as we passed them, I winked and grinned.

They rolled their eyes.

"Knees to chest, pretty boy," Taylor scolded, jogging with us again.

I turned around to face them and continued to jog backward, lifting my knees accordingly before placing a hand on my chest, "I prefer handsome, or rugged."

"Noted," Taylor's lips twitched into a grin, and after a moment they added, "...My friends call me T."

"I'm Leo," I pointed to myself, then threw a thumb over my shoulder, "This is Zaid."

Zaid slowed his jog so he could hold out a hand for Taylor to shake, "Nice to meet you."

"You too." Taylor glanced between us before cheering from the sidelines sounded. We all turned to see Signe, still sitting on her picnic blanket with her laptop in her lap, hands cupped around her mouth.

"Hot damn, look at that ass!" Signe shouted, fanning herself and dangling her tongue out of her mouth dramatically as soon as we passed by her.

Zaid laughed and shook his head at the ground.

"Your partner?" Taylor asked Zaid.

He nodded, scratching his beard and keeping up the conversation mid-jog without sounding winded, "As long as she'll have me."

I smiled at him, trying to ignore a small ache forming in my chest. It was odd, because I had no intention to settle down any time soon. I wasn't even dating anyone. The last time I was with a person was right before I moved to this country, and even then, I wasn't as into it as I had hoped to be.

Brown, scowling eyes behind gold thin-rimmed glasses filled my mind, and I shook my head once to get Jacqueline Williams out of it.

"One more!" Taylor called out, "Then we practice for our first game on Friday!"

Cheers echoed throughout the team, and I turned back around to try to focus on the workout. On the team, there were new friendships I hoped to gain. I wanted to think about almost anything else besides the small brunette who only looked at me with irritation and disdain.

THE FOLLOWING MORNING, I flicked the kickstand open with my boot, parking my bike. I rolled my head on my shoulders, letting out a pained groan because my body was so stiff.

Taylor Desmond really pushed us yesterday. For a rec team, they took exercise seriously. I didn't realize how out of shape I was until then. Thank god training was only twice a week.

I turned off my bike and grabbed my work bag before wincing off of the vehicle, standing tall and stretching my back and shoulders out.

"You, too?" I heard Signe ask from my side, and I turned to see her and Jacqueline walking toward the office building. Jacqueline gave us both a polite nod before continuing onward, but Signe approached me to walk into the building together.

"Is Zaid sore?" I asked.

Signe nodded, her bottom lip jutting out a little as she replied, "He had to take some ibuprofen this morning. He is feeling very humbled."

"He and I both," I grunted in agreement, hearing the doors open ahead. I resisted the urge to lift an eyebrow at the sight of Jacqueline propping one open with her foot for us.

"Thanks," Signe smiled as I gestured for her to step through first. I turned to Jacqueline and reached above her head to hold the door open, so she could follow after Signe.

"After you," I offered with a tilt of my head.

I glanced down at Jacqueline, which is how I saw that she blushed. It made me do a double-take.

It wasn't a subtle double-take either. I looked like a cartoon, getting ready to keep up my small talk with Signe when my head jerked back at our Human Resources representative, to double-check that her cheeks truly were filling with a warm color. Her gaze was on my arm that hovered near her head as I held the door.

Jacqueline blinked once, then frowned and turned away from me to march forward.

I was left with a subtle whiff of her perfume, something floral and mouthwatering.

After I followed the women inside, hearing Signe press the call button for the lift, I glanced over my shoulder as I wondered what made Jacqueline's cheeks turn that flattering shade.

Was it the leather jacket I wore? Was it my proximity?

Was it not related to me at all?

I stood behind the two women, the conversation lost on me as Signe chatted animatedly and Jacqueline politely listened.

I glanced down and stifled a groan.

Jacqueline was wearing another pencil skirt.

A khaki-colored thing with a pink blouse that complimented her warm skin tone.

It wasn't inappropriate for the office, but as the doors to the lift opened and the women stepped inside, I indulged myself in the movement of Jacqueline's arse moving under the form-fitting fabric. Allowing myself a few seconds to remember how my pale English hands looked against her California sun-kissed skin. Holding her hips just right for me. How I still wondered if she wore a cheeky swimsuit to keep up her tan, or if the tan lines I had seen all those months ago were faded now.

The women turned around, unaware of where my thoughts went. I forced those memories to the back of my mind while I pressed the button to send us to Sun Steer Technology's floor.

"...How close are they?" I heard Signe ask.

I glanced over my shoulder to see both of them staring at me, "Pardon?"

"The architect team," Signe clarified, "How close are they to winning the bet?"

I grinned, "Close enough to where I practiced my dance moves before leaving this morning." Signe laughed at that. The architect team was Zaid's team. It was a group of software engineers who were mostly new hires, people we recruited from other software companies in the area. The goal was for them to finish constructing the bones of the newest branch of code designed for the feature Boson Motors wanted for their machines. The caveat was that they needed less than two bugs in their code during the beta trial to win the bet.

We had a farm in Northern California that was getting our very first prototypes, and Boson Motors was preparing to send the first-ever Sun Steer-powered agricultural equipment. Solar-powered, self-driving tractors were being built for that farm at this very moment.

The bet included me, the CTO, humiliating myself for the sake of company morale.

Every single time Zaid tested the code that his team wrote, it all came back performing flawlessly.

Jacqueline lifted an eyebrow at me.

Signe added, "I love that you're willing to do it."

"Of course," I lifted a shoulder in response.

Jacqueline glanced down at her phone, as if bored, "Be sure to make it worth everyone's while, for working so hard under deadline."

I gave her a friendly grin as I replied while stepping off of the lift, "I'm happy to reward good behavior if it's earned, Jacqueline."

Jacqueline's dark eyes lifted behind her glasses and met mine, her face darkening again with another flush. I froze, because the look on her face was far from amused. I panicked, wondering what I said that justified such a reaction from her.

"Be sure to tell the team they've been such good girls, while you're at it," Signe said, noting my accidental innuendo while oblivious to the glare Jacqueline was giving me behind her back.

Fuck.

"This conversation is over unless the two of you want to be written up," Jacqueline snapped, dropping her eyes from my face and marching past the two of us before we could form a response. Her head was down, her shoulders were tugged up, and I felt like the biggest prick for making her start her day like this.

"Damn," Signe murmured, dropping her bag on the

front desk, "It's one of those days, I guess." I had to give it to her because even though Jacqueline threatened us, Signe acted very unbothered by it. As if Jacqueline's words didn't affect her at all.

I nodded, "I apologize, I didn't mean to make it weird."

Signe shrugged, "I've said worse in the office."

I believed her. How Signe and Jacqueline were friends, I had no idea. They were opposites. Signe was friendly, uplifting, and generally happy to exist. Jacqueline was... usually like this.

I nodded my goodbye to the redhead and walked toward my office. I turned into the wing where upper management's offices were lined up, mine being across from Jacqueline's. I had just seen her march into her office and close the door enough to leave a crack open when two software engineers were giving each other wide-eyed looks. They had just seen Jacqueline storm in. They were on Mary's team, but I wasn't familiar with their names yet. We hired a lot of new employees since I started working here.

The two men stood a few feet outside of Jacqueline's office and began speaking to each other with hushed tones.

"Remind me not to look at her wrong today," one of them said, a blonde, white man who smirked as he glanced over his shoulder in the direction of her open office door.

"Looks like she's in a bitchier mood than usual today," replied a short brunette man who adjusted his shoulder bag. The two of them stopped their hushed conversation as I approached, smiles spreading across their faces, "Hey, Leo."

I didn't return their smiles, "I hope you're not referring to our overworked and understaffed Human Resources Director."

They both blinked at me, "Oh—well, what I meant was

—" The blonde man jutted his thumb over his shoulder, but I interrupted his excuse.

"I know exactly what you meant," I lifted a dark eyebrow, "Do not speak about her like that again."

I waited for both of them to nod their heads and drop their gazes.

"You're right," the brunette murmured, "Sorry, man."

I left them there, my point made and employees sufficiently scolded, while ignoring the path to my own office to rap my knuckles on the cracked open door of Jacqueline's.

"What?" was her reply. I pushed her door open a little more and poked my head in.

"May I come in?" I asked. Jacqueline was just getting settled at her desk, her frown in place, and her eyes locked on mine. She stayed silent as she set her phone on her desk and pulled other items from her purse. Her iPad. A bag of granola. A small case that I assumed held the earbuds she always wore.

I ignored her silence and pretended it was an invitation as I entered her office.

"I, um," my hand lingered on the doorknob, my fingers desperately tapping out a nonsensical rhythm as nerves erupted, "I wanted to apologize. For earlier."

Jacqueline didn't say anything to that. She just dropped her gaze to her items and organized them on her desk, before pulling her keyboard towards her seat and clicking her computer to life.

It was incredibly awkward.

I was both humiliated and in awe of how powerful she was in this setting. How she made herself the biggest person in the room, making a man like me want to cower under her judgment.

"Anything else?" Jacqueline asked when she glanced at where I stood. I gripped the handle of the doorknob tighter, something aching in my chest at her words.

"Um, no," I shook my head, "Just the apology bit. I didn't mean to imply anything untoward."

Jacqueline scoffed in disbelief, "It's not the first time a man has humiliated me in the workplace. It unfortunately won't be the last."

I blinked in confusion, defensiveness for her that I didn't deserve to feel filling my chest as I stumbled out, "I—what? Jacqueline, that's not—"

"I think we're done here." She interrupted me.

I shook my head, ignoring the voice in my mind screaming at me to let it go, "I think you misinterpreted—"

"I didn't misinterpret anything, Mr. Turner," I winced, knowing there was no convincing her of anything when she called me that, "An inappropriate innuendo is one thing. Humiliating me in front of employees is another."

I raised both my eyebrows, glancing over my shoulder as if the explanation to her words would appear, before looking back at her, "What?"

"Though I may be a one-person department at the moment, I am more than capable of doing my job," Jacqueline shook her head once, "Trying to repent for your slip of the tongue in the elevator by scolding employees— who will always, *always* call me names behind my back— and implying that I am nothing but an overworked, rung-out and emotional woman isn't the way to go."

"Whoa," I held both of my hands up at her words, "It was not my intention to offend you so thoroughly this morning."

"Wasn't it?" she asked, lifting an eyebrow at me.

I gaped at her, flexing my fingers nervously before I shoved both of my fists into my pockets to still them.

"What would I gain from trying to humiliate you?" I asked.

"Why does a man ever try to humiliate a woman?" Jacqueline challenged.

I couldn't believe this.

Jacqueline truly thought the worst of me.

I ground my teeth together as frustration simmered beneath my skin, my fingers aching from how tightly they were clenched. I wanted to ask her what the problem was. I wanted to ask if this had anything to do with our one night together. I had so many questions, but none of them were appropriate to ask here. I was desperate for answers, to understand how Jacqueline arrived at this conclusion so quickly. It was like that nervous, flirty, fun side of her I met at the bar didn't exist anymore.

But I kept my mouth shut.

My jaw ached from how hard I was grinding it, so I opened my mouth and rubbed my hand along the side of my face in an attempt to loosen the muscles there.

"I see," I couldn't keep the edge out of my tone, "Again, my apologies. I will be more mindful going forward."

I saw something waver in her expression, or perhaps I was just desperate to see something that she would never reveal to me again. Regardless, I nodded at her before seeing myself out of her office and closing the door behind me.

I scraped a hand down my face, finally walking back to my office as if I had a tail tucked between my legs. I slumped down into my desk chair, running my hands over my face again and again in an attempt to calm myself.

I'll never get her to like me, I thought to myself, *She'll never like me. She decided to hate me the moment I walked into the conference room all those months ago.*

Logically, I knew that it was fine. That I didn't need to be liked by everyone. I didn't need to be friends or on good terms with all of my coworkers in the past, so this shouldn't hit as hard as it did.

And yet, I felt like I wanted to sink into a hole in the ground from the discomfort of it.

A message popped up on my laptop, the chime echoing from the notification pulling me out of my *woe-is-me* thoughts.

> Mary: Here's a list of suggestions for when you lose.

I found myself grinning at the song selection she gave. Some of them were new releases, some of them older songs we used to listen to during our teen years. I was hit with a sudden wave of memories from one song listing in particular, a guilty pleasure of mine, and I found myself staring at the name of the title in thought.

Jacqueline would never like me.

She'd always assume the worst in me, no matter what I did.

Oddly enough, the thought made a sense of spiteful determination fill my chest, and in that moment as I stared at the third song Mary suggested for my performance, I decided to make the fucking most of losing this bet.

Chapter Four

JACQUELINE

"ARE YOU ALRIGHT?" *He spoke the question against the back of my shoulder, his hot breath fanning over my skin. I arched against him, grinning when he groaned from the movement.*

"I think I need a Gatorade or something," I replied. A yawn took over the end of my sentence, but I didn't let myself be embarrassed about it. I was exhausted, in the best possible way.

"If I order food for us, do you want to stay for a little longer?" he asked, before peppering my neck with kisses. I reached out and smacked around for my phone on his nightstand. It was only about nine-thirty at night.

"Yes, please." I sighed as he pulled out of me.

"I SEE," Mariam nodded at me once, her ringlet curls bouncing around her head with the movement. Her dark eyebrows raised a bit while she gave me a look that I was now very familiar with, "...Do you want to say it, or do you want me to?"

I groaned and covered my face with my hands, my

fingertips digging into my hairline. It was an attempt to relieve the anxiety I had after filling in my therapist on the last panic attack I had at work. As well as the conversation with Leo that almost resulted in another one.

"I did the thing again," I mumbled behind my hands. The "thing" in question was assuming negative intent, and being wrong about it. My brain operated like a Rolodex of past experiences whenever I found myself in a social setting I didn't know how to navigate. I recalled how things played out in the past and attempted to navigate them accordingly.

The problem was a lot of my past experiences were traumatic. They involved toxic dynamics that required more guessing games on my part than they should have. Thus, I didn't always handle situations with grace.

"You sure did," Mariam's soothing voice was encouraging, and I thought I detected a little hint of pride as well, "But the good news is, you know you did."

"That...doesn't make me feel better," I kept my hands over my face. I was lying back against her couch in her office. It was one of those large, fluffy cloud-like couches. It wasn't a lounge bed thing you saw in the movies, but it was a spacious enough couch that I could easily sink into it as if I were lying down. I had my weighted blanket on my legs, knowing I'd need it to get her up to speed in today's session.

"That's also good," Mariam nodded, "Because that means you can take the opportunity to look inward and explore ways to make it right."

I lowered my hands, "How do I make it right?"

"How do you think you need to make it right?" Mariam asked. I frowned, and she smiled.

"I...don't know what you want me to say," I muttered. She knew I didn't respond well to open-ended questions. Questions designed to lead me to the right answer.

Questions that felt like a trap. I usually took questions and words at face value.

Leading me to the "right" answer is what my ex used to do. It took me years to understand what was happening. It took me years to learn that no matter how hard he tried, my brain wouldn't work the way he wanted it to. I was always responsible for solving his riddles, while he was never responsible for simply being honest with me. If I guessed wrong, or answered his question in a way he didn't like, that was also my fault for ruining his day.

"I don't have a specific thing I want you to say, Jacqueline. This is me just asking you a question. If you were to look back on those conversations with Brandon and Nicole and again with Leo, what would you take away from them?" Mariam leaned back and took a sip of her tea, adjusting her seat in her bean bag chair to the side of her desk. She stayed silent after that, giving me the time to think through her words.

"...That I overreacted," I murmured, "That, I assumed the worst in the moment when my body was feeling anxious. After calming down, I can see that I may have just been feeling threatened. That...I don't know, maybe their words weren't that deep."

Mariam nodded, setting her mug down on her desk while she gave me a reassuring smile, "Rewiring our brains, especially after leaving long-term problematic relationships, will always be a hard thing to do. The fact that you were able to recall those interactions, and step back to see what was really going on, is already a huge improvement. You could just dig your heels in, determined to prove that your coworkers were maliciously attacking you. But you know that's not what was happening, right?"

"Right," I sighed, my shoulders slumped because I didn't

exactly feel lighter during this conversation, "I was the problem both times."

"You're not a problem, Jacqueline," Mariam reminded me, "You're a human who is learning and *willing* to learn. You're allowed to make mistakes. Now, how have things been at work since those two discussions?"

I winced, "Awkward."

"Why?" Mariam pulled out her iPad and started jotting down notes. Or doodling. I had no idea what she did on that thing during our sessions. She could be playing games for all I knew.

"Because..." I inhaled a deep breath to get it out, "I feel like everyone's walking on eggshells around me now. It's been a week since Leo apologized to me and I was rude back to him. Usually, if I reprimand him for being inappropriate in the office, he bounces back and still smiles all the time and tries to joke around with me. But it's almost like...I don't know, he's been avoiding me."

Mariam nodded, giving me a thoughtful expression while she let me marinate in that for a few moments. Finally, she spoke up again.

"My job is an interesting one," Mariam started, "Usually, I have a client in here and they tell me these stories of how everyone else around them is the problem. Everyone else around them is rude, inconsiderate, or problematic. It takes a lot of work for someone in my position to find the truth. The reality is, that there are always two sides to every story. No matter what. My clients aren't always the most reliable narrators, because our brains instinctively try to protect ourselves from the part of us that feels shame, embarrassment, whatever else," Mariam waved her hand in the air at the end of that sentence, before settling in and focusing back on me, "What makes you one of my favorite clients is," my lips twitched with humor at her words, "that you're in here, recalling conversations you had at work, and you're doing so in a way that makes me think you are more self-aware than you give yourself credit for. You're not afraid to admit when you're wrong."

I frowned, "I didn't think I was wrong in the moment, though."

"Fight, flight, or freeze are all normal responses, Jacqueline," Mariam shrugged as she pushed her purple glasses up her nose, "You just happened to cycle through all three. You fought in the moment, during the conversation. Attempting to protect yourself by pointing an accusing finger at someone like Leo. But when you realized you misjudged the conversation, you froze and stayed away. Now, enough time has passed that I'd argue you're engaging with flight through avoidance."

I blinked at her, "I...I am?"

Mariam held back a giggle of some kind while she nodded her head at me, "Since I've started seeing you, you're quicker to apologize. Admit fault and responsibility for a tense situation. Willing to go out of your way to improve... but you haven't done that with Leo. Why?"

I frowned, "It's weird with Leo."

"Because you slept together?"

"Obviously."

"Ah," Mariam nodded, "So because you two slept together before he started working at your company, he doesn't deserve an apology from you when you assumed the worst in him?"

I widened my eyes but kept my frown in place, "I didn't assume the *worst* in him."

Mariam gave me a look, before lifting her iPad and scrolling a bit. When she reached the part of her screen she wanted, she cleared her throat and said, "Leo asked something along the lines of 'why would I want to embarrass you' and you responded with 'why does a man ever want to embarrass a woman' and then he walked out, angrily."

I nodded, "Yeah, that's right."

Mariam sighed, "If I was Leo, and I was apologizing to you for accidentally referring to our hook-up in the office, and you implied that I was lumped in with the kind of men who get off on belittling women, I would be very offended by that question."

My frown loosened, guilt filling my stomach, "You would?"

"Yes," Mariam set her iPad back on her lap, "Let me ask you this. Do you want to change the environment you're feeling at work right now? The feeling that you're being avoided or that people are walking on eggshells around you?"

I nodded, "Yes. I want things to go back to normal—well, relatively normal. I don't think I need to be best friends with Leo or anything."

"That's fair," Mariam lifted a shoulder, "You don't need to be best friends with someone for them to deserve an apology, though."

My eyes started to water, my nose started to burn and my throat constricted as if it was closing up. A large rock formed at the base of it, making it feel like I was about to start suffocating. I closed my eyes and focused on calming my body, just like Mariam had instructed me to do many times before.

She stayed quiet, giving me space to calm my anxious heart. The lump in my throat slowly started to shrink, and the burning in my nose was starting to simmer, able to be sniffed away. A tear escaped one of my eyes, and I wiped it off with my fingers.

Finally, I took another deep breath and asked, "How would you suggest is the best way for me to apologize to him?"

THE NEXT DAY I found myself standing outside of Leo Turner's office. I was wearing my work jeans, my canvas sneakers, and a cream button-up shirt that was a size too big for me. It was looser, and comfier this way. I needed my comfiest work clothes to prepare for this. I even wore my hair half up and half down, in an attempt to look more friendly. Non-threatening. Less like the uptight Human Resources representative that everyone saw me as.

The morning started off unusual, which didn't help my nerves. I felt safe with routines and predictability. So when I entered the office to loud music playing on the overhead speakers and Leo Turner dancing on top of a clump of desks, needless to say, my morning routine was disrupted.

Employees from all departments of the office gathered around, laughing, cheering, and holding up their cell phones to record the CTO of Sun Steer as he twerked and sang along with the song.

It was "Club Can't Handle Me" by *Flo Rida and David Guetta.*

I was pretty sure this was on my work playlist.

His dancing was...awful. Not good at all.

He was awkward and lanky and downright uncomfortable to watch.

But he was smiling, ear to ear. Mouthing the lyrics I was

vaguely familiar with but couldn't quite focus on because there was too much happening around me.

I stood next to Signe, who was laughing so hard at the performance that she was crying. She was wiping tears from both eyes when she laughed, "Good morning," to me. Everyone else was having fun.

There was so much positive energy in the space.

And I hated that I didn't know how to react to it.

A nervous smile took over my face, torn between watching Leo swing his hips in a way that was probably meant to look seductive, but just reminded me of awkward preteens from the one middle school dance Marco made me attend with him.

The old pop song eventually ended, and Leo concluded his performance by slumping over and supporting his weight on his knees as he gathered his breath.

Cheers erupted throughout the office, and even though I winced from the unexpected sound, I found myself raising my hands to join in with the applause.

And that's when Leo looked up from his crouch and made accidental eye contact with me.

It felt accidental because I saw a small pinch in his brow form before he looked away from me.

"Oh no, look away!" Mary was suddenly standing directly in front of me, lifting her arms up in an attempt to conceal Leo from my view, "Nothing untoward or unprofessional is happening over here!"

Mary was smiling, and obvious humor filled her tone, but I still felt my own half-smile flatten at her words.

You're the office buzz-kill.

No one wants you here.

I gave her a grin that probably looked more like a grimace before shouldering my purse and turning away from the crowd, heading toward my office. A nervous and embarrassing pressure started to expand in my chest. I knew about the bet Leo made with the engineers. I knew about him dancing and embarrassing himself for the sake of office morale. Perhaps that was why Mary's words felt like an attack.

"Wait!" Mary's voice made me pause and turn back toward her, allowing her to catch up with me, "I'm just kidding, Jacqueline." Mary looped her arm through mine, and I squeezed her limb against my ribs without a second thought as we continued towards my office arm in arm, "What did you think of his moves?"

I snickered, still wounded from Mary's teasing but feeling a little better knowing she confirmed that that's all it was, "I think he needs some more practice."

"You're not wrong," Mary halted, pulling her arm out of mine and jogging toward her girlfriend, who had just arrived, "Babe! You missed it!"

"Aw, man!" Jamie slumped her shoulders and pouted before Mary wrapped her up in her arms.

I let the two employees have their moment before everyone else got settled into their workday and did my best to settle in my own office for the time being. I opened my laptop, knowing exactly what my to-do list had on it and what my schedule was going to look like. And yet, I couldn't stop thinking about my conversation with Mariam the day before.

So after going back and forth with myself for a few hours, I grumbled and stormed out into the upper management wing.

I marched with determination before I knocked on Leo's office door, my heart jumping up in my throat when I heard his very British, "Come on in," on the other side.

Deep breaths, Jacqueline.

I let myself in, keeping my gaze on the ground until I was able to close the door behind me. I leaned back against the wood, crossing my arms over my chest, and finally forced myself to look at him.

Leo sat at his desk, braced on his elbows. He looked surprised, but he quickly masked his expression into a neutral, almost bored one before turning toward his monitor.

"How can I help you, Ms. Williams?" Leo sat back in his chair and set his hand on his mouse, clicking on something without meeting my eyes.

"I..." I blew out a puff of air and tried again, "I need to apologize to you."

Leo stiffened. He flicked his blue eyes to me for a moment before glancing back at his screen, "No need."

"Yes, there is a need," I decided to lean into being a chicken and dropped my eyes to the carpeted floor instead. Eye contact when I was anxious, was nearly impossible for me to maintain, "I offended you last time we spoke."

"...I'm pretty sure I offended you," Leo countered.

"You did," I nodded, "I thought you were messing with me. I thought that you were reminding me of..." I copied Mariam's waving hand movement to the side of me, before dropping my arm, "You know. How we met."

Leo was silent, but I still didn't look up at him. I was anxious, I thought my heart was going to race out of my chest. I might even throw up.

"I wouldn't want to do that, Jacqueline," Leo's voice was lower, softer. I nodded once, an attempt to validate him.

"I know," I sighed, "I didn't know in the moment, obviously. I assumed you were out to get me. But I thought about it after the fact, and I can see that I was overreacting." I glanced up at him, sitting still at his desk with his hand lingering on the mouse. His other arm rested on the table as he studied me, "When I asked you 'why does a man ever try to humiliate a woman' I implied that you were the kind of man who *enjoyed* humiliating women...I shouldn't have done that. That wasn't fair of me, at all."

My lip trembled. I hated the fact that I was an anxious crier, and bit my lip to keep the tears in. I didn't want to cry through my apology, I didn't want to come off as someone who manipulated forgiveness from others. I either deserved forgiveness, or I didn't.

"When I asked that," I continued, "I was trying to explain why I was suspicious of your comment. My perspective as a woman in the office. I didn't see in the moment how *accusatory* those words are in that context. But I know now. I don't want you to think that I think that...I know you're not like that, Leo. I was just being unfair to you."

I finally dropped my gaze again, right when I heard the creak of Leo's office chair indicating that he adjusted his seat, "Thank you...we're good."

I looked up at him, wiping my clammy palms on the thighs of my jeans, "You don't have to forgive me so easily. I...didn't exactly forgive you as easily."

"I know," Leo lifted a shoulder, "But I understand your perspective now, which makes the words you said sting a little less." I winced as he scooted back from his desk and stood, tapping something on his keyboard to lock his computer screen, and pulled his phone out of his pocket, "Wanna go get some lunch?"

I flinched, "Are you asking me out?"

I couldn't believe this.

It was so inappropriate; I was literally the entirety of the Human Resources department.

Leo halted, both of his dark eyebrows raised, "No...Mary and I were going to try this new burger place down the road...I was wondering if you wanted to join us..."

My cheeks burned with embarrassment, my veins feeling a little cold from the fact that I once again assumed things, not even seconds after apologizing for assuming things, "I'm sorry, I just...no, I brought my lunch today."

Leo shrugged, "Maybe next time." He shoved his phone in his back pocket and snagged his keys off of his desk before approaching me, "I know how we met makes this a little...odd." His eyes met mine then, and I was immediately taken back to that night.

How kind and confident he looked sitting next to me at the bar.

How he knew that I was trying to go home with him immediately.

I remembered it all as if it was yesterday.

"It's *so* weird," I admitted on an exhale, "I hate it."

Leo quirked his lips to the side, his brows lowering over his handsome face, but he didn't look super offended, so I didn't apologize for my choice of words. Because I *did* hate it, I wished I could move past it. I wished he was just some other employee who hadn't seen me naked and vulnerable, making obscene noises.

He was currently the only person on Earth who knew both what I looked and sounded like when I came, and I had to work with him every day.

"I wouldn't have taken the job if I didn't think it was the best choice for me. I...I didn't accept the position just to fuck with you." Leo spoke, pulling me from my thoughts.

I nodded and frowned, "Language."

"Shit, you're right," Leo sighed.

"Leo," I warned.

"Sorry, sorry," Leo smirked a bit, and I noticed myself focusing on that expression a little more than I should have. How I felt a bit of relief from seeing him in a better mood, "If you'll excuse me."

I gave him a confused look, before his gaze flicked over my shoulder toward the door I was still standing in front of.

"Oh," I jumped and opened the door, no longer trapping us in his office as we stepped through the threshold, "My bad."

Leo chuckled, "Have a good day, Jacqueline." before he strutted down the hallway toward the elevators. I stood there outside of his office, blinking at his retreating form, wondering how that went so smoothly. How laid back he was. All it took was for me to explain my side of things and apologize for being a dick to him in the workplace, and we were good.

Was it...really that easy?

Apologizing to my ex was always my gut instinct, but I prepared for about twenty-four to forty-eight hours of silent treatment regardless. Once my ex figured that I had suffered in silence enough, it was like a switch was flipped. Like I never offended him in the first place. We never spoke about the incident again, until I offended him again.

Then of course he'd throw my past grievances back in my face.

Standing there in the hallway, watching Leo glance over his shoulder to see me right where he had left me, I realized I was waiting for that kind of silent treatment.

It wasn't until Leo smirked and saluted two fingers from his forehead at me, and then turned the corner out of sight, that I realized I wasn't going to get his silent treatment.

Leo was genuine, and if he said we were good, I believed him.

It was unsettling.

It was also a relief, even though I still felt physically exhausted after getting through that apology. Instead of returning to my office, I walked towards the sensory room.

Why was I expecting Leo to react to me as if we were partners? As if we were romantically involved? We slept together once, but that was months ago.

That may be enough for my body to make the connection. I still struggled with working with him every day without constantly remembering how he looked that night. How much fun we had together. How the night was perfect, exactly what I had hoped for.

How I sure as hell didn't plan on him coming into the office the very next morning for his interview with Signe and me.

Chapter Five

JACQUELINE

He GROANS, *loud and unashamed, and I realize at that moment that Leo is the noisiest sexual partner I have ever had.*

I'm obsessed with his noises.

It's an obvious cue that he's also enjoying himself, and I want to see how loud I can make him before we part ways. Before we never see each other again.

"You don't have to—" he pants, looking down at me through hooded eyes as he runs his fingers through his sweaty hair.

His words get cut off as soon as my lips wrap around him.

AFTER HEARING laughter and loud chatter coming from Leo's office, I released a frustrated groan as I ripped out my earbuds and stood from my desk. The man was incapable of conversing in a low volume. I didn't mind noise if it was a noise I had prepared for and wanted to seek out. Like my music, or if I attended a bar that I knew would be filled with music and loud voices.

For some reason, hearing Leo's voice echo throughout the management wing where all the single offices were set up, irritated me more and more each day. At first, I thought it was because I could remember his voice from *that* night. The night we met, hours before he came to interview for the first time at Sun Steer.

His voice drew you in, and I knew firsthand how easy it was to fall under his spell.

Leo Turner was excellent one-night stand material.

Which made working with him every day so, so uncomfortable. I wasn't sure I'd ever be truly over it.

One thing at a time, though.

I marched across my office and pulled my door open, hearing his laugh boom once more before music started to play from his office across the way.

Seriously? I thought to myself.

I marched up to his open door, surprised to see Brandon and Nicole standing just inside the threshold.

Well, crap.

If the CEO and CFO were part of this, I was probably the one overreacting.

Again.

I froze, stuck between wanting to tell Leo to quiet down, while also still raw from feeling like three members of upper management implied that I was overworked and run down from my job within a week.

I was nervous, I didn't want to make them think I was incapable or that I couldn't do my job with distractions around me. Anyone would be able to work with coworkers laughing and playing music in their office, right? I was just sensitive.

You're too sensitive.

You need therapy, Jackie.

Two things I already knew about myself, but my ex's voice still rang loud and clear in my mind. I frowned, getting ready to turn on my heel and hide in my office the rest of the day when Mary's voice echoed from the space.

I hesitated, curiosity getting the best of me, because she was singing.

In Leo's office.

I turned back around to face the backs of Brandon and Nicole when I realized the song that Mary was singing along to was *Blink-182's* "Feeling This."

Nicole noticed me behind her. She leaned over to whisper to me, "They're testing out the product team's newest feature. Mary is merging it now, so we're waiting to see if it worked."

I nodded as if that was the part I was curious about before peeking in between their bodies to see inside the room.

Mary and Leo were sitting in the two chairs in front of his desk, heads bobbing to the energetic music as Mary sang the first verse and plucked away on her laptop. Signe had her phone out, recording the two while Zaid sat on the leather couch of the office, grinning from ear to ear with a computer on his lap.

Leo was also singing, but he had the easier part of the song. His phone was in his hands and his eyes were glued to the small screen. He only seemed to chime in to say, "I'm feeling this!" while Mary sang the gist of it.

The cousins were smiling, and acting goofy, and everyone else in the room was encouraging it. Everyone was having a good time while Mary and Leo performed their own rendition of the song, nodding along with the tune.

While also...working?

Suddenly, Mary stopped typing and crossed both of her fingers.

Zaid crossed his fingers too.

Leo's brow scrunched as he harmonized with his cousin.

Then the chorus hit, and my skin broke out into goosebumps.

This happened to me on occasion. I never spent the time to figure out why this phenomenon happened to me, or what triggered it. But for some inexplicable reason, hearing Mary and Leo harmonize while singing the chorus of, "Feeling This" something felt scratched in my ears. My brain too. Leo's deeper voice took the lead for the chorus, while Mary's alto filled in for the round.

I forgot all of my duties. I just stood there, pleasantly surprised at how much I enjoyed hearing Leo's voice sing like this, even if he wasn't particularly skilled.

A new auditory stim of mine was born that day, hearing Leo's voice layer with the original vocals of *Blink-182*.

Mariam was the one who informed me what stimming was. A repetitive action that my body relied on to regulate my nervous system. It was a behavior commonly found in neurodivergent individuals, and when I pointed out to her that I had not sought out any formal medical diagnosis saying I was, she reminded me that just because a doctor didn't write anything down on a piece of paper, didn't mean that I wasn't neurodivergent.

It wasn't like the symptoms of neurodivergent behaviors would wait to appear until a licensed professional permitted them to do so.

That being said, I still had no desire to seek out a medical diagnosis. Was I autistic? Was I ADHD? OCD? Or did I struggle with some type of generalized anxiety disorder? Did hypotheticals like this matter, when I had made it this far in my life without those formal labels?

That's what I told myself most of the time, anyway.

All I knew was that I needed to rely on a specific set of coping mechanisms to make it through situations that neurotypical people wouldn't necessarily struggle with as much.

Stimming was one of them.

It could look different. Sometimes it was tapping my foot, sometimes it was humming or swaying in my chair from side to side.

Sometimes it was listening to a song on repeat, back-to-back, because every time I heard the music in its entirety, I felt a rush of serotonin or even dopamine that I couldn't get from anything else.

And I knew at that moment, watching Leo and Mary goof off in his office, eyes focused on their screens, harmonizing the chorus to "Feeling This", that I was hooked.

Especially when the song neared its conclusion after Mary and Leo had made some hilarious impromptu dance moves in their seats when they sang the chorus again and again, and every time those same chills raced down my spine.

It wasn't like Mary and Leo had spectacular singing voices, but you didn't need to have one to sing with this song. It still soothed something in my ears and mind in a way I couldn't possibly explain. I didn't want the moment to end, watching the two of them perform this random song for our coworkers while they worked together.

Zaid sat forward in his seat, both of his hands gripping his laptop as his eyebrows rose above his glasses.

Eventually, though, the song did end.

"It works!" Mary stood from her chair and held her laptop in her hands, eyes wide as she hopped on the balls of her feet. Zaid tossed his laptop on the coffee table in front of him and leaned back in his seat, removing his glasses to rub at his eyes with a grin on his face.

Leo joined his cousin, standing and wrapping an arm around her neck as they both bounced in celebration. His grin took over the entirety of his face.

Everyone chuckled at the antics as Leo turned his phone out for Brandon and Nicole to see. It was some sort of code I had no chance of interpreting myself, but Nicole gave the room a thumbs up, and Brandon laughed and clapped his hands together.

And then everyone in the office clapped, including some employees who were standing behind me. I jumped when I heard their sudden applause, realizing I wasn't the only one standing outside the office watching it all happen.

Leo and Mary didn't either, because they looked past the CEO and CFO to see where the additional applause came from, and that's when Leo's icy blue gaze locked on mine.

My breath caught in my throat, so I frowned and walked away.

Cheers continued without me as I left the scene. Congratulations were given for Mary and Leo's performance and the new feature Zaid's team had built.

As soon as I shut myself in my office again and took a seat at my desk, I pulled my phone out to type in the song.

And I listened to "Feeling This" for the rest of the day.

Trying, desperately trying, to gain that similar feeling I had watching Leo sing it.

I got close, but something was off.

It wasn't until a couple of days later, enough time

passing after hearing Leo sing it, that the song started to hit me again.

I had my earbuds in at all times, getting away with the occasional smile and wave to others in the office while I focused on reaching out to candidates to hire on my personal team.

While I focused on my work.

All with *Blink 182's* "Feeling This" playing on repeat in my earbuds for the entirety of my workday. Obviously, I would take breaks, take meetings, and call potential interviewees or answer phone calls from coworkers, but I would itch until I could get my earbuds back in again.

Even when Signe, Mary, and Jamie all invited me out to lunch to eat with them, I felt like I was stiffly going through the proper social etiquette motions. To avoid coming off as a nonresponsive robot, I used listening to "Feeling This" again as motivation for checking off the "socialization" box that going out to lunch with the girls provided.

So when I left the office at the end of the week, waving goodbye to some newer employees who were also getting in their cars, I really set myself up for tremendous disappointment. I had been looking forward to turning up the volume in the car, cranking *Blink-182's* vocals as loud as my speakers could handle, and being able to feel completely absorbed by the song without the feeling of anything in my ears to do so.

I had driven home like that the last few days and found no reason for me to not continue the pattern.

That is, until my car didn't start.

I turned the key in the ignition, and nothing happened.

I tried again, holding my phone in my left hand, ready for it to automatically sync with the car's Bluetooth before I realized no matter how many times I tried, my car wouldn't start.

"Shit," I grumbled, dropping my phone and removing the keys before trying again.

There was a clicking sound, but nothing happened.

I groaned, slamming back in my seat and grinding my teeth together, trying again.

And again.

And again, smacking my hand on the steering wheel and feeling like ants were crawling over my skin. Like I had an itch in my bones I could only scratch with sound in my ears.

I was just about to pull out my earbuds to get the song pumping in my veins before I considered troubleshooting what was going on with my stupid car, when I heard tapping on my window.

I jumped with a yelp as I looked over and saw Brandon, Zaid, and Leo all standing outside my car with varied expressions. Brandon looked concerned, backing away a step when I yelped. The pinch he already had between his blond brows deepened at my reaction. Zaid stood to the side, both of his hands in his pockets as he crouched to meet my eyes through the driver's side window. Leo stood behind the two men, his arms crossed and his lips twitching as if he were fighting a smile.

"Is everything alright?" Zaid asked, his dark brows rising above his black-rimmed glasses.

I nodded before rolling down my window and replying, "Yeah, why?" I asked, flipping my phone over so it lay face down on my thigh. Why I felt like I needed to hide what I was listening to was beyond me.

"It looked like you were cussing out your vehicle," Leo

explained, nodding his head toward the front of my car, "Is it not starting?"

I felt a blush start to stain my cheeks as I frowned and tried again just for good measure.

Nope, still just that stupid clicking sound.

"Sounds like the battery, can you open the hood?" Brandon asked. It took me a moment to remember where the release was, but then he walked to the front of my car and propped the hood open to take a look. Leo joined him, and I grumbled, opening the car door and standing up while these two men started inspecting the damage.

"Do you have jumper cables?" Zaid asked, pulling his phone out of his pocket and smiling at whatever notification he received.

"I...don't think so?" I walked around to my trunk just to double-check, but I couldn't remember the last time I had needed a jump. My car was older, but it wasn't a piece of garbage.

"When was the last time you changed the battery?" Leo asked. I rolled my eyes and silently mouthed his question with an ugly and dramatic facial expression, my tongue sticking out at the end in a gag before I glanced up and saw Zaid standing there with his hand over his mouth, his shoulders shaking as he looked away from me.

"I don't remember," I replied to Leo, covering my face with my hands. I couldn't believe Zaid had just seen me act like an immature child because the new CTO asked me a simple, non-annoying question.

I was just annoyed because it was *him*.

And I was cranky because my stimming was interrupted.

"What's going on?" Signe's voice echoed across the pavement. I dropped my hands and smiled at my friend as she walked up to Zaid's side to bump her round hip with his.

"Jacqueline's car won't start," Zaid explained with a chuckle, wrapping an arm around her waist and pulling her close to him.

"Wow," Signe's hazel eyes widened as she turned to me with a smirk, "How many men does it take to start a car?"

I snorted.

"We were all talking when we saw Jacqueline start to hit her steering wheel," Brandon spoke up, "But everything looks fine, does anyone have jumper cables?"

"I don't," Zaid shook his head, "My car doesn't need them."

"I rode my bike today." Leo scratched the back of his head, a small frown turning his pink lips down as everyone gathered on the driver's side of my car again.

"Actually, I think I might have some," Brandon nodded to himself, before walking toward his car.

I studied my fingernails, refusing to look up at Leo who stood next to me. I leaned against the closed back seat door of my car, embarrassment flooding my cheeks because I mostly wanted the car to start so I could listen to my music again.

"We should probably go," Signe spoke up after a silent moment, "You got this?" she asked, her voice indicating that she turned to the side. I glanced up to see Brandon returning with the cables.

"Yeah, this should do the trick," Brandon waved goodbye to Zaid and Signe, and I thought I noticed a look flicker across his expression as he watched his old friend walk away. It almost looked...sad. It was hard to tell because he quickly composed himself and focused on attaching the cables to my battery.

"You're lucky that I parked next to you today," Brandon

murmured as he walked over to his car and attached the cables there too.

I thought I heard Leo make a grunt after that comment, but I ignored him as I watched Brandon finish whatever he was doing.

Then, both men turned to look at me.

"...What now?" I asked, tapping my fingers on my folded arms.

Leo chuckled, making me turn around to see him brace one of his large hands on the top of my car, his head nodding to the open driver's side door, "You start the car."

I frowned and glanced at the large jumper cables connecting the two vehicles.

"...It won't blow up?"

Leo snorted while Brandon fought a smile and explained, "Your battery has no juice. Starting the engine just means it'll take some of mine to start yours. It won't blow up."

I shifted from foot to foot, knowing that my impatient urge to start listening to music again was making me anxious.

"...Do you want me to—"

"Yes please," I interrupted Leo's offer by stepping back and gesturing for him to take a seat. Leo nodded, a smirk on his face as he folded his large body into my driver's seat.

"Damn, you have short legs." He yanked the seat back just enough for him to fit with one of his legs stepping outside the car, his foot flat on the asphalt. I noticed that my phone was face down on the center console still, and I felt a little bit of relief that he couldn't see my screen.

Then Leo turned the keys and started the car.

The sound of my little engine roaring to life made my shoulders sag with relief.

The sound of *Blink-182's* "Feeling This" blasting from my speakers a second later, made me want to throw up.

I dove into the car to grab my phone.

I knocked it into the passenger seat, so I crawled after it.

Finally grabbing my phone in my hands, I tapped the screen and paused the song.

I sighed, hanging my head for a second before I noticed a pair of large warm hands on my waist.

I jolted, realizing that I was currently bent over Leo's lap, still sitting in the driver's seat of my car. I panicked again, trying to crawl back out of the car so I was no longer inappropriately draped across him, but his fingers flexed on my waist, holding me in place.

"Please don't," Leo groaned through gritted teeth. I looked over my shoulder and saw his eyes squeezed shut, his face twisted in a grimace, and a muscle popped in his cheek.

"What?" I asked, before noticing exactly where my knee was.

Right on top of his groin.

"Oh no!" I gasped, immediately adjusting my position so that no part of my leg was resting against him. This caused my feet to dangle out of the car uselessly, my weight supported by both of my hands and his. With his eyes still closed, Leo used his grip on me to slowly guide my body out.

"What just happened?" Brandon asked, his dark blonde brows pinched in confusion while I regained my footing. I ignored Brandon's question and crouched over the driver's side door to look at Leo, who released a large exhale. He was still hurting.

"Do you need...ice?" I asked, unsure how to handle a situation like this. I had never kneed a man in the groin before. I hadn't even accidentally hit a man in the groin before. I had no idea what to do here.

Leo huffed out a small, unimpressed laugh, shaking his head, "Just give me a minute."

"I'm so sorry," I leaned forward to rest a hand on his leg, the one still hanging out of my car, "I didn't mean to hurt you."

"Oh...sorry, man." Brandon looked uncomfortable after realizing exactly how I had hurt our coworker.

"It's alright," Leo sighed, "Heaven forbid we learn about Jacqueline's taste in music." He finally opened his eyes, and though they weren't as light and humorous as they usually were, I found myself removing my hand from his leg and standing tall enough to cross my arms over my chest.

"I just didn't want to blow out your eardrums," I lied.

"I'd take your car to get checked out, maybe order a new battery," Brandon added, completely changing the conversation as he pulled his vibrating cell phone out of his pocket. He frowned at it once before answering with a "Yeah?"

He glanced at the two of us, and I waved him off to let him know I didn't need him to stick around.

I watched Brandon fold himself into his sports car, frowning at whoever he was listening to on his phone as he eventually drove out of the parking lot. I glanced back down at Leo, whose eyes were lowered and unfocused on some point on my lower body. I glanced down, my pencil skirt perfectly in place and not revealing anything inappropriate.

I snapped my fingers once in Leo's line of sight, pulling him out of whatever distant thought he was in. After blinking a few times, he shook his head once and made his way to unfold himself from my driver's seat. His movements were slow and careful, clearly still in some amount of pain but not enough to be immobile.

"I'm really sorry about hurting you, I promise it was an accident," I sighed, stepping back so that he had room to stand. My car was still running next to us.

"I don't know, it was very sudden and aggressive," Leo shrugged, "You could have fooled me."

"I just wanted to get my phone, I didn't even realize what I did until after," I added, rubbing one of my hands on my neck. It was a nervous tick of mine. I kept my palm flat on the base of my throat, over my collarbone. My fingers massaged the side of my neck and my thumb brushed against the dip at the hollow of my throat. I didn't even realize I was doing it until I saw Leo's pale blue eyes lock on where my hand landed.

And suddenly I was transported back into his hotel room.

"Can you—maybe—" I grabbed his hand and dragged it up, up, up. His rough palm scraped against my skin as his fingers brushed against the base of my neck. We locked eyes together as I kept his hand moving, his palm resting gently where I guided him. Right when his hand was where I wanted, I curled my fingers around his to show him how much pressure I wanted him to apply on the sides.

"What's your safe word, Jacqueline?" Leo's voice was raspy, his eyes hooded and his cheeks flushed as I removed my hand from his.

"Glacier." I breathed out.

"Do you want to use it?" Leo asked, his thumb brushing against my skin in gentle swipes.

"No." I shook my head to emphasize my seriousness.

"Just don't forget that you can," Leo groaned, pulling his hips back and slamming into me.

"Jacqueline?" Leo's voice pulled me out of my memory, and even though my skin was already warm, I felt my cheeks redden under his stare even more.

Did he also remember those kinds of details?

Was that kind of night a normal occurrence for him?

"Sorry, what?" I asked, dropping my hand and hugging myself.

"Did you like our performance that much?" Leo asked, a dark eyebrow raised in challenge.

I glared at him, "No."

"Are you positive?" Leo asked, tilting his head as he crossed his arms, his regular playfulness was slowly coming back, "Because I find it interesting that you're listening to the same song that I know you heard Mary and I sing earlier this week."

"It's a weird coincidence," I ground out and threw myself into the driver's seat of my car. I went to slam the door shut, but Leo's large hand caught it before I could.

"Jacqueline," Leo's voice was almost taunting, but I thought I detected a hint of something else. Something soothing. Perhaps it was just his English accent. Perhaps I wanted to hear something else in that warm voice of his. Regardless, I found myself looking up at him. My hand on the handle of my door, his on the frame, holding it open.

I didn't verbally reply to him, I just gave him my eyes.

He met my gaze, his grin softening with the rest of his facial features, "You know I'm just taking the piss with you, right?"

I ground my teeth together and nodded, but it was one stiff movement. I wasn't willing to touch "taking the piss" with a ten-foot pole, because at least he didn't curse at work.

"You know I'm not arrogant enough to think that our mediocre rendition of their song got you hooked on a band that's been around for decades?" Leo lifted both of his eyebrows. Little did he know, that is quite literally what happened. Sure, I had heard the song before. I was familiar with the band's hits. But the reality was that I didn't know all the words to this specific song before I started hyper-fixating on it this week.

All because I heard him, specifically, sing it in his office.

Why did my brain do this to me? I couldn't say.

"I don't know," I inhaled a deep breath before giving him a smile I didn't recognize. It was a smile I wasn't familiar with; one I hadn't made often at all. It was as close to a shit-eating grin as I could muster, "I know how cocky you can be when you think you've earned it."

I gave his body a long, lingering perusal as I delivered that statement. When I finished dragging my eyes up his form, meeting his gaze, I got to see his clear eyes widen a fraction. I got to see his smirk relax into a surprised, parted lip *something* that made me feel like I had finally won an interaction between the two of us. I took half a second to scan his features, ensuring that no anger or embarrassment was coming off of him.

Instead, all I could see from him was stunned silence.

And it was the power I felt, catching this flirty man off-guard with a very thinly veiled innuendo, that made me bite my lip and pull the door shut. Leo stood there, having removed his hand so that his fingers didn't get caught, as I tapped on my phone to resume the song. I was mouthing along with the chorus, the part that Leo's voice harmonized beautifully with, as I waved my fingers goodbye to him and drove out of my parking spot.

I glanced in my rearview mirror, shimmying in my seat with giddiness when I saw Leo standing exactly where I left him, his head tilted towards me before he shook it once and started walking to his motorcycle.

I gave him a glimpse of who I was with him that night, so many months ago.

Before he started working here, and I had to introduce him to Work Jacqueline.

The person who allowed him to pull orgasm after orgasm, almost effortlessly. The person that was sore in the most delicious way the next morning, before he walked into the office.

I hoped that it wouldn't come back to bite me in the ass.

Chapter Six

LEO

"You didn't expect to spend your whole night in your hotel room?" Jacqueline asked me, brushing her long hair over her shoulder to conceal her breasts from my view.

"No," I admitted, before gently reaching forward to skim my fingers on her bare shoulder, "But I'm not upset about it at all."

I haven't wanked this much since I was fourteen years old and discovered the beauty of deleting the browser history off of my mums' computer. The weekend went by as normal, now including a recreational rugby match with my new team and slowly befriending Taylor Desmond. Running errands. Going for rides along the beautiful coastline on my bike. And in between all those things, bashing one out to the thought of Jacqueline Williams. It was now Monday morning at 6:13 am, and I couldn't start my day without releasing this pent-up energy that had been burning in my veins ever since Jacqueline left me in her dust last Friday.

I gripped myself in my bed, prone on my back as I

recalled those memories that I constantly tried to push away during work. How soft she felt underneath me, how her voice rang beautifully when I did something *just* right for her. How she guided me so that she could finally fall over that edge again and again. I had never been with a woman so responsive before. Though I tried to go out of my way to ensure my partners had a good time and reached their release at least once, if not multiple times, Jacqueline was different. It was as if we were two bodies designed for each other. Effortlessly reacting and responding just as both of us needed. I had never felt the need to keep going. To take a break, simply to regain the energy to do it all again.

It was a bloody miracle that I was able to roll out of bed on time the next morning.

Picturing the look in her eyes as I hovered over her, the feel of her soft body underneath mine. Completely compliant, ready for me. It's what sent me over the edge that morning.

It wasn't until I regained feeling in my legs and the stars cleared from my vision that I realized my cell was buzzing on my nightstand. I gathered some tissues from my bedside table and cleaned myself up before grabbing my mobile to check the notifications.

It was a group text.

> Signe Lange: Hi friends. Jacqueline's car won't start this morning, but Zaid and I have the day off and are up in the Bay Area. Can someone carpool with her?
>
> Brandon Moore: I'm already in the office.
>
> Mary Jiang: I'm carpooling with Jamie. I'm pretty sure we live on the other side of town from her, but we could probably swing by.

> Signe Lange: That might be good, she's onboarding a new hire today and doesn't want to be super late. She just wants to avoid paying for a ride-share.

I sat there, holding my phone, picturing Jacqueline hitting her steering wheel in annoyance and frustration. I guess she didn't take her car in over the weekend like Brandon suggested.

> Me: Where does Jacqueline live?

I watched the three dots of both Mary and Signe's contact float for what felt like an extraordinary length of time before their responses came in simultaneously.

> Signe Lange: Costa Mesa, a few blocks from me.

> Mary Jiang: Costa Mesa.

The thing is, I was also a few blocks away from Signe. We had seen each other on the road a few times driving home from work but hadn't discussed where the other lived.

> Me: I can pick her up.

> Mary Jiang: You're closer but let me know if she tells you to fuck off, and Jamie and I will get her.

I smirked, giving the group chat a thumbs-up emoji before opening the company app. I found the employee directory and pulled up Jacqueline Williams' information, tapping on her phone number and adding it to my contacts.

Me: Your ride is on the way.

Jacqueline: What?

Jacqueline: No.

Me: Do you want to be on time or not?

I finally got up from my bed and started rummaging around for some clothes as I watched the three dots appear and disappear. I chuckled to myself while pulling a t-shirt on over my head. Then her message came in.

Jacqueline: Fine. You'll need to bring me a spare helmet though.

I raised both of my eyebrows.

Perhaps she didn't know that I also had a vehicle besides a motorcycle. However, I wasn't about to correct her assumption. If Jacqueline Williams was agreeing to ride on my bike, I wasn't going to look a gift horse in the mouth.

Jacqueline: Also here's my address:

Jacqueline: I guess you could have looked that up the same way that you got my number, but whatever.

Jacqueline: Also no weaving in between cars.

Jacqueline: Also what do I wear?

I smirked before hitting the dial on her contact and turning on the speaker.

"What?" Jacqueline asked, her annoyed voice rang while I waltzed over to my ensuite bathroom to fix my hair.

"You're overthinking this," I replied, turning on the

water to tame the ends of my hair that were sticking up all over the place.

"I've never—" she stopped herself, but I waited. I set the cell down while I put some paste on my toothbrush and started scrubbing at my teeth, "I've never been on a motorcycle. Is my hair going to be crazy by the time we get to the office?"

Perhaps I should have told her that I had a car to drive if she preferred, but I never said I was a perfect person.

"Braid your hair, it'll fit the helmet better," I replied before spitting in the sink and rinsing my mouth, then I continued, "Wear jeans, I have a spare bike jacket you can use."

"Bike jacket?" Jacqueline asked, her voice broadcasting how nervous she was.

"It'll protect you, and also keep you warm." It was early in the morning, and the marine layer from the Pacific Ocean still clouded the sky and filled the air with salty humidity.

"Okay," Jacqueline's voice sounded a little breathy.

"I'll keep you safe, don't worry," and just because I couldn't help myself, I added, "I won't do any wheelies either."

"Absolutely *no* wheelies," Jacqueline snapped, ending the call.

I laughed as I walked out of my bathroom, grabbing my work bag to take her for a new kind of ride.

THIS WAS A HORRIBLE IDEA.

I had just wanked this morning, so there was no reason for me to be struggling with an erection in the middle of the motorway.

All it took was for Jacqueline to walk out of her building, her hair braided over her shoulder just as I instructed her. Her jeans were loose around her ankles but snug against her ass. Her long-sleeved shirt was just loose enough that I could grab a fistful of it and use it to tug her towards me.

But I didn't do that.

Instead, I offered her the bike jacket that was too big for her but would protect her regardless. I helped her zip it up and strap it over her sleeves. Then I helped her with the helmet. She truly hadn't worn one before, because she struggled to tighten the strap under her chin. My helmet was already on, so I gently patted her hands out of the way to tighten it for her. Safety first.

Jacqueline nudged my hands out of her way and struggled with the strap again. After watching her for about ten seconds, I shook my head and replaced her hands with mine. She tried to fight me, but I gripped the jaw of her helmet and pulled her close. Making eye contact with her through the visors, silently telling her to stop. She made a frustrated, muffled noise under her helmet before her hands dropped, crossing them over her chest. I immediately tightened the strap under her chin. Once we confirmed that the mics in the helmets worked and we could hear each other, I apologized for not having spare gloves for her.

She said it was fine and listened to my careful instructions on where to place her feet and how to hold onto me.

With her arms snug around my waist.

So not only did I suffer with the feeling of her warm thighs wrapped around mine, but her entire front also pressed against my back. Now, her hands were slowly trying to sneak under my leather jacket without me noticing. Her hands were cold from the breeze riding my motorcycle created.

"Jacqueline," I spoke into my headset, "What are you doing?" I checked over my shoulder to ensure no vehicles were in my blind spot, before taking the exit into Irvine.

"Please?" Her voice was so small, so desperate, that I immediately gave in. We pulled to a stop light at the end of the off-ramp, and as I loitered with the bike by placing one of my feet on the pavement to balance us, I helped her tuck her hands under my jacket and shirt. The feel of her cold fingers on my bare skin made me twitch.

"I'm sorry," Jacqueline whispered, as she placed as much of her cold hands on my stomach as possible.

"You're fine," I tried to sound soothing, and not like I was trying to figure out how to hide my hard-on as soon as we arrived at work and stepped off of this thing, "I should have just given you my gloves."

"No, you're driving. It makes more sense for you to wear them." Jacqueline countered.

"Perhaps," I shrugged, glancing over my shoulder. My helmet didn't allow me to see a lot, all I could see was her leg pressed up against mine, her arm wrapped around my waist, and the hint of her shoulder under my spare jacket, "But now we get to go through the day pretending that you didn't spend the entire ride feeling me up."

Jacqueline stiffened behind me, and I felt a sick thrill race through me when her hands under my shirt tightened so that her nails teased my skin, "I'm not feeling you up."

"Sure," I nodded, watching the light turn green, "Tracing my abs is a very normal way to warm up your hands." At that, her thumb stopped its casual, passing movement on my stomach, and I couldn't hold back the chuckle I released.

God, I loved messing with her.

"That's not—" Jacqueline sighed, "Never mind."

"What?" I pressed.

She released another irritated sigh before trying again, "I mean, sure, you have nice abs—"

"You knew that already." I didn't try to hide the smile on my face as we wove through suburban Irvine traffic on the less busy streets.

"The point is," Jacqueline sounded like she was speaking through clenched teeth, "I'm anxious. It's loud. It's scary. I'm one wrong turn from being smushed into a pancake on the road." I frowned, silently scolding myself for not taking her anxiety as seriously as I probably should have, "I'm... fidgeting. Please don't be concerned about me making a pass at you. I promise I'm not trying to."

Why not, though? I wanted to ask. *Isn't it painfully obvious that it would be reciprocated?*

"I'm not worried, Jacqueline," I removed one of my hands from the handlebars and placed it over my jacket, right where her hands were slowly warming up under my clothes. I pressed against hers through the material, "I'm just tossing you some banter."

"I don't always understand when that's happening," Jacqueline replied. It was a quiet reply, I probably wouldn't have heard it had I not been focused on every hitch in her breath, on every sound that escaped her lips.

"How about this," I asked, as I turned onto the quiet road that led to our office building, "If you are ever unsure whether I'm taking the piss with you," I lifted a shoulder, the movement making her fingers flex on my stomach once, as if she was afraid that I would shrug her off, "Just ask me."

She was quiet as we turned left one last time into the longer drive that led to the car park. The office building wasn't huge. It was only five stories tall, and there were three other buildings in the same complex. The only indication that Sun Steer headquarters set up shop here was the giant block letters on the top of the building that Brandon ordered, facing the nearby motorway.

"Okay," Jacqueline finally replied. I wasn't sure she would. I patted her hand on my stomach once, before pulling into a spot near the front. Other employees were filtering in through the lot, doing double takes when they realized who was on the back of my bike this morning.

I flicked the kickstand open and propped the bike up, before pulling my helmet off and doing a quick pass through my hair with my fingers, attempting to tame the helmet hair as quickly as possible.

It wasn't until I rested the helmet on my lap that I glanced down and noticed something with a smile on my face.

Jacqueline was still clinging to me, her hands stuck against my stomach. Her front plastered to my back as if we were on the road and not parked.

"Jacqueline?" I called, glancing over my shoulder.

"Hmm?" came her reply from under her helmet.

"We're here." I placed my hand on her forearm, my thumb pushing the sleeve of the oversized jacket back so I could swipe gentle strokes against the inside of her wrist.

Jacqueline's head snapped up as she pulled away from me, cool humid air brushed through our bodies as her heat left mine.

"Oh thank god," Jacqueline wheezed, as she slid her hands out from under my clothing. Her fingers scraped against my abs; a movement that made me flex against her touch. As soon as her hands lifted to start working on the clasp, I tried to subtly rearrange the inappropriate bulge in my pants as I hopped off the bike. It was awkward, because

Jacqueline stayed in her seat, still struggling to remove her helmet.

"What babyproof garbage is this?" Jacqueline grumbled.

I chuckled, setting my helmet on my seat, before stepping forward and grasping her wrists.

"It's not childproofed," I replied, "Let me." I lowered her hands before taking over the clasp, releasing the latch effortlessly because it truly wasn't that complicated to do. I gently guided the helmet off her head, and the breath whooshed from my lungs at the sight of her.

Her hands lifted to tuck stray strands of her hair behind her ear, at the same time that her dark brown eyes lifted to meet mine. Her cheeks were flushed, her lips a little glossy and swollen. Was she biting them during the ride over? Was she wearing some sort of lipstick designed to make me want to bend down and suck her bottom one into my mouth?

I took a moment to collect myself, backing away a good step so that she had room to hop off the bike. Though she had given me permission to be intimate with her in the past, it was very clear that permission wasn't still permitted.

Jacqueline had bent over backward to ensure our relationship stayed strictly professional.

...Unless her hands were cold, then she had full access to anything underneath my clothing.

Yeah...I'd take what I could get.

"How was it?" Mary's voice echoed across the pavement. I held my arm out to help Jacqueline off the bike, as both of our heads turned to see my cousin and her girlfriend walking hand in hand towards us.

"Fine." Jacqueline shrugged a shoulder, before releasing my hand and shrugging out of her oversized jacket. I held my hand out to take it, and she draped the material over me before seeing the two helmets in my hands.

"Here, I have yours." Jacqueline turned around to grab both of our bags out of the basket on the back of the bike.

"It's okay, you don't—"

"I'm going to," Jacqueline shook her head once and shouldered my laptop bag on her back, her purse looped on her arm, "Let's go, the new hire will be here soon."

Mary and Jamie were grinning at us as Jacqueline marched past them on her way to the doors.

I lifted an eyebrow at my cousin, who wiggled her eyebrows back at me.

Mary had no idea that Jacqueline and I had an intimate history, which made me give her a questioning look.

"I love riding on the back of Mary's bike," Jamie spoke up, ignoring the silent conversation my cousin and I were trying to have.

"Oh?" I asked, jogging ahead in an attempt to get the door before Jacqueline, but I was too slow. She already propped the door open and was holding it for the three of us.

"Yeah," Jamie sighed as Mary dropped her hand her to lower back, guiding her girlfriend through the threshold first, "At first I was terrified."

"I understand that," Jacqueline replied as she waited for me to pass her as well. Then she followed us to the elevators, "I think every muscle in my body has been clenched for the past twenty minutes."

"Now, though," Jamie pressed the button to call the lift, "I like it. Every time I get on the bike with her, I want to pat myself on the back for stepping out of my comfort zone."

I glanced down at Jacqueline, and I got to see how her eyes studied one of our sales reps. Did Jacqueline also appreciate stepping out of her comfort zone? I doubted it. Jacqueline seemed like the kind of person who thrived on routine and familiarity. Trying something new didn't seem like an easy feat for her, now that I know what she was like on the back of my bike.

Shit, I really should have just driven my car.

"That's a good point," Jacqueline lifted her hand and patted herself awkwardly on the shoulder, avoiding my backpack, "Go me."

Mary snorted as we all stepped onto the lift, "I think it's important to note that I don't ride my motorcycle to work, because I'm not an attention-seeking douche."

I lifted my middle finger at my cousin, dropping my hand just in time before Jacqueline turned around and saw the gesture.

"Leo flipped me off." Mary pointed at me accusingly with a bored expression, which somehow made Jamie laugh. Jacqueline turned to glance at the two of us, me holding my breath, Mary keeping her deadpan expression perfectly in place.

"...I'll be sure to add it to the long list of complaints." Jacqueline shrugged before facing forward again.

Hold the fuck up.

"Long list of complaints?" I repeated with disbelief.

"Mhmm." Jacqueline held her wrist up to check her digital watch, keeping me at her back.

"May I ask who wrote these complaints? Besides..." I trailed off.

"Me?" Jacqueline finished. The lift dinged and the doors opened, allowing the women to step off first, "You can ask, but I will not tell you. Confidentiality, and all that."

"Sure," I smirked, narrowing my eyes at her backside before catching myself, "Confidentiality."

"Of course," Jacqueline nodded, pulling her phone out of her bag and widening her eyes, "Shoot!" and then she scurried off towards her office. I stood there, standing with my cousin, admiring how her legs looked in jeans. I wondered if there was anything Jacqueline could wear that wouldn't look flattering on her when I felt a sharp elbow in my ribs.

"What?" I asked my cousin as she glared up at me.

"Stop checking her out," Mary whispered with an eye roll, "Fucking *men*."

I shared a guilty smile with Jamie before the blonde was tugged away past the front desk.

Mary was right though.

I needed to do better.

Progress was being made with Jacqueline, and I didn't want to ruin any chances of friendship (or more realistically, simple amicability) by letting my mind wander whenever it had the chance.

Chapter Seven

JACQUELINE

"Again?" I asked him through a giggle. He mumbled something against my chest I couldn't understand, so I tugged on his hair to make him come up for air.

His slow, mischievous grin greeted me right before he pulled out of my grip and licked a hot stripe between my breasts.

I was distracted, and I blamed my car not starting and having to get a ride to work on Leo's stupid, dangerous—but confusingly sexy—motorcycle.

"So no holes in our jeans, obviously," the new hire sitting in the chair across from my desk spoke. Her voice made me blink up at her to focus, "How does Sun Steer feel about tank tops?"

I tilted my head in thought, "Tank tops?"

"Like..." She pulled her cardigan to the side, revealing a thick strapped forest green tank.

"Oh, that's fine." I waved her away while I finished filling out the form on my iPad and filed it away under her name. A quick peek at the employment badge I had just given her reminded me that her name was Violet Thompson.

And yet, her hair was a bright electric blue.

It reminded me of Leo's eyes.

Get a grip, Jacqueline.

"That's a fun color." I nodded towards her hair, tied up in a braid that hung over her shoulder. Similar to how I wore my hair today.

"Thanks," Violet perked up at the compliment, "I'm glad it's not an issue here."

"Has it been an issue before?" I asked, puzzled. Most tech companies didn't mind how their engineers looked on the job. As long as the products they developed worked, that's all that mattered.

Except for my last job, where my boss asked me not to wear jeans to the office. Working at my old company Blix was the worst, for many reasons. I was still unlearning a lot from that organization.

"Well, I worked at another small startup in LA before this. It was cool, but the company ended up being bought out. And the people that took it over, um..." she trailed off as she gave me a once-over. I followed her gaze to wonder what she was seeing but couldn't come up with anything before I met her eyes again, "They wanted their employees to present a certain way."

"That's stupid," I shook my head, then I dropped my forehead in my hand, "I apologize. That wasn't professional."

Violet grinned at me, her smile glowing as she replied, "No problem. I'm glad you all seem more relaxed here."

I smiled at her in return, "You've only spoken to me so far."

"Yeah," she lifted a shoulder at me, "But if Human Resources is this chill, that's probably a good thing, right?"

I did my best not to gape at her.

No one, not since starting here, had ever referred to me as "chill."

My brother Marco has told me to "chill out" numerous times. Chill was Signe. Chill was Mary. Chill was Leo.

I was not chill.

But Violet thought I was chill right now.

And I desperately wanted to cling to that image she had of me for as long as possible, before working with me inevitably dulled it.

"I'm going to introduce you to a few team members before we head over to the all-hands meeting in thirty minutes," I opened my phone to check the time, trying not to smile too much at Violet's compliment, "Feel free to ask me any questions that come up."

"Sounds good." Violet and I stood and made our way out of the office, and part of me wondered if I was capable of becoming someone chill. If working here over time would soften the prickly personality that I had.

I thought I was already smoothing out a bit. Mariam thought I was doing better, simply by going to brunch every other week or so with Signe and the other women in the office. I didn't socialize much outside of work, preferring the silence and solitude of my apartment after a long day. However, according to Mariam, going to brunch in the middle of the workday still counted as a social engagement.

I thought perhaps I should push myself to be better friends with these women. It wouldn't hurt to hang out with someone at my apartment maybe once every other week, too. If they were into being couch potatoes, that is.

But what if I became friends with Violet, only to

discover that she's one of those people who was into things like hiking?

"Is this her?" I heard Mary ask from down the hallway. I snapped my head up and threw on a smile.

"This is Violet Thompson," I gestured between the two women, "One of our new systems engineers."

"Oh, I'm so excited that you're here," Mary grinned and shook Violet's hand with enthusiasm, "We're getting so close. We're just working out the bugs we've found between Boson's engines and this new feature we developed. I'd love to get your input once you have time to look everything over."

"Sounds awesome," Violet's eyes lit up, "I love problem-solving."

"Thank f—god," Mary caught herself with a smirk in my direction, "We can now use two hands to count the number of women who work at Sun Steer."

"Yikes!" Violet laughed before we continued the rest of the office tour. I pointed out where all the facilities were, including the mother's lounge and sensory room. When we passed the restrooms, I remembered Signe's fit about a year ago when she discovered the coin-operated tampon dispenser for the first time.

How I watched her hold her palm out to Zaid, who was CTO, waiting for him to drop quarters into her hand.

That felt like such a long time ago.

Signe definitely would have been written up if we were working at Blix, my old company.

But Violet was right; things were more relaxed here.

I needed to remember that.

"Whatchya listenin' to?" Signe asked as I approached the women at the table.

It had been a week since we hired Violet, and she had readily accepted Signe and Mary's invitation to girls' lunch.

"My work playlist," I replied, feeling the heat of embarrassment flood my cheeks.

You're beautiful, but your taste in music is trash, Jacqueline.

Goddamn, not this again.

Why do you insist on making me want to claw my ears out?

I frowned at the memory of Vincent's words. How he hated my music. He thought it was tasteless, meaningless. He refused to listen to more than one song I chose in the car, or around the apartment we used to share. Whenever I turned on my music to listen to in the shower, he would sneak into the bathroom and turn it down so he wouldn't have to hear it in the other room.

"Oh, gimmie." Signe made grabby fingers for my phone. She waited patiently for me to remove my earbuds and put them away in their case before I showed her the screen on my phone. My playlist was still up, and it had the last song I was listening to fully on display.

"I forgot about that song," Violet said, leaning around Signe to get a view as well, "That's on your work playlist? What else is on it?"

I hesitated for a moment.

Then I forced myself to recall Mariam's words.

If someone feels that comfortable putting down your likes and interests, they are the worst kind of person. They're not your friends. Don't hide that part of yourself, just give people the opportunity to prove that they care about you and your friendship. If they don't, let them go.

That session with Mariam was about a year ago, the day before I discovered Signe's secret romance novel that was essentially fanfic of Zaid. When I confronted her about it, she was distraught that I had gone to Zaid first. When she said she thought we were friends, it felt like a physical punch in my gut.

Later, after sorting the mess out with Zaid and learning that he was hopelessly in love with her (and nobody felt harassed in the workplace), Signe and I had a heart-to-heart where I admitted my music taste to her.

And she never made fun of me for it.

So with that in mind, I handed my phone over to Violet, who eagerly scrolled through the songs.

"Jacqueline," Violet shifted her gaze toward me, "This playlist is fire."

"Is that good?" I was horrid at keeping up with the newest slang.

"This is basically what I would listen to back in middle school and high school," Violet replied.

"I still listen to half her playlist," Mary added, smiling at me "Because you reminded me how fun the music is."

I grinned, before finally taking my seat next to Mary, "There is something so nostalgic about recession pop."

Signe threw her head back to laugh, making me jump in my chair at the abrupt sound. The other women started laughing too, even shy Jamie.

"Recession pop," Signe wiped the corner of her eye, "That's amazing. I'm making a playlist like this and titling it that."

My phone buzzed, and Violet's eyebrow shot up before she held it out to me, "Someone named Marco just texted you."

"Oh." I took it from her hands and sat in my seat, excited for what he had to say.

Signe leaned over, pressing her body against mine as she

looked over my shoulder to see my text thread with him, "So...who's Marco?" I could practically hear her eyebrows wiggling suggestively.

I smirked, "My brother."

"Oh," Signe leaned back, "Boring—wait, you have a brother?"

> Marco: Sorry I didn't respond, Dad and his new girlfriend dropped by unexpectedly last night.

> Me: Oh really? How did that go?

> Marco: As well as it usually does, except I was balls deep inside Samuel when they knocked so that part was awful.

I clapped my hand over my mouth, secondhand embarrassment for my brother flooding my veins.

"What's going on?" Violet asked.

I glanced up before replying, "My, um, *traditional* dad practically walked in on my brother and his boyfriend."

"Yikes!" Signe's mouth dropped, and my heart rate spiked when I glanced around the table to take in everyone's surprised expressions. Nobody seemed offended, though. They just looked at me curiously, as if waiting for the rest of the story.

"Another drop of Jacqueline's lore," Mary steepled her fingers together conspiratorially, "Interesting."

I shook my head at her, "I don't have lore."

"You do," Jamie nodded while playing with her salad, "You just haven't opened up to us about it."

"I open up," I frowned, glancing around the table.

"You allow us to open up to you," Signe countered,

"You're an awesome listener. But we still don't know much about Jacqueline Williams."

Violet grinned at me, taking a sip of her soda before asking, "Are you close with your parents?"

"Who are you, my therapist?"

"She goes to therapy," Signe nodded. Then she turned to glance at Violet, who was sucking down her milkshake through a straw, "Do you go to therapy?"

"Off and on," Violet lifted her hand to splay her fingers, tilting it back and forth, "It's hard to prioritize my mental health when I have a child I want to focus on instead."

At Violet's words, Signe turned to me, her hazel eyes wide as she jutted a thumb over her shoulder toward the newest employee at Sun Steer, "See? That's how you drop your lore to your friends. Violet offered additional information without much prompting. Now we all know that she has a kid."

Violet laughed, her green eyes bouncing between us all as she continued to sip her milkshake.

"I told you that I have a brother."

"And that your dad is 'traditional'," Jamie added with a thoughtful expression, "...How does your brother deal with that?"

"He kind of...doesn't," I furrowed my brows in thought, "Marco doesn't hide any aspects of his life from our dad. But he doesn't go out of his way to share, either." I sighed, smiling at the waiter when they brought me a salad of my own. I had come here often enough that the waiter who usually works this shift remembered my order, "My dad isn't really part of our life, though. He lives on cruise ships now that his children are grown and can take care of themselves. Occasionally, we suspect guilt gets to him, and he will show up at Marco's to 'catch up.'" I lifted my fingers in air quotes.

"That sounds stressful," Mary frowned, "Does he show up and surprise you?"

I shook my head, "No. My dad only ever really wanted a son. He's never really cared about what I'm up to. We keep in touch via email whenever he reaches out."

Silence settled around the table, and when I glanced at all the women watching, I felt unease start to turn in my stomach.

"...And maybe I shouldn't have lore dropped during girls' lunch." I started to shrink in my seat, their gazes making me nervous that I crossed a line. Perhaps my "lore" wasn't truly worth sharing at all. I didn't want to bring the mood down, but it also didn't surprise me that I did, either.

Typical Jacqueline, being a party pooper.

"I'm so sorry," Signe sighed, patting my leg once with her hand before grinning, "Your dad is missing out."

I lifted a shoulder, "Maybe." I didn't want to keep talking about myself, I looked across the table to meet Violet's eyes, desperate to pivot the conversation, "Tell us about your kid."

Violet's grin spread across her face, her eyes lighting up, "Oh, she's the best. She's going to be five soon."

"Aww, happy birthday," Jamie smiled. Everyone shifted, letting the newest member of the group start talking more about herself as my phone buzzed in my hand again.

Marco: Anyway, have you downloaded the new app I told you about yet?

Me: Not yet. When I'm ready to date again I might consider it, though.

Marco: Good. Unrelated, how is it working with Handsome-British-Man? Still weird as hell?

I blushed, glancing around the table to ensure no one was looking at me texting while Violet spoke about her daughter.

"She's autistic," I thought I physically felt my ears perk up, and I momentarily forgot about my conversation with Marco while I tuned into the conversation around me, "Also nonverbal. So she's in a specialized preschool classroom for neurodivergent kids. Thankfully, the school district provides her with additional resources like OT, PT, Speech therapy, etc."

"What's speech therapy for, if she's nonverbal?" Mary asked around a mouthful of food.

"Her AAC device," Violet explained, "It's like an iPad that vocalizes for her. That way she can still advocate for herself. Her teachers also sign and sound words out, in case she does end up speaking one day."

"Is there a pretty high chance of that?" Signe asked.

I was fascinated by watching Violet talk about her daughter's special needs like this. So casually, as if it was all no big deal. It was obvious Violet loved her daughter and enjoyed talking about her with us. I couldn't imagine having a child; it wasn't something I ever planned for myself.

Violet had a deep maternal side, evidenced by the positive way she spoke about her daughter's special needs and educated us about them.

"We really can't know for sure," Violet drummed her fingers on the table, "She used to say 'mama', but has since regressed—which is very common for autistic kids. I have spoken to parents who say that one day their five- or six-year-old randomly started speaking in full sentences, and I've also spoken to parents whose kids never vocalize without AAC. So, it could go either way."

"Wow," Signe sighed wistfully, resting an elbow on the

table to support her cheek, "I can see why you'd prioritize meeting her needs over having consistent therapy for yourself."

"Yeah," Violet grinned, glancing down at her phone resting on the table. Screen up. She lifted it to show us all her lock screen, "She's worth it, though." The image was of her daughter. She had blonde hair held back in two braids, sporting a wide cheeky grin. Her daughter was laughing, her big green eyes shining brightly.

I had no idea what autistic children looked like. I had little to no understanding of how children were supposed to look or behave. However, looking at this picture taken in the middle of her daughter's laughter, I wouldn't have guessed that this little girl had challenges at all.

"She's beautiful," I spoke, my own phone clutched tightly in my hands.

I wondered if Violet and I could speak privately at another time, where I could pick her brain about her daughter. When did she first see the signs of autism start to present themselves? How has that affected her daughter's development? What will her life as an adult look like? ...Would her daughter and I have things in common?

A diagnosis won't wait to present itself until a doctor has deemed it to do so, Mariam's words echoed in my head, *Seeking out a diagnosis is a personal choice, don't gaslight yourself just because a doctor hasn't confirmed or denied one yet.*

I wasn't sure if I was neurodivergent or not.

I didn't want to jump the gun.

What if I just hyper-fixated on learning about autism and convinced myself I was when I wasn't? What if I was inappropriately claiming a label for myself that belonged to others? Would someone like me, someone high functioning and able to act as expected (for the most part), invalidate someone like Violet's daughter's diagnosis?

I shook my head, focusing back on my conversation with Marco.

Me: Still weird as hell, especially since he had to drive me to work recently.

Marco: Oh, hot.

Me: No, not hot.

Me: Well.

Me: Maybe a little hot.

Marco: REALLY?? Tell me everything.

I sighed, getting ready for the onslaught of messages I was about to receive from him when I replied.

Me: ...He rides a motorcycle.

Marco: JACQUELINE MARIE WILLIAMS

Marco: YOU RODE ON A MOTORCYCLE WITH HIM??

Marco: How does this guy keep getting hotter and hotter?

I bit my lip to stifle a giggle, ignoring Mary's curious glance in my direction.

Me: He's just a guy.

Marco: Is he seeing anyone? Maybe the universe is trying to tell you to tap that again.

Me: Absolutely not. That would be so inappropriate.

Marco: Okay but hear me out…

Marco: Who cares?

Me: Me. Human Resources. I care about hooking up with someone in upper management. That's so messed up for so many reasons.

Marco: That just makes it hotter, honestly. Forbidden. Dare I say naughty?

Me: Ew.

Me: Don't you have a boyfriend you need to apologize to for last night?

Marco: Shoot. You're right. Ttyl.

I grinned, pocketing my phone and attempting to focus back on the conversation happening around me.

"Wait, you're cousins?" I heard Violet ask right when I dug into my protein bowl.

"They're also best friends." Jamie grinned, leaning against Mary when she rolled her eyes at her girlfriend.

"He's a pain in the ass," Mary smirked, "But yeah, we're close."

"That's so cute," Signe sighed, "Did I tell you that Zaid was lowkey intimated by Leo when he was first hired?"

I raised my eyebrows at that, "What? Why?"

"Before he was hired," Signe gave me a secretive look, "I kept referring to him as 'Mary's Hot Cousin'." I snorted at the same time Violet laughed.

"Why?" I asked.

Signe's eyes widened, "...You've seen him, right?"

Yeah, I'd probably seen more of him than anyone else at this table. That didn't mean I'd give him juvenile nicknames like "Mary's Hot Cousin".

"But wait," I shook my head, trying to remember the timeline correctly, "Weren't you into Zaid, writing romance novels about him?" At that, Violet's eyes widened as she turned to Signe.

"I'm sorry, what?"

"I'll explain that another time," Signe promised Violet before turning back to me, "Yeah, but that doesn't mean I don't notice when other people are attractive. I'm madly in love with Zaid, and I'm also sitting here right now looking at you and thinking, 'Wow, that top is doing good things for your boobs."

I blushed before glancing down at my button-up today. It was a more form-fitting one, I didn't wear it that often. It was laundry day, and my more comfortable clothing was dirty.

"Really?" I asked.

"Yes," all the women at the table replied, before Mary asked, "Are you going out after work or something?"

I instinctively went to button up another button, but Signe made a whining sound, "Don't hide the ladies. They deserve to be flaunted every now and then."

I froze, my hand stuck on my button I hadn't done up yet, "I don't want to be inappropriate."

"You're not," Jamie assured me with a smile, her blue eyes shining, "You're just attractive, Jacqueline. Whether you button your shirt all the way up or not, you still have nice boobs."

I felt another blush, memories of Leo's words filling my head, *Fuck, they're perfect.*

"I'm just saying you're attractive. That doesn't mean I'm going to make a move on you. It was the same with Leo. Then he got hired, and I promptly reminded Zaid how much more attractive I found him as often as I possibly could." Signe explained.

I smirked at her, "I'm sure Zaid appreciated that."

"He did," Signe's eyes glazed over, a loving expression covering her face as she thought about her boyfriend, "God, I love him."

"Aww," Violet rested her chin on her palm, "You almost make me want to believe in love again."

"You should," Signe grinned.

"Nah," Violet shook her head, "The love for my daughter is more than enough for me."

My thoughts started to wander after that, thinking about how casually comfortable Signe was able to dish out flattering compliments like that. How confident she was in her relationship with Zaid, and how she wasn't blushing or too embarrassed to lift other people up.

Sometimes, I looked at Signe and how she behaved, to get an idea of what I could work on myself.

I wanted to be a girl's girl. I had never been given a real opportunity to be a girl's girl until I befriended these women. So I took note of that subtle comradery we shared during lunch. Even if it started with everyone (except Mary) agreeing that Leo was conventionally attractive.

He was more than conventionally attractive, though.

I thought he was one of the most beautiful men I had ever seen. His eyes were my favorite part of his face, as cheesy and basic as that made me sound. They were such a specific light shade of blue, emphasized by how dark his hair was, that I had to intentionally stop myself from making direct eye contact whenever I saw them.

I had to force my gaze away more often than not, not wanting to come off as creepy or inviting. Eye contact was generally hard for me, mostly because I didn't realize that it wasn't a literal term at all.

Growing up, I thought you had to lock eyes with people to maintain eye contact, but apparently, no one actually did that. People looked at eyebrows, cheekbones, foreheads, whatever, and that still counted as eye contact.

I didn't realize that until Marco explained it to me in high school.

It made me feel both relief and also annoyance. I had stressed so much about how uncomfortable eye contact with people made me, and I never needed to actually look someone in the eye this entire time.

Leo's eyes though? I remembered getting lost in them the night we shared. I didn't feel intimidated by his eye contact in an uncomfortable way. I was intimidated by his eye contact because of how much I loved it.

Which was why I needed to maintain a distance between us in the office.

Because as much as Marco would like to argue otherwise, stirring up anything like that with Leo was out of the question. Unprofessional. Irresponsible. Even unethical of me.

I was finding myself going through this mantra more and more often as the days went by. I refused to acknowledge my resolve, attempting to crumble every time Leo passed me in the hallway at work, or every time I heard him laugh with our coworkers.

We had a decent thing going when he wasn't driving me up the wall or causing me undue stress.

He and I had to keep things professional, especially since he probably had no idea that I still struggled with an attraction to him. This daily pull I felt whenever he was near, and how desperate my body was to feel those same feelings I experienced that first and only night we shared.

No.

I was a grown woman, capable of using a vibrator.

I could deal with this.

I had to.

Chapter Eight

JACQUELINE

"WHERE ARE YOU FROM?" *I asked, panting on his chest. I needed a breather, but sitting here in awkward silence didn't feel normal.*

"London," Leo replied, "You?" He rested a hand behind his head, flexing his bicep in a way that made me want to lick it.

"Here," I sighed, snuggling into his chest, "Orange County has always been my home."

"That sounds..." Leo inhaled a deep breath, making my head rise and fall with his chest, "Wonderful."

"It is," I grinned.

I FINALLY GOT a new battery for my car, but after two weeks of no issue, my car died again. Something was wrong with the car itself, not the battery. But the mechanic was busy, and couldn't troubleshoot for me in a timely manner, which brought me back to a situation I wasn't ready for but had to deal with again anyway.

Leo: Sure, but Mary has my bike. So we
need to take my car this time.

I blinked at his message.

Me: You have a car?

Leo: With a reliable battery and everything.

Me: And you never felt the need to offer that
as an option when I was terrified to ride your
bike?

Leo: To be clear, you never asked. You
suggested riding the bike, and I obliged.

Me: Leo.

Leo: Jacqueline.

Me: Why are you like this?

Leo: Is that any way to talk to your charming
coworker? The one who is willing to carpool
your grumpy self to work?

Me: 😊

Me: Thank you.

Me: Going forward, let's assume I want to
ride in your car whenever we carpool.

Leo: I look forward to your warm and friendly
companionship during the ride.

Leo: 😊

Me: 😊

Leo:

Me:

Leo:

Me:

Leo: Wait.

Leo: What does that mean?

Leo: Did you mean to send that one?

Leo: Jacqueline.

Leo: Leaving now, be there in five.

PART of me wondered if I was becoming friends with Leo Turner.

Another part of me wondered if we were destined to have some sort of camaraderie between us. I fought against it often. But I realized that when you have firsthand knowledge of what someone feels like, thrusting inside of you and grunting out expletives about how good you made them feel, you're bound to develop a causal relationship faster than expected.

The following week of carpooling made our (maybe) friendship grow.

I couldn't lie and say I wasn't immediately thrilled when he asked what music I preferred one Wednesday afternoon. I was ready to annoy him with it. But no, Leo surprised me.

As soon as the music started playing, he turned it up.

"I think Mary is the only one who knows this," Leo

announced on the way home from work, "But after she showed this one to me as kids, it became one of my favorites."

My eyes widened, double-checking the title to make sure my ears weren't deceiving me.

"Every Time We Touch" by *Cascada* was blasting out of his car speakers.

"Really?" I asked with a laugh.

"Of course," Leo rolled the windows down and turned the music up some more, "It's brilliant." A car with two women, who both looked like they were driving home from a long day of work, pulled up next to us, before he started fist pumping and singing along with the lyrics, serenading them.

They laughed and rolled their windows down, singing along with the old pop song just as enthusiastically before we had to drive away.

I was laughing, a sound that made him turn his head to wink at me before continuing his performance to the cars around us. I slumped in my chair, covering my face with my hands. I was torn. I was fully embarrassed, but also loved listening to my music this loud and this proudly.

Later the next day, when Leo sent a group text asking about lunch, I surprised everyone by responding.

Leo: Who wants tacos?

Brandon: I'm good.

Mary: Jamie and I are getting sandwiches.

Signe: Zaid and I have leftovers.

Nicole: I'm good.

Part of me wondered where Nicole had been lately. She

had taken a few days off work unexpectedly, and when she did come in, she didn't linger or socialize with everyone.

I sat there, watching everyone turn his invitation down, when I rattled off a response before I talked myself out of it.

Me: I could go for tacos.

Leo: I have a feeling you're joining me out of pity because everyone else refused, but I'm going to take it.

Mary: LOL

Things were going well. Nobody was walking on eggshells around me, and Leo acted like he and I never bickered at all. When we pulled up to the taco joint a few blocks away from the office, I could feel the ache in my cheeks from laughing at Leo during the ride over.

He was still enjoying my playlist.

"Oi!" I heard him shout with a hand cupped to his mouth. I didn't jump at his raised voice, but my heart did as I quickly looked around to see who he was yelling at. A person with short brown hair turned right as they were leaving the taco shop, and then their lips pulled back into a wide grin.

"Oi, look oo we 'ave 'ere!" The person repeated in the thickest, most cockney British accent I had ever heard. It was very similar to Leo's accent but hilariously exaggerated. I laughed as Leo and I approached. Leo chuckled too, clapping hands with them and doing a weird half hug, half back pat, half handshake thing that men usually did with each other. I wasn't sure this person was a man, though.

"T, this is my coworker, Jacqueline." Leo introduced the two of us, and even though the person was wearing joggers and an athletic long-sleeved shirt, the moment their dark blue eyes landed on me, I could feel the confidence they exuded.

I studied them for a moment, feeling their hand wrap around mine as we shook, still slightly confused.

"Nice to meet you, I'm Taylor," after releasing my hand and shoving theirs in their pockets, they added, "They/them."

Oh, thank god they made it easy for me, "Jacqueline. She/her."

"Are you leaving? Want to join us?" Leo asked, nodding his head towards the entrance. Part of me appreciated how he attempted to add a third person to this lunch. We hadn't ever eaten lunch with just the two of us before, and I wasn't too nervous about it, but I wouldn't hate having a third-person buffer.

"I'd love to, but I already ate and I have a client in thirty minutes," Taylor responded.

"What do you do?" I was curious about what involved "clients" but allowed them to wear the equivalent of sweatpants to work. Then I winced, wondering if that was appropriate of me to ask seconds after introducing ourselves, "If you don't mind me asking."

"I don't," Taylor lifted a hand to brush their hair off their forehead, making it look perfectly casually styled, "I'm an occupational therapist."

"For children with special needs," Leo added.

I winced, thinking of Violet's daughter, "That sounds like a stressful job." I was not a kid person. I panicked whenever I was around kids, even Zaid's nephew. And he was the most well-behaved kid I knew. But I still didn't feel comfortable around kids.

There wasn't a single maternal bone in my body, which was probably for the best.

Taylor shrugged, "It has its moments. The kids throw tantrums sometimes. But it's flexible and I love it. Plus my coworkers are all wonderful."

"That's good," I glanced between the two of them, "... How do you know Leo?"

Taylor grinned, "He's on my rugby team."

I raised my eyebrows before giving Leo an impressed look, "You play rugby?"

"Don't look too surprised," Leo held both of his arms up, flexing his biceps with a suggestive eyebrow wiggle, "How do you think this happens?"

I snorted, something that Taylor laughed at as their gaze bounced between the two of us, "Are you coming to the game this weekend?"

I blinked, thinking that they were directing the question at Leo, but Leo dropped his arms and let surprise flicker across his expression before I realized it was for me. I turned back to Taylor, "Oh, I wasn't invited."

Taylor gave Leo an unimpressed look before stepping forward and murmuring to me, as if sharing a secret, "I'm inviting you right now."

I blushed, their face was much closer to mine, and I instinctively stepped closer to Leo to avoid breathing in theirs. They watched me move out of their space, but they seemed relaxed, their eyes were focused on Leo as I responded, "Oh—I, I don't know if I should."

"You can if you want." Leo lifted a hand and plopped it on my shoulder. It wasn't flirtatious or sexual to any degree, but for some reason, his large palm on my shoulder relaxed me. I glanced up at him and gave a nervous smile.

"I'll check my calendar."

"I hope to see you there. Maybe Leo here will play better with a pretty woman like yourself cheering him on." Taylor winked, and then saluted the two of us before sauntering off down the street.

"Jesus," Leo grumbled, removing his hand from my shoulder and continuing to the front door, "and they think *I'm* the flirt."

I shrugged, "It's nice to know I still got it."

Leo gave me a once over as he held the door open for me, but clamped his mouth shut as I walked past him. It was noisy, and the taco joint had a large bar centered in the middle of the farthest wall. The two of us naturally wandered over there instead of taking a table, and it wasn't until we both took places on barstools that I realized how familiar this was.

If Leo was getting flashbacks to how we met like I was, he wasn't showing it.

We had just received chips and salsa from the bartender when my name was spoken behind me.

I froze, recognizing the voice immediately.

I took a second to blink away my surprise and sudden jolt of fear, before I turned around to face the man who demanded my attention.

Vincent.

My ex-boyfriend.

The man I once lived under the same roof with.

Vincent, who wore me down until I was a shell of a person. Changing every aspect of my life to cater to his fragile ego and manipulative personality.

I tried my best to look relaxed, but I wasn't. I was panicking.

"Long time no see." Vincent grinned. His eyes scanned my body as I stayed perched on the barstool. It felt repulsive. He shaved most of his blonde hair off, looking almost bald. His receding hairline must have gotten the best of him, but his hazel eyes still glinted with that look that used to make me panic. It was a look designed to put me on edge, to challenge me. To get me to try to read his mind.

Basically, Vincent looked awful.

Like he hadn't been sleeping well for a long time.

Dark circles sunk underneath his eyes.

I was able to take all that in, but it only took about three seconds for me to remember Mariam's words.

You don't owe him anything.

So I just stared.

I didn't reply. I didn't acknowledge him with more than my eyes.

I remembered that I had a tortilla chip in my hand and munched on it, waiting for him to do anything else besides ruin my day.

He lifted an eyebrow at my silence, "That's all I get?"

I frowned, before getting an idea for no other reason than because I was a petty woman, "...I'm sorry, who are you?"

Vincent chuckled, "Really? That's how you're going to play this?"

I shrugged, glancing to the side and feeling a wave of mortification at the sight of Leo, turned in his barstool, with his icy blue eyes watching the back and forth between me and my ex.

"I don't have anything to say to you," I felt like my heart was going to race out of my chest though. I didn't want to stay here. I wanted to run. As calmly as I could, I brushed off my hands from the salty chip crumbs, and stood from my stool to tell Leo, "I'm going to head back to the office."

Something shifted in him, though it was subtle and I didn't have enough time to focus on what it was. But as soon as I turned to step away from the bar and make it towards the exit, Vincent widened his stance in an attempt to block my path.

"I see you're still the same cold bitch you've always been." Vincent almost rolled his eyes, but he caught himself, narrowing them at me. Eager to see my reaction, my wince when his words cut through me like they always did. Excited to see that almost three years after I left him, he could still get in my head.

I sucked in a sharp breath of shock because while his words hit me like they used to, I was also surprised at how everything my therapist predicted about him came to fruition. Vincent still felt powerful putting women down. He still went out of his way to "win" arguments, even if he wasn't actually in one.

He still didn't even *like* me.

His words proved that he never actually did.

I felt something icy and cold sink in my chest under his scrutiny. A terrible, heart-wrenching confirmation that this man did waste my time. There was no alternate reality where he saw me as someone he liked or respected.

I was too caught up in my spiral, still frowning at Vincent as his eyes flared, getting his fill on how his words broke me at that moment. I almost missed the warm body positioning itself beside me, if it wasn't for that cockney accent snapping me back into the present.

"Nah, mate," Leo's voice was dangerously low, a tone I'd never heard him use before. It gave me chills, "Speak to me how you spoke to her." I thought I remembered Zaid mentioning how Leo was six-five, which was a solid ten inches taller than my five feet and seven inches in height. Watching Leo square his shoulders, resting his large palm on my lower back as he stared at my ex-boyfriend, I could have sworn he was the tallest man in the world.

Vincent narrowed his eyes up at my coworker, running his fist across his nose in a nervous tick I recognized as fear, "I wasn't talking to you—"

"I don't care," Leo dropped his hold on my back, stepping forward so that half of his body was in front of me, shielding me from my ex, "You're a grown man. You don't talk to women like that." He lifted a fist and pounded his chest with emphasis, "You want to talk like that? Talk to me. Not her. *Never* her."

Vincent lowered his eyes, his jaw clenched as he huffed out through his nostrils in anger and humiliation, before his hazel eyes lifted and met mine.

I felt my heart jump into my throat, and it took every muscle I had in my body not to flinch under his stare.

Leo wasn't having it. He stepped forward abruptly, making Vincent retreat once as he blocked me from his view.

"You don't *look* at her," Leo's tone was enough to imply the threat behind his words, "You don't *speak* to her. You look at me, or you speak to me. Those are your options."

Vincent glared up at Leo, before swiping his nose once with his thumb and sniffing, stubbornness squaring his shoulders. I felt my heart drop in fear for Leo at that moment. Vincent wasn't ever truly violent with me, but he made it clear that it was just because I was a woman. I had seen him be violent in a bar one previous time, with another man.

I didn't want Leo to end up like that man.

"Leo—"

"And who the fuck are you? Telling me how to talk to her. I'll talk to her however I fucking please." I cringed and panicked at Vincent's choice of words.

He hadn't changed

He'd never change.

I wasted *so much* time on him.

Years of my life spent attempting to make something work with him when it wouldn't. He would be the same, selfish, prideful, immature asshole until the day he died. I fell victim to the sunk-cost fallacy, the more time I spent trying to make it work, the more time I ended up wasting. Frustrated that I wasn't happy with him, no matter how hard I tried. Determined to make all those years of pain and anxiety worth it.

"Leave," Leo replied. I gasped, *no, no, no.*

Vincent sneered before he balled his hand into a fist and pulled back.

No, no, no!

Before Vincent's hand could strike, Leo's left hand came up and palmed his punch, preventing the contact to his face that my ex aimed for. I swore time slowed in those seconds. Watching the surprise on Vincent's face as Leo's long fingers flexed over his meaty fist. Seeing Leo's hand perfectly engulf the entirety of Vincent's. How Vincent was shaking and Leo...wasn't.

I was holding my breath, watching Vincent's eyebrows slowly rise in fear as I saw Leo's head lower towards him. Still holding his fist in one hand. When he tried to pull out of Leo's grip, he couldn't.

"I wish I was a better man than this," Leo's voice was lethal, and I widened my eyes when in a blink, Leo's right fist pulled back and snapped across Vincent's face.

Right when my hands came up to cover my mouth in shock, Vincent dropped to the ground.

He groaned, but he stayed down.

A small cut started to bleed across his cheekbone, and

his eyes were unable to stay open as he struggled to orient himself.

"Jacqueline," Leo's voice was by my ear as I stared wide-eyed at Vincent on the ground.

This man, who I feared for so long. Too long.

He was just...on the ground.

Vincent looked so small down there, at our feet, his hand slowly coming up to rub at his cheek. Pulling his fingertips back enough to see the blood. He was upset about it, but still unable to sit up from his disorientation.

"Jacqueline," Leo's voice was paired with his hands on my biceps this time, "We need to go."

I glanced up, seeing the bartender stalking over and pointing to the back exit of the bar, nodding at Leo and me in farewell as he pulled out his phone to dial someone.

"Okay," I nodded, though my feet felt heavy.

"Can I help you?" Leo asked.

I just nodded, unable to take my eyes off of Vincent.

Even when he managed to finally look up at me, I didn't feel this crippling panic I used to. This desperate need to win his approval. For him to love me.

No, instead, I released a surprised laugh of disbelief, covering my hands over my mouth again to hide my hysterical grin as Leo used his grip to tug me out of the bar.

I felt weightless as he pulled me out of the building, into the cool day. The sound of him pulling his keys out seemed louder than normal, as did his car beeping to indicate it was unlocked.

Leo just punched Vincent in the face.

Leo Turner just punched my ex-boyfriend in the face.

...You don't look at her, you don't talk to her...

"Jacqueline," Leo murmured with a hand on my lower back. He had opened the passenger side door for me, but I just stood there. My brain was trying to make sense of what had happened, "I'm so sorry. I didn't mean to escalate things."

I turned to look up at him, blinking.

His blue eyes filled my vision. I was hyper-aware of the dark lashes that surrounded them. The pinch between his dark eyebrows as he studied me, concern on his face.

"You..." I breathed the word, unsure what I was trying to say.

"I'm so sorry, but we should really go—" Leo was cut off, my lips trapping any words in his mouth before they could escape. I was clutching his shirt in my fists, pulling him down while also stretching up on my toes, because he was so stupid tall. I released a little sigh in the back of my throat at the feel of his warm and smooth lips against mine, feeling just as I remembered, but also somehow better.

I released one fist from his shirt and slid my palm up his chest, towards his shoulder, before I realized something.

Leo wasn't kissing me back.

He wasn't moving at all.

He simply stood there while I kissed him.

I froze, my lips parting so I could gasp my humiliation at the realization. Our top lips lingered against each other for a second, before I opened my eyes in a panic and pulled my hands off of him as if he burned me.

Leo's eyes were wide and his dark eyebrows were up, his cheeks had a faint flush and his lips were a little pinker. His dark pupils were expanded.

I stood there, looking between his lips and eyes in horror over what I had just done.

My mouth opened.

Then, my lips closed, I even went as far as to curl them

between my teeth. As if I could hide the evidence of what I just did from him.

Leo blinked at me, his chest rising on a deep inhale while his eyes dropped to my mouth.

"Come back," he whispered. Suddenly, one of his hands slammed on the roof of his car behind me. The other cupped the back of my neck. My mouth parted in shock just in time for his smooth lips to meet mine again, but as soon as I felt that familiar warmth of his kiss, I responded.

My blood was pumping, my heart was pounding, and I moaned in his mouth when my hands found the bare skin of his neck. I tangled my fingers in his dark hair, holding him to me just in case he changed his mind too soon.

Leo took control.

Just like I asked him to all those months ago.

It was as if he remembered what I needed.

He encouraged my lips to part for him, not wasting a moment before his tongue was tangling with mine. I almost couldn't keep up, but when his hand left the roof of the car to snare his arm around my waist, pulling me flush against the front of his body, I felt my knees buckle.

Leo shifted us, and then my back and butt hit the closed door to the backseat. The passenger side door that he had opened for me moments ago was now forgotten as he towered over me, his hand tilting my head back so he could reach my lips.

I went to lift my leg, but my skirt restricted my movements, so I settled for hooking my calf around his.

In response, I swallowed his groan.

I couldn't get close enough to him.

"Relax for me, love," Leo murmured against my lips.

A piece of myself thawed at his words.

I dropped my leg, but Leo made up for that loss of

contact by pressing me almost completely against his car. His hardness against all my softness. Even though my toes were on the ground, it felt like I was being held up against the car by the front of his body. Leo's kisses slowed, but their intensity grew.

At the beginning of this kiss, I was meeting him halfway. I was matching his energy, and I wanted to be an equal participant. Now, trapped between his body and his car, I surrendered to him.

I slid one of my hands out of his hair and snuck it underneath the collar of his t-shirt, feeling the hard warm skin of his shoulders.

Leo kissed me leisurely, and I simply held on so he could take his time. What was a frenzy seconds ago was now savored. It was as if he and I had nowhere else to be. Time didn't exist here, our lips reuniting after too long.

I felt a buzz against my hip, and I tried to clench my thighs together to shield myself from it.

We broke the kiss, and it was obscene. The feel of both of our wet tongues sliding back where they belonged, the extra kiss Leo gave my top lip with his damp ones, and the glazed look in his eyes as he pulled away enough to reach one of his hands into his pocket.

He frowned at his phone screen before saying, "It's Zaid."

For some reason, that made me flinch. His words made all the blood rushing in my veins suddenly halt. My heart jumped, and I released my hold on him to cover my mouth with both hands in shock.

Leo immediately noticed my reaction, leaning back and standing taller, as he pocketed his cell, "Jacqueline?"

"I'm sorry," I shook my head once, and I saw something flicker over Leo's face as I spoke behind my hands, "I shouldn't have—we shouldn't—" his stare pinned me, his mouth snapped shut and a muscle popped in his cheek.

"It's all right," Leo backed away a step, no longer caging me in against his car, "It's okay."

"No," I shook my head, stepping to the side and sitting in the passenger seat, my feet still on the asphalt as I rubbed at my temples, "No, no I shouldn't have—oh my god—the reports I need to fill—"

"Jacquline," Leo crouched down, "You're okay. We didn't do anything wrong."

"I—that was so inappropriate of me."

"I didn't exactly push you away," Leo murmured.

"I shouldn't have initiated. This can't happen. We can't —" I stopped myself and shook my head, and silence filled the space between us. I couldn't look him in the eye, my tongue was just in his mouth. He was just lazily sucking on it. I lifted a hand to trace my lips, but dropped it back in my lap, hiding my lips from him again between my teeth.

Leo stayed crouched in front of me, letting me stare at his black boots before he hummed in agreement and finally stood.

"You're right," he didn't sound positive about it, "We shouldn't have crossed that line."

"I'm so sorry—"

"Don't fucking apologize," Leo pinched the bridge of his nose as he squeezed his eyes closed and faced the ground, "Just, don't."

I snapped my mouth shut, sitting up straighter in my seat and nodding my head even when he wasn't looking at me.

Leo shook his head once, before sighing and walking around to the driver's side door of the car. I took the moment to wipe my lips with the back of my hand before folding my legs into the car and shutting myself in. In silence, Leo sat at the wheel and started the car.

We didn't speak a word the entire ride back to the office.

It was tense, so tense I could feel my hands shaking a bit. At one moment, I snuck a glance over at the brooding Leo, only to find that his gaze was studying my trembling fingers. I immediately folded them under my thighs, desperate to calm my nerves.

Running into Vincent, and then making out with Leo in the parking lot, was not on my to-do list for the day. My nervous system was shot.

Leo parked his car silently, not even waiting for me to unbuckle my own seat belt before throwing his door open and stepping out. We walked together into the building but didn't say anything at all. Everyone knew we went to lunch; it wasn't a big deal. Nobody reacted to the two of us entering the office together, silent.

Employees did notice Leo, though.

Because Leo was scowling.

I probably looked upset too, but I knew my resting bitch face was a thing already. Our coworkers were used to me looking upset, even when I wasn't.

A scowling Leo was rare, though. And various employees steered clear of him until he shut himself in his office. I didn't hesitate to follow suit and locked myself in mine.

I felt my heart racing still.

Pressing a hand to my chest, as if that ever worked to help slow it down, I plopped down on the floor behind my closed door. I didn't want anyone to see me at my desk like this. Flushed. Anxious.

I should have gone to the sensory room.

But I was here, so it would have to do.

I didn't think I could make it to my desk to get my earbuds, so I slid my phone out of my skirt pocket and quietly turned on my soothing playlist. String instruments accompanied soft piano keys, and I set my timer.

I would freak out over kissing Leo Turner for fifteen minutes.

And not a minute more.

Chapter Nine

LEO

SHE HAD DOZED off on me.

I wasn't too surprised, because she and I had been through quite a bit the last few hours. So I used the arm I had wrapped around her back and shoulders to pull her closer to me. She adjusted, her hot breath fanning over my naked chest, and stayed asleep.

Turning my head just enough to glance at the ancient digital clock, I saw that it was 12:53 am.

Being the selfish bastard I was, I didn't wake Jacqueline up. I indulged myself, allowing my nervous system to soak up the skin-to-skin contact I still desperately craved from her.

***

I COULD STILL TASTE JACQUELINE.

I felt like I had gone mad. I had to apply chapstick throughout the day because I was licking my lips too often. Desperate to remember the feel of her mouth on mine. My hands couldn't hold still. Zaid and Brandon had both stopped by my office for random questions after lunch and while I couldn't quite recall the details of our conversations, I could remember the curious glances they gave my restless hands.

I had to stop myself from tapping a pencil against my leg multiple times.

Did Jacqueline regret our kiss that badly?

She wanted to at some point, otherwise she wouldn't have done it.

I told myself later that night that she probably wasn't in the proper state of mind. Perhaps she was just confused after I had clocked that prick in the bar, whoever he was. I had to push down the anger I felt when I remembered how he spoke to her. How comfortable he felt speaking like that to her.

I shouldn't have gotten my hopes up, kissing her back with more than enough enthusiasm to let her know that yes, I too had been thinking about kissing her again since my interview.

But no.

I was immediately humbled.

So that night I poured myself two fingers of scotch and wallowed in self-pity.

A poor attempt to soothe my fragile ego over the fact that the one woman who had been taking up space in my mind for months still wasn't thinking about me like that.

And I would go to work the next day and pretend like that car park kiss never happened.

I COULDN'T BELIEVE that I was dealing with this so fucking early in the morning, the Monday after the kiss. Jacqueline and I hadn't talked much, because the morning after, she texted me saying her car was fixed again and she didn't need a ride.

It was probably true; her car was due to be fixed any day.

But I still worried that she was avoiding me on purpose.

As she had every right to.

Because we hadn't texted, joked around, or really spoken to each other in any way, I was even more surprised when she decided to rip me apart this morning.

I was giving a quick presentation to Mary and Zaid's teams. We were in one of the conference rooms surrounded by glass walls. I knew my presentation was boring but mandatory, so I tried to make it not mind-numbing so that employees would appreciate a meeting that couldn't have just been an email.

Personally, I thrived when I had background noise of some kind. If the room was too quiet and monotonous, I struggled to stay focused. It was part of my brand, the fun relatable CTO that's just like everyone else.

I didn't think that adding popular pop music would be so controversial.

"Do you think playing songs like that for your employees during a meeting sets a good example?" Jacqueline was glaring up at me, her company iPad tucked to her chest with both arms, and one hip popped out.

She had two strands of hair framing her face today, which was unusual whenever she wore her hair in a tidy bun like this.

"I think it's fine," I replied as I crossed my arms, glaring down at her as well.

I was so tired of this fucking shit.

"Why on earth would you think that's fine? That song has so many expletives I lost count," Jacqueline rolled her eyes with her reply.

"Because we're all grown adults," I threw my arms out, glancing over my shoulder to see half of the engineers were pretending this conversation wasn't happening outside of the conference room, whereas the others were intently staring to watch the show, "There was not a single word in that song that hasn't been uttered in this office before."

"By *you*, you mean," Jacqueline threw back.

"By everyone!" I pinched the bridge of my nose and inhaled, praying to anything to give me peace so I didn't rip that stupid iPad out of her arms and angrily snap it in half, "Jesus Christ, isn't it exhausting being this kind of person, Jacqueline?"

She had her mouth open, ready to retort with something before she froze at the end of my sentence.

Jacqueline snapped her mouth shut, her eyes widening a little bit, "What person?"

"The kind of person who is constantly on everyone's arse. Honestly, are my employees coming to you to complain about my behavior? Or about what slang I throw around in the office?"

Jacqueline frowned, before glancing to the side toward the conference room full of people watching this whole thing.

All the engineers who were practically missing their bowls of popcorn suddenly turned in their chairs and looked very busy on their phones and laptops.

"Because if there are employees who file complaints about me, the music I play in the office, or the language I use, then yes. I will do better. But *come on* Jacqueline," I lowered my voice, realizing I was getting more heated than I needed to, "It feels like all the issues here are yours and yours alone."

Jacqueline flinched.

I thought Jacqueline had been treating me with a cold, unfeeling nature before, but that was nothing compared to what I saw come over her now. I stood there, glaring down at our human resources rep, and saw in real time how each piece of her mask slid into place. The tightening of her eyes. The natural downturn of her lips. The way her body stiffened and her shoulders inched higher.

It wasn't until I started to see her eyes get red, a small glassy layer filming them, that I realized I had said something horribly wrong.

"Jacqueline—"

"You're right," her voice was flat. It felt robotic, unfeeling, numb, "I'm the issue." I stood there, the anger and frustration in me slowly starting to simmer when I heard her murmur, "As always."

And then she turned and marched back to her office.

I groaned, scraping a hand down my face before turning back into the conference room. An oddly quiet conference room, considering the number of employees inside.

I looked up to meet too many curious eyes, before I shook my head and marched to the front to gather my laptop, "This meeting is canceled. I'll send an email summarizing things instead."

I heard the slow, unsure squeak of chairs moving, "I thought this was mandatory?" A newer intern asked, clearly nervous to voice his question.

"I decided that it isn't." I slammed my laptop closed and stood tall to face the room, "And I apologize if my music was inappropriate. If anyone here felt uncomfortable, I'd encourage you to meet with Jacqueline about it."

"Oh, please," Mary stood as she gathered her things as well, "No one here was upset, right?" She glanced around the room, where many head nods took place, "That song has been trending for weeks. We all listen to it in our earbuds at our desks. It's fine."

I nodded once, annoyed that Mary's words didn't make me feel better.

"...She was just being a bitch."

"That's enough," I snapped at one of the engineers from Zaid's team who whispered the words. Someone who had worked here much longer than I had. The man froze, staring wide-eyed at me, "Jacqueline is doing her job to ensure everyone feels safe in the office. She has to feel comfortable confronting problematic behavior like that so *you* don't have to. You don't get to call her crude names because of that."

The man kept his eyes down as he left the room, before a flash of blue hair caught my eye. I glanced over to see one of the newer systems engineers we hired. She slowly approached me while most everyone else started to file out of the room, and she glanced over her shoulder one last time before looking up at me.

"Thank you for defending her," the woman said, with a lift of her shoulder, "If the guys feel comfortable talking about Jacqueline like that...well, they'll feel comfortable talking about all of us like that."

I blinked at the employee, before giving her a stiff nod in acknowledgment, "Of course."

"Maybe check in on her though," the woman's brows pinched together, "Whatever that was, it wasn't about the music you played."

Don't I fucking know it, I wanted to say.

Chapter Ten

JACQUELINE

I FELT like I was floating.

Or maybe I was freefalling.

Before him, I had no idea that intimacy could be like this. That I could feel like this. That I could understand and conceptualize what all the hype has been about. How asking for exactly what I wanted truly did have its benefits.

All it took was for me to pretend I wasn't nervous and proposition the handsome stranger at the bar.

As I lay there, gasping for breath, my heart racing and my limbs loose, I opened my eyes to see him grinning down at me. Simple, male satisfaction coated his features as he leaned forward and kissed my lips once, twice.

I eagerly, lazily kissed him back. A shocked giggle escaped my lips as I thought how much of a shame it was that he and I would never see each other again after tonight.

"WE NEED TO FIGURE THIS OUT," I snapped my head up from my desk, my heart jumping from Leo's voice suddenly filling my office. Hours had passed since our argument in front of the conference room, and I felt my face heat with embarrassment as I watched him step in and shut the door behind him.

"Figure what out?" I asked.

"This," he pointed between us, "We can't keep doing this. I can't keep doing this." He strode across the space until he was standing just behind the two chairs that sat in front of my desk. He gripped the back of one, drumming his fingers on it.

"There's nothing to figure out," I looked down at my workspace, saving all my work on the iPad while I exhaled a defeated sigh, "You're right. I'm the issue. I'll be less annoying."

"That's not—" he lifted a hand and dragged it across his jaw as he stared at the potted plant against the wall, "Clearly, we're both at fault here."

"Leo, I don't want to talk." I shook my head and checked the time on my phone. Holy crap, it was six thirty. Most everyone was probably gone already.

"Too bad, we're going to talk," Leo stood tall and crossed his arms, and I felt my hands tremble at the thought of confrontation with him, "We should start with who that bald prick was yesterday—"

"—I don't want to talk about him. Ever." I snapped.

Leo frowned.

"Fine. Then tell me what your problem is with me."

"No."

"Jacqueline."

"Leo. I don't want to talk."

"That's too *fucking* bad." Leo raised his eyebrows, "I just swore in the office, can we talk now?" I ground my teeth together, "I played more pornographic music in my office today, will you talk to me now? Or are we only allowed to talk when you're ripping into me in front of my employees?"

I felt my bottom lip tremble, "I'm sorry. I shouldn't have—"

"I don't want an apology," Leo shook his head, "I want to know what the fuck is going on. What is it about me that ruins every day of yours?"

I shook my head; a rock was forming in the base of my throat, and my eyes were starting to sting with tears. I was a dam about to burst, and even though I actively fought against it, I didn't want to.

I was so *tired*.

"I—" I inhaled a shaky breath, "I struggle with how we met."

Leo stared at me.

And stared at me.

It wasn't until he realized I wasn't going to say anything more that he tilted his head and asked me, "That's it?"

I frowned, "What do you mean, that's it?"

"So we shagged one time—before we worked together," Leo had the audacity to lift his shoulders and inspect the crinkled leaf of my potted fig, looking totally at ease having this conversation in my office, "It's not a big deal."

Most everyone was home right now, but still, this was not the building to have a conversation like this.

"But it's a big deal to me," I spoke through clenched teeth. I felt my knuckles strain against the tight fist I was making, gripping the company iPad to my chest like a shield to protect me from the handsome, charismatic Brit, "And it feels impossible for me to pretend otherwise."

"Why?" Leo furrowed his dark brows before turning those icy blue eyes towards me. I felt my heart thump, remembering how those eyes looked hovering over me.

How they looked hooded, concentrated, in the shitty lamp light of his hotel room all those months ago.

I felt myself squeeze my thighs together, my body also remembering the last time he looked at me like that.

"*Because*," I grumbled, turning to practically slam the iPad down on my desk.

"That's not good enough, Jacqueline," Leo's voice lowered on my name, and I found myself closing my eyes because my skin heated at the sound of him saying it like that, "What can I do to make you more comfortable? To make you hate me less?"

I was ovulating.

I was horny.

I hadn't had a sexual partner since *him*.

Those were all the reasons I was so flustered right now, and nothing else.

"I don't *hate* you," I spoke behind the safety of my closed eyelids, "I can't *stand* you."

A frustrated sound came from him, making me snap my eyes open to see him with both hands on his hips as he tilted his head back to glare at the ceiling, a muscle in his jaw popping as if he was grinding his teeth together.

"I am failing to understand what I did, exactly."

"Me," I replied without hesitation. He was getting ready to say more, but I interrupted and he snapped his lips closed to turn his glare on me, "You did *me*. I don't think you understand what that night *meant* for me."

Leo's brow smoothed, "Jacqueline..." he took a step or two closer, coming to brace his hands on my desk. He had to bend at his waist, but it helped maintain some distance between us. I wasn't on the opposite side of the desk; I was on the right side. We had ninety degrees of desk keeping us apart, "I...you said it was just a hookup."

"It was." I was confused about where he was going.

"A no-strings-attached thing...if I had known—"

"Oh my god!" I threw my hands up in the air, "I'm not in love with you."

Leo threw his arms out wide, fingers splayed as he looked around and he practically yelled, "Then *what* is the problem?"

"I haven't—" I stopped myself, grinding my teeth together as I dug my fingertips into the back of my neck in frustration, before trying again, "You're the first that—ugh. I mean, I've had sex before. Lots of times, actually."

"Okay?" Leo was shaking his head, shrugging his shoulders, looking hopelessly confused.

"But you," I finally squared my shoulders, pointing at him accusingly, "You *ruined* me."

"I *ruined* you?" Leo sounded appalled, and by the way his eyebrows shot up, I knew he was still lost.

"You ruined sex for me," I whisper-hissed at him, widening my eyes because please, for the love of god, get it already.

His brows immediately lowered, a harsh frown taking over his face as his eyes darted in between mine, "...It was bad for you?"

"It was *life-altering* for me!" I slammed myself down into my desk chair, turning so that I was facing him on the opposite side of my desk now, more space was needed for this horrifying admission, "I never knew that sex could feel —that *I* could even..." I grumbled and dropped my face in my hands, my shoulders heaving as I struggled to calm my heart rate, "You made me *want*, Leo." I released a heavy exhale, making myself breathe in and out slowly once more before adding, "...Every time I look at you, I just...*want*..."

Silenced filled my calm little office.

I could feel him standing there, quiet as a mouse as he let the room absorb my words. I could barely, barely hear his uneven breathing. After a few unbearably silent moments, I finally lifted my head from my hands to look him in the eye.

His brow had the smallest crease in it, not from irritation. From the way his eyes studied me, I knew he wasn't angry or frustrated with me anymore. Instead, I felt a new emotion from him, one that made my heart skip a beat and embarrassment stain my cheeks.

Understanding.

Maybe, even a dash of pity.

And I did *not* want his pity.

I shook my head and sat up in my chair, pushing myself away from the desk so that I could stand, "Now you know," I refused to look him in the eye as I bent down to grab my purse, "So if you'll just—"

"What do you want, Jacqueline?" Leo asked, his voice soft.

The question made me freeze while I was grabbing my phone to drop it into my purse. I turned and looked up at him. He had one hand braced on my desk; his eyes locked on me.

"What do you mean?" I asked, trying to ignore how my skin started to hum under his look.

"You said that looking at me makes you want..." Leo took a step around the desk, slow, cautious, waiting for some sort of reaction from me. When I stood still, he took another, and another, until he rounded my desk and stood no more than six inches from me. I had to crane my neck to look up at him, "What, exactly, do I make you want?"

I wheezed.

My muscles locked in anticipation, my hands fisting my phone and purse tighter than I thought was possible.

"I...It doesn't matter—"

"The fuck it does," Leo took a step closer and yanked my purse out of my hands, dropping it to the floor. I gaped at the motion, prepared to tell him off when he crowded my space. I considered holding my ground, but I couldn't stop myself from backing up and stumbling into my chair, "You don't get to be rude to me, rip into me in front of my team," he braced each of his hands on both armrests of my chair, caging me in. I thought my heart was going to explode out of my chest. I felt my entire vagina pulse at the visual of him towering over me again, "When you're telling me that there is a simple solution to our problems."

I shook my head, swallowing around a dry lump in my throat, trying not to lean in closer because *good god* his scent was intoxicating, "There isn't."

"No," Leo's voice was authoritative and demanding, one I had only ever heard him use *that* night. "You said that I make you want, so you need to tell me *what* you want. Because I swear to god Jacqueline..." When I tried to look away, he used his grip on my chair to turn me back into his line of sight, and blood rushed in my ears from the excitement of it, "If you're telling me that the solution to our problems is for me to bend you over this desk right now, I'll do it."

Oh my god, I squeezed my thighs together at his crude words, a movement he tracked as he glanced down. A flush of arousal coated my skin, and suddenly, the bra I wore today was very sensitive against my breasts. This was wrong, *so* wrong. So many violations were happening just being in this position with him. We were at *work*. It was still technically the workday because we were both here after hours, working.

Except we weren't working.

Leo was crowding me in my desk chair in a way that made me want to melt into his touch. His cologne was making me dizzy in the most pleasing way, and I was so, so desperate for connection again that I was considering it.

"...You're bluffing," I murmured, trying to blink confidently, not that slow horny blink I did when I was overwhelmed with lust.

A slow, lazy grin spread across Leo's lips as he held my eyes, and he released one armrest to gently brush his index finger down my cheek, "I wish I was, Jacqueline," I was clutching either side of my seat for dear life, "But I won't offer it again. If you say no, I'll walk right out your door," he used his finger to point at the closed door, making me widen my eyes, "And you and I will never speak of this again."

I licked my lips, my chest heaving, desperate for oxygen to clear my mind, but only the clean, earthy scent of Leo suffocated my senses, "We...shouldn't..."

"That isn't what I'm asking," Leo shook his head once before leaning in, using his hand to gently cup my jaw, "Look me in the eye," his gaze dropped to my parted lips for a beat before he continued, "And tell me you don't want me to touch you. That you don't want me to relieve all this... *tension* you're holding in." His gaze dropped to my chest, and his hot exhale brushed over my skin at the sight of what was poking through my bra and shirt, "Otherwise, I'd be happy to be of service."

I felt my lip tremble, a fire burning in my chest from the myriad of emotions I was feeling, "This is wrong."

"This," he lifted one hand, keeping his hold on my jaw

with the other, to gesture between the both of us, "Needs to be addressed. Because ignoring it, clearly, isn't working."

I nodded my head once, barely, a movement he probably wouldn't have been able to track had he not been holding my face in his hand, and I whispered, "I don't need pity orgasms from you, Leo."

His eyes widened a fraction, surprise coating his features before his lips tugged up on one side and he leaned closer, closer, close enough for his top lip to brush against mine as he whispered, "Oh Jacqueline...if only you knew the things I've thought about doing with you..." my lips parted and tingled as he teased me with his, not quite kissing me, but brushing them against mine in a delicate touch as he spoke, "The ways I wanted to get you to stop glaring at me across the room, to take me seriously here..."

His lips left mine, brushing against my jaw as he leaned to the side. The warm, wet glide of his tongue brushed against my earlobe, "How desperate I have been to feel you underneath me again." I moaned, my head lolling back to make room for him. At that movement, he pressed his warm lips against the sensitive part where my jaw met my ear, "Maybe even bend you over my knee." I whimpered at the visual, "And slap that tight little arse of yours; retribution for wearing all those skirts designed specifically to drive me fucking *mad*."

I bit my bottom lip as he trapped my earlobe between his teeth and tugged.

I was a goner.

My hands lifted to fist the hem of his jacket hanging off of his torso between us, "I want that."

"Good," Leo practically growled the word before hauling me out of my desk chair and plopping my ass right on my desk. His large hands shoved my pencil skirt up, up, up, so he could spread my legs wide enough to step between them.

"Leo—" I was cut off by his lips capturing mine, which was probably for the best because I had no idea what I was going to say. So I moaned inside of his mouth instead, grabbing his jacket again and pulling him as tight against me as possible. Even sitting on my desk I had to lean my head back to meet his lips. My leg wrapped around his waist and pulled him closer to me, and I was rewarded with evidence in his jeans that Leo did, in fact, want me, too.

"Christ," Leo gasped against my lips before shrugging out of his jacket and dropping it to the ground. I nodded encouragingly at him as I lifted his shirt up, and he responded by grabbing the back of his collar and pulling it off of his head. I smiled, and a satisfied, emotional laugh huffed out of me at the sight of him shirtless in front of me.

My hands planted themselves on his waist, beginning to roam up the dips and planes of his chest before he captured both of my wrists in his grip, "Ah, ah," he shook his head at me, a devilish grin on his face as he took my wrists and pinned them behind my back.

"I want to touch you," I whined, lifting my head to kiss him again. He dodged my lips and instead planted a kiss on the junction between my neck and shoulder, making me squirm against him because *holy shit* that felt good.

"You're not in charge right now, Jacqueline," Leo murmured, making warm chills dance down my spine, "I am. You need to ask me nicely if you want something."

I was shaking, because he trapped both of my wrists in one of his large hands while his other brushed his knuckles up the inside of my thigh, finding the seam of my thong and teasing me where I was already wet and aching for him.

"I—" I had to inhale a deep breath. My eyes were

hooded. My senses were in overdrive. It was difficult to keep my thoughts in order, "I can ask?"

"You can ask for whatever you want from me," Leo murmured, kissing me as one of his fingers hooked my panties to the side. His thumb swiped my clit and made me gasp.

"Okay," I whimpered as he dipped his thumb lower, lower, using my wetness to circle my entrance, and then sliding his finger up, up, up, to circle my clit in tight, small swirls, "Can...can I get a ride to the airport tomorrow morning?"

Leo's lips moved to the corner of my mouth to let me ask my question, and when I did, he froze. His thumb paused its ministrations, and for half a second, I wondered if my stupid ass joke had killed the mood between us.

Until his shoulders started to shake.

Until his lips pulled back into a smile against my face, his breath puffing across my cheeks as he struggled to contain his laughter. I found myself giggling too, mostly from insecurity and nerves, but giggling, nonetheless.

Leo leaned back to grin at me, before planting one firm kiss on my lips and pulling back just enough to give me a raised brow, "Yeah, I think I need to fuck that sass out of you."

I grinned back at him before he gripped my thong and tugged it roughly down my thighs, making me laugh again, "I don't know," I lifted a shoulder, "I'm feeling very sassy tonight."

"Glad to hear it," Leo murmured, releasing his hold on my hands. He smiled when I held them where he left them, and lifted my legs so he could tug my thong down the rest of the way, "This is mine." He lifted the material to his face, and I dropped my smile at the visual of him closing his eyes and inhaling the scent of my panties for a moment, before shoving my underwear in the back pocket of his jeans.

"Leo, those are—"

"Mine," Leo interrupted while grabbing my hips and tugging me off of the desk. I stumbled into him, feeling the vibrations in his chest from his chuckle as he turned me around. He shoved my hips against the lip of my desk before pressing his entire front against my back, even going as far as to grind his erection into my ass.

It was then that I remembered the kind of equipment he was packing.

"Bend over, love," his voice was at my ear, and I leaned my head back against his shoulder at the sound, "Show me what I have been missing." His warm hands brushed underneath my skirt, shoving it up around my waist, exposing my ass to him in the cool air of the office.

"I need more," I spoke up, hoping he wasn't about to just shove himself in quite yet, "I need—oh god." I glanced over my shoulder to see that Leo had dropped to his knees, his hooded eyes on my ass as each of his hands grabbed their fill.

"I'm a lucky man," Leo sighed. I bit my bottom lip to keep from laughing because it looked like Leo was kneeling before the beauty of my ass. I grinned at him, loving how his words did this for me every time he spoke. It wasn't his accent; I was pretty confident it was just *him* that got me wet.

Then he leaned forward and sunk his teeth into one of my cheeks, and I squealed.

It didn't hurt, but I had never had someone bite my butt before.

"Goddamn," Leo groaned, dragging his tongue where I thought his teeth might have left a small indent, "Perfect, just perfect."

I preened, and I refused to hate myself for it.

Then his hands moved between my legs, encouraging me to widen my stance while he left kisses down my cheek, to the top of my thigh, before his lips moved inward.

"Oh," I blushed, just now realizing what his goal was, "Leo, you don't have—" He grunted and gripped my hips, shoving me more forward on my desk. I slid the iPad and the pencil cup off of the other edge of it in an attempt to brace myself as I lay across it.

"I do, Jacqueline," Leo moaned, almost sounding pained as he used his hold on my hips to get me to arch my back, allowing my center to be exposed for him on my stomach, "If I don't, I might not make it. You don't want that, do you?"

I tilted my head in thought because a lot of the time I wanted to strangle him, before glancing over my shoulder to respond, "I guess not."

He smirked at me, before licking his lips and saying, "Then come all over my face, so you'll be ready for my cock."

I gaped, heat flaming my cheeks at his words. But he didn't care, he just chuckled before he dove in. The man *feasted*, and I had to grip my fingers on the other edge of my desk for some sense of stability. My legs were now trapped between my desk and his body as he ate me out with my face down and ass up.

I hadn't ever had anyone give me oral like this. I hadn't gotten off in this type of position before, but I knew that Leo was about to (yet again) accomplish what I used to think was impossible.

Within minutes of me moaning, squealing, and him adjusting his ministrations based on my physical cues, I was racing towards the finish line.

"Leo," I gasped, "Please, please don't stop. Just—just like

that—" And then my body tensed, and I found myself holding my breath as my orgasm ripped through me. I could feel his groan of approval as he lapped at me, keeping the pace and pressure of his tongue exactly as it was when I started coming. It felt like he was dragging every last second of orgasmic bliss out of me.

Waves and waves of pleasure coursed through me, my abs locked, my legs shook, and suddenly I exhaled a loud moan because my body demanded more oxygen so I could keep coming on Leo's face.

After an indiscriminate amount of time, my legs loosened, and I rested my cheek on the cool wood of my desk.

Leo adjusted so that I wasn't trapped between him and the desk anymore, loving the way his hands gently gripped my hips to help him stand, but I couldn't move. I was still catching my breath on my desk. It wasn't until I heard the sound of his belt and zipper being undone that I finally glanced back at him, while still keeping my cheek on the desk.

"Look at you," Leo smiled, his lips were wet and glistening, "Exhausted little thing." He shoved his hand inside the waistband of his boxers, and I found myself licking my lips at the sight of Leo pulling himself out. Hard and heavy.

Goddamn, I tightened my thighs together in anticipation again.

Leo tsked his tongue again, pulling my legs apart and stepping between them before reaching into his jeans pocket, pulling out a wallet, and revealing a foil wrapper, "You still want this?" he asked, as he ripped the foil open with his teeth and covered himself with the condom.

I nodded, but he leaned over me to gently grab my jaw again, "I need your words, Jacqueline."

"Yeah," I sighed, "I want it."

He smiled before pressing a firm kiss to my temple and whispering, "Good."

He gripped himself and lined up with where I was drenched, even though I was pretty sure I was still feeling small waves of aftershocks.

"Hold on," Leo started to slowly sink into me, and the moan I released was loud. I heard it echo off of the walls, "Fuck, you should see how pretty you look taking me like this." I whimpered, the stretch of him making me clench and flutter again, the sensation almost overwhelming. My brain couldn't comprehend anything more other than the feel of Leo, holding my hips, sheathing himself inside of me.

"Yeah?" I asked because that's all I could manage.

"Yes," Leo groaned, "I just—I'm almost in—" He thrust a little harder, making me gasp, but it was a type of invasion that my body loved, "Once more should—" He thrust again, and his legs finally meet the backs of my thighs, "Oh fuck... oh fuuuck..." He was barely moving, but he was to the hilt, and I was gasping from the pleasure of it.

"God, yes," I moaned, gripping the edge of my desk for dear life. I managed to wiggle my ass a little, desperate for him to move that massive pipe otherwise I thought I'd explode.

I was rewarded with a sudden, gentle slap on my ass.

"You're going to make me come if you keep that up, Ms. Williams."

I laughed, "Isn't that the point?" I wiggled against him again, earning another palm against my other cheek. He immediately rubbed the sting with his fingers, soothing the pleasurable burn away.

"Behave, woman," he chuckled before thrusting once, twice, "God, I really do need to fuck the sass out of you."

"Good luck," I replied before he pulled almost all of the way out and thrust back inside me again, "Fuck."

"Say that again," Leo demanded, repeating his thrust.

So I did, "*Fuck.*" I gasped.

"Ha, I'm a mess," Leo laughed to himself as he started to find a rhythm with his thrusts, and it took me a minute of squirming and gasping to realize that he was adjusting his movements based on what I responded to best.

"Why—why is that?" I asked, trying to keep up the conversation for whatever reason.

"Hearing the proper and professional Jacqueline Williams curse while I sink my cock into her cunt just does things to me," I could tell because his voice started to shake a little. Like he was losing his composure. Perhaps that explained why he was talking about me in the third person.

"Oh, *fuck*, Leo," I moaned, amping up the act a little bit, "You feel *so* good."

It was his turn to curse now, and I started to meet him thrust for thrust, shoving my ass against him, "Please stop talking," Leo groaned, "Otherwise this won't last."

I grinned, because what an exhilarating game of chicken. The idea that I could make him lose control like that was too good to give up.

"Oh," I whined, "You're so *hard.*"

"Jacqueline," Leo's voice was low, a warning as his hips started to lose their rhythm for something more unstable.

"You made me so, fucking, wet," each word was punctuated by the thrust of his hips, "I came so, fucking, hard."

"*Jesus—*"

"No one has made me come that hard before," or at all,

but that was neither here nor there, "You make me *so* horny."

With a growl, Leo slammed his hips against me, sinking in as deep as he could possibly go while he grunted through his release. Feeling him throb inside of me, filling the condom, made me grin as I tried to make it last for him by shoving back against him as hard as I could.

His grip on my hips loosened, one finger at a time, and I was excited to see if his fingertips left little bruises or not.

With a labored exhale, Leo pulled out of me, and a second later I heard the sound of him removing the condom and tossing it in the trash bin under my desk.

I was smiling when his hands pulled me up off of the desk, stabilizing me on my feet because I was a little wobbly. I sighed in contentment I hadn't felt since the last time we hooked up. He tugged my pencil skirt down my legs, even going as far as to brush away the creases from having it scrunched around my waist.

As I turned around to face him, I was startled when his hand came up and closed around my neck. It wasn't a hard clasp or one that made me feel like I was in any danger. It was a grip to get my attention, to get me to meet his clear blue eyes that were somehow both glaring at me and smiling at me at the same time.

"You..." Leo shook his head, his chest heaving as he used his free hand to shove himself back inside his boxers, zipping his jeans up but leaving the top button undone, "You're going to pay for that."

I rolled my eyes, "Oh no, you had an orgasm inside of me." I lifted my hands and wiggled my fingers in a mocking gesture.

"But you," he lifted a finger to my chin at the same moment he tugged me closer to him, again, not hurting my neck, but encouraging my movements all the same, "Didn't come on my cock." My neck flushed with the heat of embarrassment, now that I'd had some time to come down off of my horny orgasm high, his words startled me. But the fog of arousal lingered just enough for my body to react to his tone, "And I'll be damned if the woman I'm with doesn't come at least twice."

I bit my lip and lifted a shoulder, "Sounds like something you should work on, then."

Leo smirked before slamming his lips on mine, hungry, sexual, and demanding. I wasn't expecting it. I didn't know what I was expecting, because when Leo entered my office forty-five minutes ago, I couldn't have guessed that the conversation would lead to him bending me over my desk.

I met his kiss with a hunger of my own though, something raw and heated unlocking inside of me now that I experienced that unique high that only he could pull from me again.

With his grip still on my throat, his thumb brushed the skin under my jaw. Then he pulled me away from his face just enough for him to give me a heated look and say, "I see my work with you isn't finished, Ms. Williams."

I raised my eyebrows at him, "No?"

He shook his head, the movement making his nose brush against mine, "The next time we do this—because I'm betting that there *will* be a next time—" I snapped my mouth shut, surprised that he anticipated my protest, "I won't be so easy on you."

I swallowed under his grip, making the corners of his mouth tip up in a devilish grin that promised many, many orgasms in my future.

"...Bold of you to assume I'll want to do this again," I

could hear the lie in my own voice, so I wasn't surprised when he narrowed his eyes at me in disbelief.

What I wasn't expecting, though, was for him to follow up my snark with some of his own, "Until you find another partner who can make you finish, I feel like our chances of a repeat experience are high." I gaped at him, my eyes widening in humiliation, because I had momentarily forgotten that I had practically told him about his particular skillset before he got under my skirt a second time. "Until then," with a casual lift of a shoulder as he dropped his hold on my neck to pick up his jacket and shirt off of the floor, "I'm all yours."

I blinked. Flustered, embarrassed, confused.

"I—I—" I shook my head, snapping my mouth closed. I glanced down at the iPad and cup of pencils that were discarded over the front edge of the desk, and I circled the desk while Leo shrugged his leather jacket on and strutted toward my office door. That was the moment I froze. A cold feeling of horror washed over me.

Jesus fucking Christ, I had just had sex in my office with a coworker.

I was literally the head of Human Resources, and I just had a man bend me over and fuck my brains out.

Oh my god, oh my god.

"Wait," I called to Leo as he opened the door. Thankfully all the lights behind him were out, indicating that we were still the only ones left in the office. Thank god the custodial crew didn't come in until later.

I grabbed my purse and phone and hooked it on my shoulder before meeting him at my door, holding my palm out, "I need those back."

Leo tilted his head, "What?"

I glared at him, glancing at the still empty hallway

outside the doorway before meeting his eyes and raising my eyebrows expectantly, "My...my panties."

Leo's lips pulled back into a wide grin before he quickly dropped the smile and shook his head, "No."

And then he waltzed out of my office.

"Leo," I grumbled, scrambling after him, "They're mine."

"I earned them," Leo called over his shoulder while pulling his phone out of his pocket to scroll through his notifications. As if he hadn't just orchestrated the hottest sex of my life.

"You did not, they're mine."

"And yet..." he reached into his back pocket to pull them out, dangling them on his index finger as he grinned and winked at me. I gasped, terrified that someone could walk by and see him casually waving my panties around and reached for them.

But Leo was a tall man, and it took no effort for him to snatch my thong into his fist and lift it up above my head.

"Mr. Turner," I grumbled, stomping to emphasize my seriousness.

"Oh, say that again," Leo chuckled darkly before shoving my underwear into the pocket of his jacket. We made it to the elevators in front of Signe's desk. He pressed the button to summon the car.

"I'm serious." I reached around him, attempting to sneak my hand into his pocket myself before he stopped me with a firm grip on my wrist.

"As am I," Leo grinned as he turned his pocket out of my reach, and pulled me into the suddenly opening elevator doors, "These are mine. They'll look so nice in my nightstand drawer, right next to my lotion."

Heat stained my neck and cheeks as I heard the elevator doors close behind me, yanking my arm out of his grip, "Are you for real?" I asked, holding my breath as he reached behind me to punch the button to the first floor.

"As I'll ever be," was his casual response. I grumbled, making my way to the other side of the small elevator cab, before his long arm looped around my waist and pulled me into his chest, my back to his front.

"Jacqueline," Leo murmured against my ear. I could feel every muscle in me physically relax in his hold, at his words brushing over my skin, "You don't like the thought of me keeping your panties?"

I blushed because his question made me think for a moment.

Why didn't I want him to have them? Was it embarrassment? Definitely a bit of embarrassment.

"W-why do you want them so bad?" I asked in a whisper.

"I thought that was obvious," Leo pressed his lips against the skin behind my ear, making me shiver, "They're going to hold me over until next time."

I swallowed, melting at the bluntness of his words.

"Okay..." I was a weak, spineless woman when it came to Leo Turner, "And, um...when is next time?" I mean, if it was going to happen, I might as well pencil it in.

Leo chuckled as the doors to the elevator slid open, tightening his hold on my waist for a second, gently nipping at the shell of my ear before releasing me and stepping around my frozen stance to leave the elevator, "The next time you antagonize me, or when I irritate you, probably."

I released a laugh of disbelief as I followed him out, "That's probably going to be like," I checked my nonexistent watch for theatrics, "Twelve hours from now."

"Then prepare yourself, Ms. Williams," Leo held the door leading to the parking lot out for me to walk through, not being subtle in the slightest as he tipped his head and dropped his eyes to stare at my ass as I passed him, "Because I like being in this position."

"What position?" I lifted a brow as I stopped my walk to watch him step ahead of me, heading straight to his stupid, dangerous motorcycle. He turned around and walked backward, letting his blue eyes rake over the entirety of my body as he shoved his hands in the pocket of his jeans to pull out his keys.

"Being the only one who can give you what you need."

I gnawed on my bottom lip.

Was that...really that appealing?

"Don't overthink it," Leo called over his shoulder as he turned around to swing a leg over his bike, taking the helmet off of the back seat and sliding it over his head.

The visual of him putting his helmet on, complete with his leather jacket and dark jeans, made my lower belly fill with warmth.

This couldn't have been healthy.

Leo didn't say anything more, instead, he just nodded at me as he started his bike and carefully pulled out of his parking space, lifting two fingers to salute me over his visor before he sped away.

I stood there momentarily, trying to figure out when our dynamic had changed so suddenly.

...It was probably the moment he ate me out ass up, if I had to guess.

I shook my head, determined to pull myself together. I had just gotten another mind-numbing orgasm, so I should be good for a while. It probably wouldn't be within twelve hours when I had my cravings again, which made me feel a little more confident attempting to resume the normal routine I relied on.

Chapter Eleven

LEO

"Wait—" Jacqueline sat up, her hair beautifully disheveled, "You actually eat baked beans in the morning? That isn't just some made-up British stereotype?"

I laughed in response, not bothering to smother the sound with any of the pillows surrounding us.

Her smile kicked up a notch, so I reached for her again.

I was fucked.

And now so was Jacqueline, by me, which was a problem.

I was pacing back and forth the next morning, checking my mobile in case Jacqueline needed a ride to work again. But it didn't look like it. I was about to pocket my cell and get ready to head into the office when it started buzzing, and I practically dropped it from my fingers in an attempt to see who was calling.

My mum.

Shit.

I pressed answer, "Morning, I'm about to head into the office."

"Oh, I'm so sorry!" My mother, Victoria (who I lovingly call Mummy), pouted as her dark eyes, which reminded me of Mary's, widened, "I was hoping to catch you before you had to rush out the door."

I double-checked the time, and nodded, "I don't have a meeting until ten, so I can be a little late." Plus, it would reduce the chance of Jacqueline and I awkwardly bumping into each other in the car park. I was confident when we left yesterday, and I blame that on the mind-numbing orgasm that Jacqueline pulled from me.

After a full night's sleep, though, I was feeling anxious about where she and I stood. How to move forward.

"Thank you for making time for your parents, even though you're such a busy boy with a busy big-boy job," she lifted a dark eyebrow, giving me a look that reminded me so much of Mary. My mother and Mary's mother are sisters, but Mary and my mother shared their sense of humor the most.

"Please don't refer to me as a big boy," I rolled my eyes, "I'm a fully grown man."

"But you'll always be our special little boy," my other mother, Lisa (Mama), spoke up from off-camera, "No matter how impressive your job title is." Being raised by two mums wasn't the easiest way to grow up in South London. Homophobia was alive and well during my adolescent years, which made navigating which of my schoolmates I formed crushes on much more complicated. Looking back, after figuring out societal expectations and finding friends and family who became safe spaces, I wouldn't have had it any other way.

There was about a year where I wondered who the

sperm donor my mothers used was. Where he was. I was curious if he would provide a piece of my upbringing that I didn't know I was missing. It was easy to look at my classmates who had fathers and feel left out.

It wasn't until secondary school, when a teammate of mine saw both of my mothers sitting off of the pitch, cheering and waving hand-made signs for me, that I realized how well I had it.

"...I'd rather have two mums than my father any day," he had murmured the comment under his breath during warm-ups before our rugby match, and those words stuck with me ever since.

"Where did you go?" Mama asked.

I had her blue eyes, but she had blonde hair whereas I had black. Genetics from the sperm donor pulled through for our family, because even though I was a white man, my black hair still looked similar to Mummy's dark Chinese hair. I looked like a blend of the two of them.

"I just miss you both," I sighed as I took a seat at my kitchen counter. My flat was still very bare because I was dragging my feet on decorating. Every time I thought about hanging up the art I bought, I sat on the couch and scrolled on my mobile or watched the telly instead.

"When can we come visit you?" Mama asked with her hands clasped under her chin, "We didn't want to visit too early. We wanted to give you time to settle into your new home."

I grinned, "You can come whenever. I know Mary would be excited to see you both."

Mary was also an only child. Her parents ended up moving to California when we were very young. Thankfully, our mothers helped Mary and I maintain a close relationship through writing letters and later, when technology allowed, video calls. Social media also helped us stay close throughout adulthood.

We would take turns visiting each other's families for the holidays, so while I wasn't completely unfamiliar with Orange County, it was still the first time I was *living* here full-time.

"Tell us about Jamie," Mummy wiggled her eyebrows, "Though, I have only heard good things."

"Based on what I've seen, Jamie is perfect for her," I agreed, "They're very happy, even in the office. She seems like the perfect balance for Mary."

"Oh, I'm so glad to hear it," Mama sighed.

"She seems to smooth some of Mary's rougher edges," I drummed my fingers on the countertop, fidgeting.

Jacqueline had rough edges, but I didn't consider those to be negative in any way. It just was who she was. A part of her that helped make up that beautiful brain that I still craved to learn more about.

"Are you interested in dating at all?" Mama asked. I panicked because it was as if she had just caught me thinking about Jacquline. I opened my mouth to respond but clamped it shut. I hesitated, but my mothers knew me too well. I saw both of their faces squish closer onto the little phone screen they were using to call.

"Oh my word, is he blushing? Leo, who are you seeing?" Mummy asked.

"He? She? They?" Mama followed up with.

"Um," I cleared my throat, "I haven't been dating, no. But also...she."

Both of my mothers squealed, which made me want to simultaneously groan with embarrassment and hide in their embraces.

Perhaps I wasn't as much of a grown man as I claimed.

They would always be my safe space. They were the ones who held my hand to help me understand my own sexuality. That I was allowed to be attracted to more than one type of person. They were the ones who sent me with condoms off to university. My mums never made me feel embarrassed or ashamed talking about the intimate matters of sexual relationships. They were the perfect balance of a listening ear, or a helpful sounding board when needed.

"Tell us about her," Mama rested both of her fists under her chin, her blonde eyebrows rising.

"I...work with her," I started with a wince.

"Lovely," Mummy added, "Does Mary know her?"

"Yes—but she doesn't know about our—or I guess my... feelings?" Why did I make it sound like a question? Like it was much more romantic than it was?

"What? Why?"

"They're friends," I frowned, "And she's my coworker. Technically, I'm her superior. So, it's not exactly the most ethical situation...she's in Human Resources."

"...What's her name?" Lisa asked. I was surprised that she ignored my concern so quickly, but I ran with it.

I couldn't stop a grin from spreading, "Jacqueline."

"Oh, what a beautiful name," Mama nodded in approval, her blonde bob bouncing with the movement, "Does Jacqueline know you fancy her?"

Well, I'd assume so, based on how eagerly she took my cock last night.

...I decided that it was okay to keep some secrets from my mums.

"Yeah, we've tiptoed around it," I lifted a shoulder, "I don't know how to navigate this at work, though. It's very new, very early."

"Well, you're both adults who can keep things professional at work." Mummy nodded.

Well, looks like I already fucked that up.

"And just be yourself," Mama added, "Is she shy? You've always gravitated towards shy partners."

I smirked, "Very."

"Just let her be shy," she continued, "You're such a caring man, and I'm sure she'd be lucky to—" a loud beeping started echoing off camera, and both of my mother's gazes lifted toward the kitchen, "Oh, bloody hell!"

"Lisa, why is the stove even on?" Mummy exclaimed. Both women scrambled, sharing amused laughter as they struggled to distinguish whatever my mother caught on fire this time. Unfortunately, her cooking randomly catching fire wasn't an irregular occurrence.

"I need to head into the office anyway," I smiled at the blurry image of both of my mums struggling to maintain the call while attempting to turn off the smoke alarm, "I love you."

"We love you!" They yelled in unison before I ended the call.

I chuckled to myself, pocketing my phone, and ignoring the racing heart behind my ribs as I forced myself out the front door.

However, my mums' reminder was a good one. Jacqueline was definitely what I would refer to as shy, unless of course, she thought she needed to step in and fulfill her duties as human resources. Then, she squared her shoulders and wouldn't hold back giving employees a piece of her mind.

Maybe I was still under the spell created by her reciprocated lust, but I was able to view all those times she gave me grief in the office with a new light.

A light that didn't make me feel guilty or problematic.

Sexual frustration was a real thing, one that I had been experiencing myself for the last few months.

I could only imagine how frustrated she'd been feeling around me, especially while knowing that *I* had been the only one to make her orgasm. I understood just how needy she had been feeling this whole time. Because I was the first partner to help her reach her pleasure.

That was why she looked so surprised every time she came that night. She *genuinely* was. The realization was shocking since it felt like she was so responsive to me. I had just assumed Jacqueline was a woman who had no difficulty getting off.

And getting off again.

And again.

This is how I knew I identified as a man because something primal filled my lungs at the knowledge that I was unique to Jacqueline in this way. Something borderline barbaric, that made me eager to see if I could continue to prove this phenomenon true for her.

Something that made me want to see that wide-eyed, shocked, and euphoric expression coat her features as much as humanly possible.

But, as I straddled my bike and took off towards Sun Steer, I knew I needed to cool it. There was a very good chance that Jacqueline wouldn't want me in that way again, and even though I would respect her boundaries if that was the case, I really hoped she would.

THE NEXT DAY, I could feel burnout approaching me.

No amount of caffeine was helping me stay focused.

Adderall had some side effects, and it was affecting my depressive state more than it had in the past, so instead I relied on caffeine to maintain what I needed to get done every day. Sure, my heart would probably end up failing me in my fifties or so, but at least I could say that I had lived a full life until that happened.

Currently, I could feel the exhaustion in my body and my inability to keep track of basic conversations in the office. Meetings felt more monotonous than usual.

I had even missed a few glances from Jacqueline a moment too late, making me internally kick myself. What if she had been giving me an inviting look and I missed it? I didn't want to miss any unspoken signals from her in case she offered them. But I was starting to find it difficult to manage my focus between taking meetings and preparing reports for managers, instead of remembering how divine it felt to be inside of Jacqueline.

I was a simple man, after all.

Jacqueline and I had kept our distance. It was as if we were back to how we were before. Except less hostile. I would never describe Jacqueline as a woman filled with sunshine and roses. Instead, Jacqueline was reserved. Quiet. Willing to share a laugh with her louder coworkers, like Signe and Mary, but never willing to be the center of attention herself.

I would pass by her in the hallway, unable to help myself as I noted every detail I could. How when she wore jeans into the office, they complemented the soft curves of her hips and arse. How they flared near her feet, showing off her sneakers. Her work blouse was appropriately buttoned, but she would tuck a small section in the front of her jeans. This made the shirts look less oversized.

She definitely preferred her hair up, I realized. Either in

a bun or a pony-tail. She hardly ever wore it down, unlike how I first met her.

"Leo—" Currently, everyone was sitting together in the largest conference room while Brandon went over what he claimed to be an exciting announcement.

We had already had an all-hands meeting a few weeks ago. That is what Sun Steer called a quarterly meeting where the entire company got together and went over the numbers regarding how well we were doing. What goals we met, what goals we didn't, things like that.

So for Brandon to call another all-hands meeting a few weeks later, everyone seemed to be on edge. There was a nervous energy in the room up until Brandon walked to the front, getting things started with an excited look in his eye.

As soon as he started speaking, everyone realized it was good news.

Boson Motors had finished building what we hoped to be the very first machines powered by Sun Steer Technologies. Tractors, combines, and ATVs were getting polished and ready to upload the software everyone had been busting their arse to build.

Relaxing a bit helped, but my brain wasn't cooperating with me today.

I struggled to stay focused during the meeting. Perhaps it was because of my ADHD, or perhaps it was because I was sitting next to a certain brunette who I had recently shagged on her desk.

Who's to say, really?

Thankfully, when Brandon mentioned my name and I jerked my head forward, it was obvious he was simply mentioning me. Not addressing me. I relaxed a little in my seat, my legs stretched out underneath the long conference table as I fought the urge to move my hands.

I eyed Mary across the table from me, who looked very bored and unfocused in the meeting. Whereas I was struggling to stay focused, Mary looked like she didn't even bother to pretend to. She could have been sleeping with her eyes open for all I knew.

But I was in upper management.

I needed to set an example, and look excited about this update, instead of also wishing this meeting was just an email.

I shoved my hands in my pockets, but my fingers still tapped. The movement was restricted, and it didn't satisfy the need I had to ground myself with repetitive movement.

Suddenly, Zaid's name was mentioned followed by a soft round of applause.

I clapped too, smiling at the former CTO when he looked bashful from the attention, ducking his head a little as he faced the conference table in his seat.

I tried to look back up again, but my eyes kept wandering against my will. It wasn't like I actively tried to think about something else, sometimes my brain just took over. All I kept thinking was *Jacqueline is sitting next to me in jeans. Jacqueline is sitting next to me in jeans. Jacqueline is sitting next to me, smelling like vanilla and roses, in jeans.* Jeans that were just as distracting as those bloody pencil skirts she loved to wear.

I scraped a hand down my face, struggling to sit still.

Fidgeting helped ground me, and I couldn't find a single pen or anything on this massive table. Working at a tech company, pens and paper were rare. Everything got done on computers or iPads or phones. Nothing needed to be written down traditionally. I only kept a package of pens at my desks specifically for me to fidget with.

But did I remember to bring one to this meeting? No.

I didn't think excusing myself just to grab a pen to twirl in my fingers seemed appropriate or respectable, so I sat here and suffered instead.

I released a sigh, annoyed with myself for again losing focus when I felt a gentle tap on my thigh.

The thigh closest to Jacqueline.

I froze, wondering if I imagined the contact. We were in a meeting, surrounded by dozens and dozens of employees who weren't working from home today. Would she really be so bold as to touch me?

Tap, tap.

I guess so.

Attempting to be sly and not on the verge of jumping out of my chair, I glanced down to see a pen against my thigh. I looked around, confirming that nobody was looking at us, before I focused on her.

She wasn't looking at me.

She was scrolling on her iPad, following along with the presentation Brandon had up on the projector. In her hand, below the table where nobody else could see, Jacqueline silently offered me the digital pen that was paired with her iPad.

Something warm and thrilling filled my lungs at the realization of what was happening. Though I was taking too long to respond, because without looking up at all, Jacqueline tapped the pen on my thigh again. *Tap, tap, tap.*

I fought a grin when I finally slid the pen out of her fingers, careful not to touch her skin with mine.

Underneath the table, one hand resting on my leg, I twirled the pen like I usually did.

My mind and body almost immediately relaxed.

I inhaled a deep breath to help calm my anxious nerves,

focusing on the familiar movement of twirling the pen again and again.

I snuck another peak at Jacqueline by my side, but she still didn't look at me. She lifted her gaze and, I swear to god, was entirely focused on Brandon's meeting.

So I tried to do the same.

Suddenly, Brandon stopped talking, and everyone checked their phones and watches while he pulled something else up on his laptop for the meeting.

"This is so exciting," I heard the blue-haired woman murmur on Jacqueline's other side. I leaned forward in my seat to glance at her, wondering if she could provide additional context for what was happening.

"It's pretty cool," Jacqueline whispered back with a nod. When she saw me leaning forward, listening to her, and the other employee's conversation, she gave me a frown.

But not a disapproving frown.

No, this was one of my favorite Jacqueline frowns. It was a frown that looked like an upside-down smile. Her eyes crinkled in the corners, and her lips softened with the movement. It was a frown designed to hide her true feelings, which I assumed was something positive as her gaze dropped to the pen moving in between my fingers.

I gave her a small, professional smile in return in an attempt to communicate my appreciation.

"Okay, here we go," Brandon announced, making us all sit straighter while the screen displayed a FaceTime call.

The name at the top of the screen just said "Graham" and I was still lost.

Finally, the call connected, and a moment later the screen was filled with what looked like a dirt field.

"Graham," Brandon spoke as he smiled up at the screen, "Flip your camera."

"Huh?" A deep voice responded, echoing through the conference room.

"Oh, my," the blue-haired woman whispered to Jacqueline. I glanced to my side just in time to see Jacqueline smile at her before facing forward again.

"We see the field," Brandon explained as he turned his own laptop to face all of us, "Flip your camera. Say hi to everyone."

The image blurred for half a second before a man's face filled the screen. His eyes were squinting under the rim of his cowboy hat, and then he turned to face away from the sun so he could properly view his screen.

"Oh my god," the blue-haired employee—Violet! Her name was Violet—breathed.

I fought a laugh at her response before I glanced over and saw Jacqueline staring wide-eyed at the handsome man's face projected on the screen too.

Pardon?

I focused back on the call, taking in all his features.

He looked a lot like Brandon, and after clocking his hazel eyes and sandy blonde hair, I figured this must have been Brandon's brother up in Northern California. The only difference was that this man spent way more time in the sun and had a full blonde beard. Suddenly, everything was making sense. Brandon had mentioned FaceTiming his brother when we were ready to merge Boson Motors' and Sun Steer's tech, letting everyone in the company meet the owner of the first farm who would be using the machinery.

It was a momentous step in the company, and if all the machinery worked well, who's to say how it would change the agricultural industry as a whole.

But based on how the women in the office looked staring up at the rugged man with a baritone voice, I had a feeling none of them cared at all about the company's progress. They all might as well have had hearts in their eyes. Well, not every woman. Mary and Nicole were looking very indifferent.

"Hello everyone." Graham Moore clearly wasn't comfortable on video calls, his wave was awkward and stiff, and he swallowed once after saying hello. He even went as far as to tug on the collar of his t-shirt, which was sweat-stained and covered in patches of dirt.

"Hi!" Everyone in the office waved, but the women specifically projected their greetings. I glanced down at Jacqueline, having heard her enthusiastically greet the CEO's brother. I lifted an eyebrow at her, and when a warm flush stained her cheeks as she scowled at me, my smile kicked up a notch.

"Is it hot in here?" Violet asked in a whisper meant to be heard by those surrounding us. I chuckled, whereas Jacqueline shook her head in disapproval, fully pretending she wasn't as infatuated with Brandon's handsome brother as the other women.

I pulled my phone out, keeping it close and low under the table, so no one could read over my shoulder.

Me: Is he your type?

I lifted my head, barely paying attention to Graham's awkward greeting and introduction to Moore Farms. That was because, in the corner of my vision, I saw Jacqueline shift to pull her phone out of her jeans pocket.

I held my breath as I waited for her to respond, counting to three before checking my phone after it buzzed in my hand.

Jacqueline: I don't have a type.

I raised my eyebrows, but Violet's sudden, "Huh?" made me forget the text thread.

I glanced up, seeing color bloom across Violet's cheeks, somehow making her blue hair look brighter.

"I said," Brandon nodded toward her, not registering her surprise at all, "Once Boson ships their equipment, you'll be traveling to Northern California to maintain and oversee the technology there. To provide onsite maintenance."

I lifted an eyebrow, wondering why this was a surprise to Violet. She was a systems engineer. She was hired specifically to oversee the tech in action. Perhaps she was expecting to work remotely?

"Oh," Violet cleared her throat and nodded, "Yes, of course. I'm looking forward to it." She threw a thumbs up back, which weirdly, didn't convince me of her confidence.

Graham squinted his eyes on the screen, "I didn't quite catch that. I can't see everyone that well, who exactly is coming?"

Brandon repeated, "Our systems engineer."

"Ah, perfect. I don't know what the fuck I'm doing." Signe cackled, slapping her hand over her mouth. Zaid's shoulders were shaking with silent laughter too, and Brandon pinched the bridge of his nose while fighting a smile of his own.

"You're in a company meeting, Graham."

"Oh shi—sorry. I'm sorry everyone," he waved again, "I should go. Thanks for introducing me to all the talented minds making this possible." He sounded genuine, which was nice and all, but I didn't actually care because my focus wasn't on this meeting at all. Even with the iPad pen to fidget with. I couldn't help but side-eye Jacqueline next to me.

She kept her phone face-down on her leg, scrolling on her iPad, ignoring everyone around her.

So I finally replied.

> Me: If you happen to be in the mood for your favorite Englishman again, just say the word.

I WAS WALKING BACK to my office after the meeting, finally getting a bearing on what was going on with the company. Jacqueline never responded to my text, but she did read it, and I thought I saw her lips twitch positively before she tucked the phone back into her jeans.

I felt a little better about where she and I stood. Even if she and I didn't shag again, perhaps we could maintain this positive comradery. As I walked toward my office, the pen in my fingertips twirled and twirled. I was in a better, more stable mood. I smiled at the employees I passed, before glancing down.

...Jacqueline would probably want her pen back.

Though I couldn't lie and say I didn't feel the equivalent of butterflies in my chest at the realization that Jacqueline had just helped me in a very unique, observant way. Somehow, during all the months that I worked here and she bickered at me, Jacqueline picked up on this very unique tell I had.

I did my best work when I had something to keep my hands busy. A physical type of anchor to get my mind to focus on what I needed to focus on.

Did she know I had ADHD? Did Mary tell her? Did Jacqueline discover this all on her own?

What was my body language like in that meeting for Jacqueline to pick up on my angsty energy, so much so that she gave me the pen to her iPad?

I turned, ignoring my office and heading for hers, determined to give her pen back.

Before I left, I looked around the empty room. Jacqueline's office was calm, a fig tree planted in a pot against the wall. The colors were painted a neutral warm cream, with no overhead lights on. Only two lamps cast a soft yellow glow. She had a seat cushion on her desk chair and a snake plant next to her monitor.

I trailed my finger up one leaf of the snake plant, before noticing the note attached. I flicked it open, seeing what looked like an apology note from Zaid Ansara.

I snickered, wondering what wrath Jacqueline set upon him to justify such an apology.

Part of me was wondering how I missed the detail of this plant on her desk the last time I was in there. How this plant didn't get knocked off of her desk during our tryst.

I shook my head, scraping a hand down my face to get my mind back on less perverted memories. I pulled open the first drawer on her desk and found a small pad of sticky notes, before peeling one off and finding a real pen to use.

Thank you

Then I set the iPad pen right next to my note, before strolling out and making my way back to my own office.

This doesn't mean she wants you to fuck her again, I reminded myself as I plopped down in my desk chair. I would need Jacqueline's explicit verbal consent to revisit something like that, and nothing less. I used the toe of my boot to kick open my mini fridge, before reaching in to grab a can of soda.

I ignored all the terrible ingredients the US pumped into their beverages and took a few large gulps of the caffeine, Red Dye 40, and all. After setting the can on my desk, I reached over my keyboard to find one of my own pens to twirl in my hand.

I just had one more meeting at the end of the week, and then I could take the weekend to myself to recover. Everything was starting to become too much, but also not enough.

Chapter Twelve

JACQUELINE

"You have a freckle right here." The pad of Leo's fingertip gently tapped against the back of my shoulder, but I couldn't be bothered to acknowledge the random observation. I moaned into the pillow, too focused on how his other hand gripped my hip just as he needed. I relished the feel of his wet tongue gliding over where his finger just was, followed by his warm lips pressing against my skin.

I was nervous, biting my lip in my office as I held my phone in my hands. It felt like another pinnacle moment. Something that started a new timeline. And yet, I didn't think I was going to back down. It had been several days since Leo was here. Since I disinfected the surface of my desk immediately upon entering my office after...well.

I knew he was in a less-than-thrilling meeting today. I heard Brandon and Nikhil discussing it yesterday after the random all-hands meeting where we met his unexpectedly handsome brother.

179

I also had just walked past Leo's meeting in one of the conference rooms with Brandon and some older men. Probably potential investors. Leo didn't look as entertained as he usually did. He had dark circles under his eyes. His smile didn't reach them like it normally did.

It bothered me.

And part of me wanted to shrug that feeling off. Remind myself that I wasn't responsible for making him feel better or wondering why he wasn't as elevated today. The other part of me, however, cared. I didn't think too much about it. I figured it was normal to care. Signe would care if one of her friends was acting a little more lethargic or withdrawn. It wasn't because I could still remember the feel of him inside of me.

I nodded to myself, clutching my phone in my hand and standing from my desk, leaving my office door open behind me in case I chickened out and wanted to dart back. I rounded the corner, leaving the upper management office wing. There was a vending machine just across the open concept area dividing the break room from where the conference rooms lined the perimeter of the building.

I stood near the vending machine, leaning against the wall and holding my phone to my chest. I nodded politely at some passing employees while I found the conference room Leo was in.

He was facing me, his back to the windows that let the cool morning light in. The marine layer hadn't quite burned off yet, coating everything in a hint of grey. It was a sleepy morning for a lot of employees, based on the number of yawns I had heard already.

Leo didn't see me across the way, though. His tired eyes were locked on one of the old men he was meeting with. His head would nod occasionally, but I noticed how he leaned to the side of his chair. How he rested one elbow on his armrest to hold his cheek in his fist. His brow had a small pinch in it, and his pink lips were in a line with a small curve in the corner. The man was struggling this morning but doing a decent enough job of looking engaged with the meeting.

I inhaled a breath of confidence and glanced down at my phone, pulling up my text thread with him.

> Me: Were you serious about repeat experiences?

I sent the message off, holding my phone close to make it look like I was still doing important work things on it, even though my eyes kept glancing up at Leo across the way.

He shifted in his seat, using the hand that was propping his head up to reach into his pocket and pull out his phone. I could see him keep it under the table, in an attempt to not be too obvious about checking his messages during a meeting.

I held my breath while I waited for his reaction. Any sort of physical cue that he was excited to get a text from me. But after Leo took a moment to read what I assumed was my message, all he did was turn the screen down on his thigh as he lifted his head and started talking to Brandon and the potential investors.

My shoulders slumped a bit, disappointment making my stomach feel tight. Leo said something, his eyebrows raising and a smirk tugging on his lips as he engaged in the conversation.

And I felt like the biggest ass.

Why I thought a stupid flirty text from me would maybe help lift his spirits was silly.

I had just stood off from the wall, ready to sulk back into

my office, when the older man laughed loudly and turned to say something specifically to Brandon. When the attention was no longer on him, I saw Leo flip his phone back over, keeping it close to his thigh as his thumbs tapped over the screen.

I froze, holding my breath.

Leo settled back in his chair, keeping his phone out of sight and face down when he was done, and locked his gaze on the men in the room with him.

My phone buzzed in my hand. I stepped back to lean against the wall once more and opened the message, my heart racing in my chest.

My nerves were so frantic, like I was a teenager texting her first crush again.

Leo: I was deeply serious.

My cheeks heated. I glanced up at him again, surprised at how he looked so professional and unphased. He even laughed at something Brandon said, multitasking like a pro.

Me: What would that look like for you, exactly?

I watched as he waited for the attention to be off of him again before he flipped his phone over and read my message. His face didn't change at all. Leo had an excellent poker face as he tapped his response.

My phone vibrated against my chest right when he leaned back in his chair, looking a little more alert than he was before.

Leo: However you want it to look. You can call the shots.

I fought against a smile at that. My heart was still racing, because I couldn't remember the last time that I had a discussion like this over text messages. It was fun, being able to have a secret conversation with him like this during the workday. Watching him play the role of a professional CTO while also discussing the terms of a sexual relationship with me.

He yawned a bit, covering his mouth with his hand as he nodded at something someone said in the room.

So I decided to kick it up a notch.

> Me: I thought it was obvious how much I liked it when *you* called the shots.

I inhaled a breath and held it until I saw him flip over his phone again to read my newest message.

He stilled in his seat, before I saw him lift a hand and mindlessly drag his thumb back and forth across his bottom lip.

He focused on this message for a few seconds longer than the others. I could see a pinch in his brow as he stared at his phone. Forcing myself to release my breath, I tried not to spiral about how I may have made this a little too forward. Perhaps there was subtlety etiquette when it came to having text conversations like this that I didn't know about.

Trust him to tell you when you cross a line, I silently reminded myself.

Finally, Leo thumbed away on his phone again. Mine buzzed in response, but I took a moment to watch him adjust in his chair. How he shifted his position so he wasn't laying back as much. He was sitting straighter, and I thought I saw him quickly adjust how his pants folded in his lap.

I finally made myself read his newest message.

> Leo: Be careful what you ask for, Jacqueline.
> I have quite an appetite when it comes
> to you.

> Me: I know. I can still feel your tongue.

Leo glanced up at the ceiling after reading my response. The way his head tilted toward the overhead lighting let me see a very, very faint flush on his cheeks. I saw his chest expand as he inhaled through his nose before he dropped his head again to reread my text. As he thought about how to reply, I watched how Brandon and the other old men were deep into their conversation. Paying little to no attention to Leo during this part of the meeting.

Then I decided to send another text before Leo had the chance to respond.

> Me: Let me know when and how you want
> me, Mr. Turner. I also have an appetite. One
> that only you can satiate right now.

> Me: In the meantime, I can enjoy watching
> you get flustered during your meetings.

After that, I stood from the wall and turned to face the vending machine, giving the conference room my back. It wasn't a clear view, but as I pretended to study the snack options, I focused on the reflection coming from behind me. I saw Leo shift forward to rest his forearms on his thighs as he read my newest message. I bit my lip to keep myself from grinning when I saw him slowly lift his head from his lap, not facing the men in the meeting, but facing where I was standing across the way.

I couldn't stop my grin from peeking out then, because even through the glass wall of the conference room, across the way from the open hallway, I could feel his gaze on me. I could feel his eyes take in exactly what I was wearing today.

Another pencil skirt.

Something I now knew got to him.

So when I let him get his fill of me standing there, pretending to decide on my choice, I went the extra mile by bending a little at the waist, as if reading the names of the snacks on the lower levels of the machine.

Giving Leo Turner an unobstructed view of my ass in this skirt, my knees bending just enough to make the pose look less suspicious to anyone passing by.

I glanced up to the conference room's reflection in the glass of the vending machine, just in time to see Leo rub a hand over his mouth. His eyes locked on me. Well, my ass, probably.

I stood tall again, propping a hand on my lower back as if pretending to stretch out, and I got to see Leo drop his head as he thumbed away on his phone.

Leo: You're going to need to save up some
money for a new wardrobe.

I frowned, keeping him at my back as I finally left the hallway and made my way to my office.

Me: Why is that?

Leo: Because after work I'm going to rip that
skirt off of you with my teeth.

I gasped as I read his newest message, my hand coming up to rest against my racing heart as I entered my office. Heat coursed through me.

I didn't think I could come back from this.

I HAD JUST LOCKED my computer and shouldered my purse when my phone vibrated again. It wasn't until I rushed it out of my bag and pulled open my newest message that I realized I was hoping it was Leo, confirming the plans we alluded to earlier today.

Instead, it was Marco.

> Marco: I'm just checking in to make sure you're alive since I'm single-handedly maintaining our sibling relationship.

I laughed as I left my office, but the sound of another door shutting across the way made me lift my eyes away from my phone.

Leo was locking the door to his own office, his eyes slowly dragging from the tips of my toes to the top of my head. I felt his gaze as if I was standing in front of a heat lamp, warming me up for him.

"Hi," I whispered.

Leo's lips twitched in the corners, "Hi."

I pressed my lips together while scrambling to respond to my brother, then tossed my phone in my bag.

"Are you finished with your workday?" Leo asked, falling into step with me as we walked down the hallway. He kept about a foot of distance between us, but my heart reacted as if he was rubbing up on me in the office.

"I am." I nodded.

"Are you taking the lift down?" His face was guarded, his expression perfectly masked. This was the face of a coworker shooting the shit with another coworker.

"I'm taking the *elevator* down, yes." I fought against a smile.

His eyes danced over to me, narrowing as we turned the corner to find the elevators.

"You mean the *lift*?" He emphasized the word, "No need to add more syllables than necessary."

I snorted, pushing the button, "I'm not being *lifted* anywhere. If anything, I'm being lowered." We both walked into the elevator, and Leo removed one of his hands from his pockets to reach his long index finger toward the buttons.

"Ground floor?"

"What? No, the first floor. I'm not trying to go to the basement."

Leo smirked, "I keep misspeaking. Back home, what you call the first floor we call the ground floor."

I widened my eyes, "Well, considering the button you want to push has a *one* on it, I'd say our vernacular makes more sense."

Leo chuckled at my snark and looked up at the ceiling after hitting the button for the first floor. He tucked his bottom lip in between his teeth and shook his head once, closing his eyes along with the elevator doors. The cab started to descend when he asked, low and intimate, "Do you remember your safe word, Jacqueline?"

My heart skipped a beat behind my ribs; giddiness and excitement flooded my veins at his question before I replied, "Yes."

"Good," Leo reached forward to punch the emergency stop button in the elevator, jerking us to a rough halt in between floors, "Take off your panties."

My breath caught in my throat.

My heart skipped a beat for another reason, and I found myself looking around to remind myself that we were, in fact, still in the elevator. At work.

"What?" I asked.

"Take off your panties." Leo's eyes lowered as if he could see through my skirt. I released a nervous laugh, before slowly resting my hand at the hem of the fabric.

Leo leaned against the wall of the elevator, crossing his arms as if he wasn't staring at my skirt with a hungry expression. As if his eyes weren't darkening when I tucked my fingers beneath my skirt.

"Are—" I swallowed around a dry, nervous lump in my throat, "Are you serious?" I asked.

"Extremely," Leo replied, lifting one of his hands to rest his thumb against his bottom lip. He brushed it gently, and the view of his lip softly being tugged back and forth distracted me for a moment. Leo's eyes lifted to lock on mine, the icy blue becoming less and less visible beneath his growing pupils, "I have all day, Ms. Williams."

I bit my own bottom lip, wishing I was tasting his.

So I tucked both of my hands under my skirt, keeping my purse on my shoulder, while I dragged my skirt up, up, up.

Leo's eyes stayed glued to every inch of exposed skin that was slowly revealed, his thumb continuing to tease his bottom lip while I curled my thumbs into the waistband of my lacy thong.

Because I didn't want panty lines today.

Definitely not because I hoped Leo would see and appreciate the lace.

I had to bend to feed my feet through the holes, careful not to snag my sneakers on the lace as I finally pulled them off.

I stood straight and pulled my skirt back down, my panties bunched in my hand while I maintained eye contact the best I could. I was trembling from anticipation. What else did he have planned for inside the elevator? Why was I excited for it? We were still in the office. The elevator wasn't in the plan to start anything physical with him.

Was it because he bent me over my desk earlier this week? Was my threshold for what I was willing to do with this man expanding the more time I spent with him? At what point would we escalate things to the break room? The sensory room? Who's to stop us from doing it on Signe's front desk at this point?

"Jacqueline," Leo shook his head once, stepping forward and brushing his fingers over mine, uncurling my underwear from my hold, "I can see you overthinking this. Don't."

I stood stock still as he gently brushed his lips against my temple, taking my underwear and pocketing the lace in his jeans pocket.

And then Leo stepped back, pushing the button and continuing our descent.

I exhaled the breath I was holding, the sensation almost made me dizzy in his presence.

"Your flat, or mine?" Leo asked.

"Um. Mine." I replied, gripping the strap of my purse for dear life.

The elevator doors finally parted, and I took the first steps out of the threshold as Leo said, "I'll follow you."

Something spiked in my pulse from his words. I hesitated in the building lobby, glancing over my shoulder at him. Leo's hands were back in his pockets, his eyes lifting from where they were previously staring at my ass. He waited for me to either say something or keep moving forward.

So I turned and walked out of the building, calling over my shoulder, "I'll see you there."

Chapter Thirteen

JACQUELINE

DID *he realize how beautiful he looked like this? Flushed above me, panting, and satisfied? Something awakened in me here, lying with this handsome stranger. Something I couldn't name for myself, but acknowledged regardless.*

It wouldn't matter, because I was still walking away in the morning.

———

CHECKING my rearview mirror to see Leo following me on his bike, covered in his helmet, and leather jacket, and gloves, was one of the top five most erotic experiences of my life.

It was as if he was pursuing me, like a predator who was waiting for his prey to give up the chase. It wasn't like that at all, obviously. Leo never made any dangerous turns on his bike. He never revved his engine in a way that other douchey motorcyclists did at stoplights. He never got his bike dangerously close to my car. But I still knew *why* he stayed behind me the entire drive back. What our plans were.

It gave me some ideas, and I gnawed on my bottom lip the entire twenty-minute journey wondering if I could be brave enough to ask him for it. When we finally parked in front of my building, Leo conveniently found an empty spot directly next to mine (as if the universe itself was like, "Yeah, you two *definitely* need to have sex today"). He dismounted his bike and removed his helmet, before running his fingers through his hair.

Eventually, he tucked his helmet underneath his arm and shouldered his work bag, approaching me on the sidewalk.

"Do you still want me to come upstairs with you?" Leo asked. As if I wasn't impatient to be alone with him.

I swallowed again before nodding my head.

"Words, Jacqueline."

God, I loved when he ordered me around like that.

"Yes," I stood straighter, "Yes, I want you to come upstairs with me."

"And what's going to happen when I do?" Leo took a step forward, then another.

"Um..." I shrugged, before squeezing my eyes closed for a second and gaining determination to not act like a stumbling, bumbling, sexually inexperienced woman, "Pretty much whatever you want."

Leo hummed, the feel of my purse strap tugging away from my shoulder made me open my eyes. He was tracing the strap between his index finger and thumb, his eyes on his hand as he asked, "What if I want to raise your skirt and take you against your front door?"

I exhaled a shocked gasp, my lips twitching around a

smile because *holy shit* that sounded awesome, "If that's what you want."

"What do *you* want, Jacqueline? This isn't just for me." Leo tugged on my strap, gently tugging me into his space. The move didn't look inherently sexual, but still made my body heat.

"...I don't want to be in control, I think," nerves swam in my belly at my words, "I don't really want to think, or stress. I just want to...feel."

"Feel what, exactly?" Leo pressed.

I lifted my gaze from his hand on my purse strap, and locked with his icy blue eyes when I breathed out, "...What only you can make me feel."

Leo's lips parted at my response, his eyes blinking as he nodded once and dropped his hold on my purse, "I'm never going to get tired of hearing you say that."

I grinned, before stepping to the side in a silent invitation to follow me up. We silently walked into my apartment building, but my body was buzzing. I wasn't sure how obvious it looked to my neighbors who were passing in and out of the lobby. Could everyone tell that he and I were about to get intimate in my apartment?

I pressed the button to call the elevator, and his heat enveloped me as he stepped closer, waiting. His hand came up, and his fingers gently dragged over the skin on the back of my bicep, making me shiver as I waited for the doors to open.

When they did, I stepped through the doors and to the side to make room for him. Then I hit the button for my floor.

As soon as the doors closed, we both stood still and silent. He had his hands in the pockets of his jacket, and I remembered that my damp panties were stored in there. I wondered if he had a grip on them, or if he was playing with the lace in the obscurity of his pocket. I had my arms folded across my chest, both of us completely quiet as I drummed my fingers on my arm.

The elevator doors revealed my floor, and the two of us silently stepped into the hallway before I led us to my unit. I found that my hands weren't steady as I dug around my purse for my keys.

Then Leo's warm voice brushed over my ear, "You better hurry, Jacqueline."

The heat of his body pressed against my back as I finally found the ring and started flipping through the keys. Still trying to find the one that unlocked my door.

"I don't know if I can wait any longer, love," Leo's hot breath fanned against my skin before his lips teased against the shell of my ear, "If we don't get inside soon, your neighbors are about to have a show."

My entire body was trembling, my hands shaking as I finally found the key and struggled to jam it into the lock.

"Three...two..." his words teased me as I finally twisted the lock and threw the front door open, bolting inside and dropping my purse in the entryway. I lingered just enough for him to enter and close the door behind him. Leo met my eyes as he flipped the lock on both the deadbolt and the doorknob. His helmet and bag dropped to the floor.

"My safe word is 'glacier'," I said, sliding out of my shoes as I watched him do the same, "Not 'no', not 'stop', not 'don't'." Leo's eyebrow lifted a bit as he shrugged out of his jacket. I almost forgot to keep speaking when I saw him grab the back collar of his shirt and tug it over his head, "...I want to play." Based on the wetness coating the skin between my legs when he was up against my back, threatening to take me in the hallway, I had a strong suspicion this kind of play was something I wanted to explore further.

"What do you mean by play?" Leo asked. He used one hand to flip open his belt buckle, before dragging the leather through the loops of his pants in one smooth motion. It was the move of a man who had taken his belt off one-handed many times before. The move of a man who was just as eager as I was.

"I...want to be...taken."

"Taken?" Leo asked, warmth starting to fill his cheeks as he stepped toward me. I stepped back, making him hesitate his approach. I nodded at him.

"By you," I explained, unbuttoning my blouse. I watched as his eyes stayed glued to my hands as each button came undone, revealing my white lacey bra, "I like the idea of you pursuing me. Catching me. Fighting for me."

"Jesus fucking Christ," Leo rasped, as he dragged a hand over his face, his eyes almost completely black as I parted the panels of my blouse and slowly slid it off my shoulders. He took another step toward me, and I retreated one to match. He didn't stop this time, understanding what I was asking.

"Do you want me, Leo?" I asked, a giddy smirk tugging on my lips as I continued slowly backing away from him.

Leo released a low grumble before he ground out, "Terribly."

"Then you better catch me." And then I turned on my heel and ran. I went down the hallway, and the sound of his heavy footfalls closing in behind me made me laugh. I loved the thrill, but before I made it through the door of my bedroom, his large arms wrapped themselves around my waist.

My feet left the floor, my back pulled against his chest, as he turned and pinned me against the hallway wall.

"You're going to have to learn to be faster than that," Leo ground out, licking a hot, wet stripe up the side of my neck. I was squirming in his hold. My hands tried to push his arms off of me but failed, "I've been looking forward to sinking into you since this morning."

I gasped through a giggle when his face buried itself in my neck. He didn't release his hold on me. He kept me successfully pinned between the wall and his body as his hardness rutted against my backside through his jeans.

"Do you want to use your safe word?" Leo checked as he teased the sensitive spot between my neck and shoulder.

"No." I shook my head as much as I could while his lips tortured me like this.

"Good," he ground out, releasing one of his arms around my waist and wrapping his fingers around my thigh. His hot palm slowly dragged itself up my leg, his fingers curling inward towards where I was aching for him the most.

I thrust back against him, attempting to free myself, and earned another groan from him.

"Do you like fighting me, Jacqueline?" Leo captured my earlobe in between his teeth, the gentle scrape making me moan as I gripped his arm around my waist tighter, "Do you like pretending that you aren't desperate for me?"

"Yes," I wheezed, my head falling back against his shoulder as I tried to shove myself off of the wall again. His hard length twitched against my back before he suddenly dragged me away from the wall and through my bedroom doorway.

"Do you like the idea of being at my mercy?" Leo asked as he dumped me on the bed. I bounced on the comforter face down, before throwing him a smile over my shoulder and attempting to crawl away to the other side.

Both of his hands wrapped around my ankles, dragging me back down to him. He used the grip on my feet to flip me over, pressing one of his knees on the bed next to me. I panted as I watched him use one hand to unbutton his jeans and pull the zipper down, and when that hand disappeared inside his jeans, I tried to escape again.

I was giggling, so fucking horny and happy.

I couldn't remember the last time I had this much fun with foreplay.

Before I could get far at all, Leo's large body was over me, pinning me on my stomach to the mattress.

"Looks like I need to find a way to keep you put," Leo murmured, as he pressed a kiss to my shoulder, "Even though I enjoy the chase."

I looked up as his arm reached ahead of us and found my fluffy robe hanging next to my bed. I widened my eyes when his fingers wrapped around the tie for the robe and pulled it out of the loops.

"Oh my god," I breathed, attempting to buck him off of me but, thankfully, failing.

"Use your safe word any time." He shifted up my body some more, keeping me pinned underneath him as he captured both of my wrists and started to gently tie them together with my fluffy robe tie.

"Oh my god, oh my god, oh my god," I was mumbling into the comforter of the mattress as he secured my wrists. The tie was tight, but not tight enough to cut off circulation. If I truly struggled with my full strength, I could easily free myself from this. He must have done that on purpose, because then he was flipping me over onto my back underneath him, shimmying up my body that he now straddled, before he started tying the other end of the restraint to something. I glanced up, seeing that he was securing me to the post of my bed frame.

"It looks like you're still into this," Leo murmured, finishing up his knot and leaning back to look at me prone underneath him, "Which is good, because I love playing with you."

"Fuck." I arched underneath him, and I saw him close his eyes as his lips parted and he hung his head over me.

"I love hearing you curse." Leo shook his head and leaned forward to kiss me. It was the first kiss on the mouth throughout this entire ordeal, and my body lit up underneath him. Our tongues were dueling for dominance, something he smiled about as he finally won. I surrendered, letting both of his warm hands cup my head and position me just how he wanted as he plundered my mouth. The kiss was wet and messy, just like I was tied up underneath him.

One of his hands released its grip on my head, sliding down my body and tracing his fingers against the lace at the top of my bra cup.

I gasped into his mouth, bucking against him as his fingers slowly peeled the lace down. My breast was revealed to the room, the tip puckering just as he brushed his thumb against the hardened bud.

"You're sensitive here," Leo murmured against my mouth. I pulled gently against his homemade restraint, thrusting against him again just to feel his erection against me through his jeans and my skirt, "Very sensitive, if I remember correctly." He grinned at me before tugging on my lip once and kissing my jaw, my neck, and the dip at the base of my throat before his lips continued their path toward my chest.

"Oh." I bucked against him again.

Leo grinned at me, "Look at you, writhing underneath me. Needy little thing, pretending you don't want this." I bit my lip to hide my smile, because yeah, I was needy. I was *so* fucking needy. I wanted whatever he had in store for me. I was practically trembling with need. I wanted him to take me and do whatever he wanted. I wanted to lose control with him.

"If you—oh god," I was cut off because he pulled the other cup of my bra down, before dragging his tongue across my hard nipple slow enough to make me moan, "If you do that, I'm going to come so fast."

"Good." his free hand dragged down my waist to the side of my skirt, where he found the small zipper keeping the skirt on my body and roughly pulled it down. The skirt loosened, and he lifted himself off of me just enough to rip it down my legs and throw it across the room, "Because then you'll be ready for me."

I whimpered as he dropped onto me again, his wet lips closing around the peak of my breast while his thumb teased tight circles around my other one. It was like a live hotwire lit up inside of me, leading down to my clit.

I was panting, whining, and thrashing against the weight of him. He hummed, and I looked down to see him smiling against my breast. I could see his hooded eyes focusing on his task, his smile showing off his teeth as his pink tongue flicked against my nipple at the same fast pace his thumb flicked across my other.

And I exploded.

White hot euphoria erupted through me, and my back arched against him. He kept me in place, keeping up his ministrations against my chest while I throbbed around nothing, clenched my core tight, and moaned through my release.

My eyes squeezed closed, and moisture pooled around the lids. My makeup would probably be smudged, but I didn't care. All I could focus on was every muscle in my body responding to Leo's mouth and touch.

I didn't drop down immediately after he tipped me over the edge. New waves of pleasure would take me by surprise, inducing obscene sounds through my clenched teeth. I finally started to feel the pleasure ease its hold on me, and at the same moment, his hand slid down my stomach. His fingers gently curled as they teased the most sensitive area.

"Don't let me stop you," Leo murmured against my breast right as he started circling me again. I screamed behind clenched teeth as another orgasm ripped through me. My back was arched off the bed, basically shoving my chest in his face as he fingered me through this next one. I started to see stars in my vision behind my closed lids.

Eventually, after drowning in orgasmic bliss for much longer than I ever thought was possible, I twisted my hips out of his reach.

"No more—I can't—" I couldn't get anything else out as he hummed against me. Thankfully he understood, removing his hand from between my legs and releasing my nipple with an obscene, wet pop. Leo hummed as he started peppering kisses up my chest, up my neck, and across my collarbones.

"Are you done?" Leo asked against my skin.

"No," I shook my head, unable to open my eyes quite yet, "I want to keep going."

Leo captured my lips with his, and I moaned into his mouth without shame. He wasn't turned off by it. If anything, my sounds spurred him on.

"Do you want me to untie you?" Leo murmured against my lips.

"I think so," I nodded, "I want to feel you."

Leo smirked, before reaching forward and loosening the hold on my wrists. I flexed them for a moment when they were free before I froze. I looked up at him, staring at his handsome face while still very clearly delirious from my orgasmic bliss.

"What?" Leo asked, kissing the tip of my nose once.

"You," I replied, grabbing his shoulders and pushing him onto his back.

Leo followed my movements without hesitation, and as his hooded eyes watched me throw one leg over his waist, I preened when he groaned and closed his eyes. His large hands flexed on my thighs, and I teased myself on his hard length before he ground out through gritted teeth, "Condom."

"I know." I smiled, gently scraping my nails down his chest. He shuddered under my touch, and I felt like the most powerful woman in the world, "I just wanted to try teasing you. I can't believe you did that for me."

"Hmm?" He asked right when I started to shimmy down his legs towards the side of the bed where my nightstand was.

"Played with me like that," I reached over to the bedside drawer and pulled out a condom, gently peeling it open and making eye contact with him, "No one has."

"I will," Leo panted when I shuffled back up him and gently started unrolling the condom down his length, "Whatever I need to do to see you like this, I'll do it."

"Whatever?" I asked, lifting an eyebrow as I finished putting the condom on. I trailed my index finger up his erection once. It twitched, and I licked my lips at the sight, "You're not turned off by it?"

"I don't think—" he breathed, his hooded eyes watching

me lift myself on my knees and line him up with where we both wanted him to go, "I don't think anything about you can turn me off."

"Are you sure?" I bit my bottom lip as I slowly started sinking down onto him, and his hands gripped my thighs almost painfully. Leo threw his head back, the tendons in his neck straining as I slowly worked myself onto his shaft.

"What are we even talking about?" Leo ground out through gritted teeth, "I can't focus with you clenching around my tip like that."

I'm sorry, tip?

Oh my god.

"That's fine," I smirked, sinking onto him some more at a torturous pace that made a bead of sweat start to drip from his brow, "I—shit, Leo. I'm actually trying here." I laughed at myself, my hand still holding onto him because I wasn't seated fully. I had managed to fit him inside of me multiple times now, but for some reason, me being on top was proving difficult.

Leo grunted something unintelligible before one hand left my thigh and brushed between my legs. His thumb started to gently tease my sensitive flesh. Warmth started to swarm in my lower belly again, rocking against him as I struggled to fit.

"Goddamn, did you get *bigger*?" I gasped in mock outrage as I rocked again, making Leo cackle and slap a hand on his forehead.

"That's the nicest thing you've ever said to me," he chuckled, removing the hand from his head, gripping my hip, and thrusting his hips up.

I yelled or gasped, or made some type of embarrassing sound when he finally helped me get settled on him. He thrust again, and soon we were rocking against each other.

Which made talking impossible.

"Do you like this, Jacqueline?"

Well, impossible for me at least.

"Huh?" I asked, bracing my palms on his chest to keep up the pace. I could feel heat unfurling between my legs, a string tightening in my core, and I couldn't believe I was capable of this kind of thing now.

"Do you like pretending that you're in charge right now?" Leo asked from underneath me.

I lifted my head, unaware that I had let it hang as I rode him, to meet his eyes. Leo's gaze was half open, hooded above flushed cheeks. He bit his bottom lip as we made eye contact, and it took me a while to realize that he was still the one doing the work. At some point, my movements started to lag. As soon as another orgasm started to build inside of me, I struggled to keep my body moving.

It was Leo who was keeping the pace. Impaling me from underneath with a smug look that made me want to shove a pillow over his face but also, mostly, kiss him all over.

"Want me to take over, love?" Leo panted, both of his hands gripping my thighs now to keep me locked in.

"M-maybe," I stammered. My nails were starting to dig into his chest, leaving little crescent indents on his skin. Leo groaned when I canted my hips forward, grinding against him in a way that made me go mindless with the need to chase the building release, "So close."

"Look at you," Leo groaned, his hips punching up into mine while his grip kept me as close to him as possible, "Devastatingly beautiful."

Maybe his words of encouragement helped, but suddenly, I was falling over the edge. Every muscle in my body locked, and my foot start to cramp from the intensity of the orgasm that was burning through me. I released a deep, probably unattractive groan throughout the waves that hit me.

"My turn." At his words, I forced my eyelids open to see Leo's lips tug up in a slow, sly smirk, before suddenly the world was spinning. I landed with an *oof* on my back, but I was still looking into those now glassy eyes of his, "I think I like being the dominant one, Jacqueline."

I nodded my head, looping my arms around his neck and pulling him closer to me. I was still throbbing around him, "I—" I breathed through another wave when he dropped to his elbows and start thrusting erratically against me. I unhooked one of my arms from his neck and braced myself against my headboard so my head wouldn't slide into it, "I don't hate that."

"Of course, you don't," Leo grunted, dropping his head in between my shoulder and neck. His panting breath was coating my skin as his lips teased a sensitive part of my neck, "You just want to unwind after a long day, right?"

I nodded my head again, my teeth sinking into my bottom lip as another wave pulsed through me. He groaned into my neck at the feel of me tightening around him again.

"And I'm still the only one who gets to take care of you like this?" Leo asked, angling his head so that his words ghosted over my ear. I shivered, my legs wrapping around his hips in an attempt to keep us joined as closely as possible as he moved inside me.

I nodded my head again.

"Words, Jacqueline."

"Yes!" I gasped, only to start shaking my head, "I can't—I can't—"

"Yes, you can," Leo ground out, keeping his hips moving at the same pace that created another wave of heat in my core. It was building rapidly, much more rapidly than I was used to. I had already come twice. I hadn't planned on coming again, I really didn't need to. But it was happening, and I couldn't wrap my head around it.

"I can't—I'm gonna—oh no—"

"I feel you," Leo moaned, "God, I feel you coming again." I turned my head to scream into the skin of his shoulder, a poor attempt to muffle the sound, as he rambled in my ear, "You're so tight, sweetheart. Clenching around me. Fuck, I don't know if I can last—oh, fuck, you're coming again—fuck, you're soaking me, Jacqueline—fuuuuck—"

Leo whimpered before thrusting into me one last time, grinding his hips against mine as he groaned through his release. Feeling him throb inside of me made me bite his shoulder, but I stopped myself before I caused real damage to his skin.

I felt out of control.

I felt alive.

I felt fucking amazing.

I felt really, really messy.

We sat there, Leo barely supporting his body weight on his elbows so that he wouldn't crush me, both of our cheeks pressed together while we breathed and recovered from the ecstasy we shared.

"Was..." I cleared my throat and used my hand around his shoulders to gently stroke his skin, "Was that good for you?"

Leo laughed, the sound of it was muffled against me.

I stiffened, worried, before his lips started kissing my neck and ear in between his chuckles, "Yeah, Jacqueline. I haven't gained my vision back quite yet."

I laughed too, making him lift his head to meet my eyes.

A smile spread across his face, and I grinned back at him. Admiring him. How beautiful he was like this. His pupils were practically blown out, hiding so much of his clear blue irises. His pale cheeks flushed with color from exertion. How his black hair looked so messy from my fingers running through it. I couldn't wrap my head around this moment; how lucky I was that we were together like this.

"It wasn't too much?" I asked again. He had already claimed that nothing I asked of him was too daunting or off-putting, but that was during the throes of passion. I knew I couldn't possibly have a clear head while on the brink of orgasm, I wouldn't expect him to either.

"What part?" Leo asked before pecking my lips.

I waited for him to pull back again, "Any of it. Especially the beginning." I lifted my hand again, awed that I could touch my coworker like this. How comfortable we both were, tangled up in each other after a long day.

He closed his eyes and adjusted the two of us. Rolling onto his back, Leo tucked me against his side, so I could continue brushing his dark hair off his forehead while he considered his response.

"You asked me the same thing the first time," Leo sighed, leaning into my hand. If he was a cat, I thought he might have started purring. I poked my tongue against the inside of my cheek, enjoying that my touch affected him like this.

I enjoyed it a lot.

"I did," I agreed, "I asked you for things I hadn't asked anyone for before."

Leo lifted a dark brow while still keeping his lids shut, "Like choking?"

I clamped my lips together, a wave of humiliation washing over my face as I dropped against his chest. A poor attempt to hide my reaction from him.

"Yes," but my response was muffled.

"Jacqueline," Leo had turned his head so that his lips could press against my forehead, "Trust me when I say that I'll tell you if anything you ask for is too much. If you ask, and I enthusiastically oblige, it's because I'm into it, too."

I tilted my face up just enough for his lips to leave my head so I could look at him, "...I feel like I got too lucky with you," I whispered, "I don't want to put you in an uncomfortable position." Leo snorted, and my brows lowered, "What?"

"How do I say this?" Leo exhaled before tightening his hold around me, both of his arms trapping my naked body with his, "You know what I love most about you and me?" My heart skipped a beat when he threw out the word love, and I immediately told my chest to calm down, "It's not just how great you and I are together. Obviously, the chemistry we have is a huge aspect of it."

Without thinking, I immediately lifted a finger and tapped the tip of his nose once.

Leo was about to say something, but he gave me a quizzical expression after I booped him.

God, I was so weird.

"My therapist is also a sex therapist," I tried to explain, still tightly wrapped in his arms with my own partially trapped between us, "A while back she explained to me that pheromones are detected in the nose, which sends a signal to the brain. I'm sure it's more complicated than that, but I always picture how people's noses are kind of what helps us figure out who we have sexual chemistry with."

"Huh," Leo's eyes glanced down to what I assumed was my nose, "Maybe that's why I always want to kiss yours."

I gave him a small grin in return, "Sorry, you were saying?"

"Right," Leo met my gaze again before, "Regardless of

our heated nose chemistry, I also appreciate every time you ask something new of me, because it's a huge boost for my ego."

I thought about his words for a moment, which must have meant that I was frowning, because I suddenly felt his fingertip press against the corner of my mouth. I thought he was going to try tugging it up into a smile, but no. Leo pressed his finger in the corner and simply traced the shape of my lips while I thought.

"How does it boost your ego?" I whispered against his touch.

I locked in on the way his mouth twitched with another smile before his teeth sunk into his bottom lip. His two front ones weren't straight, as if he had been punched before. Maybe he had, based on how he dealt with my ex. One tooth stuck out farther than the other, almost at an angle, to make room. Standing far away, I never would have noticed this specific detail about how Leo's teeth lined up. But this close I did, and I was distracted once again by these additional facts I could store away about my coworker.

"Do you have any idea how hot it is," Leo's voice was lower, his mouth my entire focus as he leaned in to press his forehead against mine, "To have your explicit permission to touch you like that? To have your consent to ravish you just the way you want? How sexy your trust in me is?"

My heart skipped a beat, and my eyes fluttered as he rolled us again so that I was more on my back, "I guess that is a nice ego boost."

Leo snorted, "You trusted me to chase you in your flat. You trusted me to pretend to pin you underneath me. You trusted me to explore the most intimate parts of yourself, and *that* turns me on more than anything."

I tucked my lips between my teeth as I absorbed his

words, and while I took a moment to process, Leo filled the time by teasing my neck with his warm lips. Feeling his exhale skate over my skin sent a shiver through my body, and his hands gripped me tighter.

"I need to clean up," Leo pressed one last kiss under my jaw, and I whined behind my hidden lips, "Don't move, I'll be back." I nodded. It wasn't until he pulled away from me and padded to the bathroom that I thought some more.

I didn't want our sexual relationship to be so one-sided.

Leo was special, he was willing to explore my sexuality with me. To help me discover what I liked and what I didn't, but what exactly was *he* getting out of this?

I heard the water turn on and off, before he entered my bedroom again completely naked, sans a used condom, with a washcloth in his hand.

I was confused for half a second until he crawled onto the bed and gently nudged my legs apart. A protest got caught in my throat, but I remembered how he did this for me at his hotel all those months ago as well. Leo cleaned me carefully, his blue eyes flicking up to meet mine while he delicately brushed the warm, wet cloth over my most sensitive areas.

This relationship was definitely feeling one-sided.

"What do you want, though?" I ended up asking on a rasp.

Leo blinked before sitting up, finished with cleaning me, and gave me a look, "What do you mean?"

"I mean," I tucked my legs close as I sat up on the bed, leaning against my headboard. I was still completely naked, and I kind of wished I wasn't so exposed while having this intimate of a conversation with him, "What do you want out of, um, this?" I pointed a finger in between the two of us, "Is there anything you need that I can provide? Like, I don't know, roleplaying? Or spanking?" Heat bloomed across my cheeks and chest, but I was determined to be a confident woman for this.

Leo's brows rose into his forehead, and I thought I saw a flicker of amusement tug at his lips, but thankfully he stayed composed as he replied, "All I ask is that, while you and I are doing this," he repeated my gesture, using his index finger to point between the two of us, "That you let me know before exploring things with someone else. As far as I am concerned, we are currently monogamous until we have communicated otherwise."

I tilted my head, contemplative. Part of me wanted to ask why he thought that was something that would come up for me.

Clearly, I wasn't putting myself out there like that. I didn't even have additional sexual partners on my radar, so the possibility hadn't even crossed my mind.

He doesn't want a relationship, he wants to keep things casual, my inner voice told me. A pang of something cold settled in my gut, but I was determined to move past it. We weren't in a relationship. We never talked about a relationship. So far, we talked about work and sex.

That would be enough for now.

I didn't even want to jump into another relationship. I didn't think I was emotionally available enough for one. I didn't want to be responsible for the well-being of another person, yet. I had already become a numb shell of myself trying and failing to be a good partner for Vincent. Sure, maybe he designed things so I would never be a good enough partner for him. That still didn't take away the memories my body had, the stress and anxiety that would sour my stomach from failing him for years.

I had something good with Leo right now. Something

comfortable and safe. I didn't want to mess that up by committing to something with him before I fully recovered from my trauma.

"Alright," I nodded, "Though I don't think I'm interested in being intimate with more than one person at a time. So, if you find someone else you want to explore things with, please tell me, too. Safety and stuff." I didn't meet his eyes and instead chose to fidget with my fingernails.

Leo huffed before crawling up to me and pulling my hands into his, "I'll send you my last exam results when I leave tonight." And then he started covering me, tugging me down into the bed again so he could start to trail kisses up my arm. Over my shoulder.

I giggled at the sensitive touch, "I haven't been active, therefore tested, since the first time you and I...um, fucked."

Leo groaned, "You and your filthy mouth."

I playfully shoved at his shoulder, which he retaliated against by pulling me further down the bed so he could wrap his arms around me, throwing one of his long legs in between both of mine, pinning me underneath him.

"Ah," I nodded against him once, "I forgot how much of a cuddler you are after sex."

"We couldn't do this after you seduced me in your office —" my protest of how that whole thing went down was smothered by his lips covering mine in a searing kiss, before he pulled back just enough to say "—I need to make up for lost cuddle time."

I smiled as he tucked his head against my chest, his breath fanning across my breast. I managed to untuck my arms that were trapped between us, so that I could wrap them around his shoulders instead. I was fully willing to cuddle. I was craving intimacy like this. I may not be ready for a real relationship, but I was more than ready to casually lay naked with a man like him.

The fact that Leo wasn't cold and closed off after seeing me at my most vulnerable, was also comforting. I had been sharing a bed with a man for a few years, and even he would turn over and give me his back almost immediately after he and I were intimate.

I needed this form of aftercare.

So I squeezed Leo to me, smiling when he released a satisfied groan from his chest.

Chapter Fourteen

LEO

Warm lips were pressing *against my forehead, gently pulling me from unconsciousness. I was on my stomach, half my face hidden in the pillow that my arms supported for me. When had I fallen asleep?*

"Thank you," her voice was a whisper.

"Mhmm," was all I could manage.

Even though I couldn't pry my eyes open quite yet, my ears heard every soft step that led her to the door. It wasn't until after I heard the latch close, silence suffocating the room, that I lifted my head and confirmed that, yes, I was alone again.

According to the clock on the nightstand, I had just over five hours to get ready for my interview.

Three weeks had passed since our formal agreement that night in Jacqueline's bedroom. Winter had come to Southern California, and even though the rains hadn't started yet, and the sun was still shining, it was humid and cold every morning and evening. I was wearing more long sleeves to work, and Jacqueline only wore her tempting pencil skirts when she could wear thick stockings underneath them.

Jacqueline and I had managed to get together again three more times, averaging once a week. Both of us were having long workdays, and with Jacqueline finally hiring new employees to support her in HR, plus my afternoon rugby training, it almost felt difficult to sync our schedules.

But when we did manage to meet up for a quick shag... fuck, we were *so* damn good together. It wasn't difficult at all.

I still couldn't believe how responsive she was to my touch, my mouth—fuck, even my look. All it took was one heated glance, where I didn't try hiding how badly I wanted her, and her cheeks would bloom with color.

But like the mature and professional adults we were, we stayed away from each other in the office. Now that we both had security in getting our mutual itches scratched, there was no need for us to fool around on the clock.

...Even if the idea was still hot as hell.

Mary and Jamie constantly inviting me over to their flat after work didn't help either, but so far, we've managed.

Currently, I was on my way to refill my coffee. The way Americans prepared their coffees in the US was *wonderful.* Creamer isn't common back home. Usually, coffees were served black or with a splash of milk. Here? It was a never-ending stock of creamers. Signe even started stocking the fridge with holiday-themed creamers. Dairy, oat, soy, anything you could think of.

As a man who thrived by having a constant stream of caffeine flowing through his blood to survive the average workday, I practically skipped with excitement to the break room. Excited to try another flavor.

As I entered, I realized Jacqueline was just sitting down

to enjoy her lunch with my cousin and their friends. Jacqueline's back was to me, but I saw her stow away her earbuds in her purse before taking her seat.

Even though we were keeping our distance, she and I still passed each other at work. Every time she wore earbuds, I could hear her music blasting in them. I was genuinely worried she was on the verge of blowing her eardrums out.

As I made my way to the counter to start a new brew, there was a lull in the conversation between the women, so I nodded toward Jacqueline.

"I have a question for you, Ms. Williams," I made the tone of my voice incredibly serious. It made the other women hush, looking at me with curious glances. I turned, waiting for the machine to finish brewing my coffee, while I looked at the director of human resources.

Jacqueline had stiffened in her chair, her lips pressed together as she waited for me to continue.

"...Do you enjoy the feeling of blood dripping out of your ears when you listen to music?" My question made Mary laugh out loud, and Signe snorted while patting Jacqueline on the shoulder.

Jacqueline, however, looked so adorably confused.

She frowned at me, "What are you talking about?"

"The volume you listen to," I smirked, "You wear earbuds, but I can hear what you're listening to just the same."

Jacqueline's lips twitched before she rolled her eyes at me.

The look made the blood pump in my veins, and I hoped to god that she would want to see me again tonight. I'd love to make her pay for that attitude, in the most enjoyable way possible.

"My earbuds are old," Jacqueline explained, completely ignoring the humorous tone of the conversation, "I have to turn my music up louder and louder for me to enjoy it," She lifted a shoulder, "If you have a problem with it, maybe don't stand so close to me at work."

I shook my head, "It's no problem. I enjoy a blast from the past myself."

"Jacqueline has the *best* playlist," Signe brightened, affectionately squeezing Jacqueline's arm, "You should have her send it to you."

"I've heard it." I saw the moment Jacqueline stiffened at my agreement, my admission that I was already familiar with her playlist. How intimate it sounded. Would she deny that we listened to her music whenever we carpooled? Overlook the fact that I have seen her turn it on before she and I showered together at her flat.

But none of that happened.

Instead, Jacqueline's frown changed. It wasn't a frown of disapproval. It was different. The corners of her mouth were still tipped down. The basic description of a frown was still present. But her eyes brightened. Little crinkles appeared in the corners as they did. Her eyebrows even twitched slightly higher.

I was confident that Jacqueline was smiling at me.

It was just upside down.

Standing there, under the weight of her stunning gaze, something warm and terrifying expanded in my chest.

"Oh, right." Mary leaned on the table, resting her fists under her chin as she opened her mouth to say something else, but one of the new hires poked their head in the breakroom.

"Jacqueline?" A young man's voice asked. A blonde head poked around the door of the breakroom, dressed in a red and grey plaid button-up. He must have been in his early twenties, fresh out of university, "Sorry, I know you're taking your lunch—"

"What's up, Andrew?" Jacqueline turned in her seat to face the break room door, a friendly expression on her face as she addressed her new employee. In her hands, she started digging around in her purse for something.

"I was just wondering which file you wanted me to save this under." He stepped into the room and held out an iPad for her to look at. He pointed at something on the screen, and Jacqueline's brow pinched for a moment before lifting her own finger to point.

"This one," she replied. She then pulled out a small... something. It wasn't until I saw her fingers peel back the foil that I realized she was unwrapping a small piece of chocolate. She popped the candy into her mouth as she continued the conversation with her new employee.

I also realized that this wasn't the first time I had seen Jacqueline do this.

The woman always had a small piece of chocolate to eat after she finished a savory meal.

"Okay, cool," he swallowed, "That's what I thought, but I wasn't sure. So I thought I'd ask. I'm sorry to interrupt."

"You're fine, Andrew," Jacqueline smiled at him, emitting a friendly, welcoming tone, "Please keep asking me questions. I don't mind repeating things while you learn."

He exhaled, his shoulders dropping a bit before he rubbed a hand on his shirt.

As if he had sweaty palms.

I watched this interaction with interest, wondering what was so unsettling about it. Was it because Jacqueline never once showed this kind of warm understanding when I was first hired? Was it that this new hire was now blushing at Jacqueline as he said his goodbyes and left?

"What a sweet kid," Signe spoke up, digging into her meal. If I had to guess, Zaid cooked her lunch and sent her to work with it.

"Andrew's been *so* helpful," Jacqueline slumped, "I didn't realize how nice it would be to delegate some things. I don't want him to think that I don't appreciate his help."

"Maybe you'll be able to attend a girls' night now," Signe replied, around a mouthful of food, "It's been months since you've come."

Actually, it had been four days since Jacqueline had come, but perhaps Signe and I were thinking about different things.

"Yeah, that'd be nice." Jacqueline smiled, and that's when the coffee machine beeped.

"Cheers." I nodded at the table, adding a splash of a cinnamon oat milk creamer to my mug. As I left the breakroom, I gave Jacqueline some direct eye contact. I turned away just when I thought she would start blushing.

Simply knowing that *I* was the man who did that to her, that *I* was the man whom she fancied, I was more than ready to take on anything the rest of the workday.

"MARY IS ONTO US," Jacqueline whispered, clutching my face with both of her cold hands and tugging me down to her lips. She may have initiated the kiss, but I knew how much she loved when I took over. I bent my knees so I could reach my hands below her thighs, hoisting her up and stumbling like a lust-filled fool to her couch.

We broke the kiss with a gasp, before I asked, "What do you mean?"

"She noticed the flirty look you gave me today," Jacqueline replied, before I set her on the cushions. She made the sweetest little whimper as I gently pushed her onto her back. My hands made their way under her shirt, slowly dragging it up. I was ready to start worshipping her soft, warm body. I started by kissing her navel.

"So?" I asked before swirling my tongue around her belly button. Jacquline gasped, and my cock jumped to attention. Fuck, when was the last time I was this randy for a woman? I had just been with her days ago, and yet it was as if I hadn't gotten off in years. I sat up just enough to impatiently shrug out of my leather jacket.

"What do you mean, *so?*" Jacqueline's voice had a smile in it, and as I let myself glance up to see her hooded expression, I shook my head.

"I mean, so? Isn't she shagging a coworker of ours?"

"She and Jamie are an item. It's different."

I grumbled against her stomach, curling my fingers underneath her leggings and sliding them down, "I'm not worried about Mary."

"Okay, but I think that *I* am." Jacquline laughed when I roughly yanked on her leggings, a frustrated noise emanating in my chest as I realized how difficult this was. This time, the elastic fabric made it to her knees.

"I prefer your skirts." My words were quiet, more of a thought to myself, before I paused my endeavor to look Jacqueline in the eye. "If you're worried about Mary, then I'll be more mindful not to picture you naked in front of her."

"Thank y—what? *That's* what your little look was about?" Jacqueline asked with raised eyebrows.

I gave her leggings one final tug, pulling them off of her

legs completely, before holding them up victoriously and proclaiming, "Finally!" and tossing them over my shoulder, "Going forward, you should assume that I'm always picturing you naked."

I let my gaze blatantly roam over her.

She was perfect. One of her cream-colored blouses shoved up near her chest, showing off her stomach. Three buttons were undone, something she had done on her drive home since I knew that she was buttoned up at work that day. She was wearing a purple lace thong, and I dug the heel of my palm into the base of my erection to stifle the sudden wave of arousal I had just looking at her.

"Oh." Jacqueline blushed, enough for the color to spread to her chest.

"Yeah, *oh*," I licked my lips at the sight of her, scraping a hand across my jaw, "Fuck, I don't know where to start, love."

"Like, on me?" Jacqueline asked, bending her legs. She was starting to get shy, curling into herself under my perusal.

I wasn't having that.

I started undoing my jeans while kicking off my shoes and stepping out of them. Then I almost tore my shirt attempting to pull it over my head as fast as possible.

"Oh, you should *definitely* leave the socks on." Jacqueline wiggled her eyebrows with her suggestion. I paused, about to bend down to remove them, before I took in her expression. I hadn't seen Jacqueline crack a lot of jokes, if any at all. The last joke she made that caught me off-guard was the airport one during the evening we spent on her desk, and based on how exaggerated her eyebrow wiggle was now, I was confident she was joking again.

But I still wanted to be sure.

"Oh, you like that?" I stood tall, bracing my hands on my hips, showing off my prominent erection that was fighting to free itself from my boxer briefs.

Jacqueline snorted behind closed lips, grinning as she replied, "I love a man in black boxers and white tube socks. Very hot. Doesn't look dorky *at all*."

This woman.

I lifted a foot to rest on the edge of the couch, gesturing toward my feet with my hand, "They're the Costco brand. Does that do it for you, too?"

Jacqueline smiled, reaching up to unbutton her shirt to part the panels.

Fuck, her bra matched her thong.

Did she only wear matching sets?

"I'm just kidding." Jacqueline's eyes dropped to my briefs, and my cock jumped at the attention.

"Are you sure? You can be into tube socks, no shame in that." I stuck my index finger into the seam, tracing the shape of the material around my leg while releasing a very loud, very fake, whiney moan.

"Oh my god!" Jacqueline's eyes widened before she slapped both of her hands over her face, "Don't make that sound ever again."

I made the noise again.

It was my fake orgasm voice. More feminine, more dramatic. I knew it annoyed the shit out of Mary, but Jacqueline looked mostly embarrassed by it.

Behind her hands, Jacqueline squealed while turning her body into the back of the couch. Hiding from me.

"You aren't into that?" I was trying to control my laughter as I lowered myself over her, leaving the socks on, "You don't like hearing what you do to me?" I rereleased the fake moan, quieter this time. Jacqueline's body shook from her own amusement, allowing herself to be rolled onto her back as I blanketed her body with mine.

"That's not what you sound like when we're together." Jacqueline lowered her hands, her eyes sparkling with humor and embarrassment and something else I didn't recognize.

"Hmm, perhaps you need to jog my memory," I pushed her blouse off of her shoulders, allowing her to sit up just enough to toss it aside, before guiding her back down again, "It's been too long."

"It's been four days."

"All that time we've been *wasting*," I pulled the cups of her bra down, teasing her sensitive peaks with my thumbs while I locked eyes with her, "I needed you so badly today."

"Really?" Jacqueline's face lit up, because *this* woman had a certified praise kink.

"It's true," I spoke against her breasts. They were on the smaller side, perfectly proportionate with the rest of her. Perfect. Mine, "I couldn't focus on anything."

"I couldn't either," Jacqueline panted, arching into my mouth, "I need you, too."

I dragged my tongue right between her breasts, working my way up her throat to gently bite at her jaw, "You have me."

"Can we—" she cut off her question, shaking her head once, "Never mind."

I immediately pulled my face off of hers, giving her a look, "What do you need?"

Jacqueline pressed her lips together, nervous again, "It's just...I feel the air on me here." I glanced down, watching with my own eyes how her skin pebbled against the air coming in from the vents, "Can we go to the bed? Under the covers?"

I nodded, because anything she wanted, I wanted to give her.

Jacqueline giggled when I scooped her up without a word, carried her to her bed, and tucked us both under her covers.

Her bed was heavenly, and I didn't blame her for preferring it to the couch.

"Let me warm you up." I started kissing her neck again as I covered her, groaning at the feel of Jacqueline's cold hands sliding up my back, feeling the lean muscle I had there.

"Please," Jacqueline whispered. She cupped my jaw when I tried to kiss down her body again, pulling my face to hers. I loved our kisses. I couldn't get enough of her smooth, warm lips against my own. Her tongue met mine, licking into my mouth. Scraping the inside of my teeth.

The first night Jacqueline and I spent together, before the next day when we learned she'd be interviewing me, I realized something very quickly. Jacqueline didn't have a lot of experience kissing.

It wasn't a bad thing, because she kissed in a way I hadn't experienced in a while.

Jacqueline didn't kiss because she was trying to seduce me.

Jacqueline kissed because she liked the *feeling* of kissing.

I turned to putty in her hands when her lips met mine.

"What do you want, love?" The endearment always slipped out around her, and I tried to not put too much meaning behind it. She didn't seem to mind whenever I called her love, but the more I said it, the more I *wanted* to say it. To call Jacqueline *love*. I had almost slipped up in the office earlier today, but I caught myself.

"What if...we used a toy?" Jacqueline's voice was labored,

her heavy breathing interfering with her ability to speak loudly.

"Where?" I asked.

Jacqueline grinned, "Nightstand."

I scooted to the edge of her bed in search of a toy, groaning when she decided to kiss my back and shoulders and neck as I reached into her drawer and tried to feel for something made of silicon.

"You're making this hard for me," I mumbled into the pillow, my hand finally brushing against something that felt like a vibrator.

"That's the idea," Jacqueline snickered against my shoulder. I laughed, loving the opportunity to see a playful, teasing side of Jacqueline. The one willing to make jokes. It wasn't that she was loose around me, it was that she was *comfortable* around me.

I valued that more than she probably realized.

"This okay?" I asked, holding up a bright pink vibrator, no more than four or so inches long.

"Yup," Jacqueline reached over to grab the toy, but I held it out of reach while shifting to get her underneath me again.

"I want to play first," I kissed her collarbone once, before quickly disappearing underneath the covers. *Christ*, it was hot under there.

"Are you sure?" Jacqueline asked, lifting the covers so she could see me getting settled between her legs. Mine poked out on the other end of the bed, cooling off my own body for a bit.

"Positive."

I clicked on the toy, and the buzz in my hand was muted by the heavy comforter, "Any setting you prefer?"

"Um," Jacqueline thought for half a second, "The fourth setting, please."

I playfully bit the inside of her thigh, making her squeal.

"Leo!" Jacqueline hissed. I held her legs wide enough for me to lay between them, while still tucking them under my arms to hold her still.

"*Jacqueline*," I copied her tone, teasing her.

"Leo—*oh*—" her snark dissolved as soon as I started gently circling the toy over her clit, already swollen. I used the toy to tease her entrance. It was hard to see with such little light making it under the covers, but I managed to use her own wetness to coat the toy before teasing her clit again.

"That's better," my voice dropped, it got that raspy layer to it that always hit me whenever I was fighting a raging hard-on.

"Okay." Jacqueline clearly had no idea what I was saying. Her legs started trembling, so I didn't change a thing. I kept the toy exactly where it was, moving it exactly the same, watching her body tremble as she reached her climax.

Jacqueline moaned, deep and guttural, and I kissed her thigh as she came.

It was probably the fastest I had ever gotten her off.

Yeah, using toys was always fucking awesome.

I kept the toy between her legs, letting her ride out her orgasm as long as she could before her hips started to shift away from me.

I inched up her body, poking my head out from underneath the covers and grinning, "Beautiful."

She was panting, her chest and cheeks flushed in the way I often dreamed of.

"I have a condom in the drawer, too," Jacqueline whispered, rubbing her forehead, "I feel like goo."

"You mean warm and pliant and ready for me?" I asked as I retrieved the condom.

Jacqueline laughed as I covered myself with the latex, before resting over her on my elbows, kissing her jawline. She wrapped her arms around my neck, pulling me down closer to her.

"...You just should assume that I'm always ready for you," Jacqueline whispered, kissing my earlobe.

I would never, *ever* assume that Jacqueline was always ready for penetrative sex. In my opinion, consent was one of the sexiest layers of intimacy there was. That being said, hearing Jacqueline say otherwise stirred something in me. A primitive urge to prove her right. To pretend that what she said was true.

"I like the sound of that." I tucked my head near hers, wrapping one of my arms around her shoulders to anchor her body to mine. I wanted to be as close to her as possible. This wasn't one of our most adventurous shags, but my lust was still burning under my skin. I needed her so *badly*, as quickly as possible.

From the way that Jacqueline tightened her arms around me, I had a feeling she was right there with me.

I entered her slowly, feeling her body's reaction to my intrusion to ensure that it was still pleasurable and not painful. Even though Jacqueline and I felt made for each other, she always needed time to adjust to me.

"You take me so well, Jacqueline," I murmured encouraging words in her ear, smiling when she loosened around me so I could sink deeper. I loved praising her in this way, "You're so hot and tight, squeezing me so beautifully."

Jacqueline was panting, flexing her hips up and into me to help me sink deeper.

"You feel so good," she moaned.

"You've been ready for me for a while," I murmured, licking the shell of her ear, "You're soaking me. What were you picturing in that pretty little head of yours? Were you also having inappropriate thoughts about your coworker all day?"

I thrust into her one final time, bottoming out. Jacqueline tipped her head farther back into the pillows.

"So, *so* inappropriate," she breathed.

"Wicked woman." I pulled back and thrust into her, rough. I focused on how she tensed around me, ensuring that her response was a positive one and not one from pain, "Picturing how good you would feel taking me again." Another rough thrust and she already started to flutter around me. The more we fucked, the more I disbelieved her previous inability to orgasm with a partner, "Jumping me as soon as I entered your flat." This time, I ground my hips against her, earning a gasp as she clenched around me.

She felt *too* good.

It took everything in me not to lose it too quickly. The white-hot pleasure was shooting down my spine, building behind my knees.

"I needed you." Jacqueline's cheek was pressed against my neck, her arms wrapped around me as she held on tight while I plowed into her. I picked up my pace, feeling the response she had in her breath and hips as she started to chase her pleasure.

"You have me, Jacqueline."

And that's when she fell apart—moaning again, erratically clenching around me in a way that made me see stars. I tried to prolong it for her, but Jacqueline Williams unraveling in my arms would always weaken me.

I shouted into her neck as I came, grinding against her

in a pitiful attempt to expand her own release. She continued to hold me in her grip, her fingertips digging into my back as we found ecstasy with each other.

I eventually pulled out and shifted off of her, tucking her against my front so I wouldn't crush her under my weight. Silence filled her bedroom, while the two of us struggled to catch our breath under the security of her covers.

Jacqueline hummed, snuggling closer against my chest, resting her nose in between my pecks. I kissed the top of her head, loving it when she lifted her leg to settle on my hip. As if she didn't want to separate from me quite yet.

"...Are you hungry?" Jacqueline asked.

"Famished," I replied on an exhale, making Jacqueline laugh against my skin.

"Let's order something, I'm not putting clothes on the rest of the day."

I grinned.

When Jacqueline and I first started shagging, I was worried I would push her own boundaries too much by demanding aftercare cuddles. I knew we weren't in a relationship, and I didn't expect to take up her entire afternoons whenever she invited me over. However, whenever Jacqueline offered for me to stick around and eat dinner, I never said no.

Because the reality was, that I didn't want to leave.

Every time we spent the evening together, I could feel a piece of myself tethered to her flat. Anchoring me. Calling me back. I was becoming more and more comfortable, and so far, Jacqueline seemed to be feeling the same way. Instead of offering to get me a glass of water, she told me to help myself. I had a toothbrush here. I was pretty sure I had a shirt or pair of boxers around here as well.

But I tried not to read into it.

I was talented at staying in the moment.

So when Jacqueline used her leg to tug me closer to her, ensuring the entirety of our fronts were pressed against each other, I leaned into it. Holding her tighter.

Taking every single part of her she was willing to give me.

I wasn't going to ask her to repeat her name, because there was a good chance I might not need to remember it, anyway. The tall, round woman with red hair stepped aside with a smile, revealing the other woman interviewing me today.

Except she didn't need to introduce her to me.

Because I had just been inside her less than twelve hours ago.

"Where did you work before Sun Steer?" I asked Jacqueline one evening. We were on her living room couch because we hadn't been able to make it to her bedroom this time. I had dropped the food I had grabbed on my way over because she was on me as soon as I walked through the door. Her tongue was demanding entry into my mouth before I could get a word in. Within minutes I had her bent over the back of her couch. Now, we sat side by side, naked, with my socked feet up on her coffee table while she threw her legs on the long side of the couch, leaning against my side under a throw blanket.

It was my favorite way she greeted me.

From the view I had of her profile, it looked like Jacqueline frowned at my question, and not the endearing frown-smile-thing she did, but a true frown.

"Blix," she replied, before popping a chip into her mouth.

Sorry, a *fry*.

I was so glad she was someone who appreciated good takeaway as much as I did.

"That's cool," I grabbed my strip of fried potato and took a bite, but I kept my other arm around her waist to hold her snugly against my side, "Did you like it?"

She snorted before shaking her head once, "Not at all."

"Why is that?" I pried.

Jacqueline shifted against me, and even though I lifted my arm to allow her to adjust her seat so her back was more against my side, I was grateful she didn't pull away entirely from my question. She even went as far as to take my arm and wrap it around herself again once she was settled.

I wondered if physical contact was just as grounding for her as it was for me.

"Several reasons," she sighed, before pulling the blanket up higher, covering her perfect chest, "Though a big one is because my ex is kind of a huge asshole."

I tried my best not to stiffen at the mention of her ex.

"Do tell," I managed to reply.

"Do you really want to know?" She turned her head, giving me her profile as she side-eyed me. I could feel how uncomfortable she felt having this conversation, but she wasn't shying away from it either.

"I wouldn't ask if I didn't." I flexed my arm around her waist before leaning forward to grab my drink, taking a sip through the straw. It was a little more difficult to eat, wrapped up with her like this, but oh so worth it.

I was hoping my casual body language made her feel more comfortable sharing.

"Okay, so." She was working herself up for this, I realized. She held tight to her chips, flexing her fingers over the cheap cardboard box they came in, "I met him working at Blix. About seven years ago." She released a deep sigh, and her body relaxed against me as she started the story, "I wasn't a director or anything. I just worked in the HR department. It was a huge company, even back then. So when this handsome sales rep started stopping by my desk more and more, I was flattered that I was supposedly singled out compared to everyone else there." She traced the edge of her chip box with her index finger, "Within six months of officially dating, we moved in together."

I glanced around the living space, wondering if this was the same space she shared with him. If it was, I hoped she and I had created new memories in it for her. Memories that didn't involve him.

I side-eyed the kitchen counter, wondering if I could help her create more new memories to replace potential bad ones.

"That sounds fast," I muttered.

"That's because it was. Too fast, definitely." She leaned her head against my shoulder, and even though I couldn't see her face, I loved watching the back of her head lean into my body like this, "I was young. I hadn't dated seriously before Vincent, and I thrived off of the attention. Everyone at work knew we were together, too—"

"—Pause, his name is Vincent?" I interrupted.

I felt her cheek pull back, she must have been smiling against my arm, "Yeah."

"That's the most evil-villain name I have ever heard," I replied. She finally released a huff of laughter.

"You're not wrong," she laughed again before getting back to it, "The problem is, as soon as I was under his roof, that's when he started to show me who he really was. He didn't have to pretend to care anymore, he didn't have to try to win me over. As far as he was concerned, I was locked in. He even tried to talk me into marriage within a few months of living together, and when I told him I wasn't ready for something like that, I think that's when even the little things angered him."

I tried not to hold my breath, hoping that the story wasn't going in the direction most stories went when a man in a relationship started feeling anger towards his partner.

"Did he hurt you?" I asked, doing a terrible job of hiding the fury in my voice.

Jacqueline was silent for a moment before whispering, "Yes, but not physically." That didn't help my mood, unfortunately. "He's the kind of guy who feels better when he can put other people down. Suddenly, everything I did either wasn't enough for him or was something that made him upset. When I started getting more promotions than him at work, making more money than him, that's when his ego took a big hit."

I rolled my eyes, not that she could see.

I'd met a couple of men like him in the past, "I stayed with him for three years. And yeah, there were good moments. Moments that kept me with him much longer than I should have been. He would put on the mask of the guy he was when we first met, usually after a fight or disagreement. I was convinced that that mask was who he really was. I was confident that he was just going through a rough time, and I even blamed myself for bragging about my success at work too much. But it wasn't until we started going to couples counseling that I really started to see what the situation was.

"After a year of counseling every other week, I asked to see our counselor one-on-one. I was so lost, and so confused. Surely, *I* was missing something, because after a year of work, nothing really changed. I was convinced it was all my fault—Leo, I need to breathe." I blinked, loosening my grip around her waist at her words.

"Sorry, sorry."

"Don't be, I know it's upsetting," she snuggled back into me once my hold on her relaxed enough.

"So what did your counselor say?" I pressed, not ready for her to change the subject quite yet even though everything she shared made an indescribable rage burn in my chest.

"Well, she ended up risking her license for me," Jacqueline murmured.

That made me raise an eyebrow, "How?"

"So, the thing with couples counseling is that the *couple* is the client. The two of us. Which can be tricky, especially if the relationship is toxic or emotionally abusive in any way. We hired her to heal the relationship, to find a way to keep us together. So when I asked to meet with her one-on-one, and she told me what she really thought of our situation, it went against the ethics of the situation, since there wasn't any physical abuse and I wasn't in any obvious danger."

I sighed, "Okay, but what did she say?"

Jacqueline shifted to set the chips down on the coffee table before turning so that she could tuck her legs underneath herself, laying her cheek on my chest, "She told me that she considered Vincent emotionally abusive. That no matter what I did, he would look for new ways to attack me. That he had no desire to change or improve. She told me—" She swallowed before continuing, "She said he was preying on my empathy. He knew I was quick to blame myself instead of him. That if I really did want to try to continue to work things out with him, she would help us, but she was tired of trying to lead me to the conclusion herself, and I needed to hear the words 'emotionally abusive relationship' point-blank."

I whistled low, "Wow."

"Yeah," Jacqueline lifted a shoulder against me, before her index finger started tracing invisible shapes on my chest, "The problem is, I don't always understand nuance that well. So when Vincent would randomly give me the silent treatment or slam a door, I would spiral trying to figure out what exactly I did wrong. I wouldn't know we were even in a fight until he randomly snapped one day. Usually, it was for me not understanding what he said or expected of me. When our counselor tried to do the same, subtly hinting that Vincent had no intention of improving or changing, I didn't get it either. She would say things like, 'For every mile of progress you make, Vincent only makes a few inches, but he wants praise for it as if he also worked a mile.' So I just kept thinking to myself, 'Okay, I just need to be patient and work harder and wait for him to catch up.' Instead of understanding that that was her way of saying that he never had any intention of improving."

I set my drink down on the coffee table before slouching down some more, wrapping Jacqueline in both of my arms and resting my cheek on her forehead, "Can you give me an example?" I winced, "Sorry, I'm just trying to understand how not understanding nuance can cause a grown man to throw a tantrum toward his partner."

Jacqueline released a short giggle before flattening her

hand against my chest, "Okay, um..." She drummed her fingers on my skin, and every muscle in my body relaxed at her touch, "So, one day, we were supposed to go for a run together after work. I was home earlier than him, watching TV. When he came in, he slammed the front door, huffed and puffed, and was visibly upset. I asked him what was wrong, and he just said that he had a long day and didn't want to think about it anymore. This was a couple of years into our relationship, and so I was trained to try to de-escalate his moods. So I immediately replied something along the lines of, 'Hey, if you're too stressed to go for a run and you just want to hang out at home, that's fine.' But apparently, that was the wrong thing to say."

I lifted my cheek off her head to ask, "How was that the wrong thing to say?"

"Because," she turned so she could rest her chin on my chest, giving me a quick glance, "He said, 'I just want to forget about my day' again, so I repeated, 'That's fine, we don't have to go on a run if you don't want to.' But apparently, he *did* want to go on a run."

I knew my face looked confused because her lips twitched with humor at whatever expression I had on, "Why didn't he just fucking say that?"

"See!" She grinned, before resting her cheek against me again, "That's so validating. So he was mad at me for a few days after that, and when we talked about it in counseling, he explained that he felt like I didn't want to spend time with him. That I was always looking for ways to avoid spending time with him. Even though we spent that entire evening on the couch, watching TV together."

I nodded, hating that Jacqueline was ever treated this way. I loathed the fact that a man had managed to convince a goddess like her to move in with him, and yet that was how he acted because he was too emotionally immature to deal with his own insecurities.

"I'm so sorry," I managed to spit out, "So, your counselor finally told you how abusive it was?"

"Yeah. I still stayed with him for another few months after that, though. I wasn't ready to hear what she told me. Part of me was convinced that I could even prove her wrong. Another part of me wondered if therapists nowadays just felt too comfortable throwing words like 'abusive' and 'narcissist' and 'gaslighting' around. That I wasn't actually in an emotionally abusive relationship. I was embarrassed to admit that to myself, and she stayed on as our counselor until—ugh, I'm so stupid."

"Don't talk about my lover like that." I scolded, planting a kiss on the crown of her head, "You aren't stupid."

"I felt stupid in the moment, though," Jacqueline grumbled, "Anyway, I stayed with him another few months until I learned that he was cheating on me."

"I'm sorry, what?" I couldn't believe the nerve of this prick.

"Yeah, with someone else who worked at Blix."

"What the fuck," I rubbed my hand over my eyes, "You're shitting me."

"No," Jacqueline shifted so that she sat up on her knees. The throw blanket was mostly over her as she tucked it around her chest, but there was a corner of it keeping my groin from making an appearance during this vulnerable conversation we were having, "I told Marco what I found on his phone and stuff, and—"

"Who's Marco?" I asked shifting closer to her because I couldn't help myself.

"My brother—my twin," Jacqueline's dark eyes lifted to meet mine.

"You have a twin? How did I not know this?" I mentally scanned all our past conversations and having a twin had never once come up.

"I never bothered to tell you until now," Jacqueline smirked, shifting on her knees so that they rested against my thigh, "Anyway, Marco was there that same night with suitcases and cardboard boxes. He helped me pack up my apartment while I wrote my letter of resignation. I didn't even give two weeks notice. I knew it wasn't professional of me, but I just couldn't stomach the thought of seeing him and the woman he was having an affair with. I didn't even want to confront him. I just...left."

"I'm so fucking glad you did." I wrapped both of my arms around her waist, tugging her over onto my lap. She came willingly, and as she planted either of her thighs around my waist, I grinned at her.

"Yeah, me too." She looked nervous as she untucked the blanket, letting me get an excellent view of her naked body straddling mine. She tucked either end of the throw blanket around the both of us, creating a little fort with both of our bodies. It was like she was shielding us from the outside world, and I loved it, "Vincent was an asshole about it, though. I think he couldn't handle the fact that *I* was the one who left *him*. He didn't even like me, but he insisted that I come back. He cared more about how my leaving made him feel than *why* I left him. He even ended things with the woman he was seeing, but it didn't matter to me anymore. When he started to realize that I really wasn't coming back, that's when he got mean."

I frowned, so when Jacqueline glanced up from her hands resting on my chest to meet my gaze, I was surprised to see her tuck her lips between her teeth and hold back a smirk, "You look upset."

"I am upset," I admitted, "I want to do unspeakable damage to this guy."

"Well, you already punched him in the face, so—"

"Wait—" I interrupted her as I sat up, using my grip on her waist to keep her in place as I did so, because Jesus Christ I had already forgotten about that, "*That's* who that prick at the bar was?"

"Yeah," She rolled her eyes, frowning again as she started running her hands up and down my chest, back and forth, "I hadn't seen him in years before that. Since I started my job at Sun Steer, moved out of Marco's and rented this place."

I frowned, and she noticed my movement with a raised eyebrow, "What?"

I caught myself and shook my head, "Nothing."

"No, tell me," she slid her hands up my chest to start kneading my shoulders, "You made a face at a weird part of the story."

I chuckled, leaning my head back against the couch, soaking up the feeling of Jacqueline fucking Williams straddling my lap and massaging my shoulders, "I did, but it's for a ridiculous reason."

"Just tell me." She leaned toward me, her dark eyes bouncing between the two of mine.

I bit my lip in thought, and when her gaze dropped to my mouth, I finally admitted my childish thoughts, "Earlier I was just wondering if—god, I'm such a wanker for even thinking—"

"Leo, please tell me." She leaned forward more, her breasts pressing against my chest as her arms wrapped around my neck. Jacqueline laid her head on my shoulder, letting her hair fall and tickle my skin.

"Fine, fine," I sighed, wrapping both of my arms around

her back to keep us chest to chest, "I got a little excited at the idea of shagging on every surface in this flat."

Jacqueline didn't stiffen in my arms at the admission, instead, she was quiet momentarily before asking, "Why?"

"Because then we'd replace any memory you had of him in this flat with—hopefully—a better one." And that was when Jacqueline pulled back to look at me with a pinch in between her dark brows. I held my breath, waiting for the scolding. For the reprimand of how childish my thoughts were.

But that never came.

Instead, a slow, small smile pulled on the corners of her lips, "...We could still do that."

I raised an eyebrow, "Yeah?"

"Yeah." she blushed, and it killed me to see Jacqueline blush like that when she was sitting her bare arse on my bare thighs. Her warmth mere centimeters from where I was starting to harden underneath her, "I've never had an exciting sex life before you."

I grinned, pride coursing through me, "Our sex life is exciting?"

"Obviously," Jacqueline shifted against me, smirking at my hold tightening on her, "You're the only one who matches my energy like this."

I leaned forward to capture her lips, my hands on her waist dropping to cup her firm, tight ass, "I'm also the only one you feel comfortable orgasming with, don't forget that."

Instead of scoffing or shaking her head or getting embarrassed, Jacqueline nodded and traced my bottom lip with her tongue before saying, "Yeah. Just you, Leo."

And damn if that wasn't the best thing that I had ever heard Jacqueline say to me.

The conversation shifted then, and something about the

next time we were joined was different. Jacqueline didn't need me to grunt demands in her ear, instead, she hopped off the couch to grab another condom before crawling back into my lap. We didn't speak beyond groans and whimpers of euphoria when I gripped her hips to guide her over me. When I grabbed the back of her neck to bring our lips together, seconds from unraveling, she wrapped her hand around my neck, too. Anchored against each other as we raced toward that edge, much faster than expected.

Soon we were both spent. Jacqueline's head rested on my shoulder, struggling to catch her breath, as she whispered, "Thanks for letting me talk about that."

I turned to kiss her shoulder, squeezing her tight against me as I murmured, "Of course," against her skin.

I was starting to realize how this looked.

How our casual shags were slowly morphing into more.

It wasn't me coming over to her flat for a quick fuck and some post-coital cuddling before I left anymore.

Instead, we were eating dinner together more often than not. We spent the evenings together beyond having sex. We spent quality time together, getting to know one another. Tonight just happened to include some trauma dumping, which I encouraged her to open up about.

I referred to Jacqueline earlier as my lover, and she didn't question it, but part of me wondered if I wanted to ask for more.

Acknowledging how her last serious relationship ended (that also started at her workplace), I understood any potential hesitation about jumping into some type of commitment with me. Perhaps it was too early. We had only been doing this for a few weeks at this point.

I was in upper management.

She wasn't.

Even though it never felt like it, on paper, unethical power dynamics lingered between us.

So instead I focused on what I did get with Jacqueline.

How I was still the only one to get this with Jacqueline.

How I was content to keep this secret between us a bit longer, for both her protection at work and also mine.

But mostly hers.

Chapter Sixteen

JACQUELINE

Why was he here?

How was he here?

Signe was off to the side, chatting with him about Ninja Turtles or something, blissfully unaware of the panic attack I was on the verge of having. Out of all the men in that stupid bar, I had to hook up with the one she and I were interviewing today.

The one that made me see stars.

Fuck me.

"I don't know how to tell this story," I sighed, slumping against the couch cushions in Mariam's office.

"Usually it's best to start at the beginning," Mariam nodded. I looked at her hand movements going back and forth over her iPad. She was sketching today. For some reason, the focus she had on whatever illustration she was working on made me a little more comfortable opening up about my recent...thoughts.

"So," I cleared my throat, then decided to grab a throw

blanket Mariam kept on the arm of the couch and wrapped myself up in it, "You know how Leo and I are...you know."

"Having intercourse." Mariam finished for me.

"Yeah, that," I smiled even though she couldn't see it, "And, it's been going great. I mean, it's only been a few weeks, but what he and I have going on really works for us. Maybe it's just because I'm finally getting to experience what everyone else hypes sex up to be, but regardless, I'm... happy."

"That's excellent," Mariam looked up from her drawing to smile at me, then tilted her head, "Why am I sensing a but?"

I winced, "Well, two nights ago Leo came over again to— ahem, you know—"

"Boink," Mariam finished again.

I made a face, "That's not the word I'd use."

"I don't know why you're tiptoeing around it today," Mariam lifted an eyebrow at me, "You've cursed in here before. You've talked about sex before."

"I know, I know," I covered my face in my hands, "I'm just embarrassed about this next part."

"Okay," I parted my fingers to see Mariam wave her hand in a gesture that indicated I should spit it out.

"I couldn't orgasm this time," I kept my hands over my face, my cheeks flaming from this admission, "And I have no idea why."

Mariam's eyebrows rose, "Interesting. How did that go?"

I dropped my hands and instead tugged the throw blanket up, up, up until my hands held it under my chin. My face was the only part of my body that was visible against the material. I looked out the window of her office as I explained the situation the best I could.

"It went...fine? As fine as it could go without me

finishing, that is. I felt so bad for him. He went down on me for *so* long, and when that didn't work, he tried using his fingers, which was wonderful. But I still couldn't quite make it over the edge. Eventually, I got too embarrassed and stressed about it and told him it probably wasn't going to happen," I played with my fingernails under the throw blanket as I continued, "Which he was fine with. So naturally I tried to reach over and, you know, help *him* finish. Because I wasn't about to make him suffer just because *I* couldn't orgasm first."

Mariam tilted her head at me, focusing back on her drawing, "And how did he respond to that?"

I frowned, "He wouldn't let me help him. He told me not to worry about him."

Mariam lifted her head to look at me, silent.

So I continued.

"I apologized again, and even cried a little." My cheeks heated from humiliation at the memory of Leo wrapping me in his arms as I cried and apologized for not being able to perform as expected. I remembered him shushing me, whispering encouraging words with his lips in my hair as he held me tight. Until I could calm down enough, "And then, we just... hung out."

"Nice," Mariam smiled, "What does 'hung out' mean, exactly?"

I shrugged under the blanket, "He turned on the TV and ordered takeout, and we sat on my couch watching *Shrinking* for a couple of hours. Then he kissed me goodbye, which he always does, and left as if...nothing was wrong."

Mariam smirked, "Do you think something is wrong?"

I nodded my head, "Yeah. I didn't come."

Mariam dropped her smirk, "That doesn't mean something is wrong, Jacqueline."

"I—" I stopped myself, wondering if I was being ridiculous for this fear before I shook my head and remembered that *this* was where I could safely voice my thoughts, "I told him about Vincent."

Mariam gagged dramatically, "Sorry, it's a reflex whenever I hear his name," that made a small laugh sneak out of me, "How did that conversation go?"

I caught myself grinning before I tried to relax my facial expression, but Mariam caught the smile, and she pointed an accusing finger at me with a wide grin on her face, "I saw that. What did he say?"

I rolled my eyes and snuggled into the blanket more, "He seemed furious on my behalf." I remembered how safe I felt with him. "It was kind of nice to see. How he sided with me, even though I'm sure my perspective of that relationship is completely biased—"

"Stop it," Mariam lifted a hand, "Whatever you said about that little man, I'm sure you did so with fairness he didn't deserve."

I looked back out the window, "I did call him an asshole though."

"He's called you worse," Mariam reminded me, "It's fine. I'm glad Leo understood what an asshole he was."

"Yeah..." I sighed, "And then we had sex afterward."

"And did you orgasm that time?"

I blinked, thinking about it, "Yeah, I did." I scratched my chin before tucking my hand underneath the blanket again, "I thought that maybe opening up to Leo about my ex somehow took away my ability to orgasm. But that couldn't be the case, because I orgasmed hard almost immediately after the conversation." I sighed, defeated, "Now I'm not sure why I didn't this time. And I'm kind of freaking out about it."

Mariam sighed, setting her iPad pencil down and giving me a direct look, "How's work going?"

I blinked at the sudden conversation change, but I went with it. I trusted Mariam, "Um. Fine. I interviewed more employees to add to the HR department this week." Then I bit my lip, a familiar swarm of nerves filling my chest, "...I received a weird email from Brandon."

"Why was it weird?" Mariam pressed, crossing one of her jean-clad legs over the other.

"It was cryptic," I frowned, "Vague. He said he wanted to meet with me next week about potential changes and to keep him updated on who I chose to hire next."

Mariam raised her eyebrows, "Interesting."

"Yeah," I gnawed on my bottom lip, "You can see why I'm kind of stressed about that."

"Definitely," Mariam nodded, crossing her arms and leaning back in her chair to summarize the situation, "You received a vague email from your boss, and now you're going to be spending the next week spiraling about what he's going to say in the meeting." Mariam lifted a shoulder, "When did you get this email?"

I quirked my lips to the side, "A couple of days ago."

Mariam nodded again, "Before or after you had sex without orgasm with Leo?"

I stared at her, because the way she said that sentence stuck out to me. She didn't say "failure to orgasm" or "inability to finish." It was such a clinical description of what the situation was, and for reasons I couldn't explain, I felt a little less insecure about it.

"Before. I got the email the day before Leo came over this last time."

Mariam stared at me.

And stared.

And stared some more.

I shifted under her gaze, "So…" I slowly raised my eyebrows at her, "Are you saying that Brandon's email maybe had something to do with—"

"Do you know," Mariam interrupted me, "what the largest sexual organ in a woman's body is?"

I shook my head, visibly clearing my thoughts in an attempt to catch up with the whiplash she was giving me during this discussion, "Um…the clit?" I immediately tried to think of something else. There was the labia, but was that considered sexual as in *sexual*?

Mariam shook her head, "It's an important organ, but no. Any other guesses?"

Heat burned my face and neck, *Shit, did I not know my own fucking body? I needed to get home and start researching women's anatomy—*

"Before you panic," Mariam interrupted my train of thought, "Don't. The answer you're seeking is…" she leaned forward and drummed her two index fingers on the side of her desk, making me relax from the theatrics she pulled, "The brain."

What?

"The brain is a sexual organ?" I asked.

"Especially for women," Mariam nodded, "I'd argue the most important, before the clit."

I widened my eyes, "Wow…"

"I know," Mariam settled in her chair again, tucking one of her legs underneath herself, "Buckle up, because I'm about to get kind of preachy."

I glanced around myself, still self-swaddled in her fuzzy throw blanket while completely sunken into the couch. I didn't move a muscle before I looked back at her and said, "Okay."

"Before I continue, you need to understand that I do not subscribe to traditional gender roles or any idea that men are genetically superior to women. I believe doing away with the 'men are physical and women are emotional' mentality would solve a lot of problems in modern society," Mariam waited for me to nod again before continuing, "That being said, there are scientific, biological reasons why men and women's sex drives differ.

"For example, every single time a man ejaculates, he can get a woman pregnant—don't make that face, I'm not saying *you* are going to get pregnant," I laughed at how quickly she called me out on my grimace, knowing how I was purposefully child-free. She waited for me to recover before continuing, "Women, however, can only get pregnant once a month. Her fertile window is mere days, during ovulation. Usually, ovulation is when women get the horniest, right?"

"Right." I knew exactly when I ovulated. The last time I realized I was ovulating was a morning before work because I nearly whimpered at the sight of Leo dismounting his bike and removing his helmet. As he ran his fingers through his hair to fix it, I wondered if I should bail before entering the building, call in sick for the day, and go home to use my vibrator. He reminded me of every bad boy in any movie ever, even though I knew he wasn't at all. But then I remembered how he punched Vincent in the face immediately upon meeting him, and I was a goner. I was distracted by the memories of us being intimate together all day. So, near the end of the workday, I texted him, and he came over to my apartment for the next three days in a row.

"So, knowing that, it stands to reason that women wouldn't be fully aroused nearly as often as men, right?" Mariam asked.

"Yeah...but regardless, I've always been able to orgasm

with Leo. He's the *only* one I've been able to orgasm with, for whatever reason. I just, I don't know...it's been nice feeling like a normal, healthy, sexually functioning woman for the first time in my life. I don't want to lose that."

"I doubt you will," Mariam raised a shoulder, "You're stressed. You have something unsettling going on at work. You're opening up and being more vulnerable with Leo. You're probably not even ovulating."

I shook my head, "My period started this morning."

"See?" Mariam smiled, "When I'm going through my luteal phase, I'm the farthest from aroused. My wife knows I'm pretty much closed for business for that week."

"Really?" I widened my eyes, suddenly desperate for more information. I didn't have sisters, my mother died when I was young, and my father was never interested in his children. Once we turned eighteen, my dad started living part-time on whatever cruise struck his fancy. Marco was all I had, which was nice...but he was a man. I didn't have women in my life to talk about this kind of stuff with.

The closest thing I had was Signe, Mary, and Jamie. But our brunch conversations never seemed like the place for me to ask, "Hey, so do any of you have difficulty orgasming? What do you do to help with that?"

"So I understand why this freaked you out," Mariam continued, "You went from never orgasming with a partner, to suddenly becoming an orgasming *queen* with Leo. Your confidence was up, your skin was clearer, colors were more vibrant—"

I snorted at her description, "That's a little dramatic, but yeah, I see what you're saying."

"But please, please don't get so worried prematurely. If this continues to be a problem, then maybe you can talk with your doctor to have your hormone levels tested. In the meantime, I think Leo had the right idea."

I furrowed my brows, "What was his idea?"

Mariam smiled, "He tried to take the pressure off of you."

Huh, "Yeah, I guess he did."

"He didn't make you feel bad for not finishing," Mariam lifted her hand to start listing items off of each of her fingers, "He validated your feelings without making you feel like you had to get him off, instead. He stayed to eat dinner and watch TV with you. He didn't try to start things up again after some time had passed, either. He respected your body's boundaries and kissed you goodbye like normal. Have you two spoken since then?"

I nodded, "...He's sent me some funny memes. And we've been sending each other songs back and forth—he always wants to know what I'm listening to at work....I guess we've acted how we normally act at the office."

Mariam raised her eyebrows, "So he's not upset with you or ghosting you over this?"

I shook my head, "No, he hasn't given me that impression at all."

Mariam lifted a shoulder, "All I am saying is, unfortunately—though it may have felt like that for a while—there is no such thing as a magic dick. Our brain still dictates our libido most of the time." She lifted her pencil to point to her head of curls, "Give yourself time to be stressed over work, and try again with Leo another time. Be patient with yourself. Be kind to yourself. Continue communicating your needs to Leo like the confident, sexual, badass woman you are."

My cheeks blushed with the compliment, and a nervous smile tugged on my lips as I replied, "Thank you."

"You're welcome," Mariam nodded, lowering her gaze back to her iPad as she retrieved her pencil, "...Perhaps you should let Leo know how you're feeling about all this, too."

I shook my head, "That's embarrassing."

Mariam lifted a shoulder, "You already cried with him. I'm sure talking about it more in-depth would be fine."

I shook my head again, "That was in the moment, though. I was a wreck. Bringing it up after a couple of days have passed seems like...I don't know, uncomfortable. Weird."

Mariam blinked at me saying, "You're right. Anything uncomfortable or weird usually isn't worth talking about at all."

I groaned and tugged the blanket up over my head.

Because this time, I understood Mariam's sarcasm loud and clear.

I just wasn't confident enough to acknowledge the truth in her words, yet.

Chapter Seventeen

LEO

"WHAT MADE *you decide to apply at Sun Steer?" the red-haired woman asked.*

I tore my gaze away from Jacqueline, clearing my head the best I could to answer the question. It was obvious that she had no desire to admit that we knew each other.

Something settled in my gut at the realization that she wasn't humored to see me. She wasn't pleasantly surprised to find me here.

No, sitting across from her at the conference table, taking in her stiff body language, Jacqueline made it very clear that from this point forward, we were strangers again.

MY VISION WAS CLEARING, stars danced around my peripherals, and I struggled to catch my breath.

"Damn," Taylor grunted on top of me, "You really can't take a hit, can you?"

I scoffed and lifted my middle finger.

"Are you okay?" I heard Zaid's voice, followed by

footsteps of him jogging near us. Taylor had already helped themselves up, but both Taylor and Zaid lent me a hand to pull me off of the grass. I probably had green streaks all over my back and arse.

"I'm good," I gave Zaid a thumbs up after taking a deep breath, ensuring I could breathe still, "T's just a menace."

They rolled their eyes and checked their watch, before clapping their hands and ending the training for the day. Soon the team had dispersed to the edge of the pitch, grabbing water bottles and meeting up with friends and family who came to watch.

I reached into my bag to check my mobile, and my heart skipped a beat when I noticed a missed call from Jacqueline. Balancing the cell between my ear and shoulder while I gathered my things, I redialed.

"Hey." Her voice was enticing. It wasn't a high, feminine voice. If Jacqueline sang, she'd be an alto. Perhaps it was because we were sleeping together, but her voice alone could get me half-mast.

"Hey, sorry I missed your call," I plopped myself down on the grass, sweaty and gross and not willing to sit in my car with my skin this wet, "What's up?"

"Nothing," Jacqueline replied.

And then silence hung in the air.

"...Did you not mean to call me?" I asked.

"No, no. I did."

More silence

It was a thick, daunting silence.

I could practically hear her breathing.

A jolt of panic hit my chest, and a knot formed in my gut. *Holy shit, was she ending things between us?*

I knew the last time we got together didn't go as planned, but I sure as hell wasn't worried about it. Unless I *should* have been worried about it? *What if I fucked it up by being too casual?*

"What's on your mind, beautiful?" I decided to say. I wasn't above using extra flattery to convince her to keep doing...whatever it was we were doing.

A long, heavy sigh sounded on the other end before Jacqueline grumbled something to herself that I couldn't make out.

"What was that?"

"I told my therapist about you," she blurted out, "About us."

I raised my eyebrows, accidentally making eye contact with Taylor a few feet away as I replied, "And...how did that go?"

Taylor raised a dark eyebrow at me in question as they took a drink from their water bottle.

I shrugged because I had no idea what the fuck was going on.

"Good. Fine. Splendid."

"Splendid," I chuckled, dropping my gaze to my boots and unlacing them a bit, "Have you ever used that word before?"

"No," Jacqueline laughed, and my cheeks hurt from the smile I made at the sound, "I'm just nervous. I'm bad at this."

"At what, exactly?"

Please, please don't end this.

"At communicating my feelings," Jacqueline sighed again, "I talked to her about how I couldn't, um, finish...the last time we hung out."

I widened my eyes, scraping a hand down my face.

"Okay," I turned to see Taylor plopping themselves down next to me, their dark blue gaze flicking over me in curiosity, "...in the same conversation you told her about me?"

"No, no, she's known about you since day one."

I smirked a little, hopeful that this was a good thing and not a bad thing, "Really? And what does your therapist think about our situation?"

Taylor's brows raised while they shifted to face me directly, not bothering to pretend they weren't eavesdropping. I grinned at them but kept the cell to my ear.

"She said I need to talk to you about how embarrassed I am over what happened. How I reacted. I don't know. So I guess I'm calling to see if you want to come over tonight or tomorrow to do that. And like...*just* do that."

"Ah," I scraped my thumb across my bottom lip, both of my arms resting on my knees as Taylor and I sat on the grass, "I'm just finishing rugby and smell awful, I'm afraid. I'd love to stop by tomorrow, though. I want to know what your therapist has to say."

"Okay—It's all good stuff, by the way—" Jacqueline's words made me drop my head in relief, "I mean, it's awkward and weird and I'll probably fumble the conversation. But my therapist likes you. For me, that is. Well, she likes how I have talked about you in our sessions. She doesn't *know* you, and my perspective is completely biased because you made me an orgasming queen—"

I choked a laugh, covering my mouth with my free hand, "Queen, you say? Do I need to bow to you?"

Jacqueline snorted, "Okay, so. Tomorrow. We'll talk. No P's in V's. Just...talking."

"Just talking." I agreed, feeling a bit of relief from Jacqueline's words. She wouldn't lead me on. She was a straightforward and to-the-point kind of woman. If she said things were good, I believed her.

"...Maybe some kissing."

"Definitely some kissing."

"But none of your magic dick."

"What the fu—" I clapped my hand over my eyes as I laughed, "I'm glad you think my dick is magical." Taylor choked on the water they had just taken a sip of, cupping their hand under their chin in an attempt to prevent the water from spilling all over their shirt.

"Alright, I need to go so I can spiral in embarrassment over how this entire call went," Jacqueline rushed the words out of her mouth, making me laugh again at how adorable she was, "I'll see you tomorrow."

"Have a good night, love."

"You too." And then she ended the call, and I glanced at the blank screen for a second before chuckling to myself.

"What the hell was that about?" Taylor asked.

I shook my head, running my hands over my face as I laughed again.

God, I was obsessed with that woman.

Then I dropped my hands and turned to Taylor.

I wondered if the question that was on the tip of my tongue was inappropriate. Our friendship was growing, sure. But perhaps I was jumping the gun by asking for their advice.

Well, one way to find out.

"Do you date women?" I asked. I didn't want to assume their sexual preferences.

They raised their eyebrows, "Women are my favorite to date, yes."

"As opposed to?" I asked.

They wiggled their eyebrows, "Everyone else. I'm pan."

I nodded and held out my fist, "Me too."

"No way," Taylor grinned and bumped my fist with theirs, "So you *were* flirting with me the first day we met."

I laughed, "Couldn't help myself, I'm afraid."

"I don't blame you; I'm fucking gorgeous." Taylor laughed as they capped their bottle and set it aside, "So, are you having woman troubles?"

I tipped my head from side to side, "Kind of. I'm not sure. We've been seeing each other for a few weeks, but sometimes I feel out of my wheelhouse with her."

"How so?" Taylor leaned back on their palms and stretched their legs out, resting one ankle over the other. I copied their pose and looked forward toward the sunset that was halfway hidden by the Pacific Ocean in the distance.

"She's...god, how do I explain it?" I rolled my head back to look at the sky before looking forward again, "She's kind of rigid, but I don't see it as a fault like others do. I think she's just got a tough exterior. She isn't always stiff around me—anymore, at least. But she's been visibly, noticeably stressed lately. I'm not sure how to help, because she doesn't like to look weak or look like she *needs* help."

Taylor thought about my ramblings for a moment, "Well, what does she like?"

I grinned, "Music. Her work playlist is just a bunch of songs from the early aughts, it's fantastic. Stuff with a heavy beat. Sometimes I can hear the base from her earbuds if she walks past me in the office." I thought about her some more outside of work, "She also likes blankets. When there's a throw nearby, she'll always tug it over herself. Chocolates, she likes chocolates. She always seems to have a small piece ready to eat as soon as she's done with dinner—oh, she also likes the sensory room at work."

Taylor turned to look at me then, "Sensory room?"

"Yeah," I lifted my shoulder, "It's a room with a

hammock and bean bags and a fluffy rug and an essential oil diffuser. I'm pretty sure it's soundproofed. I've seen her go in there several times, usually when she's grumpy or having a rough day. Don't know how she tolerates it, it's way too quiet in there for me."

Taylor stared at me with a pinch in their brow, before opening their mouth and closing it again.

"What?" I asked, my smile fell from my face, "What is it?"

"I just—" Taylor snapped their lips closed before trying again, "Is she maybe neurodivergent to some degree?" I stared at Taylor's face momentarily, because their words clicked something into awareness for me. Like a puzzle piece sliding into place in my brain.

"I...haven't considered that."

"She may not be," Taylor quickly added, "I don't know her. But...I do have some experience with neurodivergent people, is all."

"Really?" I asked.

"Yeah," they nodded, "I work with children on the spectrum. So, I've seen just how wide and varied the autism spectrum is—especially for women."

I blinked and turned to face the sunset again, "...I have ADHD, so I feel like I should have considered Jacqueline being neurodivergent long before this."

"Well, again, she might not be," Taylor added, "But I also know that there are a lot of people out there who are walking around, high functioning and undiagnosed. It's common for autistic women to fly under the radar more than men do."

I sat up, tucking my feet near me so I could rest my arms on my knees again, "The other day, she was telling me how she doesn't always understand nuance. How that caused a lot of contention in her last relationship because she couldn't understand the vague comments her ex would say to her."

Taylor smirked a little, "I'm starting to have a little bit more confidence in my theory."

"Jesus Christ, it seems so obvious now," I dropped my head in my hands, "God, I'm such a wanker for not seeing it sooner."

"Okay, let's not be dramatic and weirdly make this about you," Taylor punched my shoulder, "Let's get back to your original issue. She's stressed, and not feeling like herself. But she likes loud music and sensory experiences...dare I ask, doth the lady like clubbing?"

I frowned because I couldn't picture Jacqueline at a club at all. I pictured her behind her desk at work, or under a blanket on the couch.

"I don't know."

Taylor quirked their lips to the side with a look of contemplation on their face, before finally pulling their phone out of their bag, "Okay, I might have a suggestion."

"Anything," I agreed, as I scooted closer to them.

Chapter Eighteen

JACQUELINE

"I HOPE to hear from you soon." Leo nodded as he shook Signe's hand before leaving. When he turned to me, he didn't look at me. He glanced at the top of my head while I quickly returned his handshake and then dropped his hold. He nodded politely at the two of us, throwing a grin over to Signe, before leaving the conference room.

As soon as he turned the corner toward the elevators, officially out of sight, I felt like I could breathe again as I promptly made my way to the sensory room.

I ALMOST DIDN'T ANSWER the door when I heard his knock.

I stood there for a moment, staring at the knob, wondering if he would walk away if I didn't answer. Then I realized that I didn't want him to walk away, and I jerked forward to swing the door open as quickly as possible.

Leo stood there, one hand in his leather jacket pocket while the other held a bag of takeout from a Thai place we both liked, "Hey."

"Hi." I sighed.

God, Leo was a handsome man.

He must have ridden his bike here because his cheeks were flushed, and his hair looked like he'd recently run his hands through it to fight against helmet hair. I stared at the way his fingers flexed over their hold on the plastic bag, almost whimpering in disappointment from how I had insisted he not use those on me tonight.

"As normal as this is," Leo's voice startled me out of my horny fantasies, and when I met his eyes with my own, he was grinning, "May I come in?" It took me a second to realize he was referring to us awkwardly standing on the threshold while I ogled him.

"Shoot, yeah," I stepped back to allow him entry, "Please, do come in."

God, I was so weird.

"Jacqueline," Leo sighed, setting the bag on the countertop before turning to face me. He planted both of his hands on his hips and lifted a dark eyebrow, "This is feeling way too formal for us."

I panicked, folding my hands over each other while I took a step toward him, "I'm sorry. I'm being weird. I know. I just—" He stopped my rambling by cupping my face with both of his large hands and tilting my head back. When he pressed his lips against mine, I practically sighed into his mouth.

He brushed his lips against mine once, twice, before murmuring, "Relax for me, love."

Just like he did that day in the parking lot.

So I did.

I melted into him, running my hands under his jacket but over his shirt, exploring the hard planes of his torso. I gripped the dips and ridges of his back, tugging myself against him so he could keep kissing me like we had all the time in the world.

After an indiscriminate amount of time, Leo pulled back and planted a quick kiss on my nose, "Better?"

"Yeah." I reached up to kiss him again, and he allowed me to. His hands stayed on my face; they did not wander like mine were. My hands never reached lower than the hem of his shirt, and they never snuck underneath to feel that warm skin I craved the touch of. But I got my feel of him, regardless.

"Jacqueline," I felt Leo's lips pull back into a smile against mine, "Are you avoiding talking by kissing me?" I responded by kissing him again. And again.

"Maybe," I murmured back against his lips.

Leo wrapped me in a tight, firm hug as he controlled the kiss to his liking. Forcing my lips open and dragging his tongue along mine in a way that promised dirty, dirty things I knew he would provide. Then suddenly, he pulled back and planted one last kiss on my forehead.

"I love kissing you," Leo breathed against my hair, "But I also want to know what's going on in that gorgeous head of yours."

"Are you sure?" I dropped my head and rested against his chest, clutching his shirt at his sides. Thankfully, he wrapped both arms around me until I pulled away first. I craved that close contact with him. Every morning I started my day feeling like I was missing something. Like I forgot my keys or my phone, something that should always be on my person.

It was just Leo.

Leo was who I was missing, who I was craving.

And that thought terrified me.

So I forced myself to pull away and start digging into the

takeout he brought over. Doing something with my hands helped me justify not looking at him as I spoke.

"Okay, so," my shoulders inched higher and higher, my anxiety desperately trying to take over my body, "... Okay, so..."

"You're killing me, love," Leo chuckled as he helped me gather our things and move toward the kitchen island. He dragged a stool out for me with his foot after taking his own seat. The moment was so casual, so intimate.

I basked in it as I sat.

When he reached his foot out again to scoot my stool closer to him, I couldn't hide my grin.

"I'm sorry," I sighed, "I don't know how to have conversations like this."

"Feel free to lead into it however you'd like," Leo took a bite of food before adding, "...Personally, I'd love if we could discuss my magic dick at some point."

"Oh god," I dropped my plastic fork and covered my face with my hands, "I'm so sorry. That's what my therapist called it—"

"—I am a *very* big fan of your therapist," Leo chuckled. I laughed too, lowering my hands to give him an amused look.

"Basically, I need to tell you how embarrassed I am that I didn't, um...finish last time."

"Why are you embarrassed?" Leo asked, lowering his eyes to his dish. He twisted his noodles around his fork, completely at ease. His casual body language helped me relax a bit as well.

"I just...it hasn't been an issue between us before." I shrugged, frowning as I stared at the way his long fingers held his fork. I watched him lift a bite to his mouth. It wasn't a sexy thing for him to do, but I was a horn-dog since becoming intimate with him. Everything he did reminded me of what he and I could do together. The pleasure he was capable of pulling from me with little to no effort.

"Is there anything I could have done differently during that moment?" Leo asked, and god, the man sounded so genuine. It wasn't a condescending question meant to lead me to some conclusion where I am at fault because the man did everything he could. If there was truly something else he could have done, he wanted to know.

Leo isn't Vincent, the words rang in my head, much like they had before.

"I don't think so, I actually think you handled it perfectly," I sighed, "I wish I didn't cry about it, though."

"I think it's okay that you did. It's frustrating," Leo spoke, "I have had times where I couldn't quite finish myself."

I lifted my gaze to his, "You have?"

"Yeah," Leo lifted a shoulder, "I had just turned thirty, I hadn't ever been unable to orgasm before, and I panicked. I thought my cock was broken."

"Oh no." I widened my eyes, realizing at that moment that while Leo was opening up to me about his inability to orgasm, I didn't hold a single ounce of judgment for him. I wasn't looking down on him. I didn't think of him as less of a man or less of a sexual partner. I just listened to him and wanted to hear the rest of his story.

Perhaps that's how he felt about me not finishing, as well.

"Thankfully, it wasn't," Leo smirked before taking a sip of water and returning the glass to the countertop, "I went to the doctor, who told me that my testosterone levels had dropped a bit. It is a common thing to happen to men in their thirties, apparently. Besides eating healthier and exercising more regularly, I was also on testosterone for a short period."

I furrowed my brows, "What made you stop taking it?"

"I didn't have the problem anymore," Leo lifted a shoulder, "That first wank where I was able to finish felt like exhaling for the first time that year." I laughed, and he grinned at my reaction, "But now I know that if I struggle with it again, that I can go back to my doctor and discuss getting back on testosterone to try to help."

The next words out of my mouth didn't feel like mine, they felt like Signe Lange's. Something she would say. Perhaps I even heard her say it before, which was why it felt so natural for me to respond with them.

"And that's gender-affirming care," I smiled at my plate, dragging my fork along the outer edge of my noodles, before adding, "My therapist also suggested seeing a doctor, but she thinks that I'm just stressed about work."

"What's going on?" Leo's brows pinched, and again, I was floored by the sincerity of his concern. Every time he asked me anything, it felt like a very intentional question. He asked because he was interested, and he cared.

I wasn't sure how to deal with a man (who wasn't my twin brother) genuinely, sincerely, caring about me and my woes.

"Brandon sent me a cryptic email about meeting with him next week and..." I frowned, "I know logically that it's probably nothing. I understand that he has given me no reason to think that he's disappointed in me or wants to fire me. But...my brain doesn't care. My gut doesn't care."

Leo was quiet for a moment, before reaching his hand over and squeezing my thigh with his long fingers, "That would stress me out too."

I looked up at him and did my best to give him a reassuring smile, but it wobbled.

"There was a while where I felt like I was just surviving," his long fingers pressed into the meat of my thigh, tightening his grip, "After leaving my ex, I kind of became a shell. This person who put everything into her job, a job that I loved. I was so grateful to get hired at Sun Steer. I was slowly starting to make friends with other women in the office, which is really difficult for someone as odd as me."

"You're not odd," Leo interrupted.

I shook my head once, "I'm odd. I'm cold, closed off, borderline rude, and bad at navigating social interactions the moment they're happening. It's okay, I'm at peace with these aspects of myself." I lifted my eyes to lock onto his icy blue ones, "I know that it's something I'll actively have to struggle with the rest of my life. I know that I need to be more cautious about the expressions I make and the words I use, and I was doing well for a while." I inhaled a shaky breath before pressuring myself to continue, "So well, that I thought it was time for me to explore my sexuality without the pressure of a boyfriend..."

Leo was silent, his eyes locked on mine as he waited for me.

"...You were the first person I felt safe and comfortable with to ask for what I wanted," I bit my lip, "And then you got hired, as you should have. You're great at your job. But I didn't know how to blend those two aspects of my life. You've seen me at my most vulnerable moments, Leo." I shook my head once, "I wasn't prepared, and I handled it horribly."

Leo shook his head, "You've already apologized for that."

"Yeah, but," I pinched the bridge of my nose, the sting of tears threatening my eyes once again, "Not being able to orgasm last time made me feel so disappointed in myself. I was embarrassed and felt ashamed. I thought I had been improving, but according to my therapist, there's no such thing as a magic dick after all. My big fat brain will still keep me from crossing over that edge if it deems me too stressed to do so."

Leo didn't chuckle or laugh at the magic dick mention again, which made me lift my gaze to the ceiling, a tightening in my chest was starting again and I desperately didn't want to cry in front of him for the second time this week.

But he didn't care.

As soon as I squeezed my eyes closed, desperate to hold the tears in, the heat of his embrace enveloped me. His arms wrapped around my torso, tugging my body into his as if I needed to accept my fate. Leo's mouth was on the top of my head, gently shushing and murmuring words of encouragement as I allowed a few tears to drip down my cheeks.

"You're allowed to be stressed, Jacqueline," Leo mumbled into my hair, squeezing me tighter as a soft sob escaped my lips, "You are not some orgasming robot. You're a human, with a beautiful brain and a beautiful personality. I don't need sex with completion to enjoy your company. I enjoy being with you, just like this."

I laughed through another sob, "You don't need to lie."

"I'm not lying," Leo squeezed me again, shifting his lips a little lower so they fell near my temple, "I'm here, eating dinner with you, instead of playing a new Lord of the Rings card game with Mary and Jamie. Because I would rather spend my evening talking to you, learning more about you, and discovering what is going on inside your brilliant mind."

I sobbed a laugh again, and he pressed his lips against my head before asking, "What is it, love?"

"It's just—" I cut myself off to swipe my hands under my eyes, still wrapped up snug in his embrace, "—you are *so* nerdy, oh my god." I laughed again, and Leo scoffed.

Without warning, I was lifted off of my barstool, his arms holding me around my torso as he practically dragged me to my living room. I was laughing still, unbothered when the couch cushions hit my back and Leo's warmth blanketed my front.

His fingers went to my sides, and I squealed.

"You think you can make fun of me, Jacqueline?" Leo was grinning wide, but it was hard to keep his joyful expression in my vision. I was very ticklish, and I had to squeeze my eyes shut to focus on playfully fighting against him, "I was a Tolkien-obsessed, queer boy raised by two mums in South London. Nothing can get to me."

I squealed as his fingers found the inside of my thighs, "Leo!"

"I'm perfectly confident with my hobbies and interests," Leo continued, successfully trapping my legs underneath him so he could continue his playful assault, "I may be a nerd, but I'm still the one who gets to spend most of his evenings between these lovely legs of yours."

"Jesus," I wheezed, giggling while also feeling a flutter of anticipation from his crude words, "You have a point." His fingers were loosening up, and I could finally catch my breath. I lay there, my chest heaving, focusing on the calmness in my body that I was starting to become more familiar with in Leo's presence.

Silence hung in the air while Leo adjusted over me, shifting to the side so that half of his body weight wouldn't crush me while snaking his arms underneath so he could snuggle in. His head rested against my breasts, but he didn't make a move. He just held me, content with the movement his head made as I inhaled and exhaled.

"...Thank you for talking to me, Jacqueline," Leo's voice was lower, calmer. A whisper. His voice reminded me of the conversation we were just having before he tickled me.

"...Thank you for listening," I hummed, as I reached up and ran my fingers through his dark hair. It was so soft. The barest hint of product in it he must have applied in the morning, and yet, I still enjoyed the sensation of feeling his locks brush through my fingers. Against my knuckles.

Leo hummed in contentment as well, and I could feel his big body relax against me even more from my soothing touch, "...Will you go out with me?"

I hesitated for half a second before continuing my grooming, "Like, on a date?"

"Yes." Leo didn't look at me, he didn't move a muscle. Part of me suspected that he was nervous, "Exactly like a date. Something with no sexual expectations. Just you and me spending intentional time together."

I thought about it for half a second before I whispered my response.

As if this was a pinnacle moment.

Maybe it was. Maybe it wasn't. It didn't matter either way, because I knew what my answer was as soon as he asked me.

"I'd love to."

Chapter Nineteen

LEO

WEEKS HAD PASSED. *I didn't get the job. It was probably for the best, considering I was over-qualified. Also, I had already shagged one of my potential coworkers.*

I was sitting at my mums' kitchen counter, listening to them toss around banter about the new recipe they were testing when I randomly checked my cell to find a new, unopened email.

It was from Brandon Moore.

The CEO of Sun Steer Technologies.

I held my breath as I tapped on the notification.

I WASN'T confident about how Jacqueline would react to a kind of surprise like this. I had a feeling she wasn't a huge fan of surprises in general. She seemed like someone who wanted to be prepared for whatever could happen next.

The Friday after our talk at her flat, she was still quiet and withdrawn at work. I saw her step into the sensory room twice. Talking with me about her stress obviously didn't make it go away, but I felt comfort in the fact that she did. I had a perspective on how she was feeling.

The fact that I could convince her to go out with me without any pushback made me realize how out of sorts she might have been. I expected the stiffness I felt in her body underneath mine, but I didn't expect her to almost immediately agree to a date.

The fact that she later requested to ride on my motorcycle to wherever we were going was another red flag. She was usually terrified of the bike.

She needed to let go.

Sometimes, people like Jacqueline needed a push to relax.

I just fucking hoped that Taylor would pull through.

We drove almost forty minutes south on PCH, the humid ocean air felt amazing even through our leather protection. The farther away we got from Orange County, the quieter life became. There wasn't much on the drive between Orange County and San Diego, besides Oceanside. But we didn't get quite that far. After finding the turnoff Taylor had instructed, I was second-guessing what they were getting us into. It was completely dark, only the half-moon was able to illuminate some of the surroundings because there were no streetlights on this gravel pathway into the hills. The ocean behind us was the only noise beyond the hum of my bike. When we finally turned onto another unnamed road, an old run-down building came into view.

"Are you about to murder me?" Jacqueline asked underneath her helmet. Her voice in my ear almost made me jump. We hadn't said a word to teach each other the entire ride out here.

"I wasn't planning on it, no," I replied, "How are you

doing back there?" I could feel her hands tighten around my waist, her fingers pressing against the skin of my abs just like that first ride we took together.

"Fine," Jacqueline sighed. I frowned. Where was her bite? Where were her quips? That feisty personality that I was starting to become obsessed with. I squared my shoulders, pulling my bike into an unmarked spot next to a handful of other parked vehicles.

When we dismounted the bike, I relaxed a bit more when I heard Taylor's voice call out to us, "What's up, nerds?"

Jacqueline also relaxed at their voice as she pushed down the protective leather pants that I let her borrow for the drive, revealing a slightly wrinkled skirt that landed just at the top of her thighs. It was the same outfit she wore the first night we met. Her top had a low-cut, square neck, with long sleeves that cropped at her rib cage. I reminded myself that I wouldn't touch her how I wanted to quite yet, "Hi, Taylor."

"How are you doing, J?" Taylor came up and wrapped Jacqueline in a side hug before reaching out and giving me one as well.

"I'm good," Jacqueline gave a concerned look behind Taylor's shoulder toward the abandoned-looking building that people were starting to walk into, "What is this place?"

Taylor wiggled their eyebrows before reaching into their pocket to grab a vial of something, "Can I glitter you?" I raised my eyebrows at the same time that Jacqueline did. She gave me a nervous look before nodding her consent.

Taylor dipped their finger in the vial of, apparently, glitter, before gently dabbing the horrid substance on the edges of Jacqueline's cheekbones. After dipping another finger, they even dabbed the top of her collarbones and shoulders.

"You?" Taylor asked, after they were finished with Jacqueline.

"Yeah," I stepped forward and allowed them to do the same to me, even unbuttoning my shirt a bit more so they could dab glitter on my collarbones and the top of my pecks, "Is this mandatory attire?"

"It is if you hang with me," Taylor lifted a shoulder before dabbing their own cheekbones, nose, and collarbones with glitter, "Let's go, it's going to start soon."

"What is?" Jacqueline asked. Taylor shoved their hands into the pockets of their loose-hanging jeans, a flannel tied at their waist, and a lime green tank top that showed off the lean muscles in their arms, shoulders, and chest.

I held out a hand toward Jacqueline, who didn't hesitate to lace her fingers with mine.

It felt like a huge win.

The doors to the building already had a line starting to form, but Taylor confidently walked up to the front where two large bouncers were managing who was allowed in.

"They're with me," Taylor nodded toward the two of us, and to my surprise, the bouncers didn't question them at all before stepping aside and holding the doors open for us.

It was completely dark inside.

"Um." Jacqueline stepped closer to me as Taylor turned around to face us. I wrapped an arm around her waist, lowering my head to murmur in her ear.

"Do you trust me?" I asked, ignoring Taylor's knowing smirk as they waited for us to follow them in.

Jacqueline inhaled a deep breath, squared her shoulders, and nodded. Taylor grinned, hopping on their feet once before sauntering inside the dark doors.

Jacqueline grabbed my hand and ended up tugging me in after the two of them.

The doors shut behind us, and we were enclosed in darkness.

"What the—" Jacqueline asked before a cracking sound echoed in the room and Taylor's sharp facial features came into view under a dim purple light.

"Are you bracelets or necklace people?" Taylor asked, cracking more glow sticks. At their feet, there was a huge box of glow sticks that they were grabbing them from. How they managed to see the box upon entry was a mystery to me.

"Both." Jacqueline nodded. I studied her in the dim light, and when Taylor placed a purple glow stick necklace around her neck, her lips were pulled back into a smile. Taylor then added blue and purple bracelets to both of her wrists.

"I'm both as well." I stepped forward, donning my own glow stick jewelry while Taylor assisted Jacqueline with hers.

"Is this like a party?" Jacqueline asked in a whisper.

"Yeah," Taylor's reply didn't sound convincing, which made me chuckle as we followed them down the dark hallway again. I could still smell the ocean, and part of me wondered how many walls or chunks of the ceiling were missing in this facility.

The farther we walked though, the temperature became slightly warmer.

Eventually, we entered a large room where everyone seemed to gather. I saw that my theory of missing ceiling pieces was confirmed because we could see the pale moonlight shining in and illuminating just enough of the room to let us know we weren't alone.

What was surprising to me, though, was how quiet everyone was.

"What is this?" Jacqueline asked, her whisper softer after hearing everyone else keeping their conversations low.

"It's a place to unwind." Taylor lifted a shoulder, "It's a secret."

"Oh..." Jacqueline glanced around as we awkwardly stood hand in hand. More bodies started to file in. More people in glitter and glow sticks and revealing attire. The three of us were more reserved with our clothing compared to the shirtless men and women with lingerie tops and corsets.

I expected to see people like this here, but I watched Jacqueline study everyone around us. She wore a curious but reserved expression on her face.

Suddenly, a light was cast on the far wall. It illuminated a metal spiral staircase that led to what looked like a second-floor fire escape. A woman in a body suit, also covered in glitter and exaggerated makeup, started to dance as the music slowly started to play.

It was loud, so I reached into my pocket to hand Jacqueline orange foam earplugs. I managed to snag them from the top of her dresser as she got ready in her bathroom. She would still be able to hear everything with them, but I knew that tonight might also be overstimulating for her and that these would help take the edge off.

I held them out in the palm of my hand, nudging her arm with mine to pull her attention away from the dancer. Jacqueline glanced down, debating on whether to use them or not. After a second of thought, she decided to put them in.

The music and the bass were growing, and I watched as Jacqueline stared at the dancer. The interpretive, modern dance moves were choreographed perfectly to the build of the music that was getting louder and louder. It made the audience focus on what was about to happen.

Jacqueline's hand squeezed mine right when the dancer decided to stand up on the rickety railing of the fire escape, looking very precarious as they somehow continued to dance. Anticipation was building within the crowd; bodies already started to bob and sway with the beat of the rising music.

Right when the bass dropped, colorful strobe lights lit up the room, revealing four more performers dropping dramatically from the shadows of the ceiling, secured in ribbons and hoops. The original dancer had also jumped and grabbed onto one of the hoops, and a surprise aerial performance took place above as the club came to life.

A loud, feminine cackle made me lower my gaze to my coworker. Her hand was up over her mouth, eyes wide as she took in our surroundings. Taylor took one look at Jacqueline before grabbing her arm to pull her further into the depths of the crowd, laughing and jumping with everyone else who started to dance.

Before she was pulled too far, Jacqueline reached back and snatched my hand, tugging me with them.

And just like that, the three of us were part of the rave.

The music was loud, so loud that I could feel it in my bones. Jacqueline pressed a hand to her chest, and I wondered if she was feeling it just like I was. It was the kind of music she listened to every day at work, but I had a feeling she had never experienced something like this before.

Her friends and past partners had failed her this way, I realized.

Because Jacqueline came to life here.

Her smile was bold and uninhibited. She didn't cringe

away from other bodies inevitably bumping into her. She didn't shy away from dancing. No, as I watched her and Taylor dance and grind and sing loudly along with the popular but fifteen-year-old song, I felt something heat in my chest.

Taylor spun Jacqueline around, making her lose her footing just before collapsing against me. I took her hands and spun her again, knowing that I would have another memory of Jacqueline's laugh burned into my memory.

The song was fitting for this moment.

As everyone in the room sang along about finding clarity in someone unexpected, Jacqueline threw her arms around my neck and danced with me.

I was on cloud fucking nine.

I glanced at Taylor over the top of Jacqueline's head, mouthing a "thank you" for helping me surprise Jacqueline like this.

Taylor gave me a thumbs-up before disappearing into the crowd's throes, and Jacqueline and I were alone.

The song eventually ended, but this was a rave, so the music never truly ended. There was no break because the DJ hidden in the far corner was blending one song into the next.

As *Swedish House Mafia* and *John Martin* started to sing about heaven having plans for us, I leaned down to speak into Jacqueline's ear. My lips pressed against her hot skin as I asked, "Is this alright?"

Jacqueline leaned back, beaming at me, and I wanted to pound in my chest which was now filled with male pride from her expression, "Yes."

And then she spun around, keeping my hands in hers. She guided my touch on her body, one held her hips and the other slowly dragged up her torso, over her breasts, until it rested over her heart. She ground her arse against me, and I didn't bother stifling the groan that erupted from my chest.

"Let me know when you're ready to leave," I spoke, licking her ear lobe.

"Do you want to leave?" Jacqueline asked. She had stopped dancing against me, her eyes wide and a concerned expression pulled her lips down. I closed my eyes and kept my mouth against her neck because the noise level made it practically mandatory to speak to her so closely.

"Not at all," I assured her, remembering her need for direct and honest communication—because *fuck me* if I ever became an asshole like some prick named Vincent, "I am thrilled to be here with you. I just don't want to wear you out too much."

Jacqueline scoffed, "You wear me out most nights of the week, Leo."

"And I'll keep wearing you out as long as you'll let me." I didn't think about the words until after they left my mouth. As soon as they did, though, I wondered if I had accidentally crossed some line. But no, Jacqueline just grinned and resumed torturing me with her arse against my groin as we danced together. Bodies bumped into us, and strangers smiled and sang as everyone lost themselves to the loud music.

Jacqueline never accepted dances with other men or women, even when they tried to sneak between us to gain her attention.

Instead, she would politely shake her head and point to me.

Or wrap my arms around her, as if she needed me to shield unwanted suitors away.

I was more than fucking happy to oblige.

Because when it came down to it, I didn't want to dance

with anyone else either. Not a man or woman in this establishment caught my eye the way that Jacqueline did. I hadn't been with anyone since I moved here and started working at Sun Steer, and I understood why now.

Watching her spin in and out of my hold, throwing me wide smiles with joy filling her expression, I realized something.

I wanted everything that Jacqueline Williams was willing to give me.

Because no one else would do for me anymore.

She was who I wanted to run home to after work.

She was the one I wanted to take to secret pop-up raves in the middle of nowhere.

She was the one I wanted to sink into every night.

She was the one I wanted to wake up to every morning.

Jacqueline had once confessed that looking at me made her want, a sentiment I had come to fully understand.

I wanted her.

I wanted *all* of her.

In every sense of the word.

JACQUELINE

"THEY FINALLY FOUND *someone to take over Zaid's position!"*
Signe cheered as she plopped into her seat at the table.

I raised my brows, because I hadn't received any information
about that. I thought that Zaid or Brandon would email me a list
of candidates they wanted me to reach out to. Not that they
would handle that process themselves.

"Who?" I asked. I was glad Zaid was finally moving in the
direction he preferred.

"Leo Turner," Mary announced, in the most flawless British
accent I had ever heard.

My stomach dropped.

LEO and I still hadn't had sex again the next week while I
waited for my meeting with Brandon. As far as I was
concerned, sex was the only thing we had going for us. It
was the foundation our relationship was based on, and I
had assumed that since I was currently closed for business,
Leo wouldn't be as communicative.

It wasn't like we got along before we started having sex.

I assumed that after he took me to the rave, Leo would wait around, doing his own thing, until I was ready to be intimate with him again.

But no, Leo was still texting me. He still came over to watch TV with me, bringing us "takeaway" to eat together on the couch. We would snuggle up together, (like we're doing now) under a favorite throw blanket of mine. It was as if we were in a relationship but without the label of a relationship.

It didn't feel like he was just waiting for me to give the green light for sex, either.

He seemed like he was enjoying himself, which was good because I was, too.

The episode ended, and while the credits rolled, I stretched my arms out, arching my back. Leo adjusted next to me so I had room to do so.

"That was delicious." I patted my very full stomach. We had Indian food tonight, and while my tikka masala wasn't the spiciest dish, I still needed to do something about the lingering mouth feel I was dealing with, "Want a kiss?"

"Always." Leo leaned forward and started smacking his lips on my cheek.

I snorted, "A chocolate kiss, you dork."

"I know," he chuckled, releasing his hold on me and allowing me to stand up to get my post-dinner treat, "What are you doing tomorrow?"

Tomorrow was Wednesday.

Which meant that I had no plans. I would probably read, watch TV, or go to bed at eight thirty. I would bask in my aloneness and lack of ability to do much, other than prepare for work again the next day. Thankfully, adding new employees to my department really helped my workload. I could actually take time on the weekend to do what I wanted.

The newest hire's name was Hazel. Like Andrew, she was also blonde. They looked like they could genuinely be siblings. So I now had Andrew and Hazel working for me.

"Nothing, why?"

"Want to come over in the evening?" Leo rested his fist against his cheek, his arm resting on the back of the couch as he watched me walk to my pantry to retrieve the chocolate. I tossed the tiny wrapper in the garbage before walking back to him.

"And do what?" I snuggled back into his side, tucking my legs underneath myself as I let him blanket us under the throw again.

"Eat, relax," Leo sighed, as he settled with me tucked beside him again, "Or we can go do something if you'd like."

"I'm still recovering from Friday's rave," I admitted, resting my head on his shoulder, "So I'd rather stay in."

"That's fine," Leo propped his socked feet up on my coffee table, "I just figured we could do this again tomorrow if you didn't have plans."

I bit back a smile, "I don't. Is this another date?"

Leo didn't hold back his smile, he let it spread across his face, "Yes."

LEO

"Bloody fucking hell," I grumbled, setting the controller down and resting my head in my hands. It was slower at the office lately, so a lot of us had all ended the day early. I met up at Mary and Jamie's flat to blow off some steam.

"I can't believe you actually say that," Jamie giggled from her reading chair, "It's so British of you."

Mary was already standing, completing a victory dance after getting first place in Mario Kart again, before mocking me with her stellar impersonation of my accent, "Oi, why don't yeh go fetch us some fish 'n chips?"

"I'd prefer something like jacket potatoes right now," I replied, rubbing my brow with my fingertips. Fuck, that did sound good. Perhaps I'd cook a meal for Jacqueline tonight, instead of just providing dessert.

"What are jacket potatoes?" Jamie inquired with her gaze back to her paperback.

"Potatoes with more beans and cheese and deliciousness." Mary replied before turning to me, "Want to make them for us tonight? Consider it your consequence for losing again. Because you're a loser."

I flipped her off. Jamie may have softened some of Mary's rougher edges, but I was grateful Mary still didn't hold back from "roasting" me, as she called it. It was a unique love language between the two of us.

"First of all, fuck you," I grinned while standing up to stretch, "I'm afraid I can't. I have plans."

That would probably, definitely, involve jacket potatoes.

"With who? We're your only friends." Mary frowned.

"He plays rugby with Zaid now; he has other friends," Jamie defended me, a grin pulling at her cheeks as she read.

"None of your business." I reached for my jacket hanging on the arm of the couch before shrugging it on.

"Tell me," Mary demanded.

"No." I grinned, loving the irritated twitch in her eye. Mary didn't care about a lot of things, but she cared when I specifically kept secrets from her.

"Are you going on a date?" Mary pressed.

Something burned in my chest, wondering if I should tell her about Jacqueline.

No, I needed to talk with Jacqueline first. The last time we talked about it, she didn't want Mary to know about us.

"If I was?" I looked around, wondering where my boots were.

"Then I could tell Victoria to get off my ass," Mary sighed, "She's been wondering if you're lonely with just me here to keep you company."

I finally found my boots, shoving my feet into them and tying the laces. I looked up at the two women, meeting Jamie's curious glance. Just to fuck with them, I looked over at Mary and gave her a wink.

"You can tell her that I'm *not* lonely."

"Leopold!" Mary sat up from her seat on the couch.

"Still not my name," I smirked as I stood tall to grab my helmet off their kitchen table.

"Are you seeing someone?" Mary's dark brows rose, which was the last expression I saw before I turned toward the door and started my exit.

I threw up a lazy wave over my shoulder before calling out, "Until next time!" and closed the door behind me.

Mary's muffled, "Oh my god," was the last thing I heard before I made my way to the store.

JACQUELINE

Two very English women were speaking, and it took me a second to realize that their voices were coming from a device of some kind.

"Slowly, slowly!" One woman was cautiously instructing.

I quietly toed off my sneakers before following the

sound. I had knocked on Leo's door, but he never answered. I heard the sound of pots and pans echoing on the other side, so I tested the knob. I had an aversion to doorbells and avoided using them at all costs. Plus, if Leo was busy, I had a feeling he wouldn't be too irritated with me letting myself in.

His apartment was...much nicer than mine.

I suddenly felt guilty that we had spent so much time in mine. My building wasn't terrible, in fact, I considered it very nice for someone like me who was single and barely in her thirties. His, however, was a step or two above. I realized right then and there, taking in the modern lines and light, and the warm wooden floors, that Leo was in a very different tax bracket than I was.

He even had large art prints on his walls and warm abstract paintings that felt welcoming.

I turned the corner, finding an open-concept space that revealed an updated kitchen, island, and dining area. Off near the far end of the room was the living space, with a black leather sectional couch and fluffy area rug.

Standing at the island, with an iPad propped up, pouring chocolate onto a pan, was Leo.

"Slowly!" One woman repeated.

"I *know*," Leo smiled as he replied, keeping his eyes on the chocolate pouring from the bowl.

I slowly stepped into the space; my eyes glued to the pan with parchment paper underneath. Leo was currently pouring what looked like chocolate kisses.

He was *making* them, filling molds with chocolate.

"You can never be too careful," another British woman replied from the iPad. Leo chuckled before turning his back to me to set the chocolate bowl aside. His apartment had a variety of smells. There was something in the oven, which I assumed was where the garlic and salty smell was coming from. But the smell of freshly poured chocolate was added to it.

It made my stomach growl.

"Are you making kisses?" I asked, taking a few steps closer to the chocolate molds to get a better look.

"Fuck!" Leo jumped, spilling a decent amount of chocolate onto the counter and himself, before catching the bowl and placing a hand over his heart. *Oh my god*, Leo was wearing an *apron*. It looked handmade, with a floral pattern on it.

Leo was officially too much.

"Is that *her*?" the first English woman asked, "Step closer to the camera, darling!"

Instead, I froze. Staring wide-eyed at a panting Leo, still recovering from the scare my presence induced.

"I didn't hear you come in," Leo explained as his eyes traveled up and down my clothing. I wasn't wearing anything special. After work, I had changed into leggings and a sweater, and some fluffy socks. I was a wimp when it came to the cold, but I also loved bundling up in my favorite layers.

The way his eyes heated on me, though, made me feel like I just walked into his kitchen wearing lingerie.

"Let us see!" both women yelled from the iPad.

Leo rolled his eyes, though he didn't look annoyed at the request. Instead, he lifted a hand to his mouth—the hand that the chocolate spilled on—and reached his other arm out toward me.

Slowly, I stepped into his embrace, in front of the iPad.

"Oh," I finally tore my gaze away from Leo's mouth, sucking the chocolate off of his fingers, to face the screen where the voices were coming from, "You're lovely."

An Asian woman with dark hair and eyes was looking at

me with a wide smile, along with a white woman with blonde hair and blue eyes sitting next to her, resting her hands underneath her chin.

"Thank you. Um, hi." I lifted my hand for an awkward wave, appreciating the comforting weight Leo's arm resting around my shoulders provided.

"These are my mums," Leo explained, "Victoria and Lisa."

"But you can call us Mummy and Mama," Victoria replied.

Something burned in my chest from the immediate inclusivity. My mom passed when I was too young. But Leo had *two* mothers. Part of me acknowledged the unfairness of our situations, but another part of me suddenly understood Leo so much better after meeting the two women who raised him.

So, I just smiled and nodded at them.

"It's nice to meet you both." I found myself leaning into Leo's body a bit more for reassurance, but my eyes kept falling to the pan of chocolate kisses, "I didn't know you knew how to make chocolate."

"He doesn't," both women replied, before Lisa added, "But his mums do."

"They're chocolatiers," Leo explained, reaching around me to grab the pan of kisses, before putting them in the fridge to set, "They were willing to instruct me on this."

"Wow, that's so cool." I gave his parents my profile while I leaned to peek into the oven, "Are you making...potatoes?"

"I am," Leo stood tall, reaching behind himself to untie his apron, "We are going to have a proper English dinner— if you're up for it."

I beamed at him, making him hesitate his movements for half a second as he registered how excited I was at the thought. How honored I felt that he was introducing this part of his culture to me.

"Leo, honey, we're going to hop off," Lisa chimed in, breaking us from the moment, "It was lovely meeting you, Jacqueline."

"You, too." I waved awkwardly again while Leo finally tugged his apron over his head.

"Love you." Leo blew a kiss at the iPad, which his mothers reciprocated before he ended the call, "I was hoping to have all of this done before you got here. I apologize."

"Don't."

That warmth bloomed in my chest again. The warmth that only Leo had been capable of providing lately. The warmth that terrified me when I was alone, but a warmth that I looked forward to whenever we were together.

"Are you hungry?" Leo asked, tossing the apron aside so he could wrap both of his arms around me and give me a quick peck on the lips.

"Yes." I reached up to fist his t-shirt, making him come back for a deeper, wetter kiss.

"Excellent," Leo grinned against my lips, squeezing my waist with his hands and pulling away, "But you're still not getting any of my magic dick tonight, I'm afraid."

"Why not?" I asked, leaning a hip against the island while he donned oven mitts.

He paused his movement toward the oven, throwing me a hesitant look over his shoulder. I braced myself, crossing my arms over my chest as I waited for him to speak. He reached up to turn off the oven with his oven mitt, before releasing all the heat from the chamber. Once the potatoes were on the countertop, he removed his oven mitts and placed them in a drawer.

Letting the potatoes cool, he stepped closer to me.

And closer.

And closer.

His front was pressed against mine, and both of his hands gripped either side of the island near my hips. He towered over me, pressing a kiss to my forehead before he let his lips linger there. Leo inhaled, his chest expanding near my face as I uncrossed my arms to wrap them around his waist.

Holding him closer to me.

Waiting for his words.

After a painfully heavy silence, Leo finally spoke against my hair, "You're not just a warm body to me, Jacqueline."

I tucked my fingers underneath the hem of his shirt, his hot skin warming my cold knuckles. Using his body to heat my hands, even though he said he wouldn't use mine for such.

"What do you mean by that, exactly?" I asked. My voice was a nervous whisper, trapped between our two bodies. A conversation only meant for us.

Leo exhaled, his breath fanning over my messy bun, "I don't know, yet. What I do know, is that I have been looking forward to you coming over tonight. I wanted to impress you."

I squeezed him, lifting my head so my chin could rest between his pecks. He looked down at me, brushing one strand of my hair behind my ear, "Consider me impressed."

"Yeah?" He smiled, but it was smaller than normal.

"Very much so. Tell me more about your kisses." I bit my bottom lip, grinning.

His hand that tucked my hair behind my ear came forward to rest his thumb against my lip, pulling it free from my teeth, "I know you like snacking on a piece of chocolate after dinner. So I wanted to make you some."

That warmth from before was spreading inside of me.

"Thank you," I squeezed him to me again, "But full disclosure, I hate cooking. I don't see myself making you dinner anytime soon—but I'll think of something nice to do for you as well."

Leo rolled his eyes, "I'm not expecting some transaction from you, love." He leaned back to grip my waist and plop me on his kitchen island, "I just wanted to do this tonight. No need to read more into it than necessary."

I tucked my lips in between my teeth, "Are you sure?"

"Yes," Leo pressed his lips once more, lingering there, nipping my top lip once more, "If I feel otherwise, I'll tell you."

My shoulders relaxed, believing him, "Okay."

Leo chuckled before turning back to the potatoes, "Okay."

Chapter Twenty-One

JACQUELINE

It has been months since I saw him. I stood near Signe's desk, both of us getting ready for when we started the onboarding process for his first day. Signe was babbling about her most recent book developments, and any other day I would be curious to know how that was going. Today, I was barely holding it together.

The elevators finally dinged.

And there he was, stepping off with his leather jacket and backpack hanging on one shoulder.

Just as gut-wrenchingly beautiful as I remembered him.

So I frowned.

⁂

On Friday, exactly one week after the rave, I asked Leo to come over.

He didn't have time to knock before I flung my front door open, startling him before his handsome smile stretched across his face.

"Are you that excited to see me?" Leo asked, as he

291

wrapped his hands around my waist and pushed us back inside. He kicked my front door closed and immediately dropped his lips to my neck.

"Yes, but guess what," I closed my eyes and savored the feel of him wrapped around me like this. He kicked his shoes off without letting me go or removing his lips from my skin, "I'm getting a promotion."

"Yeah?" Leo leaned back to look at me, "To what?"

"Chief Human Resources Officer," I grinned up at him, running my hands up and down his chest, "CHRO." I still felt the residual anxiety in my body, but it was fading little by little. I made a trip to the sensory room right before my meeting with Brandon, and even though it ended up being nothing but good news, I visited the sensory room right after, too.

"No way," Leo's eyes lit up and he bent down to wrap me tighter, standing and twirling me in the entryway, "That's amazing, Jacqueline!"

"Churro, for short," I mumbled into his shoulder with a laugh, "The pay raise is insane."

"From what I know about Brandon, I'm not surprised," Leo chuckled, stepping into my kitchen and plopping me onto my small island, "You more than deserve it, love." He brought a hand up to cup my cheek, and I beamed up at him. He looked genuinely happy for me. I realized earlier that day that I was *excited* to tell him my news. I wasn't nervous about telling him, because he had given me no reason to be. Leo wasn't threatened by my job or what my goals were. He was supportive, as simple as that.

I rubbed a hand on my chest at the realization that I hadn't experienced a sexual relationship with someone who *also* supported me and encouraged me as Leo did.

Was that what a real grown-up relationship was supposed to be like?

But I didn't have that with Leo.

As far as either of us had spoken, we were just hooking up.

But the way Leo kissed me, stepping between my legs as I sat on my countertop, it felt like more. It wasn't a filthy kiss. It wasn't a kiss that would lead to more. This was an... appreciative kiss. A gentle one, and I responded to it the best I could.

I wanted to thank him for being so...perfect.

Because apparently, a man congratulating me on my promotion instead of feeling immediately threatened by it was the bar for me.

The bar for men is in hell, I recalled Signe's words from a brunch a while ago.

"I have something for you," Leo murmured against my lips before pulling away. He removed his bag from his shoulder and started unzipping it, "Do you like surprises?"

I winced, "Not particularly."

"Then keep your eyes open," he smirked as he dug around his bag, pulling out a small white box with clear plastic wrap over it, "These are for you," he announced, placing the box in my hands. His fingers wrapped around my thighs briefly as he stepped between my parted legs again. I felt relief with his return, missing his warmth for a couple of seconds when he stepped away to reach into his bag.

I felt the pinch in my brow form, before attempting to smooth it. I didn't want him to think I was upset about receiving a gift from him, but I was confused. Why was he giving me one? It wasn't my birthday, and he and I didn't have an anniversary to share.

I glanced up at Leo, already prepared to apologize for my frown, before he flipped the box over.

"You said your earbuds were old." Leo was smiling, excited. He wasn't turned off by my facial expression at all, "These are the highest-rated earbuds on the market today. They can also be noise canceling, either with or without music playing in them."

I sat there on my kitchen counter, frozen.

Holding the little white box with the small image of white earbuds on top.

My heart was racing in my chest.

I suddenly found it difficult to take an even breath.

Heat filled my cheeks.

"Also," Leo dug around in his backpack again, this time pulling out a larger white box. Same brand, same packaging, "These are the highest-rated headphones, in case you would prefer the feel of these instead of earbuds. I was thinking you could have a pair that stays stationary at your desk, and the earbuds could stay in your bag throughout the day. We could also get you a pair of headphones to have at home, if you'd like—"

My eyes were starting to burn around the edges, a lump was forming in my throat. He said home, not *my* home. Just home. Did he feel at home here? Was he just as happy to be here, as I was to have him here?

"—but no pressure. I figured you should try these two out and see if they work for you. If not, we can always return them and go back to the drawing board to find a brand that feels better. I understand that not all earbuds and headphones feel the same. I guess I wasn't sure which you'd like to prioritize: sound, clarity, or comfort. Which is why I just got you both."

He set the headphone box on the counter next to me,

gently removing the smaller box from my hands so he could tear the clear plastic off and open it up, "But we should try these out first since they're closest to what you're used to." His brow had a small pinch in it as he opened the box and removed all the fancy packaging. His clear blue eyes flicked toward my phone resting to the side on the counter, so he reached over to grab it. He held the camera toward my face to unlock the screen. My face, which was still frozen in shock.

Leo didn't react to my silence. He just kept going, giving me time to sit with my feelings.

Once my phone was properly paired with the earbuds, which he then renamed "Jacqueline's Earbuds," he set my phone down. With gentle, slow movements, he lifted his hand to push my hair out of the way, before delicately inserting the earbuds in my ears.

If anyone else touched me like this, my skin would crawl with the impulse to flinch away. But with him, I just held still, holding my breath while I anticipated his fingertips brushing against my skin.

The earbuds had those soft silicon tips, molding to my ear canal and immediately blocking excess white noise out.

My lips tugged up. My body and mind immediately felt more relaxed without the sound of my AC unit and refrigerator running.

Leo grinned, clocking my own grin immediately, "How do they feel?"

"Good," my voice croaked.

Leo nodded before grabbing my phone again and opening up one of my playlists. I could still hear him, but his voice was muted with the noise cancellation, "I think you're going to like the spatial audio, and how much more of the bass you'll feel."

He picked a song to test out.

"Party Rock Anthem" by *LMFAO* started playing.

The sound was perfect. I heard everything, and it sounded like the two artists were singing on either side of me. When the bass dropped, I could feel it in my body in a way I had been desperately trying to seek out with my old earbuds.

Leo's eyes kept bouncing between both of mine, studying me. Gauging my reaction.

After the song played for a minute, he finally asked, "Does it sound okay?"

I pressed my lips together, the corners still turned up, as I nodded my head.

"I can't hear it at all," Leo grinned, "The sound stays exactly where it's supposed to."

I sucked in a shaky breath. My heart was swelling, pressing on my lungs. I almost felt dizzy. I could almost hear the sound of blood rushing in my ears underneath the music. I thought I was going to pass out or burst into sobs.

Though I tried to hold them in, tears finally started to streak down my cheeks. My lips were pressed together so tightly that I was worried my teeth might puncture through them.

Once my tears finally made themselves known, Leo's gaze widened, "Oh, is it too loud?" He immediately reached forward, gently removing the earbuds and reintroducing the hum of my apartment. But his calm voice was clearer now, a trade-off I'd never hesitate to take.

"No." I swallowed, the lump in my throat made the movement almost painful. I lifted my hands to wipe at my cheeks.

"I'm so sorry," Leo shook his head before stepping between my legs, his hands came up to my cheeks, moving mine out of the way. His thumbs swiped away the moisture, "Did I do something wrong?"

"No," my reply was watery, holding in a sob, "I love it."

Leo's lips tipped up in the corner, "These are happy tears?"

I nodded, "So, painfully, disgustingly happy. Thank you." I sniffed, pulling out of his hold so I could swipe my own cheeks again. Leo stepped to the side to rip some paper towels off of the roll near the fridge and came back to hand it to me.

I wiped under my eyes, frowning at the smudged mascara there.

I tried to absorb the mascara and clean up my makeup around my eyes, before using the black-spotted paper towel to blow my nose.

Finally looking up at Leo again, I tried to plaster on a wide smile, "Do I look okay?"

Leo was studying me, both of his hands braced on either side of my legs on the counter. Inches separated us as he leaned closer, his gaze locked on me. I knew I wasn't the prettiest crier around, but I hoped it wasn't enough to turn him off.

I fucking hate it when you cry, Vincent would always tell me.

"You're stunning, Jacqueline," Leo replied, "...Did the gifts stress you out, though?"

He knew I didn't cry when I was sad. He knew I was an anxious crier. I cried when emotion felt overwhelming. When a lump formed in my throat and my chest felt tight. I had always accompanied those bodily signals with negative emotions. A suffocating emotion.

I did feel a little like I was suffocating right now, but not because of anything bad. I didn't feel negativity, sitting on my kitchen counter with Leo looking between my swollen eyes, red nose, red lips, and flushed cheeks.

I felt something a lot scarier.

Something too good to be true.

A feeling I didn't think I would ever have the ability to acknowledge again.

"Yes, but..." I thought about my words for a moment, desperate for him to understand, "In a good way, I think."

Leo smirked before leaning forward and pressing a kiss to my forehead. "I didn't want to snuff your excitement, but Brandon told Nicole and me about your promotion before we left. I wanted to celebrate your success, so I picked these up."

I sniffed, successfully fighting back another wave of tears.

"You didn't have to."

"I know," Leo lifted a shoulder before reaching for the box of headphones and tearing the clear plastic off, "But I wanted to. Let's try these next."

I inhaled a deep breath and nodded, feeling more in control now that I let my body release what it needed to.

I truly didn't deserve him.

Leo was a caring, wonderful, loving man.

But I didn't want to let him go, either.

Chapter Twenty-Two

LEO

THE FOLLOWING Monday I was securing my bag into the basket on the back of my bike with a big, stupid grin on my face.

Because I was excited to see Jacqueline today. We didn't get together again because of a rugby match, which Jacqueline was invited to but politely declined because Zaid was on my team, and she was still wanting to keep our relationship to ourselves. Then I had dinner with Mary and Jamie, followed by playing board games the rest of the night. It was only two days apart, but I was motivated to go into work as soon as possible just to see Jacqueline blush when she remembered what happened between us last night.

I pulled my phone out of my jeans to double-check our messages, because I couldn't stop looking at them.

Last night Jacqueline sent me a risqué selfie.

She was in a black lace bra and panty set, her face off-camera, as she lay in bed in the most mouthwatering pose. Underneath the image, she asked if I would be willing to take one for her.

Following her lead, and leaving my face out of the shot, I donned my motorcycle helmet and sent her an image back.

I was proud of my work. I put in effort so the lamp in my room cast flattering shadows over my lean muscles. I had some definition to show off for her. I angled the camera in a way I had seen many female boudoir photographers suggest for men who wanted to send their partners spicy, flattering, pictures.

It took a while, but I managed to set up the shot just how I wanted.

I sat in front of my standing mirror, looking like I was taking a casual selfie. Except I was shirtless, in loose sweatpants that didn't hide my erection from her, with one leg propped up suggestively. My head, with the motorcycle helmet on, was cocked to the side as I placed my hand dangerously close to the low, low band of my pants.

When Jacqueline received the picture, she immediately FaceTimed me.

Which proceeded to the hottest dual masturbation session of my life.

I was just admiring Jacqueline's picture when a woman's voice caught my attention.

"Leo Turner?" I lifted my head, locking my phone so no one else could see what I was drooling at before work. A blonde woman with a cream sweater and jeans was walking toward me, a curious look on her face.

"Hmm?" I asked.

She paused a couple of feet away from me, just outside of my building, to reach into her shoulder bag.

"Are you Leo Turner?" she asked.

"Yes." I tilted my head, wondering why anyone would need to approach me at seven in the morning.

She nodded, before removing a folder from her bag and handing it to me while saying, "You've been served."

Oh, fuck me.

"I HAVE a question for you and I apologize in advance for it." I was an anxious mess, the pen I snagged from my desk twirled around and around in my fingers. I didn't take a seat in Brandon's office, instead I paced back and forth. He studied me from his chair, his hands casually crossed over his chest as he furrowed his dark blonde brows.

"What is it?"

I gave him what I hoped was a charming, self-deprecating grin, before deciding to drop it with a shake of my head.

Charm wouldn't help me here.

"I messed up," I managed to get out, "I know that Sun Steer is sponsoring my visa while I go through the clusterfuck of American citizenship, but..." I pulled the file from my bag, showing him the papers discussing the assault charges that Vincent Lee was pressing against me.

"What is this?" Brandon asked, still not looking disappointed quite yet, but more confused.

"I need a lawyer. Not my immigration one," I rushed out, finally dropping my weight into a chair across from him. I didn't love going to my boss for something like this, but he was the one who got me a job here in the first place. It felt less scary going to the CEO of Sun Steer than Mary Jiang, who would rip me a new arsehole if she found out I had been in the States for less than a year and already had assault charges under my belt.

My mums didn't need to know about this, either.

"...Want to tell me why you're being charged for assault?" Brandon asked after going through the papers in the folder.

"It was self-defense." It was true, even though Vincent never stood a chance against me. Growing up in my specific area of South London, I learned how to fight bullies before I learned how to code in JAVA. In my neighborhood, being targeted by everyone and their mother for—*gasp*—having crushes on girls *and* boys in my class, I also had to learn how to end fights as quickly as they started.

If I was the toughest kid on the playground, nobody could shove my head in the toilets.

"I see," Brandon frowned, studying the papers, before scraping a hand down his face and pulling his mobile out, "Lucky for you, I know someone."

"Thank god." I sighed. Brandon gave me an unimpressed look before dialing and setting his phone to speaker.

It rang three times, with no answer.

Brandon rolled his eyes and dialed again, and this time someone answered on the second ring.

"Yeah?"

"Graham? You busy?" Brandon asked. I raised my eyebrows. I thought his brother was a farmer. Not a lawyer.

"Not at the moment," Graham grunted, and then a loud thud echoed over the speaker before he shifted the phone and his voice became clearer, "What's up?"

"I have a case for you," Brandon lifted his eyes to mine, and I fought the urge to shrink into my seat, "One of my employees is being charged with assault but needs someone to help him prove it was self-defense."

"Ah," Graham grunted again, and part of me wanted to ask what the hell he was doing, but I refrained, "Was there video footage of the incident?"

Brandon gave me a questioning look, so I leaned forward to respond, "I can ask the pub we were in. I'd be surprised if they didn't."

"Excellent, send me the details." Graham hung up the phone after that.

I gave Brandon a nervous look as I spun the pen right out of my hand. It flew across the room, smacking against his wall. I jumped out of my seat to retrieve it, before turning back to the CEO.

Brandon was just studying me, a blank expression on his face.

"I apologize," I scratched the side of my head with the cap of the pen, "I know this doesn't look good for me. Or you."

Brandon shrugged his shoulders, "Vincent probably deserved it."

I blinked at Brandon, "What? You know this prick?"

Brandon sighed and nodded, "He came here a few weeks after Jacqueline started." I widened my eyes in shock because I had no idea, "He heard I was interested in hiring employees from Blix and tried to convince me to hire him on. But he gave me an uneasy feeling," Brandon frowned, "I tend to trust my gut about these things."

I sat down in the chair again, my attention completely focused on the CEO, "I kindly turned him down. He wouldn't take no for an answer and kept emailing me. Even showed up a handful of times, inviting me out to lunch with him. As if I didn't have a full schedule." Brandon shook his head, "When I was following him out of the building, he noticed Jacqueline leaving the lot," I held my breath as Brandon leaned back in his chair and crossed his arms again, "Let's just say, he felt too comfortable voicing his thoughts about her in my presence. I told the building's security not to let him back on the premises. He then sent me a very colorful email letting me know what he thought of that."

"Jesus Christ." I leaned back in my chair, surprised to hear this from Brandon Moore of all people.

"I ended up reaching out to my connections at Blix, which filled me in on some unfortunate circumstances that, I assumed, led to Jacqueline being interviewed and hired here." Brandon raised an eyebrow, "What I want to know is, how *you* got involved with him."

The heat of embarrassment rushed under my skin before I realized that the answer to this question wasn't as scandalous as it could be.

"Jacqueline and I went to that new taco joint a couple of blocks away, for lunch," I jutted a thumb over my shoulder, probably in the entirely wrong direction, but whatever, "He saw her there and started saying some crude things about her."

"Not surprised," Brandon chimed in, a frown pulling at his lips.

"I told him to sod off—then he threw the first punch," I rushed to say, because for some reason that detail felt important, "Though, I threw the last. I didn't realize it would knock him on his arse...but I wasn't upset about it, either."

Brandon nodded, his eyes landing on the stack of papers on his desk.

"I never told Jacqueline that Vincent came here after she was hired," Brandon pressed his lips together in thought, "I didn't think it was worth mentioning. There's a reason we promoted her to CHRO, we don't want to lose her. However..." Brandon sighed and rested his elbows on his desk, a pinch forming in his brow, "I'm wondering if we should tell her about this."

"This," I pointed to my assault charges, "I don't think she needs to concern herself with. This is between me and him. Her name isn't anywhere on these documents. I checked."

Brandon nodded, "I'll check in with building security to make sure he's still not allowed on the premises. It's not a good thing that he's still so bitter years later. A man who is willing to hold a grudge for that long is probably dangerous."

I agreed. It made me sick to my stomach, but I also didn't want to ruin Jacqueline's day with drama from her ex-boyfriend. I didn't want my assault charges to give her any reason not to keep seeing me the way I wanted to keep seeing her.

Perhaps it wasn't fair to keep her in the dark.

He was her ex-boyfriend, after all.

But I wasn't a perfect man by any means, so I decided I would tell her about it after it was all taken care of.

A WEEK LATER, I met Graham Moore in person.

And the lad was fucking fit.

Brandon gave me Graham's number after I approached him in his office, and Graham and I have been in contact since. Thankfully, the pub did have video footage of that night and was very happy to hand it over for our case. They also had statements from employees working that day who had already dealt with Vincent's volatile behavior before Jacqueline and I showed up.

"As you can see, it's a reach to try to call what happened, assault. It's in your best interest to drop these." Graham didn't take a seat at the conference table. We weren't meeting in Sun Steer's building; we were meeting two buildings over on the same campus, where Vincent was allowed to go. The four of us sat in the otherwise empty conference room, where Vincent glared at me from across the table, next to his lawyer. His face looked healed, minus the tiniest scar on his cheek from when my fist broke his skin.

"But—" Vincent spoke up, but his lawyer lifted a hand as she spoke over him. He tensed at the action; a vein started to bulge in his neck right when she started to speak.

"My client and I would like a moment to discuss, if you wouldn't mind." She glared at Vincent, properly annoyed at the inconvenience this arsehole was causing everyone.

In response, he pounded his fist on the table in irritation and glared at me.

His lawyer jumped from the motion but straightened her posture as she frowned at him.

"Of course." Graham turned his massive frame toward the doorway, keeping a wary eye on Vincent, and I followed him out. I had an inch or two on him, but the bloke was solid muscle. It was like looking at a rugged, beefy, cowboy version of Brandon. With a full blonde beard.

"Do you think they'll drop the charges?" I asked my new friend and lawyer in a low voice. Graham removed his cowboy hat—because he wore a fucking cowboy hat to this —and brushed his hair back before placing it back on his head. He glanced over his shoulder, keeping his gaze where we could see Vincent and his lawyer bickering with low voices. Based on the way Vincent's face reddened and his nostrils flared, I'd say things were looking good for me.

His lawyer, though, was clearly on her last straw. Vincent pounded both of his fists on the table before hissing something between his teeth at her, and she responded by shaking her head and gathering her things, refusing to look at him.

"They'll drop them," Graham murmured, "I don't know how good you are at reading body language, but that woman fucking loathes him." Then he pulled out a small black box, no bigger than the palm of his hand, brought it to his lips, and inhaled.

My lawyer had just taken a hit of a vape pen.

Welcome to California.

"I managed to pick up on those not-too-subtle signals, yes," I leaned against the wall, keeping our conversation low so our voices didn't echo across the lobby, "Could you do me a solid and connect with my immigration lawyer? I don't want this to fuck with any of that."

Graham winced, before lifting a massive shoulder in a casual shrug, "I would hope it wouldn't, since you weren't at fault here. But I'll see what I can do."

"Thanks, mate." I clapped him on the shoulder.

He nodded, and took another hit of his pen, before pocketing it.

Fucking legend.

The doors to the conference room burst open, and Vincent stomped toward the two of us with his hands balled into fists. Graham and I immediately straightened our postures, and in response, Vincent halted his approach. He huffed through his flaring nostrils, and his narrowed eyes bounced in contemplation between Graham and me.

I was in disbelief that this man was clearly considering starting another physical altercation with me.

Seconds after being humbled by our lawyers.

Vincent shook his head once and spat on the ground, before shoving his hands in his pockets and turning toward the exit. I was so shocked by the insanity of his behavior that I chuckled, loud enough for Vincent to glare at me over his shoulder, letting me know he did *not* find any of this amusing. His shoulders were scrunched high enough to almost cover his ears as he stormed out of the building.

Moments later, his lawyer stepped into the lobby and approached us, "My client has decided that all charges will be dropped," she held her hand out for Graham and me to shake, "I'll send everything to the address here?" She held a piece of paper, and when Graham double-checked the address, he nodded his confirmation. Then she nodded her head and followed her client out of the lobby.

Then I buckled over, with my hands supporting my weight on my knees, as I wheezed through my relief.

"Oi, I could kiss you on the mouth," I gasped, as I stood tall again.

Graham lifted an unimpressed blonde brow, reminding me so much of his brother, "I'd rather you just pay me like everyone else."

"If you insist." I nodded, wrapping him up in a hug.

Graham grunted, patting his rough palm on my back twice, and pulled away.

"Are you excited about the new equipment being built for your property?" I asked as we exited the building to walk through the courtyard.

"Huh?" Graham was checking his phone now, his Timberland boots thudding loudly with each step he took, "Oh, yeah. Super thrilled."

I snorted, "So that's a no."

"What do you mean?" Graham's voice was laced with thick sarcasm, "It's not like every movie ever has specifically warned society about what happens when you give computers too much power."

I threw my head back and laughed, "Are you worried the tractor will run off with all your produce?"

His lips quirked under his thick facial hair, "I can barely check my email. Why Brandon thinks I can launch his fancy new tech for his fancy company, is beyond me."

"Well, that's why we are sending an engineer to you. To help with the transition. It's a learning process." I saw a flash of blue out of the corner of my eye, and grinned.

Speak of the devil.

"Hi Vi—" She bulldozed between the two of us, her phone to her ear and her bag clutched in her hands as she sprinted towards the car park. She was rambling something about waiting until she got there, and I shook my head.

I'd check in with her another time.

Graham grunted, and when I turned to look at him, he was holding his side, "Small thing knows how to work through a crowd." He lifted his flannel shirt as if to check for injuries, and I laughed again.

"Are you coming up?" I asked my lawyer.

"Sure, I want to say hi to Brandon." He pulled his shirt back down, threw a puzzled look over his shoulder, and shook his head before following me into Sun Steer's building.

Chapter Twenty-Three

LEO

IF I THOUGHT her loose black skirt was distracting that night we met at the bar, I was in for a rude awakening for when I first saw her in a pencil skirt.

It was probably the longest first day of work I'd ever had in my entire life.

———————

"GOOD MORNING!"

I glanced over my shoulder, seeing Violet jogging to meet up with me.

"Morning," I nodded before waiting for her to fall into step, "How was your weekend?"

Violet sighed, "Good, but I'm exhausted. My daughter is going through another sleep regression."

Today I learned that Violet had a daughter, "I'm sorry to hear that."

"It's alright. I'm just worried about relocating so soon." I nodded, suddenly distracted from our conversation at the sight of Jacqueline stepping into Brandon's office, where Violet and I were currently headed.

Jacqueline didn't notice me, which made me want to run up to her and wrap her in my arms until she did, but I refrained.

"Change is already so hard for her, but everyone has been so supportive about preparing me and her to move up north." Ah, yes, Violet was getting ready to move to Moore Farms in a few weeks. She could have had the opportunity to meet Graham Moore in person a few days ago, considering they'd likely be neighbors. But instead, she elbowed him out of her way to rush to her car.

They'd meet eventually.

That was probably why she was joining us for our bi-monthly check-in. Brandon hosted these in his office, and even though they were mandatory, he was excellent at making sure we didn't take up more time than needed. If there were no questions or updates from any department, he excused us.

Brandon was quiet, introverted, and short with his words.

But he was a great CEO.

We finally entered his space, and when Violet spotted Nicole, slouched on Brandon's couch, she made her way to sit next to her. So I not so subtly stood near Jacqueline. Against the wall, waiting for Brandon to show up.

Jacqueline was staring at Nicole, a pinch in her brow as if she was deep in thought. She didn't acknowledge my presence yet. I wasn't expecting a hug or kiss, but for her to not notice me at all let me know how focused she was.

"Are you alright?" I asked, my voice low.

"Hmm?" Jacqueline glanced up at me, clearly distracted by whatever she was thinking about. I saw in real time how her brown eyes studied my face, doing the quickest scan of my concerned expression. After assessing whatever she found, she pulled her lips back into a smile.

It looked forced; the smile tight. It didn't reach her eyes because the delicate lines that crinkled the corners of her lids were missing.

I hated it.

"I'm good," Jacqueline replied through her grin, "Just tired."

"Don't do that," I spoke without overthinking the intensity of my tone.

Jacqueline stiffened at my side for a moment, her smile slipping a degree as a pinch formed between her perfectly groomed eyebrows, "What do you mean?"

"Don't give me a smile I didn't earn, Jacqueline." I glanced around the room, ensuring none of our coworkers were paying attention to this conversation between the two of us.

Jacqueline blinked at me, before pushing her glasses up on the bridge of her nose some more.

"I just wanted to show you that I'm okay," her voice was soft.

I tried my best to soften my voice as well, I didn't want her to think I was upset at her, "I appreciate that," I inhaled, attempting to find the correct words to explain myself, "But I am not interested in any fake smiles from you."

Jacqueline's grin slowly, slowly dropped. Her lips were relaxed in that natural downturn that I was growing to love more every day. Sometimes, when she was smiling at something I did at work but didn't want to seem too obvious about it, her lips would still turn downward. Creating her upside-down smile. But it still counted because her eyes crinkled. Sometimes she would blush and release a huff of laughter as well.

"...I know that when I'm not smiling, I look mad," Jacqueline was whispering to me now as she took her turn to scan the office that we stood in the back of, "If I don't smile, people assume I am upset at them when I'm not."

"Okay," I lifted a shoulder, "But you don't have to do that with me."

She lifted a brow at me, "I don't need to smile around you?"

I shook my head, "Not if you don't feel like it."

She stared at me, unblinking. I could practically see the wheels turning in her head. The confusion made her lips part the slightest bit. I wanted to bend down and take her plump bottom lip in between mine, but alas, we were standing in Brandon's office.

"If you tell me that you're okay, I'm trusting you to tell me the truth." I nudged her arm with my elbow, a casual touch. It was the only contact I could get away with during the workday, "You don't need to force a smile for me. I would much rather wait until I earned a real one. Besides," I glanced up from where I bumped our arms to meet her gaze, an attempt to show just how serious I was, "Your smile is beautiful, but so is your relaxed expression. Your frowns. Even your glares." Jacqueline's breathing staggered a bit at my words, but I never broke eye contact with her, "You don't need to put on a mask with me. I want to see you. All of you."

When I saw her tuck both lips between her teeth, I threw her a grin and broke eye contact. I crossed my arms in an attempt to still my hands that ached to pull her into me. To hold her against me. But I couldn't, because Brandon was standing just outside his office door, finishing up a discussion with Zaid.

The meeting was going to start, and Jacqueline and I were still a secret.

———

Jacqueline: I want you.

I GRINNED AT MY PHONE, before leaning back in my desk chair and thumbing out a reply.

Me: That's good, because I need you.

I didn't set my cell down; I watched those three little dots appear as she typed her response. Nothing else mattered. The code Mary sent me was meaningless. The meetings I had later in the week were not important.

Jacqueline was texting me during the workday.

She was my priority now.

Jacqueline: I can't focus on anything. It's been forever since you touched me, and I want you so badly.

I smirked, fucking thrilled with her direct communication about her needs.

Me: I like this. You, distracted in your office, thinking of how much you want me.

The three dots danced and disappeared.

Then they appeared again, before stopping again.

I twirled a pen between my fingers and held my phone in the other, my eyes glued to my screen. I hoped to god she'd respond. Keep the conversation going. There was no chance in hell I could easily focus back on my tasks.

Minutes passed.

Suddenly, she responded.

But it was a voice message. I hadn't ever received one from her before. I immediately pressed play, glancing up to ensure my office door was, indeed, closed. I lowered the volume on my cell, but crouched close so I could hear everything.

"I'm serious, Mr. Turner," Jacqueline's voice was a low whisper. I pictured her holding the mobile up to her luscious lips as she recorded this, "I don't think I can wait any longer. I'm *aching*...maybe...no, I really shouldn't..." I was holding my breath, because I could hear how aroused she was. How her voice gained a raspy, low edge to it.

We were both at work, I could hear Brandon's muffled voice talking during his meeting through the shared wall of our offices.

And there was still a decent amount left of her recording as she breathed through her pause, "...Maybe if I just...yeah —" the sound of shuffling and a zipper being undone made my pulse spike, my chest and groin heated, and a flush bloomed across my cheeks. I glanced at my closed office door again, *was Jacqueline really about to—* "Oh my god, I shouldn't be doing this. But I can't—oh my god, Leo...*Oh...*"

I was rock hard, my cock pressing against my zipper painfully as I focused in on the sounds of a repetitive motion, like a hand moving back and forth.

I glanced at the time at the top of my cell; it was 4:37 pm.

"...Yes, yes, god what have you done to me, Leo?" *I don't fucking know but don't you dare stop,* "This is so wrong. I shouldn't be touching myself like this—but I can't..." A low moan from her ended the voice recording, and I practically knocked my chair over from how fast I stood from my desk. My chair was probably still spinning by the time I reached my office door and scoured the space between our respective offices.

No one was loitering around. Jacqueline's employees were probably gone already. Brandon was still deep in his meeting that I knew would last at least another hour.

Nicole had left early today, as she usually did.

I marched across the hall and threw Jacqueline's office door open before catching it, and gently pushing it shut.

Jacqueline jolted at her desk, standing as she saw me barge into her space.

She placed a hand over her chest, "Christ, you scared—"

"Come here," I interrupted her. I leaned my back against her closed office door, not sure if I could control myself.

Jacqueline's lips parted, and even though her cheeks were already rosey, I saw them darken some more from across the room.

"What?" Jacqueline breathed. I saw her hand shift, reaching down for the undone zipper at the side of her skirt, pinching it between her fingers. She pulled it up an inch before I pointed a finger at her hand.

"Don't you dare zip that up," my voice was low, quiet enough that no one could hear me from the other side of the door. There was a window right next to the frame, allowing anyone in the hallway to look inside. Which was why it was so important for Jacqueline to come to me, before I lost control.

"R-really?" Jacqueline asked. Her chest was heaving, and her hand froze. A sliver of her thigh was revealed from her undone skirt. I could still hear the sound of her unzipping it in her voice message. I was about three seconds from charging across the room.

"I'm fully serious. C'mere, Ms. Williams." I pointed to my feet, holding her gaze with mine. I held unwavering eye contact with her, and she swallowed.

I almost shouted with joy when she slowly moved around her desk.

She was nervous, but just as desperate as I was.

Eventually, after a painful amount of time, Jacqueline stood directly in front of me. She held her pencil skirt up with one hand, biting her lip as her gaze dropped to the window next to me.

Well, I could fix that issue.

I grabbed her hips and turned, pressing her back against her office door as I stepped forward to crowd her space.

"Oh—" I cut her off, not a single kind or gentle muscle in my body. My tongue invaded her lips, taking everything. She ground into me, her hands gripping either side of my neck as she struggled to meet my kiss. To duel with me. To kiss me back as heavily as I was kissing her.

Jacqueline Williams could ruin me, and I wasn't sure she had any idea.

"Did you come?" I asked against her mouth.

"N-no," Jacqueline whispered, before biting my bottom lip. She traced her tongue over it, her teeth a gentle hold. I moaned, before grinding my erection against the apex of her thighs. Her skirt and my jeans created a thick barrier between us, but I didn't care. I knew she could still feel me. Feel what she did to me.

"You're going to," I responded, "You're not allowed to do any more work until you do."

"W-we shouldn't," Jacqueline panted. But she gripped me tighter and met my own thrusts with hers.

"I don't care." I dropped my lips to her jaw, kissing and sucking on her delicious skin. I was ravenous. A man starved, and the only thing that could satiate my craving was Jacqueline's body, "Get ready."

"Oh god," Jacqueline wheezed, and I smirked against her jaw before sucking a little harder than normal, "You're going to give me a hickey."

"Mhmm," I sucked again, and she leaned into me, "Seems only fair since all the blood in my body is rubbing between your legs at the moment."

Jacquline sighed, shifting on her toes in an attempt to get the bulge from my shaft where she needed it. I lifted my hands, my touch against her skin bold as I finally found the lacy cups of her bra.

"I don't care how you come, Jacqueline," I murmured against her neck, "I'm going to touch you. I'm going to play with you. I'm going to keep doing so until you come. I'm not going to stop." I grinned when she whimpered, knowing that my thumbs gently flicking over her taut nipples were quite possibly enough to tip her over the edge, "Not even if someone knocks on this door. Right now, you're mine until you're soaked." I lowered my voice with a growl on the last word, knowing that, for some reason, she melted from it.

My strong, bossy, independent Jacqueline liked it when my voice was rough and demanding.

"Okay," she panted, making my blood sing. God, nothing made me feel more powerful than feeling her turn to putty in my hands. Gasping from my touch. Knowing that I was the only man who got to see her like this. The only man who ever saw her like this.

"I could play with your perfect tits all day." I pinched her nipples once, making her head lean back against the door. She was still in too much control because she didn't let her head thud against it. She held the movement so it wouldn't make noise, so it wouldn't call attention to anyone potentially out in the hallway, "How wet are you, Jacqueline?" I didn't expect her to actually answer. Instead, I released one breast while I trailed the back of my fingers down her stomach, letting my knuckles tease her until I got to the loose, unzipped waistband of her skirt.

It took no effort to tuck underneath the material to find her completely bare.

"Fuck, you planned for this," I accused, biting her earlobe just enough to send a shiver down her body. Feeling the tremble made my cock throb, but I knew I probably wouldn't find release like her, "You like the idea of me touching you in the office."

"Yeah." Jacqueline admitted, her eyes were squeezed closed and her hands were braced on my shoulders, tensing their grip as I traced a knuckle against her center.

Jesus, she was so fucking wet.

"You feel bloody divine," I moaned against her neck, mindful enough to keep my voice quiet, "You feel like *mine*."

Jacqueline whispered back, "Only yours, Leo."

I was grinding against her thigh, unable to help myself. Eventually, my fingers were soaked, making it easier to bring her to the edge. I barely dipped my middle finger inside, gently curling as my palm worked against her wet clit.

Her hips were rolling against my hand, doing half the work.

Removing my other hand from under her shirt, I decided to cup my fingers behind her neck. Holding her to me as I ground my erection against her thigh, using the door for support. I was mad, lust consuming my thoughts as she panted hot breaths over the skin of my ear. My neck. Her fingers dug into my shoulders, painful enough to turn pleasurable with each grind of her hips against my hand.

"I could do this all day, Jacqueline." I wasn't lying. I

wasn't going to last much longer, but I'll be damned if I stopped touching her, "I could play with your soft, pretty cunt for hours. Until the sun goes down. Until you've come so hard, so many times, you pass out from exhaustion."

"Please, please," Jacqueline whispered against my neck.

"Up to you, love," I whispered back, "I'm just enjoying myself. You come when you want to."

"*Shit*," Jacqueline buried her face in the space between my neck and shoulder, and I groaned from the satisfaction of feeling her start to flutter around my fingers. I slowly inserted another, taking my time to tease her just how she liked.

"I love how you tried to tease me," I spoke against her hair, her bun that was becoming more disheveled with each movement, "As if I wouldn't immediately make you pay for it."

"Leo, please." She sucked on my shoulder in an attempt to stifle her moans, and I prayed to anyone, anything listening to *please let Jacqueline leave her mark on me*.

I hummed against her, slowly dragging my fingers into the bottom of her hairline as I started to feel a white-hot pleasure zing down my spine. Shooting up from the backs of my knees.

"You're going to make me come like this, Jacqueline," I whispered, "That's what you do to me. You make me unable to control myself. *Fuck*."

Jacqueline's entire body stiffened, and her inner walls started to flutter erratically before clamping down on my fingers. She was so tight that I almost couldn't continue to draw out her orgasm. I prevailed, though, sliding them in and out of her just like my cock would, when she tipped over the edge. Grinding my palm against her clit.

Jacqueline whined in my ear as she came, the sound

intimate and desperate, and that's when I groaned into her shoulder and accepted my fate.

I spilled in my pants.

Just like I said I would.

And I had no regrets.

Chapter Twenty-Four

JACQUELINE

"Can I call you Jackie?"

"I'd prefer if you didn't."

"Jack?"

"No."

"Hmm, Jacqueline it is then," he smiled before bracing my shoulders and pushing me onto my back.

When I was a child, I struggled with (what I would later learn is called) self-injurious behaviors. This wasn't behavior designed to harm myself. It was behavior that I practiced in an attempt to regulate my body when I was feeling very, very dysregulated. But the behavior still wasn't safe. It didn't happen often, because I quickly learned how problematic it was. I already felt weird, and alien around my peers. I didn't want them to see me do these things and find another reason I was different. I only had a handful of memories of these behaviors. Memories that stuck with me because of the big reactions I received when other adults saw me do it.

One time, we couldn't have been much older than five or six, Marco was chasing me around our house. I remembered turning a corner, cackling loudly, feeling adrenaline course through my body when I had accidentally bumped into a housecleaner and spilled her bucket of dirty water all over the floor. It soaked me as well.

Marco, being a typical brother, pointed at me and laughed.

The house cleaner scolded me, instructing that I help her clean it up.

But I didn't want to stop and help. I knew I *should*. I knew how to clean up messes. I know that helping her clean it up was the right thing to do. But I still had energy buzzing in my veins. I wanted to *run*. I wanted Marco to keep chasing me. I needed to release the pent-up energy itching in my arms and legs and stomach.

So I lifted my forearm to my mouth and bit down, and my insides started to feel better. All the focus and restlessness buzzing inside of me suddenly had an outlet as I dug my teeth into my skin hard enough to leave a bruise, but not hard enough to break it.

Marco wasn't surprised, because he'd seen this from me before. The housecleaner, however, gasped and quickly pulled my arm from my mouth. Her reaction was so big, so frightening, so *concerned* for me, that it was then that I learned that biting myself wasn't socially acceptable.

Marco ended up helping us clean up the mess.

I ended up biting my arm only when I was alone and no one would see me do it.

Later, our father was lecturing us before school. I guess

Marco had been disruptive in class and was trying to use me as an example of how to behave. We were both slouching at the kitchen table, Marco resting his head on his crossed arms, me with my hands in my lap and my chin resting on the wood.

Our father always demanded eye contact whenever he spoke to us, so while I understood what was happening, all of my energy was focused on staring at our father. Not looking away. Not getting distracted. It was why I was deemed "good" in school because I had mastered how to make it look like I was paying attention when really every muscle in my body was trembling with the need to escape.

My dad raised his voice, snapping his fingers in front of Marco's face to get his attention.

So I pressed my chin against the wood.

It felt good, it was grounding me. I felt more in control.

I dug even harder, slowly adding more pressure as my dad went on and on about proper classroom behavior.

Finally, the wood cracked underneath my face.

I had a bruise on my chin for a few days.

And the memory of my father's scream that I could still hear to this day.

It had been a while since I had behaved that way, but today, I was reminded of it. Why I did those things as a young girl.

Mary knocked on the doorframe of Leo's office before poking her head in and asking, "Can I interrupt?"

I nodded and took a seat on Leo's leather couch that was up against the wall, throwing Mary a smile as she let herself in. Leo and I were chatting about the emails I was about to send to a couple of engineers, offering them unscheduled bonuses. Pizza parties were great, but upper management at Sun Steer Technologies understood that nothing expressed employee appreciation more than money.

My mood was so elevated lately. I caught myself smiling more and more, and I knew others could see it too.

I'd heard talk, when I walked past the break room, from employees saying, "The ice queen seems to be melting."

I didn't hear those words and feel offended, because they weren't exactly wrong.

"I need to talk to you about the file Zaid just forwarded us." Mary held her laptop in her hands, a dramatic frown on her lips as she stood in front of Leo's desk. He leaned back and rested both of his hands behind his head as he addressed his cousin.

"What about it?"

"First, I fucking hate Excel," Mary started with.

"Language," I sighed, as I added another note to my iPad. I was not as concerned about language as I used to be, but it was a habit to say something at this point.

"Sorry," Mary threw over her shoulder, before turning back to Leo, "There are over three hundred and fifty million rows on this thing."

"So there is." Leo grinned at Mary.

"Second, I know no one has ever told you this before," Mary's tone was so dry that even I could pick up on the comedic one-liner incoming, "But it's too big."

I snorted, scrolling on my iPad as I murmured, "That's not true."

And then my heart stopped before it jumped into my throat.

My hand froze over my iPad.

I glanced up as my eyes widened, petrified.

Mary was staring back at me with her own set of wide, horrified eyes.

Leo's jaw was practically on the floor as he gaped at me.

"Oh god," I set my iPad on my lap as the flames of embarrassment scorched my cheeks, "I mean—"

"Oh my *god!*" Mary's head swiveled as she darted her gaze between the two of us, "Did you just—" I stood, letting my iPad fall to the couch cushion next to me. I didn't know what to do with my hands, which were suddenly moist. My heart finally kickstarted again, and embarrassment flooded my body. Sand was rushing in my ears. My breaths were becoming shorter and shorter.

I looked towards Leo, hoping he understood that I was so, so apologetic.

Everything was officially fucked.

You just messed everything up.

He's so pissed at you.

Leo stood from his desk, clear eyes still wide and a light dusting of color forming on his cheeks, "Mary, calm down—"

Mary set her laptop down on his desk before pointing an accusing finger at me, "Are you implying that you—you know what his—" her finger pointed to Leo, who just laughed with a roll of his eyes, making Mary's widen even more as she clutched her hands into her hair, "*Oh my god!*"

My lungs were shrinking, my heart was starting to hurt. That stupid lump in my throat was forming. I tried to relieve the pressure, using my own hands to push on my chest and stomach. When that didn't work, I balled my hand into a fist and hit my chest once. Twice.

The movement caught Leo's eye, "Jacqueline? Breathe." He started to walk around his desk, but I stared at Mary, whose expression still looked appalled.

She ignored Leo stepping around her as she hissed at me, "Are you really telling me you *slept* with my cousin? What the fuck is wrong with you?"

Shit, shit, shit.

Everything is ruined.

You can't fix this.

Before Leo got any closer, I bolted.

I wasn't running, but I knew how to speed-walk out of a situation like a pro.

"Bloody hell." I heard Leo's curse right as I left his office. I was sweating. My vision was tunneling. I didn't try to mold my face into anything. Focusing on getting to the sensory room was my first priority. I had to make it there.

"Hi, Jac—oh," Violet's voice brushed past me. I didn't wave, I didn't acknowledge how she also seemed to greet Leo.

Nicole was just walking around the corner, and I almost stumbled into her.

"Whoa, are you okay?" Nicole asked, bracing both of my arms to avoid a collision. I shook my head and kept going, ignoring her protest as I finally, *finally*, made it.

I flung the door open, stepped inside, and pushed it shut behind me before flipping on the diffuser.

A thud echoed in the room when there should have been a latch catching, and suddenly Leo's voice was trapped in the space with me, "Jacqueline, breathe."

I shook my head at him. I didn't need to breathe. I needed to stop. Stop everything. Stop thinking. Stop seeing Mary's look of betrayal over and over and over in my mind. I needed to peel out of my skin and scoop out all the unease boiling in my stomach. I didn't remember pulling out the throw blankets and falling onto the pile of bean bags, but once my body made contact, I finally attempted to inhale a full breath.

"Jacqueline—" that was Mary's voice.

I balled my hands into fists again, pushing them against my head as hard as I could handle it.

"Fuck off, Mary," that was Leo's voice. His large hands were pulling me off of the bean bags. I was shaking, tears streaming down my cheeks as I shook my head. It was the only form of protest I could manage, but Leo ignored me.

In a blink, I was rewrapped in the soft blanket, but my back was against Leo's front. His feet planted on the ground while his long legs bent on either side of me, creating a cage. His long arms were wrapped around me, and Leo's grip on my forearms locked me against him. His head was bent forward, his cheek rested against my head as he settled me between his legs.

"Breathe, love," Leo instructed.

I gasped through a breath, letting my tears soak the fluffy material of the throw blanket. My fists were still tightly pressed against my head.

"Jacqueline, it's okay—" Mary started again, crouching next to us. I didn't hear her shut us all in here, but I couldn't find it in me to be upset. I didn't know what to do.

"I'm so sorry—" I panted, embracing the tight squeeze Leo's arms gave me, "I'm so sorry. I'm sorr—"

"Stop it," Leo interrupted, "You're safe. No one else is upset."

"Well," Mary tilted her head back and forth, "I have some feelings about this."

"I don't give a fuck about your feelings," Leo snapped, "Get out of here."

"Fuck you," Mary flipped him off.

"I'm sorry," I whispered again, my breathing slowly coming back to me. Slowly, it was still a struggle.

"Shh." Leo squeezed his legs around me. I almost, almost forgot we were at work, had Mary not been crouching next to us. She studied us with her dark eyes and red lips turned downward.

Every time I tried to speak up, Leo shushed me, flexing his limbs to squeeze around me again.

Time passed in a way I couldn't keep up with. I had no concept of what time it was while I struggled to regulate my meltdown, but I knew that at some point I had closed my eyes. I focused on the feel of Leo's heartbeat against my back, his chest expanding against me, his arms locked around me, his legs squeezing me, because it helped.

Leo didn't have to help me, but he did.

I finally opened my eyes, to see Mary sitting cross-legged on the floor.

Her face wasn't as hard, but she still didn't look happy.

My heart sank a bit more at her expression.

"I messed up," I finally whispered.

"You didn't," Leo insisted.

The three of us sat in heavy silence before Mary broke it with a gentle voice.

"How are you feeling?"

I lifted a shoulder under the blankets, relieved when Leo didn't loosen his hold on me from the movement, "Better." My hands lowered from my head, awkwardly loose underneath the band of Leo's arms.

Mary nodded; her fingers folded in her lap as she pressed her lips together.

Then she snorted.

I jumped because it caught me off guard. The room was silent, minus the hum of the diffuser.

Then she snorted again, before slapping a hand over her mouth.

"Are you—?"

"I can't believe you slept with my cousin!" Mary lowered

her voice, but she was smiling now. I had no idea how to react to this change of mood. I thought she was upset with me, but she was smiling. Holding in laughter as her shoulders shook. Eventually, she looked up at the ceiling in a way that reminded me of Leo.

"Sod off," Leo grunted behind me, pressing his cheek against my head.

We were at the office, but he was showing physical affection toward me.

I couldn't find it in myself to pull away.

My body needed what he was providing me right now.

My heart did, too.

"You're never allowed to scold me for cussing again."

I frowned at her, "What? Why?"

Mary raised her eyebrows, resting her hands on her knees as she arched toward me, "Because you're *fucking* my cousin. You don't get to break girl code, and then sit back on your high horse and scold me for dropping some colorful language on occasion."

I parted my lips, dread filling my chest from her words, "I broke girl code?"

I really was the worst.

Mary nodded, her dark eyes studying me with an intensity I didn't know what to do with, "But don't worry, I forgive you. Because I'm a good person, and you're both consenting adults."

"This is none of your business," Leo spoke, though his tone was less grumbly.

"She's the one who offered the information." Mary pointed an accusing finger at me again.

"I didn't think—I shouldn't have—"

"Shh," Leo lifted one of his hands to cover my mouth, "I

don't care if Mary knows about us. I'm not upset by your slip of the tongue."

I furrowed my brows, before nodding behind his hand.

"Especially because she gets your slip of the tongue—"

"—*Mary*," Leo scolded, but I could tell by the way his chest shook behind me that he was holding in a laugh.

Muscles that were clenched tight in my body were starting to loosen, one by one. It was a gradual adjustment, regaining control and ease in my limbs. Instead of pulling away, and getting myself together, I found myself slouching against Leo some more.

Mary studied the two of us, lifting her legs and wrapping her arms around her knees, "Does anyone else know?"

I shook my head.

"How long has this been going on?"

I sighed, lifting the covers to hide my face in them.

Leo adjusted a bit, pulling me closer to him, "It's complicated."

"Okay," Mary rolled her eyes, "When was the first time you..." She inserted her index finger between a circle created with her other index finger and thumb.

I snorted, adrenaline still coursing through me. But my body was suddenly so exhausted from the attack I had just taken on, that I felt almost loopy.

Mary knew.

Leo was cuddling me in the middle of the office.

Nothing mattered anymore.

"Before he was interviewed."

Mary's eyes practically bulged out of their sockets, "Pardon?"

"We met the night before my interview with her and Signe," Leo added, I felt him lean his cheek away from me, a thud indicating that he was now resting his head against the wall he was sitting against, "But then I got hired, and we kept things strictly professional."

I rolled my eyes, "Until a few months ago when he bent me over—" *Wait, no, I probably shouldn't say that to Leo's cousin*. I cut myself off a moment too late, because Mary screeched, pulling her black sweater up over her head to hide from my words. It was comical, making me laugh as she pretended to gag underneath the collar of her sweater.

Leo was holding back his laughter again as his voice dropped near my ear, "She doesn't need to know those kinds of details."

I blushed, thoroughly embarrassed, "Sorry."

I was ass at navigating basic social settings, I had no clue how to handle a conversation that included Leo's cousin asking us *some* details about our sex life, but not wanting to know others.

Randomly, I thought about Mariam's reaction when I eventually updated her on this particular development in my life.

"Is it serious?" was Mary's next question, muffled by her sweater as she revealed her eyes to us.

I shrugged, my brain unwilling to process more for that question. Leo cleared his throat before managing to get out, "Haven't gotten that far."

"Ah," Mary nodded.

Something buzzed on the ground, and as Leo shifted to pull his phone out from his pocket, I made my way to sit up so that he could. Without speaking, he tightened his other arm around me, keeping me there.

"I have a meeting in thirty minutes," Leo murmured.

"I should get up."

"You don't have to," Mary was starting to stand up though, "Take a beat." As she finally got to her feet, she hesitated. Mary tapped her fingers on her pant leg for a moment, debating on something.

Then she lifted her head to look at me, "I'm not upset. I was shocked at first, and I think a little hurt. I don't like feeling left out of the loop...but I shouldn't have asked you what was wrong with you. That was unfair, to let my feelings control my reaction like that."

I finally pulled out of Leo's arms, even though he initially tried to hold me down against him for half a second, standing and dropping the throw blanket at my feet. I stepped toward Mary, who was already opening her arms for a hug when I wrapped both of mine around her.

"I'm sorry, too," I murmured against her shoulder, "I don't like keeping secrets, either."

"I understand why you did, though."

I sniffled, pulling back and sighing. Mary was now the second woman in the office I had hugged while tears were still stained on my cheeks, which reminded me—

"Don't tell Signe," I pleaded. Leo finally stood, grabbing the throw blanket and tossing it back into the basket with the others.

Mary furrowed her brows, "Why?"

"I need to tell her, or—" I turned to face Leo, who raised his eyebrows in question. Staring at him made me catch my breath. He had been wrapped around me for some time, but I hadn't *seen* him since my slip.

His t-shirt was wrinkled from having me sit against him, and the movement of his arms straightening it out made me rest my hand on my collarbone.

"Or...?" Leo lifted an eyebrow.

"Does she need to know?" I asked, "I mean, we aren't, like, *dating*—"

"Aren't we, though?" was Leo's reply. His dark brows

lowered, and his clear blue eyes studied me through the soft light of the lamp.

Something blocked my throat, making me snap my lips closed.

Were we? We went on dates, *but did that mean we were dating?*

"Oh..." Mary slowly stepped closer to the door, "I think I need to be, I don't know, somewhere else." And then she let herself out, the door latching closed. Leo and I were now stuck together.

Leo opened his mouth to say something, but his phone buzzed again. He sighed before removing it from his pocket and reading the notification.

"I need to reply to this," he lifted his free hand to rub the corners of his eyes, inhaling a breath before looking at me, "Can we talk about this? After work?"

My heart started to race but for a different reason.

A reason that didn't make me want to run away, but freeze. Stay here. In this moment.

Aren't we, though?

"Okay." I managed to nod.

Leo nodded in return, pocketing his phone and stepping closer to me, "I know...I know we're in the office, but...can I kiss you?"

My own brows twitched up as he stepped closer, closer. My space was officially crowded with his. My hands lifted to his sides instinctively, clutching the hem of his shirt.

"Yes," I replied.

Leo cupped my face with both of his hands, "Thank you." Then his lips gently pressed against mine. His kiss was gentle, smooth, and simple. And yet, something broke in me from this particular kiss. A dam, except a dam that wasn't holding anything out. It was holding something very big, very real, deep inside of me. This feeling released, spreading from my chest to my gut, to my limbs. The tips of my fingers. The lips that met his with the same gentleness he gave.

He pulled back just enough to keep contact, his top lip teasing mine, "Thank you."

"Thank you," I repeated back to him. I thought I saw a smile twitch on the corners of his lips, but he bit his bottom one to hide it. With another quick peck, he released me and stepped out of the sensory room, digging his phone out of his jeans again.

And I stood there, dizzy.

I wasn't ready to go back to normal. I wasn't ready to deal with the rest of work.

So I pulled my phone out and set a timer.

I retrieved my throw blanket and crawled into the hammock at the farthest corner of the room. I instructed the speaker to play my instrumental playlist, and I worked on my breathing.

I would let myself freak out over what I was feeling for Leo for fifteen minutes, before I pulled myself together, and finished the workday.

Chapter Twenty-Five

LEO

"Do you want to have a look around?" Leo asked after following me into his hotel room. I took in my surroundings; it looked like your typical hotel room.

"Why?"

Leo shrugged out of his jacket, "To make sure you feel safe shagging in a stranger's hotel room."

I smiled, toeing off my shoes as I shook my head, "I'm free to leave whenever?"

He nodded, "Whenever."

"Cool," I stood tall, nerves swarming in my stomach as I drank him in, "...Can you kiss me again?"

I WAS LEANING against my bike, parked outside of Jacqueline's building. My helmet was in my hands, turning it over and over.

Where did one start with a conversation like this?

I had no idea how to have one of these discussions. My experience was quite limited. The last serious relationship I was in was years ago, and after he dropped the L word way before I was ready, I hadn't sought a serious relationship again.

But Jacqueline's moment at work today made me realize...I couldn't lie to myself anymore. She had to have known where I stood. If she didn't, perhaps she would understand when I communicated as such.

Jacqueline relied on direct, unmistakable communication. Reading between the lines wasn't her forte, so if I wanted her to understand everything I was feeling, *I* needed to be the one to tell her.

And whatever her response to that was...I would have to deal with it.

I hoped, though, that I wasn't alone in this. That it wasn't just me. That she felt for me what I have been feeling for her for a while now.

A car rumbled next to me, parking before the ignition got cut off.

Turning to see Jacqueline step out of the vehicle, my chest expanded and my heart started to kick up.

Would this be the last time I see her after work?

Jacqueline brushed loose strands of hair behind her ears, her bun keeping the rest off of her neck. She looked nervous as she approached me, her steps tentative as she clutched the strap of her bag.

"...Hi," she spoke first.

"Hi," I replied. I reached out to play with the strap of her bag, like I did weeks ago, "How are you doing?"

She lifted a shoulder, "I'm... I don't know. I just want to start apologizing again."

When Jacqueline tucked both of her lips between her teeth, I lifted my hand so my index finger pressed on her bottom one, releasing it.

"Don't," I shook my head, "Don't apologize, Jacqueline."

Jacqueline apologized profusely the first time she kissed me. Anxiety took over, and what I thought was pure rejection ended up just being her struggling with her own emotions. Her attraction for me.

Right now, standing outside of her building, I was hoping that her need to keep apologizing was linked to a similar struggle within her. If Jacqueline was this anxious to admit something as simple as physical attraction, I assumed that she would struggle just as much—if not more—when it came to real, big feelings.

"Want to head up?" I tipped my head toward the front of the building.

"Yes, let's go." She lifted her hand and laced our fingers together, leading me in.

We were silent on the walk to her flat, but she kept our fingers laced the entire time. We looked like a real couple; like two people who were just getting off of work and getting ready for a night of *Netflix and Chill*. Most nights, we were.

Except today, there was a very high chance that I was about to ruin this dynamic.

Shutting the door behind us and flipping the lock, I watched Jacqueline slip off her sneakers.

Panic started swelling in my chest.

My fingers itched, naturally reaching toward her, before I balled them into fists at my side. I set my helmet near my bag in the entryway, and she gave me a curious look. Her dark eyes scanned my body, the pinch in her brow an indicator of some puzzle she was trying to piece together about me.

"Are you okay?" Jacqueline asked, with her delicious frown in place. Her eyes were searching mine, stepping closer.

I exhaled a nervous breath, before shaking my head once.

She tilted her head as she shrugged out of her jacket, hanging it up. My eyes dropped to her blouse, and her jeans which were my favorite pair because of how well they hugged her arse.

"You seem...tense." Jacqueline unbuttoned another button on her blouse, revealing more of her smooth skin. My eyes homed in on her movements, and she hesitated.

I saw the moment something clicked for her, her eyebrows twitching up the slightest bit, "Do you...want me, right now?"

"Yes." I always wanted Jacqueline. That would always be the case. It was an answer as mindless as breathing.

Jacqueline nodded, "...Do you want to talk first, or after?"

I thought about her question this time, wondering which was best. Part of me insisted that we speak first, knowing deep down that if she didn't reciprocate what I was about to admit tonight, there was a good chance there wouldn't be an after.

There would just be an end.

...I wished I was a better man.

"After." I decided.

She nodded, continuing to unbutton her blouse. Not just to get comfortable, but to remove it entirely.

"Do you want me, Leo?" Jacqueline whispered her question. The tension was thick. My heart was sure to race out of my ribs at any moment.

"Fiercely." I shrugged out of my leather jacket, dropping it next to my helmet.

"...Do you want to play with me?" I could tell that was very much what she wanted. She was a woman with layers.

While she enjoyed simple missionary and was able to get off multiple times with what others deemed as vanilla sex, she also enjoyed playing.

This might be the last time I could play with Jacqueline Williams.

"Yes." I was only capable of one-word responses, apparently.

Jacqueline's lips twitched up in a smile before she dropped it just as quickly. Her chest was heaving as she shrugged out of her blouse. Her bra was simple today, a nude shade that had no lace. No front clasp. It was a bra made for function, and yet, my throat went dry at the sight of it.

I was officially wrecked for this woman.

Jacqueline then bent down to shrug out of her jeans, delicately pulling her smooth legs out of the material, and setting it aside.

Her panties were white cotton.

Simple. Functional.

I wanted to bite them off of her.

Without warning, Jacqueline turned on her heel and bolted.

I chuckled, grabbing the back collar of my shirt to pull it over my head before I marched after her. I didn't run this time. I didn't want to rush this.

I turned down her short hallway, grinning when I saw her bedroom door close. The light turned off underneath the door, and I allowed my footsteps to heavily fall in my approach. I wanted her to know I was coming.

I turned the handle, slowly pushing it open.

"Jacqueline?" I sang her name as I closed the door behind me, locking it.

I held still, waiting to hear where she was. Under her

bed? In her closet? Behind the drapes? The ensuite bathroom?

I heard a shift against the carpet, and my head turned toward the walk-in closet.

"Jacqueline," I hummed her name as I marched toward her, slowly pushing open the closet door. I left the light off, more than willing to play this game.

Clothing shifted on the hangers, so I stepped toward the rack and parted the clothing with one hand.

There stood Jacqueline, in her bra and panties, hair undone from her bun, with her hands over her face. I was breathing heavily; all blood leaving my brain and flowing south. My cock was desperately at attention, fighting to free itself from my jeans.

I didn't say anything, and neither did she.

So I crowded her space, resting my hands on the shelf above her head as I trapped her against the back wall of her closet, "...Look at you."

Jacqueline parted her fingers, one dark eye spotting me.

I grinned, determined to appreciate these moments with her. How she hid the most vulnerable parts of herself from everyone else, but not me.

"This isn't the most ideal location," I glanced around her walk-in closet, before leveling her with my undivided attention, "But I can make it work. Or you can come with me to the bed. Your choice."

Jacqueline's breathing kicked up, "...And if I want to resist you a little bit more?"

I bit my bottom lip, my grip tightening on the shelf I braced myself on, "You can try."

The corner of Jacqueline's lip kicked up the corner, liking that response.

In a blink, she swiped her hand behind her clothes,

shielding herself from me again. I laughed, pulling the clothes back and grabbing her waist, tugging her out from hiding.

"Do you remember your safe word, Jacqueline?" I grunted as she struggled against my hold. I managed to wrap my arms around her waist, carrying her out of the closet.

"Yes."

"Do you want to use it?" I stopped just at the foot of her bed.

Her hair swayed back and forth as she shook her head, "No."

"Good." Then I practically threw her onto the bed. Jacqueline squealed a bit, but I wasn't letting her pretend to get away from me for long. Playing with Jacqueline was always one of my favorite pastimes, but I was unraveling. Desperate for the connection she was willing to provide me in these moments.

I grabbed a fistful of her panties and started yanking them down.

Jacqueline laughed, moaning when I trapped her body underneath mine to keep her still.

"You're so sexy like this, love," I grunted, yanking her panties farther down. I decided to let them linger around her knees while pulling the cups of her bra down, "You have no idea."

Jacqueline groaned when I mouthed her, teasing her aroused peaks with my tongue in a way that I knew would drive her to the edge faster than anything else.

"Leo," she moaned my name religiously, but I was the one desperate to worship every part of her.

Right when her hips started thrusting against me, her breath panting shorter and shorter, I eased up. Her hands had since tangled themselves in my hair, and when I released her breast with a loud and wet *pop*, she groaned.

"You think I'm going to go easy on you?"

Jacqueline pouted, her cheeks and chest flushed, "A girl can hope."

I chuckled, enough amusement leaking through to mask my sincerity when I said, "After that little stunt you pulled today?"

Jacqueline stiffened for half a second, her dark eyes quickly scanning my face. Whatever she found relaxed her, and she tugged my face down to hers in a searing, sloppy kiss.

I allowed her to take a little of me, before I pulled back and removed her hands from my hair, "Do you have any idea what you do to me, woman?"

Jacqueline shook her head, her eyes hooded and her lips swollen and glossy. She was the most beautiful woman I had ever seen.

My hand danced across her collarbone, between her sensitive breasts, and down her smooth stomach, before finding what I wanted right between her legs. She was hot, wet, and soft for me.

Me.

"What do I do?" Jacqueline whispered, gasping when I teased her sensitive flesh.

"You drive me fucking *mad* with want." I wasn't letting up on her, flicking my thumb over her clit in retribution. She was gasping, thrusting her hips into my hand, "You make me want things I haven't wanted in a very, very long time. Then you go and tease me with them."

"T-tease you?" Jacqueline was clutching my wrist now, holding me between her legs. Chasing her release.

"What I would give," I gasped, lowering my head to suck

on the sensitive skin between her neck and shoulder. She whined, and I decided I couldn't take it anymore. I stopped teasing her clit to search for a condom from her bedside drawer, "To have everyone know exactly who you part your legs for." Jacqueline's eyebrows jumped, but she held my arm so I wouldn't let go of her too much. She took the condom from my hands, even ripping the foil off with her teeth.

"You-you want that?" Jacqueline asked when I took the rubber from her hand and sheathed myself with it.

"I want *you*, Jacqueline," I pushed her onto her back when she started to sit up, because as fun as exploring sexual positions is, missionary with me on top would always be my favorite, "I want you to be *mine*." I kissed her again, desperate to taste her plump lips. I was ravenous, biting and sucking and licking into her mouth without a chance for her to catch her breath.

She let me plunder her mouth as I dropped to my forearms above her, teasing her wetness with my cock.

"I'm yours." Jacqueline nodded, wrapping her arms around my shoulders, and widening her legs for me. I shook my head.

"I'm serious," I glanced down between us, watching as I pulled my hips back to finally, finally sink into her, "I want you in every sense of the word."

Jacqueline moaned as I stretched her out, going slow so I wouldn't cause harm.

"Then take me," she gasped.

"No." I practically growled, something hot burning in my chest. I shifted one of my forearms so that I could gently fist her hair, "Look at me, Jacqueline," her eyelids fluttered open, and the look in them only settled my resolve. I couldn't do this anymore. It was *real* for me. It wasn't us playing, it wasn't a game. I was done. She was *it* for me, "The next time I take you like this," I thrust my hips for emphasis, making her bite her lip, "I need to know that there isn't going to be anyone else." I pulled back and thrust deeper.

Jacqueline's eyes widened, redness starting to tinge the whites as she tightened her hold around my shoulders.

She was starting to hear me.

"The next time we do this..." I rocked into her again. I released the hold on her hair, pleased with her attention, while I shifted my weight to the side. My fingers found her swollen clit in between us, easier to access, when she finally kicked off her panties from around her knees to hook her knee on my waist. Her other was trapped underneath me, but it didn't feel like either of us cared, "It's not going to be a game. It's going to be real. I'll be yours, and you'll be mine."

Jacqueline's lips parted, her body working perfectly in sync with mine as moisture started to gather in her eyes, "Leo..."

It wasn't a disappointed tone, or a tone saying goodbye, so I rocked harder into her again. My chest cracked open, staring at her all pliant and soft underneath me. Her inner walls started to tighten, and I ground my teeth before speaking up again.

"I can't pretend anymore, Jacqueline," I shook my head, kissing her lips aggressively once more before continuing, "I wish I could, but—do—" I worked my fingers over her more, finding the motion that made her chest flush and her breathing catch, "Do you understand what I'm saying?"

Jacqueline nodded, rolling her hips against me and my hand in a way that made me start to see gods. Heat and pleasure shot down my spine, exploding out of me at the same time she cried out my name. Her pussy practically locked around my cock, making it difficult for me to keep up my ministrations enough to prolong her release, but not impossible.

After she felt slack underneath me, I finally released everything I had into her. Groaning into her neck, grinding my hips against hers. I wanted to embed myself in her, permanently anchor her soul to mine. Desperate for Jacqueline to understand everything I felt for her.

Silence filled the room, the sound of our breaths, our bodies shifting over the covers as I leaned back on my forearms, still inside of her.

Jacqueline was staring at me, her eyes locked on me in a way that made me almost crumble against her. But I didn't. I had to do it. The words were burning in my chest, it physically hurt to hold them in.

Gently, I cupped her face, my thumb tracing her swollen bottom lip, my eyes locked there as I whispered, "I love you."

Jacqueline's breath caught. She swallowed, and her eyes started blinking. She pressed her lips together for half a second, before opening them again.

So I gently covered her lips with the palm of my hand, shaking my head.

Jacqueline's brows pinched, confusion coating her eyes while I spoke, "Don't say anything back, yet. Just...sit with that knowledge, will you?" I inhaled another shaky breath, having to say it again, "I love you, Jacqueline. There is no other way to put it." I held in a breath of my own, gnawing on my bottom lip as I saw the pinch in her brow smooth out, her eyes softening, "I know you probably need time to process this. I can give that to you, yeah?"

Jacqueline nodded under my hand, not enough to dislodge it from her lips, but enough for me to understand. I nodded back, slowly pulling my hand back. Jacqueline's eyes dropped to my own lips, and I couldn't resist.

I was done for.

Dropping my lips to hers, I kissed her. The first kiss with everything I had on the table, bared to her. A kiss that held nothing back. A kiss with my truth out in the open, in the palms of her hands. I kissed Jacqueline like I wanted to kiss her; like she was mine and I was hers.

Finally, I pulled back, unable to stare into her eyes for long before I cleared my throat and shifted off of the bed.

I glanced down, realizing I never even got my pants off.

"I'm going to go." I cleared my throat after my words, rubbing the back of my head as I stood from her mattress.

Jacqueline slowly sat up, her bra still around her waist, before she rested her arms on her bent knees, "...Okay."

My clothing was by her entryway door, there wasn't anything for me to justify lingering in her bedroom like this. So I forced my gaze up to hers, attempting to smile, but unable to hold it this time.

Jacqueline's lips parted, a tear escaping her eye as she watched me discard the condom in a nearby bin and zip myself back up.

"I..." I hesitated at her bedroom door, squeezing my fingers against the wood, "I'm sorry." I wasn't sure what, exactly, I was apologizing for. For telling her something huge while I was still deep inside of her? For irrevocably changing the dynamic between us forever? For developing the feelings in the first place?

Perhaps all of the above.

So I stepped out, slowly closing her bedroom door behind me.

Right when I heard the latch click, I barely heard Jacqueline's muffled voice say, "Don't apologize," before I left.

Chapter Twenty-Six

JACQUELINE

"Too much?" He asked through a heavy breath. It sounded like he was really exerting himself.

"No," I gasped, pushing back into him, "You're perfect."

I spiraled all weekend.

I also FaceTimed Marco a lot. Perhaps that justified his grumpy greeting when I FaceTimed him again Monday morning before I left for the office.

"Oh my hell," Marco answered on the second ring, "I'm still in bed."

Samuel's muffled groan echoed off-screen.

"How do I go to work today?" I asked, fidgeting with my car keys. I hadn't pulled out of my spot yet, scared to even put my shoes on. Knowing the next step would be taking me to Leo.

"One foot in front of the other," Marco groaned, laying an arm over his eyes, "Tits up."

"I'm serious," I groaned, my leg was bouncing, shaking my kitchen stool "We haven't spoken since—"

"Do you love him?" Marco asked behind his arm.

"I don't *know*," I replied.

"Okay, well, I can't figure that out for you." Marco sighed, removing his arm and leveling me with his dark eyes that matched mine, "You both have survived a lot during the workday, you'll survive this, too. I promise he's feeling more insecure than you are right now."

"...Because he said it first?" I asked.

"Because he said it at *all*," Marco shook his head, "He's made it clear he doesn't expect you to say it back. The ball is completely in your court here. To open himself up like that, to make himself vulnerable to such a big rejection, is fucking terrifying."

That...didn't make me feel better.

"I just don't *know* yet."

"I think you do," Samuel said, "But take some more time until you figure it out yourself. Bye, Jacqueline." Then, the phone was tugged out of Marco's hand before the call ended.

Crap.

A few seconds later my phone vibrated in my hand, and I tapped on the notification with greedy fingers, hoping it was something sweet and funny from Leo even though I was dreading seeing him in person today.

But no, it was an email.

From Vincent.

The subject line said, "You're still a fucking bitch" and nothing else.

So, I tapped on his email address and blocked it. Just like I had blocked his number and social media accounts, pushing my childish ex to the back of my mind.

I didn't care about the random jump-scare his name in my inbox should have invoked in me.

I didn't care if Sun Steer employees whispered how much of an ice queen I was.

I cared about how Leo was doing right now. What he expected of me. What I wanted, which the more I thought about it, felt terrifying to ask for.

I huffed a breath, scraping my hands over my face, before setting a fifteen-minute timer on my phone.

I lay my forehead down on my kitchen counter, forcing myself to sit with my emotions.

Because in fifteen minutes, I would gather myself and force my feet to take me to work.

"I…THINK I NEED HELP." My voice shook as I stood in front of Signe Lange's desk.

Signe raised a dark red eyebrow, "Why do I have the feeling that this isn't work-related?"

I tucked my lips in between my teeth before replying, "Because it's not."

Signe immediately perked up.

"Oh," she wiggled her eyebrows while steepling her hands, drumming her fingertips against each other, "What do you need help with? Did you fall for a pyramid scheme?"

I shook my head, "I think I fell for a person, and I don't know what to do about it."

Her jaw dropped before her hazel eyes shifted to stare at someone behind me.

No, no, no.

But thankfully, when I turned around, it was Nicole standing there. Her bag was slung over her shoulder, and her oversized jeans hung low on her hips underneath her hoodie.

"I didn't mean to eavesdrop—" Nicole shook her head, her black hair swaying with the movement, "I just...I..." she gnawed on her lips while her dark eyes dropped to the ground, "Nevermind, this is clearly a bad time."

"What is it?" I asked, stepping aside so Signe could get a good look at her, too.

"I was—god, this sounds so frivolous right now." Nicole shook her head again.

"Spit it out, Young," Signe smiled with the words, making them sound more encouraging and less demanding.

Nicole looked up, her gaze bouncing between the two of us, "Violet said that you all were planning on having a girls' night this week."

It was true, I got the text from Signe last week, but I hadn't officially RSVP'd. I haven't gone to one in months.

"Yeah, they are," I nodded, throwing a smile toward the CFO of Sun Steer, before turning to Signe, "I think I'd appreciate everyone's help with this." I drummed my fingers on Signe's desk.

"You *have* to come," Signe emphasized, holding her phone up in her hand, "Can I add you to the group chat?"

Nicole perked up, stepping closer to us, "Yeah." Then she took Signe's phone and added her number.

"I'm glad to finally have you join the sisterhood," Signe stood from her desk, towering over Nicole and me, as she gently tapped both of Nicole's shoulders with the corner of her cellphone, "I dub thee, a girl's girl." Nicole grinned at Signe's theatrics, standing a little taller.

I snorted, "I haven't been knighted yet."

"Oh fu—I mean, really?" Signe shook her head, before turning to me to tap both of my shoulders with her phone,

"There. A girl's girl. Now that I think about it, I think Violet is the only one I officially knighted into the circle. I was super high the first night she came, but anyway, I should knight Jamie and Mary, too."

Nicole and I laughed before she shouldered her bag and got ready to walk to her office, "Send me the details." Nicole lifted her phone before waving goodbye with it and marching off.

I turned back to Signe, "Remind me what we're doing again?"

"Watching the Pride and Prejudice movie," Signe smiled proudly, "Everyone's coming over to my tiny apartment. Boys aren't allowed. Pajamas are mandatory. Edibles are optional, though."

I smiled before I asked, "What about trauma dumping?"

Signe didn't perk up at that, instead, her smile turned softer, more vulnerable, "Encouraged."

———

"WHERE DID YOU GET THIS?" Violet asked, tucking her fingers underneath the sleeve of my cream-colored matching set. I didn't really have pajamas. I mostly slept in oversized shirts and my underwear. I hoped loungewear was an acceptable substitution for the evening.

I pulled up the website I ordered the set from a while back. The brand was known for not having any paper tags sewn into their clothing and using materials that soothed sensory-sensitive people.

Like me.

"Oh, they make kid's clothes, too," Violet immediately pulled her phone out of her pocket to look at the website herself.

"Ahem!" Signe cleared her throat dramatically. She was wearing basketball shorts and an oversized t-shirt of her own, so I assumed my clothing met the standards of girls' night, "Before we get started, does everyone have their snacks?"

"Yup!" Jamie and Mary both lifted their bowls, Mary with pretzels, and Jamie with Oreos. Violet lifted her package of gummy bears while scrolling on her phone, and Nicole lifted her bottle of red wine. We were all sitting in a semi-circle on various blow-up mattresses, blankets, and pillows we all brought. In front of us was Signe's monitor on the far wall. Her studio apartment was one decently sized room, with her bed on the opposite wall of her kitchen. But it was homey.

"Excellent," Signe nodded, "Now, has everyone who wants a gummy taken one?"

There was a knock on the front door, making us all perk up as a small blonde woman with freckles let herself into the space, "Hellur!"

"Eloise!" Signe sang, awkwardly hopping around all the bedding to get to her friend, "Hi!" Eloise stepped to the side of the door, dropping a bag of what looked like groceries, before pulling out a paperback.

Once the entryway was free, Taylor Desmond cautiously stepped through the threshold right as Eloise was telling Signe, "I just wanted to drop these off and have you sign this."

My heart jumped into my throat.

For no other reason than because I knew Taylor was Leo's friend.

Not mine.

"Oh, of course! Everyone, this is my girl, Eloise!" Signe dragged her through the room, "I invited her tonight, but I guess she has plans." Signe rolled her eyes while Taylor chuckled, bracing a hip against Signe's countertop and crossing their arms, "I haven't met you, yet." Signe added, holding out a hand to them.

"Taylor," they nodded with a grin, "They/them."

"Signe, she/her."

"That's a gorgeous fucking name." Taylor's brows jumped up. Signe milled around the kitchen in search of a pen to sign Eloise's copy of her book. I still hadn't read it, mostly because I had no desire to read a book about all the ways Signe imagined doing a coworker of ours, but hey, I loved that she was finding success in her field.

"This feels illegal," Violet stood up to approach Taylor, who did a double take and grinned when they saw her, "It's like seeing my teacher at the grocery store."

"What the hell? How are you? How's little Gracie?" Taylor joked, wrapping Violet in a hug. When Violet gave me her back so Taylor's head rested over her shoulder, that's when their eyebrows jumped.

Because their dark blue eyes had finally locked on me. *Shit.*

"Wait, Jacqueline? That you, girl?" Taylor released Violet from the hug, and heat flamed my cheeks. On the other side of Violet, Nicole's head turned towards me, her black hair swishing with the movement. I met her wide, dark eyes, barely acknowledging her own flushed cheeks, before I pasted on a smile and stood up from my seat.

"Hi, T," I opened my arms when their body language made it obvious that they were going for a hug again.

"T, how do you know everyone in Orange County?" Eloise shifted her weight to one hip and crossed her arms, her light blue eyes bouncing between the two of us, then she turned to Signe who had returned with a pen, "I'm going to need a long, heartfelt message with your signature, thanks."

Signe grinned before taking her book and getting to work.

"I worked with Violet and her daughter for a few years," Taylor explained with a nod towards Violet, before looking back at me, "Jacqueline's man and I play rugby together," Taylor said with a grin, pulling me in tight against them. They smelled good, like clean laundry. I noticed how they didn't mention the fact that they helped Leo surprise me with the experience of attending a secret pop-up rave. Perhaps that needed to stay a secret, so I didn't mention it.

"Pardon me?" Violet spoke up right when Taylor released me, "You have a boyfriend? How did I not know about this?"

Taylor hesitated, their smile slipping a bit once they took in my facial expression, "Oh, shit."

"It's fine." I flapped my hand, not wanting them to feel bad for assuming things.

"Who is your boyfriend?" Nicole asked, her eyes bouncing between Taylor and me.

Taylor scratched the back of their head, scraping against the shaven strands.

"That's, actually..." I bit my lip, "What I wanted help with tonight. If you don't mind me carving out some of girls' night for myself."

Taylor's facial expression softened, "I'm so sorry. I just assumed."

I shook my head at them, "It's fine, I was going to bring it up anyway."

"Oh my god just tell us who it is!" Signe slapped her book closed before shoving it in Eloise's hands, "I'm dying here!"

Mary rolled her eyes back and released a loud, dramatic groan that gained the attention of everyone in the room, "Jacqueline and Leo are fucking. Leo is head over heels for her. Jacqueline hasn't figured things out yet."

I wanted a hole to open up in the floor and swallow me away from this moment.

But I braced my shoulders, fighting the urge to fold into myself under Mary's blunt, but truthful, words.

Signe was silent, mouth agape. So were Nicole and Violet. Eloise and Taylor shared a look with each other.

"Okay, well, we better be going," Eloise spoke up, shoving her book in her bag, "T?"

"Yeah," Taylor replied with a nod, "I'm sorry, Jacqueline."

"You're fine," I gave them a wobbly smile before they turned and delicately stepped over Nicole's legs, "'scuse me."

Nicole didn't say anything, just shifted out of their way and kept her eyes on the floor. Taylor gave me one last wave goodbye before following Eloise out of the apartment.

Then, Signe practically threw herself down on the bedding with the rest of us.

"Girls' night is officially in session," she declared.

"Start from the beginning," Violet demanded, "How did this happen?"

I inhaled a breath for confidence, before folding back into my spot on the floor and grabbing a throw pillow to hold against my chest.

And then I told them everything.

Starting from how we met in the bar, all the way to when Leo told me he loved me. I left out certain parts, assuming they didn't want to know how far inside of me he was when he whispered those words to me.

I left out the part that involved Taylor, and the pop-up rave.

But everything else pertinent stayed, including my past. My ex-boyfriend. Leo punching him in the face, and never making me feel like Vincent did.

"I think that's the scariest part," I had been talking for a while, but all of their attention was on me, and even though I was sweating under my matching set, I was determined to see this through, "I like how I feel with Leo. How he makes me feel. How lucky I am to...to even be around someone as wonderful as him. When he told me he loved me—I don't know—it didn't feel devastating. It felt elevating."

I finally lifted my eyes, locking with Mary's. He was her cousin; I was worried that my friendship with her was forever ruined at this point.

Everyone was quiet, letting my story sit with each woman in this room, before Signe broke the silence, "Do you love him back?"

I had been asking myself that question the past few days.

Did I even know what love was? Was I capable of an emotion as big and strong as love? I thought I loved Vincent, but I didn't. I was infatuated with Vincent but was eventually willing to let him go.

Leo, though, I wanted by my side. I wanted to hold him to me. I could see myself attending his rugby matches, staying at each other's apartments, bickering over English verbiage versus American.

"I do," I whispered.

Violet whistled, "Well, there you go."

"But I'm—" my lip started wobbling, my throat tightening, my eyes watering, "I don't deserve him." I sniffed, wiping away a stray tear trailing down my cheek with my palm, "He's so good. You know—" I waved a hand toward Mary, who was giving me a look I couldn't decipher, since I hadn't seen it on her before, "You know how good he is. He deserves the best. He deserves someone who makes him feel as wonderful and confident as he makes me feel. He's bright, glowing, radiant energy. I'm just, *not*—we're *so* different—"

"Stop right there," Jamie spoke up, making me slam my lips shut. I sniffled some more, breathing through my mouth in an attempt to stop my tears. She waited for me to collect myself before continuing, "Mary and I are very different, wouldn't you agree?"

I frowned, studying the two of them. Mary was wearing a black band t-shirt with black sweatpants, sitting with her feet on the ground so her knees could support her elbows. Her septum and lip piercings were glistening in the lamplight of Signe's apartment. On her fingers, were various kinds of rings. Her black hair was pulled back, showing off all her ear piercings.

Jamie's blonde hair was in a bun, no jewelry anywhere on her face or ears. Only a simple gold chain with the letter M hung around her neck. She wore a soft pastel pink sweater and heather grey joggers.

They were opposites.

"Yeah," I nodded.

"But we make sense together, right?" Jamie reached a handout to grip Mary's leg, and Mary shifted so she could tuck an arm behind Jamie, "No one is super confused as to why we are together, right?" Jamie asked that question to the room, raising her blonde eyebrows.

All of us shook our heads.

"Here's the thing," Mary sighed, stretching her legs out to cross one ankle over the other, "Leo does whatever the fuck Leo wants to do. No one can talk him out of something once he's set his mind to it. He's a stubborn bastard. Right now, Jacqueline, Leo wants *you*." My heart thumped at Mary's words, my teeth gnawing on my lips so hard I was embarrassed at how scarred they would be tomorrow, "It's none of our business *why* or *how* he came to that conclusion. So you don't need to set up some grand jury for us to determine how deserving of his love you are."

My shoulders slumped, "I'm sorry—"

"Oh my god," Mary rolled her eyes, "Do *not* apologize for falling in love with my cousin. Don't you dare," Mary leveled me with a look, "Do you love him, Jacqueline?"

I nodded, something burning in my stomach, feeling suspiciously like resolve, "More than anything."

"Then you need to tell him and let the two of you be happy," Mary shifted so she could pull her phone out of the pocket of her sweatpants, "So he'll stop texting *me*."

Signe cackled, leaning forward to look at Mary's lock screen, which showed a number of unread texts from a contact named "Annoying Blood Relative."

"What is he texting you?" Signe asked with a wide grin.

"Dude's a mess," Mary pocketed her phone, "I have never seen Leo this far gone for someone. Ever. You," Mary pointed an accusing finger at me, "Made Leo a lovesick motherfucker. Jamie and I went over to his apartment last night just to make sure the guy ate something while he waited to hear from you."

My stomach dropped, souring with the realization, "I'm so sorry—I had no idea." I shifted, getting ready to go do something, but not knowing what. What could I possibly do at this hour?

"Stop it," Signe placed both of her palms over her chest, "I can't handle how cute he is. Oh my god." Signe sighed, closing her eyes, "It's almost enough to make me forget to rip into you for—heaven *forbid*—dating a *coworker*." I shrunk in on myself under Signe's scrutiny, because she had just reopened her eyes and turned her head to stare me down.

"I know, I'm so sorry—"

"Stop apologizing!" Signe threw her hands up in the air, "I'm just not going to look past the hilarity of you, Jacqueline Williams, having a secret office romance with a member of upper management *not even a year* after you told Zaid to never, ever start a romance with a coworker. What did you say to him? Something like, 'there are seven-point-five billion people in the world. There is never a reason to get involved with someone at work'." Signe clutched her stomach with her hands before cackling again, which was echoed by Violet and Nicole, "Oh, how the tables have *turned*."

"You should do something big for him," Nicole piped up. She had been reticent this whole evening, and I don't think I was the only one surprised to see her suddenly insert herself into the conversation.

"I'm open to any suggestions," I nodded, folding my legs closer, "Leo deserves something big. He deserves everything."

Mary smiled at me as she crawled across the various bedding to push me over in a large bear hug, "That is why I think you are going to be good for him, Jacqueline." She mumbled into my shoulder, "You appreciate him. You see him." She pulled off of me, before adding, "Thank you for loving him."

My eyes got misty again before Nicole sniffled.

We all turned to look at the CFO, surprised to see her looking emotional.

She shook her head once before sniffing again, "I'm so sorry—I just went through a super bad breakup and lost all my friends. I didn't realize—I didn't realize how much I needed something like this." She waved around the room, before Violet reached over and wrapped Nicole in her arms as well.

"Thank you all for being my friends," Violet added, squeezing Nicole tight.

"I love you all," Jamie added.

"And no one loves love more than me," Signe straightened in her seat, before rubbing her hands together mischievously, "Which is why we need to come up with something good for Jacqueline to do for Leo."

Before anyone could add anything, Mary's phone started going off.

"Is that a ringtone? Can our phones even do that still?" Signe asked with pure disbelief.

Mary rolled her eyes before pulling her phone out of her sweatpants and frowning at the screen, "I told you all, he's a mess."

"That's your ringtone for *Leo*?" Violet cackled, releasing Nicole from her embrace to properly laugh.

"Every Time We Touch" by *Cascada* was echoing from Mary's phone.

An idea came to mind then, remembering Leo's confession in his car all those months ago.

"Wait," I spoke up as Mary silenced the call, watching as she thumbed a message on her screen instead, "I...I think I have an idea. Please tell me if it's too embarrassing or not."

"The more embarrassing the better," Violet replied with a shrug, "There's nothing like proving your love for someone else by sacrificing yourself on the altar of dignity."

"First of all, I changed my mind, after we resolve this, we're going to watch *10 Things I Hate About You*," Signe high-fived Violet for her movie reference, before turning to me, "Now, tell us what you're thinking."

Chapter Twenty-Seven

LEO

"I'M sorry to inform you, but as soon as the wheels of your plane touched down on an American tarmac, you have been legally obligated to refer to fried potatoes as fries." Jacqueline finished her ridiculous statement by placing a fry between her teeth and grinning at me.

I leaned forward, biting the other end of her chip, making her giggle.

"As long as you do that thing with your tongue again, I'll call them whatever you want."

I STILL HADN'T HEARD from Jacqueline.

Mary blew me off last night for some girls' night, and I was hoping that she would pull through in this situation and provide me with some intel on where Jacqueline was leaning. Women talked about men with other women, it was a universal truth.

When she texted me last night to fuck off, I figured it was because she was still there. Gaining information for me.

362

I wasn't sure how much longer I could do this. I had driven my car to work today, and was sitting in the driver's seat until Jacqueline made her way into the building. I saw her pull into the carpark at the same time I did, and I couldn't handle the pain of sharing a lift with her right now. I was too deep in my head.

Taking a deep pull of my fizzy drink I had bought at a McDonald's drive-thru on the way into the office, my heart rate started to kick up.

Not because of the caffeine I was consuming.

But because a familiar, bald man was currently marching right toward Jacqueline as she made her way toward Sun Steer's building.

Bloody hell.

I threw myself out of the car immediately, marching straight towards the love of my life. She halted on the sidewalk, surprised to see Vincent marching right toward her.

Dread filled my gut. I picked up my pace.

"Vince? What the hell?" Jacqueline asked, taking a tentative step back.

"Oi!" I called, making Jacqueline glance over her shoulder to see my approach. Vincent, not surprisingly, slowed his pace as he glared at me, "Long time, no see."

I managed to step in front of Jacqueline, shifting so most of her was hidden behind my body. Something about this man didn't feel right. I remembered Brandon's words from not too long ago, about how he tends to trust his gut with these kinds of things.

My gut was telling me to get Jacqueline the fuck out of here.

"I need to talk to Jacqueline." Vincent ground out. His hands were shoved in his coat pockets, and the way he was fidgeting inside the material made alarm bells ring in my head.

"I don't think you do." I shook my head, stepping back with my arm out in case Jacqueline had any desire to approach him.

The side door to the building opened far behind Vincent, and I almost breathed a sigh of relief watching Mary, Zaid, and Brandon all start walking toward us. Brandon had his phone to his ear, and he was angrily scanning the area. I guessed that he was looking for security.

"This is between me and her." Vincent spat on the ground, his head twitching to the side. He scratched his cheek, and the way he swayed from the movement confirmed my suspicions.

He was not sober.

"You need to leave, mate," I lowered my voice, going as far as to grab Jacqueline's arm, ensuring she was still behind me and out of his reach. I felt one of her smaller, cold hands wrap around my wrist, holding me as well.

"Fine, fine." Vincent shook his head and stepped off of the sidewalk, making our coworkers slow their approach. His eyes were on the ground as he marched off.

Jacqueline made a concerned noise behind me, so I whirled on her to scan her body. I didn't think I saw him touch her, but I couldn't be sure. I ended up grasping both of her arms in my hands, desperate to feel for myself.

"Are you alright?" I asked her, crouching to meet her eye.

Jacqueline was shaking the slightest bit, blinking as her eyes met mine, "Yeah, yeah I'm—Leo!" I was about to turn around when suddenly, blinding pain filled the back of my head.

Everything went dark.

"Leo? C'mon man," my cousin's voice didn't normally sound so shrill, but for some reason, Mary's tone made the throbbing in the back of my head feel even worse, "Wakey, wakey."

"Fuck me," I groaned, reaching a hand up to rub my eyes. Someone was trying to shine a light on them.

"Mr. Turner, I think you have a concussion. I need you to move slowly." I had no idea who the hell that was, but I trusted their diagnosis, based on the nausea I was feeling when I tried to sit up. I slowed my movements, allowing my cousin's ring-clad hands to support me. I finally managed to open my eyes. I was on the ground, outside the office.

In front of me was a medical professional of some kind, and behind them was an ambulance. I turned my head, because just behind the ambulance, Vincent was in handcuffs and being shoved into the back of a police car.

"Where's Jacqueline?" I managed to groan out.

"Here," I smelled her rose and vanilla perfume right as she dropped to her knees beside me, triggering an unexpected wave of nausea as her cold hands brushed my hair back off of my forehead, "I'm here."

"Are you okay?" I asked, reaching up to wrap her hand in mine.

Jacqueline scoffed, "I'm fine, you're the injured one."

"Fuck, am I?" I reached my hand up again toward where the pain was throbbing behind my skull. Something damp was in the strands of my hair, and when I lowered my hand, I saw a small bit of blood coating the fingers.

"It's a small cut. He doesn't need stitches," another medical professional said, "We want to determine if you need to go to the hospital. Can you make it to the ambulance or do you need assistance?"

"Ah," I winced, shifting my body in an attempt to stand up, "I can walk."

"Go slow," Jacqueline instructed. She tucked herself under one of my arms, helping support my weight as she shuffled us to the back of the ambulance where I could get properly assessed.

"Fucking prick," I heard Mary grumble, "Who sucker punches someone in the back of the head with brass fucking knuckles?"

"Those are illegal in California," Brandon added, "So he's got a lot of trouble ahead of him."

"Leo?" Jacqueline's voice pulled me from our coworker's conversation, I tried to focus on her dark eyes. She was wearing her thin golden glasses today, and I tried to lift a hand to peel them off, but my movements were stiff.

"Yeah, love?"

Jacqueline's lips twitched before she continued, "You need to rest at home for a few days." I shrugged because I wasn't going to object to that. I felt like hell, "Can I take care of you, or would you prefer Mary and Jamie to look after you?"

I frowned, "I want you."

Jacqueline exhaled as if she was holding her breath until I answered, "Okay, we need to go."

"Wait—" I resisted her when she laced her fingers in mine, "I need to be assessed."

Jacqueline released a soft laugh, "You already were. You don't need a hospital."

Shit, really?

"He might be confused for a bit," the paramedic from earlier was speaking...somewhere, "Pick up over-the-counter painkillers from the pharmacy of his choice, and if any of these symptoms show up or he needs something stronger, take him to the hospital."

"Thank you," Jacqueline nodded, her profile becoming clearer in my vision, "Let's go."

IT WAS dark when I opened my eyes, which I was grateful for. The next day after Vincent's assault, Jacqueline kept all my drapes in my flat closed so the sun wouldn't make me nauseous. I flexed my arms, sighing in contentment at the feel of Jacqueline's soft, warm body tucked against mine. Her back to my chest. Her hair braided out of the way, so my nose could inhale the vanilla of her shampoo.

Apparently, after sucker-punching me in the back of the head, Zaid and Brandon tackled Vincent down. Jacqueline caught most of my fall, preventing my head from hitting the sidewalk while our coworkers wrestled her ex.

Building security called the police while Brandon and Zaid held Vincent down. Law enforcement arrived two minutes later with an ambulance, and I gained consciousness soon after.

According to Jacqueline, Mary was in hysterics after seeing me fall unconscious so easily. If he hadn't worn brass knuckles, I doubt that a single hit would have taken me out that easily.

I also could have ended up much, much worse.

That probably explained why Mary had been blowing my phone up the last twenty-four hours, praising my thick skull for finally having a useful purpose.

After Vincent's assault, Jacqueline took care of me for the rest of the evening. The entirety of the next day, too.

Bringing me bland foods so I wouldn't get nauseated again, rubbing my neck when I felt an ache, and switching out ice packs to help with lingering pain and swelling.

She even went to the store and stocked up on my favorite fizzy drinks.

This was the second night she stayed over, and I was worried it would be the last.

We didn't talk about anything important. We watched the telly, we chatted about work and our friends, but never us.

I broached the subject before we fell asleep that night.

Jacqueline didn't stiffen or react as if my inquiry surprised her. Instead, she met my gaze and said, "We're going to talk. But not yet."

The fact that she was still here, sleeping in my bed, gave me hope.

Chapter Twenty-Eight

LEO

"I can't even move," she breathed.

I chuckled next to her, half my face buried in the pillows as I mumbled a response, "Is that a good thing or a bad thing?"

"Good," she couldn't even roll over to look at me, "Very, very good."

It was one week after Vincent gave me a concussion. It was my first day back at rugby training because Taylor didn't want me participating in any games or taking any hard hits yet. They didn't hesitate to remind me how hard I fell when I wasn't recovering from a concussion. But I needed to get out of my flat. I wasn't allowed back at work until next week, according to Brandon, and I was itching to do something with my time besides spiral over Jacqueline Williams.

Jacqueline never came over again. She never invited me over to her flat again. Instead, she would text me to check in and make sure I didn't have any additional symptoms from my concussion or to simply chat. She would send me what songs she was listening to, and we would FaceTime when we ate dinner at our separate flats.

I didn't care about my fucking concussion anymore.

I just wanted to know where she and I stood.

Could I keep casually interacting with her at work without knowing if she loved me like I loved her? I wasn't sure. Each passing day felt like torture. My mind spiraled with a constant stream of worst-case scenarios.

"Last one!" Taylor shouted when we finished the last lap of the day. Zaid was glued to my side, even though I told him he didn't have to be, he watched me carefully as we came to a slow jog, stopping by our bags at the edge of the pitch.

"Over here!" I heard Taylor call from behind us. I glanced at them over my shoulder, confused by the smirk they were wearing as they jogged toward us. They winked at me before waving their hand at someone near the edge of the park.

When I followed their gaze, I widened mine when I saw a familiar beauty walking toward the pitch.

Next to her was a man. Instinctually, I wanted to shove him away from her, but as they approached I realized the similarities. The dark chocolate hair, dark eyes, the shape of their mouths.

It must have been her brother, Marco. He was speaking low, and his dark eyes kept darting over to me with a smile on his face. Jacqueline would nod at him, but her eyes stayed locked on me.

Behind them, Signe, Mary, Jamie, and even Nicole all followed. Mary and Jamie were carrying a large speaker, and Taylor ran over to them to take it before it dropped.

Jacqueline wasn't wearing her office attire, even though she must have come straight from the office based on the time of day. She wore a cream-colored sweatshirt and sweatpants. She loved baggy clothes, but these were a couple of sizes too big for her.

She probably loved it.

"Do you have any plans right now?" Jacqueline asked as she finally approached Zaid and me, with no segue into the question.

I stared at her, wondering how in the fuck she still took my breath away when she was dressed in the frumpiest clothes I had ever seen her wear, before I answered, "Um, no."

She nodded.

Then she shifted from foot to foot, twisting her hands together.

She was nervous. But why?

I was practically holding my breath before she released a large one of her own and stepped closer to me, speaking lower.

Behind her, Marco smiled, crossing his arms.

"...Have I ever told you what I think about your eyes?" Jacqueline asked. She kept her own down, tracing a delicate finger along the collar of her sweatshirt.

I thought about it for half a second before replying, "No?" like my answer was a question.

She nodded, tucking her lips between her teeth before replying, "I think that they're beautiful."

I gave Mary and Signe curious glances, because they just stood behind Jacqueline with amused expressions, before looking back at her and responding with, "Thank you."

"You're welcome," she sucked in a short breath, holding it, and lifted her gaze to meet mine, "...They're such a specific shade of light blue. Icy, almost. The first time I saw your eye color in that bar... I thought that they reminded me of glaciers."

My facial expression smoothed at her words, but my body tensed.

Jacqueline held my eyes captive as I tilted my head at her in question, wondering if her words meant what I thought. She nodded once, her lips in a hard line as she silently confirmed my suspicion.

"...as long as we have a safety word. Do you have one in mind?"

"*Glacier.*"

I didn't know what to say.

I was speechless.

But Jacqueline didn't let me go. No, she locked me in with her stare, the two of us forgetting about our audience on the grass. It wasn't until Jacqueline tapped her collar with a finger that she released her hypnotic hold on me and turned towards Mary.

"Can you help me set it up?" Jacqueline asked.

Mary pulled her phone out, "Yes, ma'am."

"Alright," Jacqueline stepped back from me and shook her hands out, nerves taking over her body language, "Alright."

Marco stepped around Jacqueline to hold his hand toward to me, "Before we get distracted, I wanted to introduce myself. I'm the one she took the picture for." He winked at me after that.

I shook his hand and nodded as if any of this made sense.

Then he stepped back to pat Jacqueline on the back before joining the others.

"What's happening?" I asked, but all of them ignored me. Signe was beaming though, her eyes bouncing between Jacqueline and me with anticipation. I stared again at the sweatpants and sweatshirt that Jacqueline wore, wondering why this seemed important.

Jacqueline shifted from foot to foot as Mary and Taylor started doing something with the large speaker they set on the ground, "Think you can stick around for a few more minutes?"

I stared at her for a moment before nodding again, because apparently, that was all I could manage right now.

She licked her lips before her eyes shifted to something over my shoulder. I followed her gaze to see the rest of my rugby team scattered where they left their own bags, watching this interaction with curiosity.

I frowned at them, ready to tell Jacqueline we could talk somewhere else, but her back was already to me.

She seemed to be looking for a good spot, her sneaker-covered foot dragging across the grass.

I exhaled a breath and ran my hands through my hair, before scraping one down my face in an attempt to relax. I almost stepped toward her again but stopped. Instead, my leg started bouncing, a restless movement I hadn't dealt with in quite a while. I wasn't sure how I could focus on anything else after Jacqueline dropped that bomb on me.

Do you have one in mind?

Glacier.

I wouldn't get any sleep tonight knowing *that's* how she chose her safe word for us.

"How's it goin', Zaiddy?" Signe asked as she stepped toward her boyfriend and puckered her lips for a kiss. He had just put his glasses back on, now that training was over, and leaned down to comply with a loud smack of lips.

"Good, how are you?" Zaid replied and glanced up toward the random speaker, "Do you need help with that, T?"

"I think we got it," they replied.

"What is going on?" I asked again.

Taylor didn't respond, instead, they just wiggled their eyebrows at me over their shoulder while they stood back from Jacqueline and the speaker.

"Connected." Mary gave Jacqueline a thumbs up before promptly following Taylor off to the side, giving Jacqueline a wide berth.

"Oi—" I tried asking again, "What are you—"

"Calm your British-booty down." Taylor pointed at me, then pointed behind me. For some reason, I obeyed, crossing my arms and taking a couple of steps back from Jacqueline like everyone else had, as she shook her hands out.

"You ready, J?" Taylor asked.

"Wait, wait, let me record this for Violet," Signe spoke from the opposite side of the small semi-circle all of us created around Jacqueline.

"Not gonna lie, I was kind of hoping you all would have better things to do..." Jacqueline's voice sounded nervous, and my muscles tensed with the need to hold her.

"Absolutely not," Mary shook her head "Chop, chop, girlie."

"Tell me when," Taylor instructed, as they tapped on Mary's mobile.

"Fine, fine," Jacqueline grumbled, "Ready!"

"You got this, sis," Marco added, with a grin toward his sister.

Mary tapped on her cell a few times, and suddenly, "Everytime We Touch" by *Cascada* started playing from the speaker. Very loudly. It echoed across the pitch and gained the attention of some teammates who were in the middle of leaving but halted in curiosity.

Jacqueline dramatically straightened her spine. She brushed her hair behind her shoulders and lifted her chin as she inhaled through her nose. She pulled heart-shaped sunglasses out of her sweatpants pockets and placed them over her eyes. Then she started shifting her hips sensually from side to side.

It took my brain a second to catch up to what I was seeing, but it wasn't until Jacqueline stepped to the side and back, and the bass dropped that I realized I wasn't hallucinating.

Jacqueline was...*dancing*.

At my rugby training.

And the moves she used reminded me a lot of the ancient, pixelated music video to this song.

...It was then that I realized that this was a planned performance.

Behind Jacqueline, Signe had her phone out, recording it.

Cheers, applause, and laughter came from everyone else as Jacqueline stepped forward and ripped off her sweatshirt.

My eyes could not have gotten any bigger.

My mouth was hanging open in shock, but I couldn't find it in me to close it.

Because Jacqueline was making unwavering eye contact with me through her sunglasses—miraculously still on her face. When she bent down to rip off her break-away sweatpants, I almost fainted at the sight of her in a very similar outfit that *Cascada* wore in the music video.

She wore a bright orange tube top with a thick black belt around the waist and a black skirt. Instead of knee-high black leather boots, Jacqueline opted for sneakers with scrunched socks at her ankles.

Jacqueline even went as far as to run her fingers through her dark hair as she continued to dance.

There was a long break in between verses, where just the music played and the beat bumped.

During this time, Jacqueline danced.

And danced, taking up most of the space in the half-circle our friends created for her.

It was choreography that was simple and easy to pull off but didn't reduce how effortlessly sexy she looked. How her hips swung perfectly with the beat, and how her hands traced the delicate curve of her waist.

The music video that Mary and I used to play on repeat over and over as teens.

It was obvious that Jacqueline had practiced this performance many, many times.

The final bridge of the song played, and Jacqueline was panting as she strutted up to me, sensually lip-syncing the lyrics. She even went as far as to dramatically flip her hair, sliding one of her palms up my chest, running her other hand down her neck, staying in character.

I was hypnotized, vaguely aware of the cheering coming from our rugby team and Taylor. Of Zaid bringing his thumb and finger to his mouth to whistle. Jacqueline lifted her hands to her hair again, turning around to grind her arse near my groin to tease me with her dancing.

She looked up at me over her shoulder, and I instinctively leaned down to bring our lips closer together, before Jacqueline smirked and stepped away from me.

No.

There was obviously more to the dance because the chorus still needed to play two more times, but I didn't give a damn.

I grabbed Jacqueline's arm, startling her out of her routine as I tugged her back to me.

And I kissed her.

Right then and there, in front of all of our friends and my teammates.

For everyone to see.

I kissed her because as far as everyone on this pitch was concerned, from this point on, Jacqueline Williams was *mine.*

This dance of hers only proved it.

And she kissed me back, falling into my arms.

She looped her arms around my neck, pressing the entirety of her body against me as I secured one arm around her waist to hold her there.

And we kissed and kissed until I decided I couldn't keep tasting her tongue with mine with so many people still watching. Reluctantly, I pulled back.

Jacqueline was panting in my arms still. She reached up to remove her heart-shaped sunglasses and set them on top of her head before letting me see into her wide, nervous gaze.

And then she huffed her embarrassed laugh.

Which made a grin bloom across my face seconds before I realized everyone around us was cheering and clapping and whistling even louder.

Suddenly, Signe wrapped her arms around us and squealed something about "I love love!" before Zaid tugged her off. Everyone was smiling as they broke apart the semi-circle to chat with each other, getting ready to leave.

Marco nodded at me with a brotherly look of warning on his expression before he started strolling toward the exit of the park.

The entire time, I kept Jacqueline in my arms.

And she stayed snug against my chest, her breathy laughter tickling my neck in a way that really made me wish we weren't in a public space right now.

"Damn, he couldn't even wait for the song to end." Taylor grinned as they gathered their bag to leave. They stepped backward as they waved goodbye, accidentally bumping into Nicole. She had been quiet, near the back of the crowd the entire time, and as Taylor reached a hand behind them to prevent Nicole from falling over, they raised their brows.

"Oh, my bad—"

"I'm sorry—"

But neither of them finished their sentences when they made eye contact. I leaned down to rest my face in Jacqueline's fruity-scented hair as I watched Taylor's cheeks turn pink.

Eventually, Nicole smiled at them and turned away, and after a moment, Taylor shouldered their strap and decided to stick around as well.

My attention was pulled away from my teammate at the sound of Zaid's voice, "So are you two going to stop pretending you aren't dating yet, or...?"

Mary cackled at his question.

"Yeah, we're done pretending," Jacqueline replied. She looked up at me, "If that's what you want?"

"*Fuck* yes."

Jacqueline's brows raised at that, "Wow."

"Sorry," then I shook my head, "I'm not sorry. We're off the clock. Fuck, I love you so fucking much." I wrapped her up tighter in my arms, letting her feet dangle against my legs as I pinned her arms to her sides, her laughter in my ear as I murmured, "I love you."

"I love you too," she whispered as I loosened my hold on

her, "You deserved something big when I finally said those words to you. But…I don't know, was it too much?"

I raised my eyebrows as I pulled back to rake my gaze over her little outfit.

"I don't think it was enough, actually," I leaned down to kiss her neck, still feeling the rush of finally, *finally* being able to hold her and kiss her whenever I wanted, "We should go home and have you redo your dance, though."

Jacqueline's brows pinched together as her beautiful frown pulled at her lips, "Oh. Was it bad? Marco helped me practice it for hours yesterday—"

I placed a finger over her delicious lips and shook my head, smirking at the sight of her hopelessly confused eyes staring up at me.

My Jacqueline, who thrived on direct communication, widened her eyes when I leaned down to whisper, "I want you to give me a private dance, love." Her breath picked up when I slid my hand up her arm, over her shoulder, to tangle in the soft strands of her dark hair, "Do you have any idea how hard it is to conceal what you're doing to me, in front of everyone here?"

Her dark eyes glanced down between us, and I used my hand that wasn't in her hair to subtly adjust my shorts so it wasn't painfully obvious how I felt about Jacqueline dressing up as one of my old celebrity crushes.

"Oh," Jacqueline blushed, raising a hand to cover her smile as she looked at me with a sparkle in her eyes, "Yeah. Let's go."

"Do you understand what I'm saying?" I asked as we started to follow our friends off the pitch. My hands didn't let her step too far away from me, though. One was busy cupping her arse.

"I think I got it," Jacqueline laughed as she reached around to pinch mine in retaliation.

"Are you positive? I could be clearer if I need to." I offered as she laced my fingers with hers.

"I think you're being crystal clear," she giggled before snuggling against my chest, "You should shower, though."

I chuckled as I led us off the grass, leaning down close to her ear, "I will. Then I want to watch you dance while slowly peeling those clothes off," I pinched the fabric of her tube top, grinning like the Cheshire cat when I both felt and watched her shiver against me, "I want to kiss every inch of your skin, before sinking into you—officially—as your boyfriend."

Jacqueline smirked, turning to face me, our lips centimeters apart, "Why does referring to you as my 'boyfriend' feel so childish?"

I pecked her lips with a quick kiss as she led us toward my bike, our coworkers were all gathered near Zaid's car as they chatted without us.

"Probably because we're much more than that, love." I smiled down at her, "We're partners. Lovers. I'm yours, and you're mine. There's nothing casual about it, right?"

Jacqueline's lips slowly pulled back into a wide smile, before tucking her lips between her teeth in that nervous tell I adored, "Right."

Chapter Twenty-Nine

JACQUELINE

I CLOSED *the door behind me gently, not wanting to wake up anyone else on this floor. I was surprised I could walk straight, considering everything he put me through last night. And technically this morning. I turned, ready to walk to the elevator, when I hesitated.*

Should I leave him my number?

The impulsive thought made butterflies erupt in my stomach, but no, that wasn't the deal. He was leaving later today, anyway.

So I forced one foot in front of the other until I could ignore the invisible tether in my chest that tried to tug me back. The ache that built every step that took me away from him.

This chapter was closing for the handsome stranger and me, but I was determined to believe that somewhere out there, the universe was starting another.

MUCH TO LEO'S DISAPPOINTMENT, before he got into the shower, I ripped that silly outfit off of my body as fast as possible. When we arrived at his apartment, we weren't kissing and stumbling into each other. We weren't frantic with our need to taste and feel one another. I wondered if it was because we had some comfort now. Security in the fact that we would satiate the other's needs like this.

"Did I not make myself clear earlier?" Leo's hands came up from behind me, halting my movements before I could bend down and slide out of this skirt, "I wanted a proper strip tease."

"I—" I hesitated, "What if I did that another time? In a different outfit?" This skirt felt awful. Something about the fabric was horrible against my skin.

"Fine, join me in the shower, then," Leo chuckled, as he headed toward the bathroom. He gave me one last smile as he pulled his sweaty jersey over his head and stepped out of view. The sound of water running echoed in the space.

I stepped out of my itchy skirt and tube top, stripping out of my thong and bra just as he instructed. His room was warm, allowing me to stand there freely to tie my hair up in a bun and soak in the joy of this moment, before following after him.

Leo was already under the stream, his face tipped back as he already lathered his shampoo, and used the same lather to scrub his face.

The sound of the glass sliding door opening made him glance at me with a smirk before he rinsed off.

I shivered, the steam of the room created a damp layer on my skin while he took over the majority of the spray. Right when Leo reached for his bar of soap, I snatched it first.

"Let me," I whispered. Leo grasped both of his hands on either side of my waist, turning so that my back hit the spray of the shower now, but none of it touched my hair. The water warmed me up. He trailed his hands on my hips and waist as I began to lather him up with the soap. Scrubbing his arms and shoulders and chest and legs. Every inch of his skin until I started to reach where he was erect.

"You shouldn't," Leo murmured, halting my hand before I could touch him, "Otherwise this will be over before it starts." After he took care of washing that himself, he wrapped his arms around me and kissed my neck, turning us again so he could rinse his body off. Leo then took the soap and started lathering me up.

I had showered this morning, but I let him have the opportunity to roam his hands all over me again. It was as if he was surveying me, even though he'd already seen me like this. The way his palms scraped over my breasts, and my ribs, and shoulders, and neck felt like an imprint.

Like his hands were reuniting with my body.

"Stunning." His eyes darkened, and a heated grin pulled on one corner of his lips. My heart thumped when the water turned off and he grabbed a nearby towel to dry us off. Standing in his bathroom, both of us finally dried, he leaned forward to kiss me. As his lips devoured, his hands on my waist guided us out of the bathroom.

Letting him lead us, I enthusiastically kissed him back. I wanted him to know he could kiss me like this, that I was *here*. That I loved him just as much as he loved me, if not more.

After taking time to properly reunite with his lips, I placed my hand flat on his chest and pushed him toward his bed.

"Sit," I licked my lips after ordering him.

He lifted a brow, tilting his head to the side, "Are you in charge right now?"

"Yes." I pushed him again, and he obeyed. He promptly sat on the edge of his bed, though he made me stay near him with his hands on my thighs, "At least, you're going to let me pretend to be in charge until you can't wait anymore."

Leo's hooded eyes landed on my naked breasts, puckered from the cool air of the room, "That's not going to be for much longer, I'm afraid."

I shrugged, "Let's set a timer then." I padded around for my discarded clothes to find my phone, and opened the clock app, "Let's try making you wait for ten minutes."

"Thirty seconds," Leo countered, his fingers flexing into my skin.

"Five minutes," I giggled.

"Forty-five seconds."

"Three minutes?" I set the timer, not willing to let him push for more, "You can resist taking over for three short minutes, can't you?" I brushed my fingers through his damp hair, loving how his head leaned back and his eyes fluttered closed from my touch.

"I'll try," Leo grumbled as I dropped the phone on the mattress next to him.

"Good." I stepped back, out of his reach, and ran my hands across my collarbone.

"Fuck," Leo leaned forward to rest his elbows on his knees, his hands balled into fists as his gaze locked onto where my hands were.

"You wanted a strip tease," I reminded him, tracing the shape of my breasts with my index finger, "But I think I just want to tease."

Leo groaned, scraping a hand down his face and keeping his hand over his jaw, his pupils expanding. I preened, loving that I had this effect on him. Leo Turner brought out a confidence in me I didn't know I had, and I relished the feeling as I continued to trace the different dips and planes of my body, showing him everywhere he couldn't touch me right now.

I traced the curve of my hip slowly, slowly, holding back a laugh as his gaze followed the movement. As if Leo was hypnotized. I glanced at the timer, only one minute had passed. I had two more. I stepped forward, batting his hands away when they reached up to grab me.

He grumbled, trying to grab my hips again before I locked my hands on his wrists and held them behind his back. It brought our faces close together, so I took advantage of my position to delicately lick up his neck.

Leo shuddered under me, and the heat of arousal burned in my lower belly from the knowledge that I could turn him on like this.

"You always take such good care of me," I whispered in his ear. I followed him as he dropped his head back, determined to drive him as wild as he drove me, "What if I want to take care of you? Have you lay back while I do all the work?" I released his wrists to push him back on the bed. He obeyed with a dramatic thump against the mattress. I kissed his earlobe, teasing the flesh with my teeth, before sliding down his body.

His hands came up to cup either side of my face, which I decided to allow before I teased the tips of my fingers down the V-shape pointing toward my destination.

"Letting me take care of you," Leo rasped, "Is taking care of me." I had a feeling this was just Leo being Leo. That perhaps our dynamic was a habit, where he ravishes me and then gets his fill. We hadn't ever had him finish first, and I wanted to use the opportunity as another form of appreciation for, well, everything he is.

Everything he's done for me.

How much I love him.

I tsked my tongue at him before running a finger up his length just to watch it twitch. Leo's hips flexed, and I stood up.

A disappointed grumble sounded in his throat, while I studied him. Prone on his back for me.

I was just leaning over him again, teasing him from root to tip with my tongue, when the alarm on my phone went off.

Without warning, Leo pushed me off of him so he could grab underneath my armpits and pull me onto the bed. I was laughing as he used his strength to flip us over. I was now the one on my back.

"Wait!" I laughed.

"Do you remember your safe word?" Leo asked, grabbing hold of my jaw to ensure he met my eyes.

"Yes, but I wanted you to go first—" Leo shook his head before slamming his lips over my mouth as he covered me with his naked body.

"I don't want to go first," Leo rasped the words against my open lips, dragging me farther up the bed so he could spread me out. He threw one of his legs over mine, grinding his erection against me as he sucked on a sensitive patch of skin between my neck and jaw.

"But—oh god," I clutched his shoulders, an attempt to anchor myself as his fingers slipped against my aching center.

"You want me, and I want to play with you," Leo murmured against my neck. He was able to tuck an arm underneath my shoulders, his fingers fisting in the roots of my hair. He angled my head exactly where he wanted so that his mouth could ravish mine. I was burning, my heart thudding at an erratic pace in my chest.

I wanted him *so* badly.

But this was supposed to be about *him*.

Right when Leo's thumb started swirling in circles, tightening that invisible string inside of me, I mumbled out, "Glacier."

And Leo froze, his hands halting exactly where they were. He leaned back, his brows drawn together as he studied me.

"I want you so, *so* badly," I flexed my hips against his hand, in an attempt to reassure him that I still did want his touch, "But I wanted to do something for *you*."

"You are."

I shook my head, "No, I'm always taken care of first—"

"Do you not want my touch right now?" Leo interrupted, resting his forehead against mine. He kept his hand on me, his thumb scant millimeters from where I was aching for him.

"I always want your touch. I just..." How did I explain? "I want to show you how much I love you." I inhaled a breath, wondering if getting emotional during this moment would ruin the heat of it, "That I can take care of you, like you take care of me."

Leo nodded against my forehead, letting my words settle around us. I was still holding his shoulders. My fingers flexed their hold on him. I really didn't want to stop anything, but my plan was currently derailing, and I wasn't sure how to deal with it.

"I hear you," Leo kissed my cheek, "But, Jacqueline, I am *dying* to be inside of you."

I huffed a laugh at that, "But that means I go first."

"Yeah, that's exactly what I want," Leo grinned against my cheek, "Love me, by letting me have you how I have been dreaming of having you."

Warmth swarmed my chest with his words, "You don't want me to take care of you first?"

"No, no," Leo shook his head again, "I want you to go first, so I can fit in between your legs as fast as possible. I want to rock into you, holding you under me, while you tell me that you love me, and I remind you how much I love you." He kissed my lips again, leisurely, adoringly, "Please, let me take over in this moment. I promise, later tonight even, you can play with me as much as you want."

...That option really didn't suck.

"Are you sure?" I lowered one hand from his shoulders to trail down his arm, the arm frozen on my body. I gently nudged his thumb closer to where I was most sensitive.

"Positive," Leo groaned, "Can I keep touching you?"

I nodded, and before he could remind me, I vocalized, "Yes. You can touch me."

His grin was wide and warm, making butterflies take off in my stomach as his thumb immediately went back to work.

"Do you want to use your safe word?"

"No." I shook my head, biting my lip as the rest of his hand slipped under the material to where I was burning.

"Thank you," Leo settled more against me, resuming the searing kisses. His tongue plundered my mouth, I almost couldn't keep up with him. I was surrounded by Leo. His masculine scent, his hand pulling my pleasure to the surface, and his lips claiming mine in a way that felt almost primal.

I was barreling towards the edge, knowing that this was what he wanted. How he wanted to be inside of me "as fast as possible." Usually, I didn't perform well when there was pressure. I struggled in my past with feeling insecure about the fact that I didn't get off as quickly as my partners, but that wasn't a problem this time.

Leo loved me, and I loved him.

Leo wanted me, and I wanted him.

It was as simple as that.

My body understood.

So when I started gasping against his mouth, squeezing my eyes shut as my release throbbed through my core, I wasn't too surprised I was able to get there as quickly as I did. Leo murmured encouraging words against my gasp, saying how well I was doing and how much he loved me.

I finally came down from the high, rubbing at my forehead as Leo went searching for a condom.

He shuffled around in his nightstand for a while longer than normal, before releasing a low, "Shit."

"What is it?" I asked, opening my eyes to see his frown.

"I don't have a condom," he held the box upside down, dropping his head against the mattress when nothing fell out, "Fuck."

I rolled over, drumming my fingers on the comforter in thought.

My legs squeezed together a moment later as if just realizing how devastating this was for me as well.

"Um..." I bit my bottom lip, almost distracted by the way Leo brushed his dark hair off of his face as he glanced at me, "We could not use one?"

Leo immediately slammed his face into the comforter and released the deepest scream. I was glad it was muffled because otherwise, that would have been very loud.

I frowned, but laughed, "You can just say no."

"No, no," Leo lifted his face again, his cheeks flushed and pupils blown as he crawled back over me to cup either side of my face with his hands, "Are you serious about not using one?"

I lifted a shoulder, "I'm not on the pill, but I'm not ovulating...if you want to risk it."

"But do you *want* me inside of you bare?" Leo pressed, his eyes darting between both of mine. Something heated in my veins at his question. The ache that currently felt released was building. It was as if my body anticipated this connection with him, and desperately needed it.

"I've never not used a condom before," I skimmed my hands down his sides, "But I want to with you."

Leo shook his head, "We can use a condom again after this. Not using one right now doesn't mean we can't use one ever again."

"I know." I saw his neck and chest heat, and his erection twitched against my leg the more we delved into this subject. Leo wanted this. He was excited at the idea of having unprotected sex. It was thrilling, and I was happily getting caught up in it.

"I need your clear consent for this, love," Leo bent down to kiss my lips once more, "Do you want me inside of you without a condom?"

I smiled, "Yes. I want you inside of me."

"Do you want me to finish somewhere else?" he added. I immediately shook my head.

"Don't you dare." Leo wheezed at my response, before dropping his head on my shoulder to gather himself. I laughed, wrapping my legs around his waist and arching my hips up, "I have Plan B at home. Maybe we can go to my house right after so I can take it." I didn't love the idea of Plan B destroying my hormones like it had for me in the past, but it was worth it to me to not get pregnant.

"If you want," Leo groaned, flexing so that the tip of his

cock teased me where I was wet and ready for him, "But I also had a vasectomy a few years ago."

Uhhh, "Pardon?"

"So I can't get you pregnant," Leo added, hoisting himself up on his elbows so he could look between our bodies, "I've gone to every checkup, and I've come back with the same results. No fertility."

"Oh my god," I groaned, dropping my hold on him to cover my eyes, "I didn't think you could get any hotter."

Leo laughed, kissing my hands until I removed them from my eyes so he could say, "Me having a vasectomy turns you on?"

My core throbbed at his words, "Yes—but why haven't you mentioned that before?" I grabbed his waist, pulling him into me. Leo entered me slowly like he always did. I gasped through his intrusion, desperate to relax enough for him to sink as deep as possible, "We could have been going without condoms this whole time."

"Vasectomies don't negate the value of condoms," Leo grunted, a drop of sweat building on his brow as he thrust his hips, inching farther and farther inside of me, "You can still take Plan B after, to give you peace of mind."

"Oh my god," I groaned, when he finally bottomed out. In a physical sense, there was no real difference between the feel of him with or without a condom on. In an emotional sense, I felt more connected to Leo Turner than I had ever felt with anyone else. That was what made me throb with want. That was what made me reach up to grab a fistful of his hair. My grip made him pull his gaze from where our bodies connected, to my eyes.

"Fuck me," I instructed, "Fuck me like you've wanted to."

Leo's jaw clenched as he started moving, rocking inside

of me at a rough pace that made me lock my legs around him.

"God, yes," I wrapped my arms around his shoulders again, fully anchored to his body, "I love you so fucking much, Leo." The sound he made in response felt tortured, but he picked up his pace, planking over me as he did his best to get me over the edge again.

"I've wanted you for so long, Jacqueline," Leo grunted out, "I love feeling you bare like this. Feeling you take me so *fucking* well." He was shifting us up toward his headboard, so I released one arm from his shoulders to palm the headboard, keeping me put while he thrust into me.

"I love you," I breathed, "I love you."

"I love you," Leo moaned the words, his eyes filling with moisture as he looked down at me, "I love that you're mine now."

"I love—oh my god," I squeezed my eyes closed, "I—it's too much."

"Look at me," Leo demanded, "Open your eyes."

I managed to obey, enough to see him studying me as if he couldn't look away. He had a feral look to him, something deep in his core that was being revealed each time I rocked my hips in tandem with his.

"I want you to finish inside of me so badly," I whispered, "I want to make you lose control."

He whimpered even though the corner of his lip tugged up in a smirk, "Yeah?"

I was starting to forget to breathe properly. I was holding my breath and gasping for air, my orgasm building at a rate that almost terrified me. Leo could tell when it was about to happen, the look in his eyes darkened more as he pounded into me, desperate to bring me to the surface.

Right when I broke, so did Leo.

We groaned through our releases. It didn't happen often, reaching our pleasure at the same moment, but I was so grateful that we shared this experience today.

I felt Leo pulse against my inner muscles, setting off aftershocks that made silent tears spill from my eyes.

Once we managed to catch our breath, he scooped me up in his arms and tugged me flush against his chest. Laying on our sides, he breathed me in, tightening his hold. Our legs tangled together; our arms wrapped around each other. My head rested against his shoulder and neck, and his mouth settled against my hair.

After breathing me in, Leo whispered, "...That was incredible."

I couldn't nod this close to him, wrapped as tight as we were, so I whispered back, "You're incredible."

"You're brilliant," I could feel his lips pull into a smile against my hair after his words.

"You're all mine," I replied, smiling against his warm chest.

"I am."

Chapter Thirty

JACQUELINE

TURNS OUT, Leo was a very moanable name.

"I CAN'T BELIEVE I missed it" Violet whined as she shifted back into her seat.

"It was awesome!" Signe's eyes were shimmering after showing Violet the video she took the day I danced at Leo's rugby practice. It was a good thing Signe recorded the experience because I sure as hell wasn't doing that again.

...Unless Leo wanted me to.

Then I'd consider it.

It was about a week later, and the women of the office all went out to dinner at a Korean barbeque restaurant. We were each sharing space on the grill built into the table, searing our preferred meats.

Violet had been working from home, so this was the first she had been able to see my dance.

"You two are so cute together," Violet smiled before

using chopsticks to flip her steak, "I'm glad that ended up happening."

"Thanks," I grinned, scooping some rice with my pork.

"So you have a start date, yeah?" Signe asked, turning to Violet.

"I do," Violet smiled, but it quickly dimmed, "I'm so nervous about moving."

"Why?" Jamie asked. She reached over to snag some of the side salad Mary had ordered, grinning when Mary pretended to glare at her for stealing off of her plate. Jamie shimmied happily after taking that bite, before turning back to Violet.

"Change is always hard when you feel safest with a routine," she lifted a hand to tuck her electric blue braid behind her shoulder, "I'll have help. But I'm still anxious over it."

"It's just temporary though, right?" Mary asked, "You and your daughter will be back within a year or so?"

"Yeah, but it would almost be better to just move there and stay put for a few years." Violet met our gaze, before lifting her shoulder, "I've managed to stay in the same apartment since she was two. Moving was kind of a trauma for Gracie. Thankfully, my dad is going with us. So she'll have two familiar adults in the new house."

"The house looks cute," I chimed in, "Brandon was showing us pictures of the guest lodging."

"That, I'm grateful for," Violet grinned, "I think Gracie will like the quiet, once she adjusts to the change. Actually," Violet sat taller, "Taylor recently met up with us at a park and gave me some pro-tips on what might help Gracie regulate at this stage of her development."

"I love Taylor," Signe grinned, "I've met them a couple of times now. They're so chill."

"They are very fun," I added. Mary and Jamie also mentioned how well they got along with the Occupational Therapist after my performance. I guess they both helped get the speaker back in Taylor's car, and then went out for drinks.

Nicole, sitting next to me, stayed quiet.

She shifted her chopsticks side to side, pushing food around on her plate as we all talked about our admiration for Taylor Desmond.

"Anyway, I told Zaid I wanted to drive up and visit you while you're there, because Northern California is so pretty and green," Signe shifted the conversation, "Maybe we could all spend a weekend with you and your daughter or something—if she'd be okay with houseguests."

Violet giggled, "She is very much not okay with house guests, but I'm sure we could figure out something so you all could visit."

Jamie frowned, "How does that work with dating? You just never bring people home?"

Violet shook her head, "I don't date, period."

Mary nodded, "Ah. Makes sense."

Signe gaped, "Ever?"

Violet shook her head once more as a humorous grin tugged on her full lips, "I'm okay, I know how to work a vibrator."

Signe snorted, I lifted my hand to cover my mouth and laugh.

"Cheers to that," Nicole lifted her water glass, clinking it against Violet's and making us all laugh, "Sometimes it's best to take time for yourself. Romance isn't always for everyone."

"Preach," Violet agreed before taking a large gulp of her

water, then tilted her head in thought, "...I wouldn't hate to eventually ride some dick again, though."

Mary and Nicole grimaced, while Jamie, Signe, and I laughed. Mine was quieter, and I was able to collect myself before the others did.

"Just upgrade to a dildo," Mary waved her hand at Violet, "Don't settle for some mediocre man who probably doesn't know how to get you off."

I nodded, turning toward Violet, "I was with a man for years who never figured out how to get me off," I gave her what I hoped was a reassuring smile, "But I eventually found someone who proved that, if he wanted to, he would."

"Gross," Mary grunted, puffing her cheeks out as if she was holding back.

"Sorry." I blushed, realizing that Mary probably didn't want to hear how easily Leo got me over the edge.

Violet's phone started buzzing on the tabletop, and we all ate our food while she flipped it over and checked her messages. She was sipping from her water when her brows suddenly lowered, "Oh."

"What?" Mary asked around her mouthful of food.

"I think, um..." Violet's lips pulled back into a smile, "I think Brandon's brother thinks I'm a guy." She angled her phone face out to show us an email from Graham Moore. I momentarily ignored all the pictures he attached to the email, showing what I assumed would be the house Violet and her daughter would be living in, and read the text at the top of the email instead.

"Did he really start the email off with a 'Hey man'?" Jamie giggled. She reached a hand out to angle the phone more towards her so she could read it all, "Here's some pictures of the space. Let me know if you need anything else."

Signe was smiling as she asked, "Why does he think you're a guy?"

Violet shrugged, "No idea."

"Sexism," Nicole said, "He's just assuming that his tech support is a guy because it's a male-dominated field."

All of the women at the table collectively shared a groan.

"...v.thompson@sst.com is a masculine-looking email, too," Jamie tilted her head, sitting back so Violet could look at her phone again. She quirked her lips to the side as she studied the screen.

"You should respond with 'Hey girl'." Mary grinned at her suggestion.

Violet laughed, "I think I'm not going to address it at all. Let him be surprised when I show up," she waved a hand over herself, gesturing to her general appearance, "Instead of a bro coming to help him out, he's about to live side-by-side next to a blue-haired, tattooed mamma with tig-ol-bitties." She then made a gesture that looked like she was about to cup her own breasts, which were significantly fuller than mine.

"*Mommy* indeed," Signe wiggled her eyebrows, "You're going to keep up the ruse?"

"Yeah," Violet grinned, "Something about fucking with a presumptuous man gives me a thrill." She thumbed back a response on her phone, reading it aloud as she typed, "Hey man, thanks for the photos. Looks like a nice place. While I have you, do you know of any good sports bars in the area? ...Now I just gotta remove my email signature and replace that ish with a simple gender-neutral-looking letter V."

Signe snorted while Mary threw her head back and cackled.

Violet shimmied excitedly in her seat, before pocketing her phone.

Then it was my phone's turn to buzz because Leo was FaceTiming me.

Except it wasn't Leo's face that filled the screen when I answered the call.

It was Taylor Desmond.

"Hey J." They grinned, their septum piercing shimmered in the low light of the sunset. Their cheeks were flushed and their dark hair was pulled back with a thin headband. Before I could properly say hello, Leo shoved his face next to Taylor's, wearing a matching headband to keep his hair out of his face. His cheeks were also flushed from exertion, his breath puffed out of him as he gave me a wide smile.

"Hey." I smiled at him.

"Why weren't you at the game, J?" Taylor pouted, jutting their bottom lip out, "Leo needs a good luck charm."

I blushed, glancing up at my friends at the table. Jamie, Violet, and Signe were chatting to themselves as they dug into their meals. Mary and Nicole were watching me take this call.

"I'm with my friends."

"I told you she's having girls' night, T." Leo tried to take the phone from Taylor, who laughed manically before running away from him. Leo cursed in the distance, and Mary's lips twitched with a smile as she overheard her cousin being bested by someone else.

"C'mon, J," I had never formally permitted Taylor to call me by the first letter of my name, but I was okay with it. They were probably the only one who could get away with the nickname. "Leo dropped the ball so many times today. Literally. He has the worst butterfingers I have ever seen."

"I'm sorry," I held back a giggle from Taylor's antics, they were such a character, "But, how would I help, exactly?"

Taylor's eyes widened before they rolled. To my side,

Nicole muffled a giggle, "Because he'll want to show off for his pretty girlfriend and perform better."

"What if she's just a distraction?" Nicole asked from my side. I turned the camera towards her so she could be in the frame with me, and Taylor's eyes changed. I couldn't tell how they changed; I just noticed that they did.

The shift in their expression lasted half a second, before they recovered and continued, "What if she's not?"

Nicole studied my phone for a moment, a warm color touching her cheeks before she shrugged and dug back into her food.

"I'll try to make it to the next game," I promised Taylor. They grinned at me, before the camera started shaking and the image became pixelated. There was a grunt and a "hey!" from them before Leo's handsome face filled the screen again.

"Sorry for interrupting your night, love," Leo licked his lips, and I suddenly wished the girl's night would wrap up sooner rather than later.

"You're fine," I glanced around at my friends again, double checking that they were distracted with their food or other conversations before I pulled the phone closer to my chest to ask, "...But what if afterward, you were waiting for me at my apartment?"

Leo bit his bottom lip before replying, "In your bed?"

Mary started fake-vomiting all over her food, and Nicole barked out a surprised laugh. Nicole hadn't laughed like this in a while, I realized. She had been reserved and closed off most of the year ever since things ended with her last girlfriend. To see her throw her head back and laugh at Mary being dramatic, I realized that maybe she was starting to come out of her mourning phase.

Nicole's laugh was contagious, it made me huff some

giggles out too, even though Mary was teasing us at our expense.

"Obviously, in my bed," I rolled my eyes when Mary's response to that was to pretend to stab her chopsticks into her throat and die. She collapsed against Jamie's shoulder dramatically, who just patted her head, and continued her conversation with Signe and Violet as if this was normal for them.

"Hurry home, love," Leo blew the phone a kiss before Taylor jumped on his back and the call ended. I was grinning when I pocketed my phone, a feeling of peace swarming inside my stomach that I wasn't familiar with quite yet. A sense of contentment. Of love.

"Starry-eyed-and-in-love-Jacqueline is my favorite," Signe sang from the opposite end of the table. I glanced up to look at her, gnawing on my lip before picking up my chopsticks and digging into my plate of food.

"Me, too."

Epilogue

LEO

I ALMOST CHOKED *on my beer.*

Sitting next to me, looking perfectly casual as she perched on the barstool, sat the most gorgeous woman I had ever seen.

Perhaps I should...?

No, she's probably used to men hitting on her all the time.

But then she turned to look at me with a nervous lip bite. Her dark eyes widened when they took me in, and she quickly scanned my body in a way that made me want to puff my chest out in pride.

Her cheeks flushed, and I realized that perhaps I had a chance after all.

She licked her lips once, and I was done for.

"Hello."

A MONTH PASSED, and Jacqueline and I were riding home from work together on my bike. A form of transportation she started requesting herself shortly after she finally said those three little words that I never grew tired of hearing from her.

We were still deep in the honeymoon phase of our relationship, and I wasn't upset about it.

Jacqueline was getting used to riding my bike of her own volition. She requested to ride to and from work on it instead of one of our cars. It fulfilled a couple of fantasies that teenage me had of driving around with a sexy partner clad in leather, feeling me up as we showed off how cool and mysterious we were.

She still wasn't willing to wear leather pants, though. She hated the texture.

So jeans it was.

As we turned toward my street, I snatched her wandering fingers in mine for the fifth time this ride.

"Jacqueline," I murmured in a deep warning tone, lacing our digits together.

She didn't respond through the mic. Instead, she squeezed our fingers, attempting to distract me while brushing her free hand over my upper thigh, teasing where I was already stiff.

"You're not that scared of crashing anymore, are you?" I chuckled as I grabbed her frisky hand and placed it back on my abdomen, where it would be less distracting.

I needed to keep one hand on the handlebars at all times, and Jacqueline used that to her advantage to tease me the entire twenty-five-minute drive home from the office.

Finally, we pulled into my building's car park.

But Jacqueline's boldness increased as she, with lightning speed, lowered both of her hands and gripped the solid outline of my erection hidden beneath my jeans. She even managed to stroke me once or twice before I yelped a laugh and covered both of her hands with mine.

"Jacqueline!" I glanced at her over my shoulder, seeing my own reflection in her dark visor.

Suddenly, we both jerked forward. I faced forward to see that I hadn't properly parked the bike, distracted by my girlfriend's wandering hands, and the bike drifted so that the front tire bumped into the cement divider of the car park.

"Wicked woman," I mumbled, earning a pleased laugh from her. We were parked right next to the entrance, allowing anyone walking or driving by our building to see what she was doing to me.

I backed up a bit before flicking the kickstand and cutting the engine, not thinking too much of it until I heard Jacqueline cackle behind me.

I removed my helmet and smiled at her over my shoulder.

Jacqueline's laugh was hypnotizing. It pulled me in like a siren's call. Her laugh was uncontrolled, a religious experience that deserved my full and undivided attention. I wanted to worship the sound of her laughter.

"What's so funny?" I asked, stepping off the bike first.

"The bike fantasy is ruined," Jacqueline shook her helmet-clad head as her shoulders shook, laughter erupting out of her in waves.

I dropped my jaw, "What? How?"

She lifted her head to finally unclip the helmet, something she could do on her own now, to show me her beautifully flushed cheeks. Lifting her hands, Jacqueline had to wipe tears from her eyes that were smearing her mascara. She was laughing that hard.

"Watching you slowly back up today," Jacqueline pressed her lips together in a giggle, struggling to get through her explanation, "Using your little tippy-toes to balance the bike."

I gaped, before glancing down at myself. She still straddled the bike, so I used that to my advantage as I stepped forward and cupped the back of her head with my gloved hand.

"This doesn't do it for you anymore?" I asked. Jacqueline's entire body was shaking with laughter, her hand had to wipe more tears from her eyes as she squeezed them shut.

"No, no," Jacqueline shook her head, inhaling a deep breath and waving her hands in front of her face. She was losing it. I had seen this happen with her once before when we were watching the telly, and a funny, unexpected one-liner was said by one of her favorite characters. We had to go back and rewatch that scene a dozen times, and each time the line was said, Jacqueline would cackle and bury her head in my chest from the hilarity.

I thought the line was funny, sure, but I mostly replayed the scene just to keep watching Jacqueline's enjoyment. It felt like a hit of the world's best drug, hearing her laughter again and again.

According to her therapist, it was common for neurodivergent individuals to fall into giggle fits that were difficult to come out of.

I always loved learning about my stunning girlfriend's beautiful brain, and how it functioned.

"Hmm, we're gonna have to fix that, yeah?" I asked, lifting my other gloved hand to cup her neck, leaning in so our noses brushed against each other.

Jacqueline sucked in a breath from the contact, her pupils dilating just as I hoped. Except she was still giggling.

"I—I can still see it," Jacqueline pressed her lips together just as tightly as her eyelids, "Your little tippies—" with an amused growl, I bent and captured her lips with mine. My kiss was aggressive, and I nipped at her bottom lip in a way that promised retribution for her teasing. I reached down to grab her thigh with my fingers, lifting her leg so she was no longer straddling the bike but still sitting on it. I held her legs wide so I could press against her, fitting my body in between.

Right where I belonged.

"Jacqueline," I grumbled against her neck, "I'm perfectly confident in my masculinity, love."

"That's great," Jacqueline was struggling to calm her breathing, wrapping her arms around my shoulders as she leaned back, offering more of her neck to me, "But the sexy, mysterious, motorcycle rider schtick is on hiatus for a moment."

I chuckled against her skin, before scraping my teeth against her throat. Her responding shiver let me know she wasn't completely turned off by me.

"Any other fantasies you'd like me to deliver on?" I murmured, brushing my lips up to her neck and teasing her earlobe, "Want to play today, Jacqueline?"

She whined, and I rewarded myself by taking a deep breath of her vanilla and rose scent. I hadn't ever been super aroused by perfumes and smells before, but Jacqueline was the exception to the rule.

She was always the exception to the rule.

"We—we can't," Jacqueline whimpered against my touch.

"Do you remember your safe word, Jacqueline?" I lowered my voice, letting the gravel take over in a way I knew would have her panties soaked within minutes. God, I couldn't wait to sink inside of her again.

"No, Leo, we actually can't—"

"Leo!"

I froze, my teeth tucked around the shell of Jacqueline's ear as I struggled to make sense of what I was hearing.

Of *who* I was hearing.

Jacqueline gripped the roots of my hair to pull my head off of her, a nervous smile on her face as she met my eyes.

"Surprise…" Jacqueline immediately looked bashful, and I realized the blush coating her cheeks—unfortunately—wasn't just from arousal.

"Mummy?" I glanced over my shoulder, helping Jacqueline hop off of my bike.

Both of my mothers were exiting a taxi just outside the car park, and Mummy raced toward us with wide open arms. I barely had time to open mine to catch her hug before she practically slammed me against Jacqueline and the bike.

"I know we're interrupting," Mummy squeezed me hard before pulling me away from her so she could look up at me, her dark eyes scanning my features, "But I don't care. I've waited too long to hug my son."

I laughed, before bending down and wrapping her up in a hug again, lifting her feet off the ground. Mama had just finished tugging their suitcase out of the taxi and waving it off before she jogged over to join the reunion.

I missed my mums.

I didn't realize how much until this very moment, but I did.

That wasn't to say I regretted leaving London, I was still happy with the choice I made. I was in a rut over there, and something in my soul craved a move like this. Plus, moving closer to Mary and meeting the love of my life didn't suck, either.

The three of us pulled away from each other before my mums practically shoved me out of their way to get to my partner.

"I'm so glad to finally meet!" Mama cried before wrapping her arms around Jacqueline's shoulders. Instead of the group hugging her, they each took their turn.

"Thank you so much for coming," Jacqueline grinned at my mothers, but it was shy. This was a big deal for her, embracing strangers so openly.

"Thank *you* for the invite," Mummy replied after scanning Jacqueline up and down, "You're even lovelier in person."

"You invited them?" I grinned at Jacqueline, who looked up at me with a small smile.

"I wanted to surprise you," Jacqueline bit her bottom lip, her cheeks still flushed from our intimate embrace, "Is that okay?"

"I love surprises," I grinned, wrapping her hand in mine to bring her knuckles to my lips, "Thank you."

"Let's get on, then," Mama retrieved the handle to their suitcase and started shooing us toward my building's lift, "We want to hear everything. How's Mary? Are she and Jamie coming over, too?"

I glanced down at my partner for that one, my chest expanding with that cozy warmth I learned to associate with her.

"She is, she's bringing dinner with her," Jacqueline squeezed her hand in mine, and I squeezed hers back. I decided it wasn't enough, so I released our hands so I could tuck her against my side, my arm around her shoulders.

Because it was habit at this point, Jacqueline wrapped her arm around my waist, squeezing the two of us together as we entered the lift. I raised my other arm when Mummy snuggled on my other side, and I felt two parts of my world finally fitting together.

Falling in love with Jacqueline Williams was unexpected. I didn't think I was a man who desired the love of one single person. But I was perfectly happy being wrong about that. I never stood a chance against a woman like her, who was willing to risk exposing the most intimate parts of herself to me. Her insecurities, her frustrations, her concerns. But also her desires.

Her love.

A love that was so raw, so vulnerable, that I couldn't help but fall into it headfirst.

As Jacqueline chatted with my mums, asking how their flights were and what they had planned for their visit, I planted a kiss on the crown of her head.

Jacqueline glanced up at me, a grin on her face as she gave me a playful look with her eyes. Biting back a groan of disappointment, because Jacqueline and I would have to wait for another time to play like I wanted to, I rested my cheek against her head.

My mums eyeballed our casual intimacy with a soft expression on their faces, before taking each other's hands and having a silent conversation with their eyes.

I had a feeling I knew what they were saying to one another.

He's okay.

He's not alone.

No, I wasn't.

And I would continue to do everything in my power to keep Jacqueline right where she belonged.

Right here, with me.

THE END

Acknowledgments

First, I want to thank *you*, for reading this book. Thank you for picking up this story. Thank you for taking a chance on me. I keep writing love stories because of readers like you who keep reading them. I cannot thank you enough.

I'd like to thank my sensitivity and authenticity readers for educating me on how best to write Jacqueline and Leo's story. Their personalities. Their isms. Thank you for educating me about how ADHD commonly presents in men, and how undiagnosed autism commonly presents in women.

As someone who has had therapists, friends, and family members gently suggest that I may be on the spectrum to some degree, this story felt very vulnerable for me to write. I felt like I was putting parts of myself into Jacqueline's character that I had felt ashamed of for most of my life. Writing her experiences and illustrating how her brain works was therapeutic for me, and I hope other readers can resonate with her, too.

As always, thank you to all my friends and family who have helped me write my fifth romance book. Thank you to those who have cheered me on from the beginning and as I continue to make writing romance novels my entire personality.

About the Author

Andrea is originally from Oregon but now resides in southern California with her little family. When she isn't curled up on the couch writing love stories, she can be found rewatching her favorite TV shows or taking too many naps.

www.andreaandersen.com